S0-BZL-871

Other *Leisure* Books by Shirl Henke:

NIGHT WIND'S WOMAN

TROUBLE IN PARADISE

"You! What in the name of all the angels of heaven do you here, lady?"

Magdalena stared at the savage standing before her. Sweet Mother of God, what had she done! This stranger was practically naked, wearing only a small cloth about his hips, with a wicked looking knife strapped to his side. His skin was bronzed as darkly as any of the Tainos she had seen in town, and his hair was long and shaggy. The shadow of a beard glistened on his jaw, which was clenched in amazement and fury. Cold blue eyes pierced her as he awaited a reply to his question.

Her throat constricted. She took a deep breath and said, "Hello, Diego." Before she could beg leave of the Colon brothers to talk in private with her "betrothed," Bartolomé interrupted.

"A passing strange way for a man to greet the lady he is to wed after she has crossed an ocean for him." The heavyset, red-haired man stood protectively next to Magdalena, dwarfing her.

"The lady I am to wed?" Aaron echoed in astonishment.

For Alicia Condon,

who gave us the idea for the "Columbus Concept"
and the opportunity to write the books

Shirl Henke

Paradise & More

LEISURE BOOKS   NEW YORK CITY

A LEISURE BOOK ®

November 1991

Published by

Dorchester Publishing Co., Inc.
276 Fifth Avenue
New York, NY 10001

Printed in the United States of America.

"I have served God and their Majesties with as great diligence and love as I might have employed to win paradise and more . . . "

Christopher Columbus, May 20, 1506

Acknowledgments

The Discovery Duet launched my associate, Carol J. Reynard, and me into deep waters much as Columbus and his crew sailed west into the unknown five hundred years ago. All our previous books had been set in the eighteenth or nineteenth centuries in North America. The Medieval Castile of the Inquisitor Torquemada and the Catholic Monarchs Ferdinand and Isabella was a whole "New World" for us. So was the exotic Caribbean and its Taino Indian culture.

We owe the opportunity to begin this fascinating project to our editor, Alicia Condon, who first originated the concept of a set of books related to the five-hundredth anniversary of the discovery of America. Alicia not only gave us the idea, she has inspired us with her enthusiasm. When an excellent and experienced editor says, "You have the historical background. I know you can do it!" how can writers not rise to the challenge?

And a challenge it has been. While I waded through oceans of books on political and social history, Carol researched the flora and fauna of Andalusia and Española as well as the costumes, food, and furnishings of the Castilian nobility.

When we began this project under a tight deadline, we needed a great deal of help, which we received from numerous sources. My husband Jim spent his "summer vacation" in the Maag Library of Youngstown State University, looking for books with the capable help and guidance of the Director of Reference, Mrs. Hildegard Schnuttgen. If Maag could not yield up a source, her tireless searching through the labyrinths of interlibrary loan found it for us.

When I began sending my hand-scrawled chapters to Carol, a whole new set of problems occurred. We not only had a vast number of archaic terms from fifteenth-century Iberia, but the words introduced into modern European languages from Arawakan dialects, plus the names of actual *caciques* such as Guacanagari. Getting our printer to place accents on Spanish and Taino words was nigh onto impossible until Dr. Walt Magee, our computer physician, made several housecalls. Thanks to him, we are now prepared to spell and punctuate in almost any language.

The battles and weaponry of the fifteenth century were far different from those in more recent times. From his vast collection of books on antique armaments, Dr. Carmine V. DelliQuadri, Jr., D. O., selected a good number that were filled with illustrations and photographs to guide me as I wrote action sequences employing arablests and bolts, spears and broadswords. For all his technical assistance, Carol and I are once more greatly in his debt.

Prologue

The girl crouched in the marsh grasses, tense as a hare. She endured the suffocating heat and humidity of late August in silent discomfort. A sun-scorched reed scratched her slim, pale-golden arm and she muffled an oath.

"Swearing, another sin to confess to Father Alonzo on the morrow." She mouthed the words inaudibly and began to crawl along the edge of the brackish water toward the deeper, clearer pool where sounds of loud splashing and singing echoed. Her long plait of dark red hair had come partially undone and hung over her shoulder as she stalked her prey. Approaching a clump of prickly roses, she narrowed her cat-green eyes and peered through the dense low foliage.

Some twenty feet away, a young man stood with his back to her, waist deep in the clear water while his stallion drank noisily at the river's edge downstream. For a fleeting moment, her eyes strayed to the magnifi-

Shirl Henke

cent Barb whose deep chestnut coat gleamed in the hot Andalusian sun. She had often admired the horse, but it was the rider who now held her interest. His shoulder-length hair was curly and badly in want of barbering, yet it gleamed darkest gold as he splashed and sudsed, singing a shockingly ribald soldier's ditty, doubtless learned from older compatriots in the Moorish wars. *Another sin to confess*. She sighed and edged closer, her eyes widening to take in his sun-bronzed beauty.

Muscles, sinewy and corded, rippled across his lean body as he scrubbed vigorously. When he turned, nearly facing her hiding place, Magdalena Luisa Valdés held her breath. He scanned her cover and passed over it to gaze at the stand of olive trees behind which her horse was hidden. She studied his handsome face with its thick, arched golden eyebrows, blazing dark-blue eyes, high sculpted cheekbones and finely chiseled lips, now split in a dazzling white smile. He threw back his head and laughed, launching into another verse of his song. His voice was deep and lusty, resonating from that wide, muscular chest, which was generously furred with a pattern of golden hair that narrowed and then vanished tantalizingly beneath the water's surface.

"Andaluz, you should join me. The water cools and refreshes," Aaron called out to his stallion standing patiently on the bank. The Barb shook his head as if comprehending, then resumed grazing. "Enough! You will grow too fat for your cinch if I do not ride for home soon," he said, submerging quickly to rinse off, then breaking the water's surface, shaking his head and sending sun-splashed droplets of water flying.

When he began to wade toward shore, Magdalena forgot to breathe as she watched his bronzed, naked body emerge from the water. "So, it is true," she murmured in awe, as her eyes fastened on that male part of his anatomy nestling in a thatch of dark gold

12

hair. Her eyes swept his long slim legs, then once more traveled back to focus on his phallus. It did look different than those drawn in the medical books she had perused in the de Palma's library.

Magdalena had overheard her father and his friends say that Jews mutilated their bodies by circumcision. Diego Torres did not look deformed in any way to her. He looked splendid. All of him! What a penance she would have for this excursion, spying on a Jewish *converso* naked at his bath! If her father ever found out he would be livid. But having her curiosity so well satisfied was worth it.

Magdalena had been infatuated by the youth since she was a mere child of ten and he a boy of fifteen accompanying his father to the court of King Fernando and Queen Ysabel five years ago. Of course, then he had been Aaron Torres. His father was the king's most trusted Jewish physician. Under royal pressure, the Torres family had accepted conversion and their children had taken Christian baptismal names. Aaron was now Diego. But some things could not be erased so easily, she thought with a girlish smirk. If the beardless youth had been a golden vision to her, the battle-hardened young man she beheld now was infinitely more imposing. A fine scar edged his jaw and another slashed across his back where some cowardly Moorish soldier had doubtlessly attacked him from behind. A wide gash on his left leg also attested to his battle experiences. She watched him dry off on a length of white linen, then begin to dress in clean garments he took from a pack.

The clothes befitted his station as an heir of a wealthy and distinguished family. The hose that hugged those lean muscular legs were of the finest cloth, the snowy white linen shirt embroidered at the neck with silk threads in a deep blue that matched the doublet stretching across his wide shoulders. He packed away his heavy leather armor, but buckled the sword and dagger of his trade about his narrow hips and pulled on a pair of well-worn, age-softened kidskin boots.

Aaron ran his hand across his smooth jawline, freshly shaven before his bath, then inspected himself in the reflection of the pool. "This will have to suffice to greet my family," he muttered grimly, glad to at least be rid of the stench of blood and filth from battle. Odd. He felt as if he were being watched. Attributing the strange sensation to recent close encounters with death, he laughed and asked himself, "Do you expect a Moor to jump from behind yon rosebushes?"

Packing up his discarded clothing and battle paraphernalia, he considered his brief homecoming. Don Carlos had given him leave to visit with his family on the joyous occasion of his younger sister Ana's marriage into a prominent noble family of Old Christians, the illustrious ducal house of Medina-Sidonia. Perhaps his father rejoiced, but he knew his mother did not. He would withhold judgment until he talked with Ana.

Magdalena watched the golden horseman mount up, apparently deeply absorbed in thought. Good. He was far less likely to see her. Crouching low in the scratchy grasses, she held her breath lest his keen soldier's eyes fasten on her vibrant red hair amid the dull greens and tans of the marsh. When his magnificent chestnut trotted off in the opposite direction, she released a lazy, whistling sigh and stood up. Her legs ached with cramps and every inch of her skin felt abraded. Tossing a damp plait of hair over her shoulder, she stretched like a lithe young animal and began backtracking to where her horse was hidden.

Scarce had she cleared the tall, marshy grasses when she saw them, the Muñoz brothers, Juan and Pedro, nattily decked out in elegant finery. Sons of her family's closest neighbor, they were sly, crafty, and infamous as abusers of the peasant women on their estate. Straightening up to her full five feet, she faced them defiantly. She was the daughter of Bernardo Valdés, a noble of ancient and honorable lineage, if not at present great wealth.

Pedro smirked at the damp gown, clinging to her slender, half-developed frame. "What have we here, alone and lost, eh?"

"Perhaps a lady in need of rescue," Juan answered, then clucked as if reconsidering. "No, no, I think such a sweaty, bedraggled swamp nymph is merely a peasant girl."

Magdalena's eyes narrowed in fury. "You know full well who I am, Juan Muñoz. Out of my way," she commanded imperiously.

"Where is your escort? Surely your father would not permit such unchaperoned wandering," Pedro said with oily good will, moving nearer.

Magdalena saw that they stood between her and her horse. Why had she sneaked off to ride alone this afternoon? Her dueña, Miralda, had scolded and threatened for years to no avail, warning of just such consequences as this. Her mouth felt dry as she scanned the isolated marsh. Only the small dagger at her waist lent her courage. "Are you as barbarous as the Moors to accost a lady?"

"I see no lady, only a slightly damp hoyden who wants for a lesson in manners," Juan said, lunging for her.

Magdalena freed her jeweled dirk and slashed his offending arm, cutting through the heavy velvet sleeve of his jerkin to draw blood and a hissed oath.

"Take her, Pedro," he growled as his hand again shot out and this time grabbed her slim wrist in a bone-breaking hold, yanking her toward him.

Magdalena kicked at Juan as her numb fingers relinquished her tiny dagger, but Pedro was quick to come up behind her, grabbing her around the knees as his brother seized both arms. Together they pulled the small girl down to the grass and held her fast. Pedro shifted his hold to imprison her ankles and shoved her skirt high on her thighs. As she struggled, Juan stroked a slim leg and pulled the skirt yet higher.

Magdalena felt the scream ripping from her throat. Why had she followed Diego Torres to spy on him? What folly to enter this deserted backwater and risk the horror now visited upon her!

"Cry out. No one will hear you," Pedro said in a voice gone hoarse with lust. He began to unbuckle his belt while Juan held her down.

Magdalena twisted, kicked, and thrashed to no avail. Although strong and active, she was but fifteen, of slight stature with fine bones. Pedro freed his hose and pulled them down, exposing his sex, huge and hardened. How obscene and fleshy it looked as he used one beringed hand to roughly pull back the foreskin. Magdalena turned her head away from the impending horror, as Pedro began to lower himself over her.

Suddenly she heard Juan grunt and his fierce hold on her wrists was released as he twisted from his kneeling position to confront an attacker.

"Swine! Stand and fight someone able to defend himself," Aaron said tightly, his sword gleaming in the afternoon sunlight.

Pedro rolled away from Magdalena and she scrambled to her knees, covering her lower extremities and sobbing. The rapist struggled desperately to roll up his encumbering hose and free his sword at the same time.

Juan stood and faced the challenger, quaking when he saw the grim smile on the blond stranger's face. He no more than drew his sword and made one sweeping, clumsy thrust than it went sailing from his hand. Juan backed up as his taller foe pressed the edge of his blade at the panting man's throat.

By this time Pedro had recovered his wits and arranged his hose sufficiently to confront the intruder.

"Diego, look out!" Magdalena cried just as Pedro lunged at Torres' back.

Aaron whirled with lightning speed, parrying Pedro's steel with his own. He dispatched his shorter but heavier opponent in one swift, practiced stroke that nearly split his body in two. Sensing Juan behind him, sword regained, he turned and again wielded his blade with blinding precision, severing the squat heavy neck of his foe.

Magdalena had not seen so much blood since she had witnessed a sword fight in the streets of Seville two years earlier. Her rescuer methodically cleaned his weapon with the practiced calm of a soldier used to carnage, then sheathed it and looked at the girl standing before him. Filthy and disheveled, she nonetheless had the patrician features and bearing of the Castilian nobility. His eyes narrowed as he considered how nigglingly familiar she seemed to him. "You know my name, lady," he said, helping the frightened girl to her feet.

Magdalena averted her gaze from the Muñoz brothers and looked into the piercing dark blue eyes of her fantasy prince. Recalling how she had just spied shamelessly on him, she felt the heat stealing into her cheeks as she replied, "You are Diego Torres."

"You have the advantage over me. I do not know your name." In spite of its bedraggled condition, her green wool dress was of a fine cut, and her muddy boots were kidskin. He waited for a reply.

"I am Magdalena Luisa Valdés. My father owns these lands." She gestured to the north grandly.

"How comes a nobleman's daughter to be roaming alone about the countryside?" He could sense her childish guilt interwoven with an inbred sense of pride. Pride, greed, and this worthless stretch of marshland were all the Valdés family had left.

"These were my neighbor's sons. Of noble blood," she added scornfully, evading his real question. "I saw you

17

Shirl Henke

many years ago when the Majesties were holding court in Cordoba. You were there with your father, Don Benjamin. Your name was Aaron then," she said softly, her eyes worshipping his bronzed face.

Remembering the scheming Valdés woman, Doña Estrella, one of that Trastamara bastard's whores, he said coldly, "My name is still Aaron."

"You must not say that, else the Holy Office—"

"You sound as if you were rehearsed by my father," he interrupted with disgust. "I have been dutiful to my country and its one true religion, forsaking the Law of Moses. That will have to suffice. Would you report me to the Inquisition?" he asked with contemptuous amusement in his voice. "Poor repayment for saving your life."

Magdalena gasped. "Of course not! I am most grateful and the Muñoz brothers have always been hated. Everyone will hail you as a hero for killing them."

Aaron snorted in open disbelief. "Have I your leave to doubt that? When a *marrano* kills the sons of an Old Christian noble, he will be blamed no matter what the provocation. You can scarce stand witness to my valor anyway, without destroying your reputation," he added speculatively. She was only a child, but what might she know of her mother's morals?

Magdalena swallowed in horror. "My dueña has always told me sneaking off to ride alone would bring the wrath of Heaven down on me."

She looked so stricken that he chuckled. "Your secret is safe with me if mine"—he gestured to the slain men—"is safe with you. Where is your mount? How came you to be so far from it?" He looked around, seeing no evidence of a horse.

Again Magdalena felt her face flame. "My horse is beyond those trees. I . . . I wished to walk for a bit."

"In this brackish mire?" he asked dubiously.

Her shoulders slumped as she turned and began to slog toward where her filly was tethered. "It was foolish

18

of me, I know." Then she turned and gazed up at him, her face radiant with a gleeful smile. "But if I cannot report you, you cannot report me either."

He nodded. "We will let the authorities think the Muñoz brothers were killed by robbers." He retrieved the dead men's purses, pitched them far out into the bog, and whistled for his stallion, which trotted obediently toward him. Mounting, he reached down and scooped the slip of a girl up in front of him. "Now, where is this supposed filly?"

"Beyond those supposed olive trees," she said sweetly, her heart hammering as she was thrust against his hard body. Fighting the urge to reach up and touch the scar on his clean-shaven jaw, she whispered, "Again I thank you for saving my life and my honor, Don Di— Aaron," she amended.

"Just see you do not ride without escort ever again," he said with the sternness of an elder brother as he slid her from Andaluz after reining in beside her pretty white horse.

"Will you be at court when the Majesties come next to Seville?" she asked breathlessly. His face was forbidding as he said, "I only visit my family briefly . . . to settle a personal matter. The king and queen are encamped outside Granada and likely will be until it falls. I am to rejoin Fernando's armies shortly to participate in the glorious event."

"Will it happen soon?" Her eyes glowed as she envisioned the pageantry of the court, with knights in gleaming armor and ladies in jewels and laces, all marching in a triumphal entry into the last Moorish stronghold in all the Spains.

"I would expect Granada to fall early in 1492," he replied with an odd note of grimness in his voice. "Perhaps I will be at court after that," he added enigmatically.

"Then I shall see you there," she said with relish, "for

19

my father has promised that I shall be a maid in the queen's entourage." She mounted her filly with the unconscious grace of one long accustomed to riding, then smiled winsomely as she tried to smooth her tangled plait of hair. "Only wait, for I shall be a very beautiful lady when next we meet, Don Aaron."

He laughed at the scraggedy girl's spirit. "Perhaps you shall, at that, Doña Magdalena." With that he saluted her and turned Andaluz away.

Magdalena watched him ride toward Seville, then whispered low, "I *will* be beautiful for you, Aaron Torres . . . and I will marry you!"

Chapter One

North of Palos, Fall 1491

On the banks of the sluggish Rio Tinto just outside the sleepy seaport town of Palos, the mighty monastery of La Rabida stood, gray and imposing. Aaron hated the place. At the age of fifteen, he had been sent here as a newly baptized convert to complete his instructions in the Christian religion. The younger son of the House of Torres had been given over as a token of good faith by his family. He was to take holy orders. He smiled sardonically as he rode up to the gate, recalling the truculent boy who had defied and defeated his teachers at every turn, finding few allies during his wretched years under their tutelage.

But now he returned because of a lone youth he had befriended, Diego Colon, son of a visionary Genoese chartmaker. Diego's mother had died in 1485 and he had been wrenched from everything familiar in Lisbon and deposited by his impoverished father with the

Franciscan teachers. Aaron, baptized with the same name as Cristóbal Colon's son, became the child's hero and protector. Both boys suffered the taunts of the other students—for the elder was a hated Castilian Jew and the younger, an equally detested Genoese, whose countrymen had grown rich as bankers and moneylenders in impoverished Castile and Aragon.

Aaron had seen Diego seldom in the past five years, not at all in the past two since he had joined King Fernando's army in the Moorish wars. He patted the letter he carried as he hailed the tonsured youth at the gate and arrogantly gave him the care of his horse. "I seek Cristóbal Colon, the Genoese. Are he and his son Diego yet here?"

"They are to depart on the morrow. Tonight they sup with Fray Juan," the young friar replied, noting the air of authority in the soldier's carriage. Surely the tall blond hidalgo was a man of some import. He carried himself with an assurance that commanded deference. "See the light that burns—"

"Yes, I well know the location of Fray Juan's quarters, Benito," he interrupted with impatience. He paused for a moment, inspecting the gangly young man. "It is Benito de Luna, is it not?"

The round face crinkled in nervous puzzlement for a moment as Benito searched his memory. "Diego Torres?" he croaked, now genuinely afraid of the hard-looking soldier.

"Yes, the *marrano* you and your friend Vargas used to spit upon," Aaron said almost genially, one hand resting lightly on his sword hilt. He watched the young friar back away in mortal terror. With grim satisfaction he turned and strode across the courtyard toward the guardian of La Rabida's quarters.

"The river air was ever oppressive," he murmured as he inhaled the humid decay. Just as he passed a cluster of oleander bushes, he heard voices and footsteps crunched on the gravel. A tall man with faded red hair, shabbily dressed in a blue doublet and much-mended black wool cape, stood talking with a rotund little man in the brown robes of his office. The eleven-year-old boy standing beside his father saw Aaron first and raced across the space separating them, yelling a joyous welcome.

"Diego Torres! Is it truly you? I hoped we would meet again ere my father and I journeyed to France." Round brown eyes were the heritage of his Portuguese mother and now they sparkled in pure delight as the boy embraced Aaron.

"Yes, Diego, it is truly I. You did not think to lose me so easily, did you?" Ruffling the boy's curly black hair, Aaron said affectionately, "I bring good news. You need not fear having to master yet another strange tongue. The Court of Charles VIII is cheated of your father's dream."

"Torres! It is good to see you, my young friend," Colon said as his long strides brought him quickly across the courtyard. "Once already you saved my life at the siege of Baza. Now do my ears deceive me, or do I owe you yet another debt?"

The two tall, slim men clasped each other in a firm embrace as the short, plump figure of Fray Juan came trundling up to them. The Franciscan watched as Torres handed a paper set with an official seal to Colon. "Word from their Majesties? Is the Enterprise of the Indies to be pursued then?" he asked excitedly.

Cristóbal's keen blue eyes crinkled shrewdly as he broke the royal seal. "I do not think that King Fernando would have sent the son of his most trusted physician all the way from the encampment of Santa Fe unless he bore news of some import." He quickly scanned the contents of the missive. "After languishing for six years, I will at last be vindicated!"

Aaron put a restraining hand on Cristóbal's arm. "Do

not let your hopes swell too soon, my comrade. Until Granada falls, the king and queen will only study the matter. Their sole concentration is on driving the Moors from their last stronghold."

"But that surely cannot be long in coming! You fight with their armies," young Diego said with assurance.

The three men laughed at the boy's exuberance. Then Aaron replied drily, "Even so formidable a soldier as I cannot banish Boabdil's army quickly. Perhaps by year's end."

"But I am saved from leaving Castile to plead my case in France," Cristóbal said gratefully.

"I do not think King Charles would be inclined to listen," Fray Juan interjected.

"I agree. The French are everlastingly embroiled in Italian politics, but with the coming of peace in Castile, the monarchs will need the wealth that a trade route to the Indies promises," Aaron said, brushing off his dusty clothing.

"You have journeyed far on royal business and must be weary," the friar said. "I will have a meal and a bed prepared. For now, rest in my library with Cristóbal and Diego." With that, the friar scurried across the courtyard, summoning workers to do his bidding.

Once comfortably ensconced in the heavy leather chairs of the library, Aaron and Cristóbal sipped wine and discussed their plans as the boy sat between them on a stool, listening with rapt attention.

"It is most fortunate that you arrived now. At first light we would have been gone," Colon said.

Aaron's lips twisted wryly. "Some might even say it was God's will."

"I am one such." Cristóbal's voice was quiet, but his eyes glowed with fervent fire. "My enterprise will not fail."

Paradise & More

Seville, January 1492

Aaron surveyed his family home fondly, looking down on the courtyard from the second-story height of the open gallery. The orange and lemon trees waved softly in the morning breeze and the babbling fountain seemed almost to be singing to him. Yet Aaron Torres was not soothed.

"So grim, my son. The war is over and you are returned, God be praised, safe with your family." Serafina Torres' strong face was smooth and serene, belying her fifty years, even though her dark brown hair was threaded with silver.

"How long will any of us be safe? That is the question," he replied softly. "Now that Granada has fallen, those Trastamaras will turn their attention to us—Fernando to bleed us for money, Ysabel to bleed us literally in her religious zeal."

Serafina's brow creased. "But surely not, for we have suffered the loss of so much to secure our safety. We converted and accepted Christian baptism—thousands did. Your father has long and faithfully served the royal household as physician."

"And intermarried his children with the most powerful Old Christian nobles in Castile and Aragon, yes, I know," Aaron said curtly.

"Your bitterness is understandable, but misdirected, my son. Benjamin only acted to save us."

"You are a good and loyal wife, Mother. And," he sighed heavily, "my father has taken what he sees as the only course. But my brother Mateo has become a stranger, concerned only with the interests of his Catalan wife's merchant fleet. And Ana . . . I cannot forgive what has happened to Ana."

"Nor I. But when we betrothed her to Lorenzo, we did not know how unhappy she would be as his wife." Her voice broke.

Aaron swore beneath his breath as he took his mother in his arms. "Forgive me. I know you did not, nor Father."

"Ana is beyond his cruelty now," Serafina said softly. "She is retired to his estates outside Seville to await the birth of the child. Let him cavort with his whores at court. She no longer cares."

"But I do. His blatant infidelity crushed her. He will pay for her pain." Aaron's voice was brittle.

"Never speak of it! You yourself have just said how precarious the position of New Christians is in Castile. We can ill afford to have a member of our family confront a nephew of the Duke of Medina-Sedonia." Her small hands were surprisingly strong as she clasped his shoulders and met his fierce blue eyes, so like his father's.

"I will not challenge him now. I, too, have learned the value of patience. And more than a little cunning from my king. In time, when matters are settled for our family . . ." He let the half formed plan to deal with Lorenzo fade and asked instead, "Do you receive regular correspondence from Ana?"

"Yes. She is glad of the child and eagerly awaits its birth." Serafina paused and looked up at her young son, only twenty, yet more hardened by life than many a gray-haired man. "Rafaela is also with child."

He smiled. "So, Mateo will provide an heir for the family name."

"That only leaves the disposition of my younger son, ever the restless malcontent," Benjamin Torres said, standing in the doorway from the sala.

"Benjamin! You are home. Have you ridden all night? You must be weary," Serafina said, giving her husband a warm hug, which he returned lovingly.

"Yes. While in Málaga I received word that this young rascal's commander released all his men after the

26

victory procession into Granada. Did you see your friend Colon before you rode for home?" Benjamin asked as he embraced Aaron.

"We rode together into Granada. He saw the Moor's fall as an auspicious omen for his mission."

Benjamin turned to Serafina. "Please my dear, I have some matters to discuss with Aaron."

"Go inside and sit down, both of you. I shall have the cook prepare a feast for starving men," Serafina said, watching the silent interchange between father and son. They had quarreled much over the years. Aaron resembled his father physically, yet in other ways he was the exact opposite. Her gentle Benjamin was a skilled physician, quiet and bookish. Aaron was a soldier, impetuous and daring, a man of action, not introspection. Thank God Benjamin's patience was great. She walked along the gallery that encircled the interior of the house, then descended the stairs and crossed the courtyard toward the kitchens.

Father and son settled wearily on piles of brocade cushions that covered a pair of long, low couches. Aaron knew the old man had not ridden all night only to see his wife and son a day sooner. "What is brewing that brings you from your patient at Málaga?"

Benjamin chuckled grimly, "I never could dissemble with you. Isaac is in the city and would speak with us."

"Are you certain we dare risk being seen with your Jewish brother?" The moment he had asked the harsh question, Aaron cursed his own impetuosity. "I am sorry, Father."

"Isaac forgives me. The question is, my son, do you?" Benjamin asked with profound sorrow.

"You know I have. I often speak before I think, then regret my words." Aaron stood up and began to pace restlessly. "Where can we meet Uncle Isaac? We dare not go openly to his house."

"Under cover of darkness it can be done. Since today is neither Friday nor a Jewish feast day, the familiars of the Holy Office will be lax," Benjamin said in a measured voice.

"The eyes of the Inquisition are everywhere. You should have been in Granada after the triumphal procession into the city, Father. That fat old madman Torquemada, who is so in love with fire, set a great one, this time not for people, but for books—all the treasures of the Muslim libraries, thousands of volumes in Arabic and Hebrew, all destroyed! And worse, his power over the queen grows daily."

"Torquemada is only one madman," Benjamin said quietly. "The monarchs need money and we, not he, can raise it for them. King Fernando still relies on many Jewish advisors such as your Uncle Isaac. Even the treasurer of the Civil Militia is Abraham Seneor—a Jew—in charge of the most powerful law enforcement body in all of Castile."

"If it is so secure to be a Jew, then why did we subject ourselves to conversion? Better to have stood with Uncle Isaac and refused."

"You know our agreement," Benjamin said wearily. "One branch of the House of Torres had to convert in order to guarantee our survival if the worst befalls. Isaac agreed to the pact. So did Serafina and Ruth. You were too young. . . ."

"I was fourteen and Ana fifteen. Mateo was seventeen. We remember the old ways. We are neither Christian nor Jew now. Nor will we ever be accepted by the Old Christians. It does not work, this conversion at dagger's point. Families do it to save their lives and property, to keep from being dispossessed and sold into slavery in North Africa. But by becoming New Christians we are all under the Inquisitor General's power more surely than ever we were as Jews."

"We have often before had this argument, Aaron. That

is why I want you to speak with Isaac. He brings news from court. He sent word to me in Malaga. Something of great import is afoot, and it concerns you."

"Colon must have his commission for the enterprise!" Aaron said excitedly.

"Perhaps," Benjamin replied with caution, then looked at his son with a shrewd, measuring eye. "You trust this Genoese sailor?"

"Yes," Aaron answered earnestly. "He is much as we are, a foreigner in every land where he has ventured. I fought by his side in the war. He is brave and steady but of a single-minded resolve."

"He is obsessed!" Benjamin interrupted, scowling.

"I am neither a geographer nor a sailor, but I believe in Cristóbal. If he brings back riches from Cathay and Cipangu, he will receive great royal favor."

Benjamin smiled gently. "And you would share in that favor?"

"I would never trust the patronage of that Trastamara bastard, Fernando, or his zealot of a wife, but the knowledge of lands beyond the sea might bring us refuge in an uncertain future," Aaron replied, still pacing across the thick Moorish carpet in front of his father.

Benjamin stiffened. "Do not call our king a bastard!"

"My pardon," Aaron replied cynically. "You have spent years serving the House of Trastamara. You know what they are. They succeeded to the thrones of Aragon and Castile by murder—Fernando's mother had his elder half-brother Carlos poisoned and Ysabel arranged for her brother Alonzo to have a riding accident."

"Neither tale has ever been proven. But Fernando and Ysabel rule the Spains now and that is a fact," Benjamin said with finality. "Let us put aside your spleen for the monarchs. I wish to know your feelings about supporting the Genoese."

"I would join him on his voyage. Has he other

supporters among your Jewish friends at court?" Aaron asked, his eyes locked on his father's weathered face.

Benjamin stroked his blond beard thoughtfully. "Several."

"What of Ysabel?" Aaron asked. "Cristóbal has often said he felt she favored his cause more than her consort." He smiled cynically. "Of course, Colon's own religious zeal is convincing. He has often said how the riches of the Indies could finance the reconquest of Jerusalem. I know not whether he really believes that possible, but he is a devout son of Rome."

"In spite of her childhood confessor Torquemada's opposition, Queen Ysabel agrees with those who would sponsor Colon," Benjamin replied. "Perhaps she has spoken to him of this taking of Jerusalem. Think of how many Muslims and Jews could be converted en route and then be subjected to the Inquisition."

A soft knock sounded and then Serafina entered with a serving girl who placed a tray laden with food on the low brass table between them. Dismissing the servant, she sat beside her husband and reached for a cluster of grapes. "You are tired, Benjamin. Eat now, then rest," she commanded. Smiling, he complied.

"Father," Aaron said hesitantly, "I . . . I do not wish for us to quarrel."

Benjamin looked at his younger son, the mirror image of himself nearly forty years ago. "Yet we always seem to do so," he replied gently. "These are evil times we live in, Aaron. The strain of surviving them wears on us all. Only remember that we, all of us—my brother Isaac and sister-in-law Ruth, their children—all of us are one family. The House of Torres will live on in the Spains and our children's children will honor us."

His father's impassioned words echoed in Aaron's mind during the rest of that day as he waited for darkness. He was eager to see his uncle once more. He remembered the old man as gruff and outspoken, proud of his heritage. *How can he stomach serving the Trasta-maras?*

Darkness fell. Horses' hooves sounded on cobble-stone. The call of the watch echoed through twisting streets as the night passed without incident, chill and foggy—a good night for an assignation.

"I remember seders at this house during my child-hood," Aaron whispered to Benjamin as they tied their horses in the stables and walked quietly toward the rear entrance.

"You remember so much then," Benjamin said sadly. He knocked once, a sharp low tap. Immediately the door swung wide. A hooded servant gestured silently and they followed him up a dark, twisting set of stone steps.

Isaac Torres was as unlike his brother as could be imagined—short and thickset with coarse dark brown hair. Only the eyes, that same keen measuring blue as Benjamin's, betrayed their common ancestry. His homely face split in a wide smile of welcome for his tall, elegant brother and the nephew now transformed into a soldier. After they embraced and took care to blink back any evidence of emotion their eyes might betray, Isaac gestured to the round oak table. "Come, sit. I have had Ruth prepare refreshment. A cool draught of wine, some fresh fruit and bread."

They sat in the richly carved high-backed chairs around the table. Isaac fixed his guests with a firm stare and said, "This time is precious and we must not waste it. I bring news from court—some good, some ill."

"Has Colon the approval he sought?" Aaron asked.

"Yes, and in that lies a tale. He was summoned before the Majesties in Santa Fe only three days ago to have his petition again denied." At Aaron's angry outburst, Isaac put up his hand for silence. "But no more did he depart than the Keeper of the Privy Purse, Luis Santangel, and I importuned the queen. We have been in contact with a merchant of Palos, one Martin Alonzo Pinzón, who also wishes to back the enterprise. He owns two ships and happens to owe money to the crown. We struck a bargain with Ysabel, shrewd woman that she is. In time she and Luis convinced Fernando that the venture would cost little and gain much. Within hours of the Genoese's departure, we had a royal messenger racing to recall him. He has received his commission to sail west for the Indies!"

Isaac watched Aaron's eyes light at the news. "You will join him?" He knew the answer even before he asked.

"Yes, I will join him. If he pleases the Trastamaras, our family fortunes cannot help but fare better." Aaron's expression became guarded then as he studied both older men. "There is more?" He looked from Isaac to Benjamin.

"We have all been hearing rumors," Isaac began carefully.

"You spoke of tidings good and ill, brother. Let us now hear the ill. Since I worked with you to get Colon his hearing last summer, I have been away from court."

Aaron's eyes widened. So, his father had been in continuous touch with his uncle. He bitterly regretted his words earlier in the day.

"The ill is the worst we feared."

"It is to be expulsion, then?" Benjamin said hopelessly.

"I fear so, although I shall do everything within my power to stop it. We were wise to plant a foot in each camp. If I fail, you must succeed. Torquemada's power over the queen has grown alarmingly since the fall of the Moors. He rails at her night and day. Only Fernando's avarice keeps him in check. The Jews can always be counted upon to bleed ducats into the treasury."

"More might be gained in the short run if he simply expelled all Jews and confiscated their property," Benjamin said thoughtfully. "Remember the laws of Castile prohibit anyone from taking gold or silver from the country."

"Just so. Of course, after a few years without his most vital civil servants to collect taxes, conduct trade and keep his accounts—not to mention treat his ailments—he will come to a sorry pass, but only time will prove that out," Isaac replied with disgust.

"Can you smuggle money from Castile across the Pyrenees into France?" Aaron asked.

His uncle's smile was guileless. "A plan long afoot. We did not wait like sheep to be sheared."

Benjamin's face was bleak. "For a thousand years we have lived in Castile and Aragon. It will be hard to live in a cold northern clime."

"We fought for the Moors and they turned on us. We fought for the Christians and they, too, have betrayed us. Why must we ever be the dispossessed?" Aaron asked bitterly.

"All the greater reason for you to join the Enterprise of the Indies. Colon is your friend. He will take you on. If you find riches in the East, it is yet another refuge for the House of Torres," counseled Isaac.

Aaron smiled, clasping his uncle's hand. "Yes, and perhaps a refuge in a warmer clime?"

All three laughed a bit. They discussed the details of Aaron's trip to court to meet with Colon and join his expedition, then Isaac bade the youth go upstairs and seek out his Aunt Ruth, who longed to see him again. When Aaron had left the room, Benjamin faced his brother.

"There is more," he said bleakly.

Isaac sighed. "Torquemada will expel the Jews at great cost in human misery for many, but we have made our plans. I will help all others I can. Many wealthy men of our faith are so pledged. It is for those we leave behind that I fear. You now fall beneath the Inquisition's power."

Benjamin sighed. "We have converted, Isaac, may God forgive us. We no longer keep the Law of Moses. We attend the mass and eat of the bread. The Inquisition's familiars can find no fault with us."

Isaac's expression was almost pitying. "When we agreed upon this course, I did so to spare you leaving Castile. But now . . . I fear your conversion has been in vain. Do you eat pork? Have you abstained from regular bathing?"

"What has that to do with anything?"

"According to the new instructions promulgated by Torquemada, everything. Not only do his spies watch on Saturday mornings to see whose chimneys do not have smoke coming from them to learn who keeps the Sabbath, but he even sends to the butchers asking who has not purchased swine in the past month. Also, reeking of sweat and garlic in stale filthy clothes is a sign of true piety. If your servants carry overmuch water indoors for bathing, or wash clothing often, it will all be written down. In time, someone will report even the most careful New Christian. When the Holy Office confiscates his property, the Crown, the Church and the spy all get their share."

"But that is monstrous! We have sacrificed so much. My elder son, so far away in Barcelona, my little Ana, wretched with a whoremongering husband . . . all of us abide by their rules." Benjamin's shoulders crumpled, then he straightened up and pounded on the table. "No, by God, I will not let this befall my family!"

Isaac looked miserable as he whispered, "I feared you would not see reason and leave now while you can."

"Castile has been our home for a thousand years," Benjamin replied stubbornly.

"Then so be it. But I am all the more eager for Aaron to sail with the Genoese for the Indies."

Benjamin smiled wistfully. "As if we could prevent it!"

Chapter Two

The Valdés Estate, 1492

The low plains were vibrant with life as the pungent tang of lavender and thyme gave way to the balmier aromas of late spring in Andalusia. The richly fecund scents of olive trees fertilized by horse dung and irrigated by estuaries of the Guadalquivir blended with the sweetness of jasmine and roses. Magdalena reined in her filly and surveyed the vastness surrounding her. In the distance, Seville shimmered on the horizon, gleaming white, gold, and green. She took a deep breath and savored the freedom of yet another forbidden ride.

Remembering the consequences of her shocking escapade of last year, she had not ventured out alone over the winter. But now, Magdalena had other matters to occupy her attention since Diego Torres had returned to his dangerous life as a soldier. Her dreams of becoming a great lady at Queen Ysabel's court had been dashed by her mother. Doña Estrella wanted no daughter gamboling about her. Only last year she had married off Dulcia,

the third Valdés daughter, preceded by Maria and Elena.
Magdalena was to wait at least another year. Would
Diego, covered in martial glory from the war, be mar-
ried by then?

She chewed her lip in vexation, realizing that neither
Doña Estrella nor Don Bernardo would favor a marriage with a New Christian—especially not now that her
father had joined a lay order of the Dominicans.

"Odd, I never thought of Father as particularly religious. Mother certainly is not," she murmured to Orange Blossom as she patted the filly's finely arched neck.
Every possible obstacle seemed to stand in the way of
her dreams, but with the bravado of youth, she brushed
them aside. "Somehow I will go to court and catch
Diego's eye."

Miralda would be frantic with worry, but the old
servant would never dare tell her parents that she had
let her charge slip away. Since Estrella spent so much
time at court and her father was busy with local politics,
Magdalena had been left in the care of servants and
tutors much of her life. For her tutors at least she had
been grateful, learning to read and write along with her
younger brother, José. As was common among women
of the Castilian nobility, Magdalena's mother and sisters
had not learned to read. Her own highly unorthodox
lessons had been opposed by her father, but when
young José, always sickly and spoiled, refused to study
without the company of his sister, Bernardo relented.
Her lessons had stopped abruptly two years ago when
José died of a summer fever.

Always curious and willful, Magdalena stole books
from her father's library and took them with her when
she rode out on dreamy days like today. Ever since the
German printers had come to Seville nearly twenty
years ago, books on all manner of subjects were
available—even that scandalous and utterly wonderful
one on human anatomy! Of course Don Bernardo had

not bought that one. Magdalena had borrowed it from her friend Lucia, who had sneaked it from *her* father's library.

If truth were told, the Valdés family library fared about as well as their overall fortunes, ever on the decline for as long as she could remember. One look at the crumbling west wall of their ancestral estate indicated just how far the Valdés family had drifted into penury. The olive orchards surrounding them were sparse, the gnarled trees untended and diseased. The low stone walls of the main house and its outbuildings had been blasted by a thousand hot summer winds and scorched mercilessly by the Andalusian sun. Little had been done to repair cracked tiles on the roof or to rethatch the hovels of the Valdés peasants. There was no money for repairs.

Magdalena rode up to the stables, passing several scraggly chickens pecking on the sandy ground. Flies droned sleepily about a pair of yoked oxen that stood patiently in the noonday sun waiting for their driver. She dismounted at the low, open front of the stable and smelled the perfume of sweet hay and horses, the usual smells of countryside in spring. Handing the reins of her filly to an old groom, she looked across the weed-infested courtyard to the main house.

A handsome gray stallion whose saddle bore the green cross of the Inquisition stood by the door with one of Fray Tomás de Torquemada's men-at-arms patiently holding the reins. Several dozen heavily armed guards leaned on their saddles beneath the low branches of spreading oak trees, the only shade in the noonday heat. Ever since her father had joined the confraternity as a Crossbearer, one who spied on his neighbors and reported any heretical lapses to the Holy Office, Magdalena had been frightened of Fray Tomás.

She shuddered as the man holding the Grand Inquisitor's horse studied her with narrow, obsidian eyes.

Instinctively she gave him a wide berth as she stepped from the low stone steps into the front door.

Down the hall in her father's library, Magdalena could hear his voice and that of his guest rise and fall in conversation. Her curiosity won out over her repulsion. She slipped into the open courtyard in the center of the large rectangular house and walked along the shaded portico to the open window where the conversation was taking place. Magdalena eased down onto a rough pine bench beside the window. Inside the clipped voice of Fray Tomás spoke.

"You have done well, Don Bernardo, bringing the Muñoz family's judaizing to the attention of the Holy Office. Old Pedro Muñoz confessed to eating meat on Fridays and blaspheming against the statue of the Holy Virgin."

"His lands then all stand forfeit?" Don Bernardo asked tentatively.

"Since the mysterious murder of his sons last summer, his only heir was his daughter. She, too, has confessed to her father's sins."

Magdalena stiffened in disbelief. Pedro Muñoz and his children were licentious and brutal, but judaizers! They had not enough scruples to be Christians, far less to observe the Laws of Moses.

"Here is the money from the sale, ten thousand maravedies," Torquemada said, answering Magdalena's unfinished question.

"Only ten thousand?" Bernardo said stiffly.

"You have received the two orange groves and the sheep pasturage by the river where the Muñoz estate adjoins yours. That is additional compensation enough for your testimony," Fray Tomás replied with finality in his voice. "You have done the Holy Faith a service. That alone should suffice."

Although Magdalena had ample reason to dislike the Muñoz family, she felt her gorge rise at her father's treachery. She knew her old and noble house had fallen on evil days, but this was not the way to mend family finances—by selling family honor and consorting with a madman like Torquemada!

Magdalena slipped behind a large water urn and leaned against its cool smooth sides for a moment. Then she walked slowly to her quarters, remembering Aaron Torres' scornful attitude when she had told him her family name. Small wonder he was contemptuous. Would that cool disdain turn to icy terror when he, as a New Christian, learned of her father's power with the Holy Office? Somehow she knew that a man who still used his Hebrew name so boldly would not fear the Inquisition. But he would despise her for being the daughter of a Crossbearer.

"Perhaps if I cannot get Mother to take me to court in Granada this spring, I can at least use some of Father's ill-gotten wealth to travel into Seville and have a new wardrobe made," she murmured, thinking that the Muñoz brothers owed her that much after their foul attack! She felt the tightening of her old cambric shift across her breasts, which had grown considerably in the past year. Even her looser woolen overdress no longer hid her lush curves. If she had beautiful gowns with low-cut embroidered necklines and grand trains like her mother wore, she would soon catch Diego's eyes. She must remember to call him by his baptismal name. Even if he disdained the power of men like Fray Tomás, she did not dismiss it lightly.

The Torres family had a palatial residence in town, far grander than the modest city home of her family. Perhaps Diego would return to it when his military duty was done. She could learn of his plans if she could get to Seville. Magdalena entered her sleeping quarters and looked about the shabby room. Whitewash peeled off the smoke-stained walls, and dust lay thick on the bare wooden floor. She began to pull up her woolen gown, discarding it on her rumpled bed. Then the cambric shift followed it as she called Miralda.

"Where have you been?" the fat old maid said, wiping her hands on a none-too-clean linen apron. "Your mother wants you to meet her cousin, Doña Luisa." She sniffed and said accusingly, "You have been out riding again."

Magdalena shrugged as she unplaited her waist-length mane of dark red hair. "So I have. If I am to eat midday meal with Doña Luisa, you must fetch me bath water else I will stink of horses. Mayhap I should go before her like a serving woman. She is only here to see if I am comely enough for her son Gilberto." She laughed, knowing the family was far too obscure for her father to consider a marriage alliance. "I itch with sweat. Bring the water, Miralda."

The old woman went in search of a serving boy to fetch water, muttering beneath her breath, "Fah! Watch lest you be accused of judaizing with all your washing!"

The Alhambra, Granada, March 15, 1492

Isaac Torres walked with Abraham Seneor toward the enormous audience room where the sovereigns they had so ably served were holding court. The sun-splashed Courtyard of the Lions, with its ornately worked arcades, glittered with all the vanquished splendor of the last Moorish dynasty to rule in Iberia. As they entered the incredible splendor of the interior hall, neither man paid heed to the surroundings. Far more pressing matters weighed on them.

"What are you able to offer if they will negotiate?" Isaac asked bluntly. "I only wish they had given us time before this summons. I like it not."

Seneor grimaced. "Not giving warning so we could rally our supporters and raise money is exactly the plan of the queen."

"You mean of that slavering madman who stands behind her throne," Isaac replied.

"We can raise enough to send Fernando into fits of such rapturous rapacity that even the healing arts of your brother Benjamin might not rescue him," Abraham replied with grim humor. "You are correct though, a quarter of a million ducats would not move Ysabel or Torquemada."

"The Prior of Santa Cruz has not been about the palace of late," Isaac said hopefully. "Only pray he stays away until the matter is settled." He paused and said, "You truly believe we can gather a quarter of a million ducats so quickly?"

His companion shrugged. "Five years ago I ransomed nearly five hundred of our people when Málaga fell. The cost was dear to everyone who contributed. How much more so is the fate of all Jews in the Spains?"

"If only we had time to contact banking houses in Genoa and Naples," Isaac said tightly.

Abraham Seneor's face, thin and assertive, split in a surprisingly beatific smile. "We can always bluff now and raise the money later."

Isaac's short, thick frame shook with a tension-purging chuckle as he threw back his head to laugh. "Yes, my friend, let us bluff. The Trastamaras were ever good at the game when they had nothing but the backing of a handful of towns to face down all their rebellious nobility."

"Their towns and their Jews, let us not let them forget that," Seneor added gently as they approached the guards standing before the door of the audience room with their crossed halberds gleaming evilly.

Both richly garbed courtiers nodded ever so slightly to the guards and the halberds were pulled back, a signal for them to enter. The royal Jews were expected.

Isaac Torres had always been taken with the incongruity of the king and queen, who ruled with such singleminded precision yet looked such exact opposites. Fernando was swarthy and slim, with a pretty, almost effete handsomeness that might deceive a casual observer into thinking him a peacock, but the cunning in his narrowed eyes measured everyone.

Ysabel was short and plump with an elongated face that was as painfully plain as her husband's was handsome. Her nose was long and bulbous and her neck rippled with slight rolls of fat that were accentuated by a sadly receding chin. Faded red hair stuck out in wispy strands from beneath a woefully old-fashioned turban headdress. Yet, in her watery blue eyes a light of keen intelligence burned that was, in its own way, the equal of Fernando's.

The king sat back, his long, beringed fingers splayed calmly on the rich black velvet doublet he wore. Fernando Trastamara had always affected black clothing except for state occasions. Ysabel sat forward on her ornately carved chair, her small, blunt hands holding a parchment, the heavy antique material used only for official proclamations.

"We give you leave to enter," Fernando said with deceptive indolence, waving Seneor and Torres forward across the gleaming marble floors.

They made their bows formally, since Ysabel was particular about such matters. When Isaac's eyes met hers, her look was grave and nervous. *As if she actually finds this distressing.* The thought surprised him.

"You have our leave to read this. The decision is a sad one, but God's will must be done," she said quietly. Her voice was firm, yet he thought he detected a hint of uncertainty in it.

Both men sat at the low brass table across from the dais where the Majesties were ensconced and quickly perused the proclamation which—significantly—had not yet been signed. So they did want to bargain. Isaac's eyes met Abraham's. The old rabbi spoke first. "Expulsion of all your Jewish subjects would bankrupt the nation, gracious Queen."

Ysabel's mouth firmed. "There is, of course, always the alternative Holy Mother Church so freely offers. Be baptized and know the one true faith," she replied with soft fervency in her voice.

"Do you find that so unreasonable?" Fernando asked, stroking his cleanly shaven chin as he watched the two men like a cat contemplating a pair of fat canaries.

Ysabel looked at her consort and her pale eyes flashed angrily. She was here to save souls, not bargain to increase the royal treasury.

"Our faith, most gracious Highness, has sustained us for nearly five thousand years. We offer our complete loyalty to the crowns of Castile and Aragon, yet we would be Jews, not Christians," Abraham said simply, directing his words to the queen while he noted the king's expression from the corner of his eye.

"This presents a problem, for now that the Moorish heretics have been driven from our lands, we would unite all the Spains under the banner of our Holy Faith," she said, still seated ramrod-straight on her chair.

"Ah, but have the remaining Muslims not been given forty years in which to be assimilated and promised they may practice their religion unmolested for that span of time?" Isaac asked, already knowing the answer since he was one of the chief negotiators of the terms of capitulation.

"How much more worthy of such largess should your Jewish subjects be—they who raised the finances and served in the armies to defeat the Moors?" Abraham asked.

"We would pay for our Spanish birthright," Isaac said bluntly, cutting to the heart of the matter.

Fernando smiled. "Let us discuss this." He looked at Ysabel, waiting for her reaction.

She sighed, always a realist in matters of state expediency. "What would you be willing to pledge in return for a grace period such as our Moorish subjects now have?"

"One hundred thousand ducats would greatly enhance the royal treasury after the costs of taking Granada," Abraham said.

Always loving to bargain, Fernando nodded in consideration. "Surely, if the Spains have been so good to the Jews, they can pay more."

Thus began the negotiations. After nearly an hour, it appeared as though accommodation would be made. Contemplating how soon he could again ask a renewal pledge, the king said with evident satisfaction, "The price for your continuing in our lands is set at three hundred thousand ducats then." He looked at his consort, who nodded her approval.

"Your majesties are most gracious," Abraham said with a smile.

Just then a noise at the end of the hall seized everyone's attention. The guards parted without the slightest hesitation. A white-robed friar in a long black cape stormed into the room. His rounded face twisted in furious outrage as he brandished a heavy ivory crucifix inlaid with precious jewels.

"Three hundred thousand is it! Well met with the Jews," Torquemada said with a feral growl. His yellow eyes fixed first on Ysabel as he raised the crucifix and held it like a talisman before her rounded blue eyes. She seemed to shrink back on her chair. Then the Grand Inquisitor whirled toward Fernando. "Judas Iscariot sold our Lord for thirty pieces of silver—are the Spains worth so much more? Three hundred thousand pieces? Sell Him then and be damned for eternity!"

Torquemada hurled the heavy crucifix at Fernando's feet where it shattered, sending sparkling, blood-red rubies flying about the gleaming floor like an explosion of fiery stars. His voluminous cape flew about him like a raven's wing as he whirled away from the royal presence, given no more leave to depart than he had been given to enter. He vanished through a side door, leaving their Majesties and their two Jewish advisors stunned into silence.

Abraham Seneor looked at his monarchs and knew he had lost. Ysabel once more sat straight, her receding chin amazingly resolute as she stared at her consort, forcing him to meet her gaze. The king was pale beneath his olive complexion as his dark eyes narrowed on the shattered religious artifact. Abraham knew all too well how his crafty, superstitious mind worked.

"You will leave us now. We would confer on this matter . . . and I must pray," the queen said with steel in her voice.

"While we await your pleasure, royal highness, we may be able to raise yet more gold," Isaac said, hoping that Fernando's cupidity would conquer his fears.

"You are dismissed," Ysabel said, rising.

Abraham bowed, his long caftan sleeves brushing lightly against Isaac's as a subtle reminder that unseemly protest would only harm their case. Both men departed with leaden hearts.

"We cannot take their bribe, my lord," the queen said after they were alone. She turned and looked at her husband.

He sat stroking his chin, still staring at the precious gems that surrounded the fragments of ivory and gold. "No, I warrant we dare not. The Prior of Santa Cruz has vast support the length and breadth of Castile, even into Aragon. The people scream for the banishment of the Jews."

"The Church demands it lest they corrupt the New Christians back into their ancient heresy," Ysabel said, her voice rising ever so slightly.

He studied her for a moment and his old air of

confidence seemed to return as he asked, "Do you fear for my soul, beloved? After all, I am one of those with Jewish blood."

She snorted testily. "No, your Jewish grandmother is not what can cause your downfall—it is your desire to keep their council and their wealth. We do not need their council—we have Fray Tomás and many other learned Christians to give valuable advice. Anyway, why need we stoop to accept their petty bribes when by expelling the Jews, we may seize all they own for the glory of the Holy Faith?"

"And for the glory of a united Spanish Empire," Fernando added slyly.

"Do not be impious," Ysabel scolded sternly, then relented, reaching out to touch his richly embroidered sleeve rather like an infatuated young bride. "I shall pray for us and for our realms, my lord. Do you have the royal scribes make copies of the edict for our signature."

"As you wish, my queen," Fernando said dismissively, already turning over the mechanics of how he would apportion the confiscated wealth of the refugees to his best advantage. Deep in thought, he did not see the hurt in her watery blue eyes as she cast down her thin, pale lashes and silently quit the opulent room.

"It is official. I have seen the privy seal on copies signed by them both. The Edict of Expulsion will be promulgated by the end of the month," Lorenzo Guzmán said. His pewter-colored eyes glowed, changing to an icy white. His narrow face was lit with triumph, making even his sallow complexion take on a ruddy hue. He stood up and paced restlessly across the shabby room. Long and gangly in build, he nonetheless possessed surprising strength for one used to the lavish life of a courtier. The slight paunch protruding above his tightly fitted hose was the only fat on his otherwise gaunt frame. "I am certain you can do much with this information." He waited expectantly.

Bernardo Valdés rubbed his hands nervously. "If the expulsion is to be so soon, we have little time. Seville is filled with *marrano* families who will be unable to deny their Jewish relatives succor. Some Old Christians, too, will become embroiled to help save Jewish neighbors."

"You, of course, must be the one to spy these things out. As a Crossbearer to the Holy Office, you have ample means at your disposal. I am only interested in one thing—the fall of the House of Torres," Lorenzo said as he stroked his pointed beard with long, thin fingers.

Bernardo looked at the younger man, anger compressing his lips. "I take the risks while you reap the profits, it would seem."

"I am the nephew of Castile's most preeminent ducal house. I have brought word from court well in advance of the edict—you will profit well enough here in Seville and elsewhere," Lorenzo replied with steel in his voice. He loomed over the short, fat Valdés. Looking around the room, he gestured to the torn velvet on Bernardo's chair, then to the splinters on the library table's well-used surface. The carpet was threadbare and faded where once it had been a thing of plush grandeur. "You will gain excellent compensation—enough to refurbish this shoddy city place and rebuild your ancestral estates as befits the old nobility."

Bernardo shuffled papers on the table nervously. "Why do you risk so much? You married the Torres daughter and received a goodly settlement. As New Christians of great influence at court, your wife's family might stand free of involvement in judaizing."

Lorenzo's eyes narrowed and he spun on one booted foot, his heel grinding down on a cockroach unfortunate enough to have scuttled across his path. "Have you any idea how much more wealth is possessed by the

House of Torres besides my little Ana's portion? Old Benjamin, my esteemed father-in-law, has grown rich as court physician. And the largest shipping firm that plies the Mediterranean is owned by his elder son and his Old Christian wife in Barcelona.

"There is more to it than the money, anyway," he added tightly. "My family arranged that disaster of a marriage—me and a puerile, scrawny Jewess who follows me about like a damned lap dog. Fidelity! She had the unimaginable gall to come sniveling to me of fidelity. She even expected me to bed her when she grew fat and misshapen with child." He shuddered at the memory of Ana's tear-filled blue eyes and bulging belly when he had banished her to his country estate. God's balls, how he wanted her out of his life forever! Her and her whole accursedly lucky family.

"Luck. Damnable Jewish luck. That is what the Torres possess. Even the upstart pup of a younger son drew high honors from the king for his valor in the wars. While I, of the most noble house of Medina-Sidonia, have been reduced to beg crumbs from a Jewish table! But that luck will change. I will see them all crawl! Set your spies to work and report to me within a fortnight."

Bernardo nodded unhappily, afraid of the spleen of this volatile and crafty courtier. Guzmán quit the room, slamming the heavy oak door. The old man watched through the front window as Lorenzo seized the reins of his waiting horse from an old groom and hurled himself into the saddle. Yanking savagely at the gelding's bit, he dug his spurs into the sides of the frightened mount and rode off without a backward glance. Valdés decided he would tread very warily around Lorenzo Guzmán.

Chapter Three

Seville, April 1492

Magdalena rode westward through the narrow, twisting streets, heading her white filly away from the Alcazar gardens toward the open air of the Guadalquivir River. The morning breeze was cool and redolent with the fragrance of orange trees and rose bushes. Tradesmen and vendors stirred, but handsomely dressed young women of noble family were a rare sight so early in the day. Her restless spirit craved an open space where she could let her horse run freely, leaving her groom and her elder sister, Maria, far behind. Just as she sighted the Gold Tower by the river's edge, the steady stream of creaking carts laden with olives, pomegranates, and freshly butchered pigs for the markets thinned, revealing a long, clear stretch of road. Its rain-washed cobblestones gleamed golden in the morning light.

"I'm going to ride to the Church of Saint Stephen at the edge of the river," she called out to Maria, attempting to placate her sister's sense of matronly propriety.

Magdalena urged Blossom into a canter, leaning low over her neck, weaving the small filly gracefully between heavy, wooden-wheeled carts and plodding oxen, a fairy sprite flitting amid earthbound mortals. Her frustrations seemed to fade with her sister's protests. She had spent a week riding by the elegant Torres palace, watching for Diego and his family at the Cathedral on Sundays, strolling in the market to purchase cloth and trinkets she did not want.

Her mother remarked on her piety, sitting through mass three times in one week, while her father complained at her shopping excesses. Still she did not encounter Diego. She had seen his mother in church and his father leaving the house to attend a patient one day, but their son seemed to be in seclusion—or absent from Seville.

She had learned from her mother's sources at court in Granada that he had left King Fernando's army after the city had fallen. Where had he gone? Surely not into exile with his Jewish uncle. The story of the king's most trusted and honest adviser leaving Castile under mysterious circumstances had been retold for weeks. Some said Isaac Torres was on a secret mission to the Majesty's brother-in-law, King João II of Portugal. Some said he had taken all his vast wealth and fled to the south of France, bribing the king to allow him to send gold abroad in spite of laws which forbade it. As she rode, Magdalena crinkled her brow in vexation, praying Diego had not accompanied Isaac.

Magdalena had wheedled a sizeable sum from her miserly father for lavish gowns and jewels, secretly hoping to impress the worldly soldier who had grown up at court. Of course her parents had plans for her other than allowing her to marry into a New Christian family, no matter how wealthy. Since the Expulsion Edict had been promulgated last month, all Jews had until the end of July to dispose of their property and leave the kingdoms of Aragon and Castile. This cast a pall over anyone of Jewish blood, especially recent converts such as the House of Torres with near kindred who had remained in their old faith. No, the Valdés family would wish their youngest daughter married more securely to someone with political power. That was why Don Bernardo had allowed her the extravagance of the new wardrobe in preparation for her debut at Queen Ysabel's court.

"I will marry where I choose," she murmured willfully beneath her breath as she turned the plan over in her mind once more.

Of course, it would work only if Diego were here in Seville, not abroad somewhere with Isaac Torres. With the bravado of a spoiled sixteen-year-old, she dismissed that idea as unthinkable. This would be a beginning. Diego's father was the king's personal physician and a renowned healer. Meeting him would forge the first link between her and his son. For days she had turned the matter over in her mind, deciding to fall ill of a fever before she realized that such a ruse would easily be detected and scorned by Benjamin Torres. For over a week now she had watched him leave his home each morning at daybreak to attend patients in various parts of the city. One elderly man lived on the river's edge at the outskirts of the old Roman wall.

Left to run reckless and unattended in the country, Magdalena was an expert rider and had taken many a fall from ponies and horses since early childhood. How difficult could it be to throw herself from Blossom onto the roadside just as Benjamin Torres emerged from the home of his patient? A few scrapes and bruises would be necessary to make her accident convincing, but Magdalena had suffered far worse.

Because of the cool morning air, she had worn a heavy velvet gown of pale yellow. The color was becoming, but more importantly, the fabric would protect her from overmuch damage—she hoped! Flinging her mantle impatiently across her shoulders, she felt it catch the wind, pulling at the topaz broach that held it fastened at the high neckline of her bodice. Magdalena caught sight of her quarry. Benjamin emerged from the arched doorway of the house and was climbing into his cart. His driver moved the horse into a slow trot when she sped past, seeking a curve in the road where Blossom could be pulled up short and she could fall. A small swale off the cobbled road was overgrown with the weeds that flourished in the rain-dampened earth. She turned Blossom toward it as she rounded the corner, then reined her filly in sharply. The startled horse reared and Magdalena let loose a shriek, then made to slide clear of her mount. She had kicked free of the stirrups with her soft kidskin boots, but the stubbornly strong velvet of her gown caught on the pommel of her saddle, and with it her right leg. As she slid backward, her body and left leg were flung down while her right leg was held for a terrifying moment by the rearing horse's saddle. Then with a hissing rip, the cloth gave way just when Magdalena was certain she was being torn asunder. Merciful Mother, she could be killed! The thought flashed in her mind just as oblivion overtook her.

Benjamin saw the young woman ride past, noting her rich dress and splendid mount, wondering at the boldness of a noblewoman unescorted on the streets of the city. Then he heard a scream and the sounds of a frenzied horse just past the turn of the road. By the time he reached the girl, she lay in a crumpled heap on the side of the road and her small white filly stood grazing a few yards distant. Reaching for the pouch with his medical supplies, he rushed to her side and knelt to examine her just as a groom and a very distraught young woman rode up.

Maria cried and crossed herself, terrified of what

their father would do if Magdalena were seriously injured. As an elder married daughter, she had been entrusted with chaperoning her far lovelier sister. "Who are you, sir, and what has happened to my sister?" she asked in her most authoritative voice, which squeaked in spite of her resolve. Plump and breathless, Maria dismounted and rushed to Magdalena's side.

"I am Benjamin Torres, physician to their Majesties Fernando and Ysabel," he replied, not sparing her a glance as he calmly examined the girl, who was moaning as she regained consciousness. "She fell from her horse, which she was riding far too fast."

Maria was agog at meeting someone so close to the royal couple, for she had married at age fifteen and had never been to court with her parents. In spite of her provincial life, she knew the Torres name. "Can you heal her?" she asked in an awe-filled voice, impressed by his calm manner, but still afraid of her father's wrath.

"I must see if there are internal injuries after she has regained her senses and can speak."

Magdalena's eyes fluttered open and looked into the unsettling blue of Benjamin's eyes, so like his son's. Gentle hands restrained her when she tried to sit up.

"You must lie still a moment. Are you dizzy?" His fingers worked and probed lightly about her head, then up and down each arm with practiced ease.

"No, my head is clearing. I think I had the breath knocked from me." She looked down, needing to find some superficial injury, yet grateful to be alive and whole. Carefully, with Benjamin's assistance, she sat up, ignoring Maria's hysterical weeping and scolding. The moment Magdalena moved her legs a sharp pain lanced up from her groin into her belly and she bit back a scream, then fainted.

She awakened in a strange room, richly appointed with mosaic designs on the domed ceiling and heavy embroidered silk hangings on the walls. Thick Persian carpets covered the marble floors and the bed she lay upon was sinfully soft and piled high with cushions. A small crucifix hung on one wall, seeming as out of place as a pine tree in an orange grove. Instinctively she knew she was in the palatial city house of the Torres family.

"So, you have come back to us at last. I gave you a sleeping draught."

Recognizing Benjamin's voice, Magdalena turned to where he sat, reading. A maid sat dutifully in the far corner, out of earshot. "How long have I been here?" She turned toward him and winced in pain.

"A day and a half. Be careful of that leg. You have badly pulled the muscles inside your thigh, but with time they will heal." He hesitated, putting aside the heavy leather-bound volume with Arabic lettering on it.

Magdalena studied his face, sun-warmed and creased with wrinkles, yet still surprisingly handsome. There was more. She could read it in his expression. "Why has my sister left me here? Am I gravely injured?"

He smiled gently and the even white teeth again reminded her of Diego. "No, not gravely. Your sister and her husband agreed with me that it was best not to move you after I had you brought here and examined you." He paused for a moment, then continued, "I think she fears telling your parents what has happened. After all, you were in her charge."

Magdalena let out a snort of youthful derision. "Maria is afraid of her own shadow. 'Twas my own fault I outrode her and then fell. I will tell our father." She watched as Benjamin took a slim parchment roll from the folds of his robe.

"This should be ample proof of your purity. Have your father read it. He can come to me if he needs further assurances for your betrothal agreement."

Her bright green eyes widened. "My—my purity?" she croaked. Then as he approached, she snatched the

parchment from him. "I can read well enough myself."
She unrolled it and her eyes quickly scanned the
contents. Officially signed and sealed, it attested to the
fact that her hymen had been ripped when she suffered
a fall from her horse. Legally she was still a virgin, fit
property for marriage!

A sparkling blackness surged behind her eyes for a
moment. What had her insane scheme cost her? Now
her father would be certain to rush her into some
loathsome alliance before any could claim her to be
impure. Small wonder she hurt so cruelly at each small
movement of her hips.

Benjamin studied her expressive face, pale and lovely,
keenly alight with intelligence. "This is not the world's
end, Doña Magdalena," he said gently. "You were
fortunate to have me see you fall and attend you so
directly. No one will question what has happened to
you. My reputation as a physician will protect you."

Her clear green eyes met his. "I do thank you for that,
but this accident will only hasten my father's plans to
marry me off, I fear." She looked at the parchment
again.

Knowing the whorish reputation of Doña Estrella,
Benjamin felt he understood Bernardo's reasoning. Yet
this girl was young and unspoiled. "How came you by
the ability to read?"

Her smile transformed the dazed sadness of her face
into radiant pride. "I was taught Castilian and Latin by
my brother's tutors." Her eyes strayed to the volume
laying near his chair. "I would love to learn Arabic, but
'tis frowned on now."

Benjamin sighed. "More than merely frowned on, it is
seen as a sign of heresy by the Holy Office."

"Yet you read it," she said matter of factly.

"I read medical treatises by special license of King
Fernando. I don't think they would interest you," he
added drily.

Magdalena's cheeks tinged pink as she recalled the Latin medical books she had read scarcely a year ago. "Many things interest me, especially the healing arts. Tell me, is it true there are Jewish women who practice medicine?"

Benjamin was intrigued by the artless girl. "Yes, for many centuries now. The Moors will allow no male physician to examine female members of their households. This stricture led to women being trained as healers. I do not think it is feasible for you to consider such an unlikely vocation."

Magdalena sighed. "No, I suppose not, but I am curious about so many things and my father's library is so small . . ." She plucked at the bed linens nervously.

"I will have your maid Miralda bring you as many books from my library as you care to read. She awaits you next door."

Thus began the unlikely friendship between the elderly physician and the sixteen-year-old girl. The following day, Magdalena was well enough to return to her parent's city house. She was laden with volumes from the Torres family library. In addition to the books, Magdalena also took with her the medical certification and Benjamin's promise not to inform her father of the precise and permanent nature of her injury. It would be her decision alone when and to whom she divulged the nature of her defloration, thus avoiding the threat of a hurried marriage to some horrid man like Maria's aging husband.

"I tell you, Benjamin, I like it not. The Valdés family is hand-in-glove with the Inquisitors," Serafina said as she wrung her pale hands in agitation.

Benjamin put his arm about her as they walked toward the gateway to their friends' home. They were dining with the Ruiz family, New Christians like themselves. "Magdalena is nothing like her father—or her mother. Ah, yes," he said with a twinkle, "I have heard court gossip about Doña Estrella, which I am certain has filtered back to Seville. The girl is winsome and bright. She has grown up ignored by her parents, raised by servants and tutors. She is lonely, Serafina."

"All the more reason to beware. If she attaches herself more closely to our household, she might inadvertently let slip some bit of information to her father's Dominican friends. You know how little it takes to convict a *converso* of judaizing."

"Pah! We go to mass regularly and abstain from eating meat on Fridays. What more is asked of us? You are only upset because the expulsion date draws near and our son sails with the Genoese."

"At least Aaron will be safe—oh, I must call him Diego, not Aaron! You see, even our names betray us. I fear even the walls have ears, and the daughter of a Crossbearer . . ." Serafina ran her hands over her silvered hair, smoothing it into her stiffly embroidered headdress. "When will this end, Benjamin? When?"

Across the city Aaron Torres reined in his mount at the Torres palace, letting the warm, golden sunlight and sweetly burbling fountain in the courtyard welcome him. "Soon I will be far away at sea. I will miss this place," he murmured to Andaluz, forcing himself not to think of how much he would miss his parents and Ana and her baby daughter. Bidding farewell to Isaac and Ruth had nearly broken his heart.

A deep bitterness welled up inside him as he recalled the final leave-taking on that bleak mountain road high in the Pyrenees. At least his aunt and uncle were safe, along with much of their hard-earned gold. Yet tens of thousands of other Jews would not be so fortunate. In mid-July, with only weeks before the final expulsion deadline, they clogged the roads in a stream of human misery that stretched from the high plateaus of Castile to the rocky promontories of Catalonia. Aaron had seen

merchants and bankers, physicians and skilled tradesmen, all forced to sell priceless family heirlooms, thousands of acres of land, magnificent palaces, and blooded
livestock for a pittance.

In Lerida he had seen a wool merchant sell his
warehouse for less than a thousand maravedis, which
Aaron knew would barely pay his way from Barcelona
to Naples in a leaky, worm-eaten trading vessel. The
fortunate ones were highly placed politically, men who
had planned ahead pragmatically. Few Jews had believed the monarchs would expel them from their
ancient home and now the majority of the doubters
were paying a bitter price.

The noonday heat was drugging as he dismounted. A
groom took Andaluz and headed toward the stables to
give the splendid beast a thorough rubdown. A wide
grin suddenly slashed Aaron's face as he entered the
shade of the spacious courtyard. Mama always had a fit
when he had done it as a boy, but now—how could he
resist the fountain? He had ridden the length of Aragon
and Castile far south into Andalusia, spending weeks in
the saddle. Dust coated his sweat-soaked skin beneath
layers of clothing. Aaron unbuckled his sword belt and
let it fall with a clatter, then tossed his cape atop it and
began to peel his tunic over broad muscular shoulders.
He knelt beside the fountain and then plunged his head
beneath the cool, sparkling water.

Magdalena stood rooted on the porch watching in
rapt fascination as Diego appeared at the opposite end
of the courtyard, striding purposefully toward the central fountain. Her eyes widened in amazement as he
stripped to the waist and dunked himself in the water.
Entranced, she drew nearer, her silk skirts rustling
softly as she approached.

Years of survival on the battlefield had honed Aaron's
instincts. He stood up and turned with blurring speed to
confront the silent intruder, shaking long shaggy golden

hair from his eyes. "Who—you are the Valdés girl! What by all the saints has brought you to my home?" His scowl was as fierce as if he faced a Moorish soldier instead of a mere slip of a girl.

As he turned toward her, Magdalena watched the water that darkened his hair fly in a spray about his head and her eyes followed the path of the glistening droplets as they rolled over the muscles of his chest and arms. She could smell the faint aroma of male musk and horse that still clung to him. He had journeyed a great distance. Her tongue cleaved to the roof of her mouth and her hand mutely reached out to touch one lightly furred forearm. He was splendid and golden . . . and almost naked! Her glance swept from his broad chest to his skin-tight woolen hose and soft leather boots, then back up his long legs to fasten on a reddish scar that cut across his side and vanished beneath the waist of his hose. "That scar is new," she blurted out, then gasped at her stupidity.

"Yes, it is, but since we met only once last year on the Seville road, how can you know that?" His eyes narrowed speculatively on her pink-tinged cheeks and wide green eyes. The bedraggled waif of Bernardo Valdés had grown into a lush little beauty. Then he realized how she knew about the new scar! "It would seem I was bathing off trail dust both times we met." He answered his own question and was rewarded by her guilty expression and a step backward. He took a step forward to see if she would retreat again.

She did, clutching a volume from his father's library in her hand like a shield. His smile became predatory. "Have you become mute since last year? If an attack by two brigands could not daunt you, little she-cat, surely seeing me only half naked can strike no terror . . . or can it?"

"I am not afraid, merely surprised to see you returned home after so long an absence," she said resolutely. "Benjamin has been worried for you." Magdalena stood her ground, letting him run one long-fingered hand up the tightly fitted sleeve of her pale green silk gown. The warmth of his touch was like the Andalusian sun. She fought the urge to move closer to him.

"Benjamin, it is now? How come you to know my father? And to have leave to walk through our home and use our library?"

"If you stayed home more, you would know," she snapped as he snatched the book from her nerveless fingers.

His brows arched. "Ovid's love poetry. You can read Latin?" Frank incredulity was etched across his handsome face.

"Yes, I can read Latin," she replied, trying to be haughty about her erudite accomplishments while battling her mortification at being caught with such erotic reading material. Should she have denied the truth and said the book was for her mother or married sister?

He opened the volume and flipped through the pages, pausing over a few fondly remembered passages. "So, a lover of poetry who spies on men in their baths." His eyes were merry but assessing.

"If you bathed in more private places, I might not have encountered you. Is it your usual habit to pull off your clothes at every stream and fountain in Andalusia?" She felt the cool stones of the wall against her back as he pressed his advantage, stalking her, book in hand.

Aaron surprised her by throwing back his head and laughing. As he combed his fingers through the curly golden locks, brushing them off his forehead, he replied, "Some streams and fountains in the south of Castile have proven dangerous over the years, but I had assumed my own courtyard was safe."

"I am unarmed, sir, but for my poet," she teased boldly, eyeing the volume in his hand. She loved him most of all when he laughed.

"How do you know my father?"

"I was his patient. I suffered a fall from my horse and he cared for me." *It was all part of a ruse that turned on me. All I have ever wanted was to get close to you, Aaron!* she thought desperately. "When Benjamin learned I was able to read Castilian and Latin he kindly offered me the use of his library. I have come here often in recent months." She studied the veiled expression on his face.

Aaron ran his fingers up her arm and lightly across her collarbone. He could feel her pulse racing. An answering surge of lust throbbed to life in his body, so long starved for a woman. He had always been fastidious about his choice of bedmates, having learned from his father's medical practice what could happen to a man who was careless. She was young and clean and very obviously attracted to him. She was also Estrella Valdés's daughter, and that meant she no doubt possessed the morals of his gardener's pet cat. Still, there was a vulnerability about her. Experimentally, he reached up and touched the silk of her cheek. Her eyes opened wide, then closed in breathless languor.

Magdalena could sense he was going to kiss her, here in the courtyard, while he was half dressed, where anyone could interrupt them. What would Benjamin or Serafina think? She drew back and raised her hand, her eyes once more wide open. "You must not—"

He felt her small, soft hand push ineffectually against his chest as he pulled her to him, the book forgotten in his hand as his arm held her fast. Ignoring her feeble protest, he tilted her chin up and fastened his mouth on her slightly parted lips. She smelled of jasmine and tasted of honey. Aaron deepened the kiss, his tongue rimming her lips, then lightly darting between them, teasing and tormenting until he could feel her softly muffled moan. She would be his, but first he must greet his parents and assure them that all had gone as planned with Isaac. Slowly, savoringly, he broke off the kiss, his mind racing to form a plan on how to set up an assignation.

"I must show my mother and father that I am well returned from my journey and then—"

"They are not home," she said breathlessly. "They have gone to share a meal with friends across the city. Your doorman told me." Why had she spoken the words that sealed her fate?

"And you come and go from here, freely using the library," he murmured low, once more tasting her lips. She did not protest when he resumed his embrace. Aaron Torres vowed to learn why the daughter of a Crossbearer had befriended a Jewish *converso*, but first there was a most pressing hunger to be assuaged. He swept her up into his arms and headed upstairs toward his private quarters.

Chapter Four

Magdalena clung to Aaron, her mind in a whirlpool of confusion. Guilt and doubt warred with six years of languishing, unrequited infatuation. It seemed that she had loved this man forever with all her young heart, and now, for the very first time, he saw her as a desirable woman, not a child hiding behind her mother's skirts or a muddy waif to be rescued on the roadside. *I am beautiful for you, Aaron . . . and I will marry you . . . only you.*

He opened the massive oak door to his apartments and then pushed it closed behind him with one booted foot. The thick Persian carpets muted the sound of his footfalls as he crossed the large outer sala with its low couches and brass tables. Only the harsh rasp of their breathing was audible as he carried her across the room and through a ten-foot-high doorway.

As his warm lips brushed whisper-soft across her closed eyelids, Magdalena clung to his bare shoulders, her nails biting into the hard, satiny muscles of his back. Then he nipped with sure strong teeth at her earlobe and curled his tongue inside the small opening. She gasped with surprise and delight. Before she knew what was happening, he had tossed her onto a fluffy mound of pillows atop an enormous circular bed. As her drugged, breathless body sank into the silken surface, he stood over her, fixing her with passion-glazed blue eyes.

Staring into those fathomless eyes, Magdalena was held in thrall, falling deeper and deeper beneath his spell. She watched his gaze move from her wide jade eyes down her throat to her heaving breasts, then travel lower yet to where her skirts were bunched up and her slim ankles and slippered feet were visible.

"So young, so perfect," he murmured softly as he inspected her beauty, following her down onto the lush bed. One knee supported his weight as he leaned over, placing a hand on either side of her arms. Slowly, like a man afraid to drink too quickly after a long desert journey, he lowered his head to taste of her once more. "Place your arms about me," he commanded as his lips and tongue slid in sensuous trails down her slender throat, then back up to center on her mouth. She obeyed his order, clasping her arms about his bare waist as she opened her lips to meet his kiss. With a groan, he let his control slip, deepening the kiss as he lowered his full weight atop her.

Magdalena could feel every inch of him, even through the layers of her silk surcoat and gown. His hard flesh pressed her deeply into the enveloping bedcovers. Then he moved to his side and gently eased his hand beneath her skirts. His deft fingers worked their way up from her tiny ankle to trace the sleek curve of calf and the velvet softness of her inner thigh. Instinctively she arched toward him, holding him tightly as he stroked her, igniting fires she had never in her wildest fantasy imagined.

Aaron felt her respond to his touch and knew he could wait no longer, savor no more. He must have her now. With catlike grace he sat up and turned his back to her to pull off his boots. Then he stood and peeled down the tight, soft woolen hose that had revealed his desire even while covering it. He watched her eyes widen and her mouth form a small "o" of frightened wonder. *Such a consummate performer,* he thought, chuckling. "You have seen me unclothed before. I claim the right to see you the same," he said hoarsely, stretching his hand out to clasp her wrist and pull her from the bed.

Limp and pliant as a doll, she stood close beside his naked body, her palms pressed against his hard, furry chest, feeling the thud of his heart. Magdalena obeyed his silent instruction like a sleepwalker as he slid her open sleeveless surcoat from her shoulders. It whispered to the carpet as he turned her around and began to unlace her gown. As he tugged the snugly fitted sleeves down, baring her shoulders, his plundering mouth followed, wetting her soft pale skin with his kisses. Her sheer muslin under-tunic was whisked away, soft as an Andalusian summer breeze.

He had imagined her lithe young body budding to a woman's ripeness, but his fantasy did not compare to the reality. The pale pink nipples of her upthrust breasts tightened in anticipation, begging his hands to cup them and his mouth to suckle the pulsing points. Her head fell back as he obliged her. Aaron could feel her pulses racing as she let out small whimpering cries of inarticulate pleasure. His hands moved lower to her slender waist, then curved around her hips to clutch her small silky buttocks and lift her up against his aching staff.

Magdalena felt that vitally male part of him that had so fascinated her last summer now pressing against her belly with insistent hardness. He growled and kissed her lips fiercely, bruising them with his passion. She was frightened and eager all at one time, unable to think or speak, only to respond to each new maddening, magical thing he did to her. Her hair, pulled back from her forehead with jeweled combs, was contained in a sheer lace snood that his impatient hands quickly ripped away. A dark red riot of curls spilled free, filling his hands with lustrous glory. He plucked the combs away and tossed them onto the carpet, then ran his fingers through her hair, massaging her scalp with sensuous thoroughness. When he laid her back on the bed and pulled her wooden-heeled slippers off, she stretched back, hunger and languor oddly merging to obliterate all else.

Aaron slid up the bed, caressing her deliciously delicate young curves as he covered her with his body, nudging her thighs apart with one knee. Her movements were hungry and acquiescent, yet seemingly unpracticed and tentative, as if she knew not exactly what to do or how to move. Yet her hands slid over his back and clasped his shoulders as he lowered his head to kiss her. By all the saints, he would burst if he did not have her now! He kissed her fiercely as he plunged into the soft wet sweetness of her body. She was incredibly small and tight, but there was no barrier to impede his thrust. An instant's regret washed over him, but months of celibacy quickly overrode his foolish hope. He rode her with long slow strokes, savoring as much as he could of her wondrous body, which was still incredibly unsullied by her earlier liaisons.

So this is what is done between a man and a woman, Magdalena thought in wonder, holding fast to him as the beautiful core of heat low in her belly grew into an inferno. If only it might last forever—if only it might be assuaged. She felt her mind spiraling out of control, going blank as primitive instincts drove her. Suddenly, she sensed a change in Aaron's body. Every muscle, hard and tense, seemed to quiver, then turn to stone. The breath seemed to leave his body and his phallus swelled and pulsed in a series of convulsive heaves. Then he collapsed on her like a leaden weight. Her legs instinctively clamped tightly, holding him to her, desperate for him to continue the act which seemed to have ended.

Aaron came to his senses with a slow, drugged struggle. The intensity of his release had been shattering. Surely it was merely his long celibacy, not this hoyden from the court that explained it. He shook his head and rolled away from her clinging embrace, then looked at her flushed face. A surge of guilt, highly irrational and most irritating, overtook him. She lay back with her mane of dark mahogany hair tangled about her shoulders. Her expression was both dazed and hurt. He knew he had gone too quickly for her to be satisfied. His youthful male vanity was stung when he saw what he perceived as accusation in her jade eyes.

He reached out and took a glossy curl in one hand, raising it to his lips. "Do not look so stricken. My apologies for such haste, but I was a long time without a woman. It will not be so when next we come together, I promise." He sighed and stroked her silky shoulder. "I only wish I could oblige you now, but soon my parents will return—"

Her gasp of horror cut short his defensive apology. "What have I done? If Benjamin and Serafina find that I have—that we—Oh! I must go!" She slid away from him, yanking her hair free of his grasp as she jumped off the far side of the bed. Her eyes frantically searched for her discarded clothing and her cheeks crimsoned when she saw how shamelessly it was scattered about the floor. Grabbing her under-tunic, she hastily pulled it over her head. Then she surveyed the crumpled heap of her silk gown.

Reclining on the bed, Aaron watched her antics with increasing amusement and cynicism. "To see you in such a quandary, one would believe you never had a tryst before. Or is it that you would not lose my father's high opinion of you?"

Magdalena dropped the dress she had been inspecting as if it burned her fingers. Her eyes locked with his. "What do you mean? Think you I have done this before?" Then Benjamin's sympathetic words came roaring down on her, explaining about her injury and giving her the document to verify her virginity.

"I know you have done this before, Magdalena," he said simply, standing up and strolling casually over to a large chest from which he extracted a long satin robe. He slid into it and belted it, then walked back to the frozen girl and took her dress from the bed. "Allow me to assist you, since the lacings are in the back."

His cool tone of voice fueled her pain and with it her famous Valdés temper. Never, never would she deny the heinous accusation he made! Generations of Castilian pride demanded she hide her shame. She had loved him from afar since childhood, plotted and manipulated her entry into his life, desperately wanting to win his love, only to have it end this way. *And it is all your own fault, stupid schemer!*

"I appreciate your assistance," she said with a tear-clogged voice that she struggled to keep level. "I am certain you have had much practice lacing ladies' gowns. You unfasten them with consummate ease."

He chuckled as he pulled the fitted bodice tightly around her breasts and began to work the fastenings down her back. "Have you traveled often with the court?" He felt her stiffen.

"Why do you ask? Your family has spent far more time with the Majesties than mine."

"Yes, but things have not been going so favorably for

the House of Torres this past year—or for anyone of Jewish blood. As the daughter of a Crossbearer, I doubt that should escape your notice."

The grimness in his voice frightened her. "I have nothing to do with my father's activities," she replied angrily.

"What of Doña Estrella? She, I hear, is most often with the court . . . and the king." His voice was a silky insult now.

Magdalena whirled on him, her jaw clenched in pained fury. She raised her hand and gave his handsome, arrogant face a stinging slap.

He grasped her delicate wrist with bruising roughness and yanked her against him. "So, you do not like the comparison between you and your famous mother." Her flushed face was a telling admission that she was well aware of the truth of his accusations about Estrella Valdés. "I repeat my earlier question, Magdalena. Why have you sought to befriend my father? What plan ferments in that devious, overly educated mind of yours? Court politics . . . or is it the Holy Office that you serve?"

"You lured me up here, seduced me, tricked me only because you think I am plotting something for my parents!" Her voice broke now and those burning, humiliating tears gushed from her eyes as she struggled to pull free of his hold.

His smile was patronizing. "In truth, I wanted very much what you so freely offered, lady. You are very lovely and I am not so calculating as those of the House of Valdés. Perhaps you judge me by your own standards?"

"You insult me beyond endurance," she said through gritted teeth, dashing tears away with one small fist as she yanked the other free and whirled away from him, stopping only to scoop up her slippers and surcoat before she raced from the room.

"We will meet again, Magdalena Valdés," he called after her. The words echoed in the empty outer chamber and he felt oddly bereft. Once when he was a boy hawking with his brother Mateo, his favorite peregrine was cruelly injured by a larger tiercel and had to be destroyed. The scheming Valdés minx had naught to do with that. Why did the memory flash into his mind now?

He should never have given in to his lust and become ensnared in her web. He misliked any connection with her family. The temper of the times was far too dangerous for such dalliance—if a mere dalliance it had been. She seemed so genuinely inexperienced before he had taken her and so profoundly outraged afterward that she had almost convinced him of her innocence. Absurd. She was no virgin. Still, such a skilled little liar had apparently fooled his father, who was no mean judge of character. He summoned a servant and ordered a bath. He would soak and ponder until he could discuss Magdalena Valdés with Benjamin and Serafina.

Magdalena tore down the stairs to the courtyard, pausing only long enough to don her slippers. Heedless of her unbound hair flying behind her and her long surcoat billowing over her arm, she fled past the fountain and out the rear gateway leading toward the stable where Blossom waited patiently with her groom. Swinging her full skirts across the small horse as she mounted, Magdalena kicked her heels and let the horse fly into the sleepy heat of the afternoon's deserted streets with her servant in frantic pursuit.

Benjamin returned from the Ruiz home early, having left Serafina with her friend Sofia. The two women planned to stroll through the bazaar in search of some token or other. He smiled fondly, certain his wife would search out a special gift for Aaron to carry with him as a talisman on his forthcoming voyage. According to his last letter, the young rascal should return to Seville any day now. In scant weeks he would be bound for the

Indies. Pray God the Genoese was right in his plan and that Aaron would be safe.

As he pondered on these unsettling thoughts, his cart pulled up to the stable and he saw Andaluz. Aaron was home! As soon as Benjamin entered the courtyard, he spied Aaron's weapons and clothing strewn around the fountain. That devilish boy had ever teased his mother to wrath by leaping into the cooling waters on hot days like today. At least his son had shed part of his clothing before dousing himself! Benjamin quickly crossed the courtyard and walked up the low wide stairs that curved toward the gallery where Aaron's quarters were located.

His son's voice called out to him from across the long room. "Father! I hoped you would return soon!" Dressed in clean hose and boots with his leather armor over his linen tunic, he looked freshly bathed and exhilarated, ready to set off on a journey, not a man who had just returned from one.

Embracing his son, Benjamin said, "Why the full soldier's complements? Surely you must not leave so soon? Your mother will be sore beset."

Aaron's face fell. "She is not returned with you? I had hoped we would have this brief time together. I must be off for Palos at once. The town council is holding up the outfitting of the enterprise. Three ships, really only one *nao* and two caravels, to provision, but the Admiral has haggled with them since May. It is near August and we must sail soon to catch the northeast winds from the Canary Islands to the Indies."

"You are no provisioner of sailors. Why must you go to Palos so soon?" Benjamin argued.

Aaron's face grew harsh with anger. "It would seem from the wording of the royal commission, that one of the inducements for signing on this unlikely voyage is freedom from criminal prosecution. Cristobal is in need of someone to inspect the recruits and keep an eye to their behavior during the last stages of the outfitting. As marshal of the fleet, that is my job."

"How long can you tarry?" Benjamin asked in resignation as they walked toward the stairway to the court-yard.

"Of course I will not leave until I have said farewell to Mother and Ana and little Olivia. I detoured on my journey home through Barcelona. It was good to see Mateo and Rafaela again. We had much catching up to do ere I departed. I hate this dispersion—my brother and his wife in Catalonia, our uncle and aunt in France. Now I must leave you here in Seville. . . ." Aaron sighed.

"Yet you must go with the Genoese. We are all agreed on that. We will collect your mother from the market and thence ride to Ana's country house for our farewells together. Tell me of Mateo and your Uncle Isaac as we go."

Arm in arm, the two tall men walked through the green and gold canopy of trees in the courtyard gardens, deep in conversation, oblivious of the shimmering late afternoon heat.

When an exhausted Benjamin and Serafina returned, the moon hung low and full over the tall palm trees lining the streets outside their home. "Pray God he will be safe," Serafina said in a choked voice. She had spent the long afternoon and evening putting on a brave face for her son. Ana had shed tears enough to upset her brother when he departed on his great adventure. Now that Aaron was off, his mother let down her guard.

"Our son has survived the worst the Moors can do," Benjamin reminded her, "not to mention thriving among King Fernando's fiercely jealous military advisors. He will return covered in glory from the Indies, never fear, beloved."

"Yes, I know he is strong and brave and clever—just as his father is, but you always think before you act.

Aaron is so impetuous at times that I marvel he has fared as well as he has. Only recall all the scars he carries from that awful war." She shuddered.

"He is a soldier. Not an easy life, but one he has chosen and is suited for. Can you see him as a physician tending the sick?" he asked her.

A small smile quivered on Serafina's lips and she shook her head. "No. And now that the war has ended, he is well free of court intrigue. Better that he go with the chartmaker and search out the riches of the east."

"You are weary. It has been a long and trying day. Go rest. I would walk and ponder for a bit." After his wife retired, Benjamin paused at the fountain, a grin on his face. Some servant had picked up Aaron's tunic. What would Serafina say if she knew their son still violated her rules about bathing in the courtyard? Finally he walked to the stairs leading to his son's quarters. How long before Aaron would return to them? Had he taken all he would need for such a long journey?

"Sentimental old fool," he murmured as he entered the large open sala. Then as he lit a brass lamp, his eyes caught sight of an expensive volume from his library tossed carelessly on one of the couches. Picking it up, he wondered how it had come to be here. Aaron had read Ovid years ago and surely had little time or inclination to have brought it to his quarters this afternoon. Then his gaze strayed through the wide arched doorway into the bedroom. . . .

I must speak with your mistress," Benjamin Torres said urgently to Miralda, who watched the *marrano* suspiciously as she wiped her fat hands on her apron.

"Who gave you leave to enter? No one is sick in this house," she said, ignoring his request. Magdalena had come home yesterday afternoon disheveled and crying. The old servant knew she had sneaked across town to the Torres palace with naught but a groom for protection. Now the king's own *converso* physician had sought her out. What had been done to her at his home? Miralda did not trust Jews, converted or not.

Struggling for patience, Benjamin resorted to his most commanding court voice. "I have something of great value to give your lady and it must be delivered in person. You will immediately send word to her that I await her in the sala."

Seeing he was not to be deterred, Miralda turned and scuttled across the portico toward Magdalena's room. A few moments later, Magdalena appeared, her eyes red-rimmed and her face pale. She had hastily dressed and combed her hair, leaving it unbound.

Please, Holy Mother, do not let him know what Aaron and I have done! "Good day, sir. What brings you to visit so early in the morning?" She tried for a cheerful voice as the tall old man turned to greet her. Benjamin had only come to the Valdés city house when she was still recovering from her fall. Then it had been so shabby she had been ashamed of it. Now, newly refurbished by her father's wretchedly gained wealth, its opulence made her even more ashamed.

Ignoring the transformation of the sala, Benjamin reached out and took her hands, guiding her to sit on a brocade couch near the courtyard window. His eyes were grave as he studied her ravaged face. *So, the worst is true.* "I have brought you some things, my child." He took the volume of Ovid from his cloak and offered it to her. "This was your selection from my library, was it not? Our doorman said you visited yesterday while Serafina and I were away."

She knew her hands trembled as she clutched the book. Had the meddling old servant said more? She could not meet Benjamin's eyes. "I . . . I must have dropped it in the courtyard. I am sorry. . . ."

When he produced her jeweled combs, she gasped and her face turned up, her eyes locking with his. With infinite gentleness he placed the combs in her limp fingers. "You must tell me what happened, Magdalena. Did my son hurt you?"

She buried her head against his shoulder and began to sob. "It is not as you think. Aaron is not to blame for my foolishness. He did not force me. I . . . I went willingly to his bed." Her voice choked and she gulped great breaths of air in a vain attempt to calm herself.

Slowly, with careful questions and encouragement from Benjamin, the whole story of Magdalena's girl-hood infatuation with Aaron spilled out, from their first encounter at court to his saving her life on the marsh last year, then to her scheme to insinuate herself into the Torres family with such disastrous results. "When . . . when he kissed me in the courtyard," she paused, overcome with shame, "I could think of nothing but how long I had waited for his notice. I thought he returned my feelings—no, no, that is not true. I did not think at all! I merely acquiesced," she finished misera-bly.

"Magdalena, my child, you have loved foolishly per-haps, but you have loved. There is no shame in that. You, as I well know, are an innocent. And my son," he paused delicately, "is not. He will marry you before he sails. We will ride for Palos within the hour."

Magdalena's head snapped up. "Sails? He is leaving Castile?"

"He sails in a fortnight with Cristobal Colon." Benja-min felt her stiffen as he spoke. "Never fear. He will give you the Torres name before he departs. It may be many months ere he returns."

So he had seduced her knowing full well that he was leaving on an adventure to carry him to the opposite side of the earth! She was only his last female solace before the long celibate months at sea! "I will not marry him!" Magdalena replied tightly, remembering Aaron's cruel accusations about her morals and her family honor.

Benjamin sighed. "He thought you no innocent because of the accident, the young fool. I can certainly put that to right, Magdalena. Have no fear."

She stood up, clutching the combs until their sharp ivory tines pricked her fingers. "It is more than that. Much more. He thinks me to be one of my father's familiars—or a court intriguer such as my mother! Look around you, my friend, before you deny the accuracy of his accusations." Her hand swept toward the newly whitewashed walls hung with Bergundian tapestries, lined with lushly upholstered couches and elaborately carved oak chairs. "My family is accursed! And I have stooped to their level, God and all the saints forgive me! My mother would be proud of how I stalked him. I am cut of the same cloth as she!"

Benjamin stood up and took her by the shoulders. "No! You did foolish things, yes, but you acted out of love, not avarice, to gain a husband, not political advantage."

"I will not force him to wed me," Magdalena said stubbornly.

"When came your last courses?" Benjamin asked her softly.

She turned, horror-stricken, then replied, "Last week." Her eyes were enormous, glistening with tears.

Benjamin released a long, relieved sigh. "Thank heaven. You are not likely to be carrying his child. We can be grateful for that. But he has carried away your honor, Magdalena. He may be a fool, but he can be taught the error of his ways. In time I know he will love you."

"Perhaps, but it cannot be forced at sword's point. Let it rest until he returns. We have both of us acted most unwisely."

Benjamin studied the proud, lovely young woman

before him. Never in his life had his intuition guided him this surely. Aaron and Magdalena were destined to love each other. As was the custom, he had arranged the marriages of Mateo and Ana. One had been for good, the other for ill, but in neither case had he felt this way.

Some instinct impelled him to act now and not wait for Aaron's return. Taking the heavy sapphire ring with the Torres family crest from his finger, he reached out for her hand. Unclenching her cold white fingers, he took the combs from them. Then he placed the ring in her palm and closed it.

"Keep this always as a pledge of betrothal between you and my son. He will sail home by year's end. I know it. Will you be waiting for him and give him yet another chance?"

Magdalena could not deny the look of entreaty in his eyes. "Yes, my friend, I will wait for Aaron, your son."

Chapter Five

Magdalena could still see the old Jewish woman as she sat crumpled on the street corner. Her six-year-old grandson was fighting a valiant but losing battle as two older youths rifled through the meager pouch of goods his grandmother had hoarded. He cried and kicked as they threw a Hebrew Bible into the gutter and pushed him on top of it. The wizened face of the woman was beyond pain, dead to all expression, defeated. Magdalena had rushed from the courtyard into the street and driven the youths away with her riding whip. Then she took the ragged pair to the kitchens and offered them food and some coins.

Within a few hours word of her kindness had spread, and several other desolate refugees paused hopefully outside her courtyard. With Don Bernardo at Segovia having an audience before Torquemada, and Estrella at court, Magdalena was temporary mistress of the household. She had opened her gates to give whatever succor she could to these wayfarers on their journey to Cadiz, the major embarkation port of Andalusia.

Her efforts had been short-lived once word had reached Don Bernardo. Magdalena feared he had set some of those awful "Inquisitor's eyes," the street scum of Seville, to spy on his own daughter. Within three days a threatening letter had arrived and today her father came in person, livid over her "judaizing activities."

Bernardo Valdés looked at his youngest child, willful and spoiled but by far the most striking of Estrella's children. He could never be certain whether any of the four girls was his, but that was of no real significance. They were useful for political marriages . . . or other arrangements. This beautiful child-woman would be his best offering at the royal court. Magdalena's striking green eyes and mahogany hair would certainly catch the king's attention. But only if he could keep her free of the Holy Office.

He cleared his throat and placed his hands across his widening paunch. "Not only have you been giving unlawful aid to the Jews, but you have been sneaking away unescorted to visit that accursed physician, Torres. Miralda told me he even came to our house to visit you this past week. I will not have you putting this family in jeopardy."

"I could not watch people who have been our friends and neighbors start their journey with nothing. What I did was an act of Christian charity, not 'unlawful aid.' My friendship with Benjamin Torres should not upset you. He is a *converso* and the king's own physician, high in royal favor."

"*Marranos* can never be trusted, no matter how high their rank. And his own Jewish brother fled Castile with a fortune, a direct violation of royal decree."

"Since the roads are filled with Jews being forced to

leave, I do not blame him for escaping with what property he could take before this tragedy unfolded!" she replied, her hand sweeping to the window. The streets of Seville were clogged with Jewish men, women, and children, carrying what few pitiful possessions they could on their own backs, denied even beasts of burden to bear the meager loads.

Bernardo's eyes narrowed until they glinted like cold gray metal. "You will no longer associate with the *marrano*. And to keep you from succoring any more stiff-necked Jewish swine who fall by the roadside, you will go to the country—if I have to have my men bind and gag you and tie you onto a cart! Once this messy business is over, you will be grateful that I have saved your reputation. Then you will go to court and serve the queen."

Magdalena saw the look of arrogant determination etched on his florid face. He would do as he threatened if she did not acquiesce. Her shoulders slumped in defeat. "I shall pack my clothing, although I see not what it matters if I am to be locked away in the country."

"You will await my summons to court. Miralda will assist you with packing," Bernardo added with oily solicitude, having won his way. He had instilled a terror of the Holy Office deeply in the dueña. The stupid old hag had reported his daughter's every word to him.

Hurt by Miralda's betrayal, Magdalena refused her help in packing. As she folded the soft woolens, rustling silks, rich brocades and cloth-of-gold gowns, she wondered with what blood money her father had purchased the clothing. Once she would have danced with glee for such lovely things, for a lavishly decked-out home, for all the trappings noblewomen of distinguished families expected. *But not this way. Never at this cost,* she thought in horror, squeezing her eyes closed and crumpling a silver embroidered cape in her hands. She had been so foolish, so selfish as to think her life bereft when Aaron casually had taken her innocence and sailed away. Her broken heart would mend, but the very fabric of the lives of entire families had been irreparably rent by the expulsion. Their broken hearts would never mend!

If only she could get word to Benjamin before she left. Magdalena tossed the cape into her trunk and looked about. Miralda was still downstairs receiving her father's last minute instructions. Good. She stole over to her small jewel chest and unlocked it.

The magnificent Torres crest ring winked at her. It was easily the most splendid piece she owned, but the monetary value was nothing to her. Some premonition made her feel the need to hide it. Even possessing the only key to the cask was no safeguard. Since her father had joined the confraternity, all in their household lived in fear. No servant was reliable any more, she thought sadly. Pulling a large locket from the jewel box, she pried it open and took the small muslin spice bag from inside the garish bauble. The pomander was an amulet against diseases, but not noxious smelling, thank heavens. Magdalena pulled the tiny pouch open and hid the ring inside, then quickly replaced it in the locket. She fastened the gold chain about her neck and let the locket with its precious content nestle between her breasts. "From now on I shall surely be free of all illness, for I will never part with my locket." The irony of the locket's design did not escape her. It was embossed with a pearl cross.

Palos, August 2, 1492

"We have been blessed, my friend, in spite of a multitude of tribulations," Cristobal Colon said quietly when he had finished his simple mealtime prayer in the small tavern.

Aaron's face quirked in a grim parody of a smile. "I can not but envy your faith," he replied with a sigh, picking up his wine cup and downing a stout draught of the bitter red liquid, waterfront swill in a small isolated port. He grimaced, looking with distaste at the overcooked mutton and slab of coarse brown bread on his plate.

The older man smiled. "Not the elegant fare you are served at home, but far better than the ship's biscuit you will be eating in the weeks ahead."

"I have downed far worse during the war," Aaron replied, attacking the greasy mutton with his knife. "And you are right. We have been blessed—or lucky. I know not which, but without the timely appearance of that old seaman who sailed for the Portuguese, we would never have recruited the men now aboard."

Colon's pale blue eyes were alight as he replied, "Pedro Vásquez was sent as a sign, a man who was within sight of the golden island of Cipangu and then lost it in the fog."

Aaron scoffed, "The fog of his imagination, I suspect. He was, by your reckoning, off the Irish coast."

The Genoese's face betrayed a glint of humor tempered with the seriousness that always pervaded his nature. "But it matters not that he was mistaken in his sightings—or imaginings. What he did, I as a foreigner could not do—he convinced these skeptical sailors of Palos to sign on the Enterprise."

"You are disliked as a Genoese, but I as a *marrano* am hated far more, in my own land," Aaron said softly, studying the enigmatic man seated across from him.

Colon looked at the youth's bitter face. "Do not be so certain Jewish blood makes you more despised than Genoese blood. All my life I have been a stranger in other men's houses. I have sailed the Mediterranean from Gibraltar to Greece and the Atlantic from the icy seas above Ireland around the hot, still curve of Africa. Everywhere I was a stranger. My wife died in Lisbon and my sons . . . Diego left in a monastery, Fernando and his mother alone in Cordoba, while I pursue my quest.

Shirl Henke

There have been times when I doubted, my young friend, even as you do now."

"Yet you never abandoned hope."

"Have you?" Colon's eyes searched Aaron's face.

The younger man sighed. "I abandoned my faith, my heritage, my identity when I followed my family's bidding and converted. I am not a Jew, but I am a poor Christian. Is there hope for such as I? Look you at the misery along every roadside, in every port. Thousands dispossessed, impoverished, fated for death—yet they, like you, still have hope. By comparison, I must seem mean-spirited indeed," he confessed in perplexity.

"You will find what you seek. Perhaps in spite of their suffering, they will, too. And you may be the instrument," Colon said enigmatically.

Aaron looked at him curiously. "My uncle Isaac is in France. He has saved many lives and given hope to the immigrants, but what can I do?"

"Open the riches of the East—vast and exotic lands filled with diverse men and cultures. Once we bring Castile in contact with such as lies across the Atlantic, how much less menacing will your Jewish kinsmen seem? How much more room will there be for them to live and work? Think of it, Diego. The whole world, one, finally linked in harmony."

Aaron knew his friend and commander believed in his own words. Would there truly be a place for the Jews in the vast new world of the Indies? "I must believe in this, must I not? What else is there but to hope?"

Cristobal smiled. "Yes, now I see the old Diego I first knew at La Rabida, the stout youth who befriended my frightened young Diego. You have been a rare blessing to this enterprise. The merchants and mariners have proven most stubborn in the light of my royal commission. Your help with them has been invaluable."

Aaron replied drily, "I think the good citizens of Palos, especially the Pinzón brothers, mislike the royal

84

command to give over two fine caravels. You did some impressive talking to convince that Basque to give us his *nao*."

Colon shrugged his thin shoulders expressively. "Convincing Juan de la Cosa to join us with his *Santa María* was far simpler than dealing with the Pinzóns. I like not the wallowing pitch of his *nao*. Another caravel like *Niña* would be better."

"The Admiral of the Ocean Sea deserves a *nao*, not merely a caravel," Aaron said, echoing Colon's gentle good humor. "*Santa María* is the flagship."

"The Admiral is first of all an explorer. Those who would chart the Indies' unknown waters need caravels with shallow draft, not grand flagships." Cristobal's eyes gazed out the narrow window to where torches danced like golden sprites at the river bank.

"To sailing at first light!" Aaron raised his cup, echoing the words with a toast, and Cristobal joined him, returning the salute.

August 3, 1492, dawned gray and calm in Palos. Carried out with the morning tide, a *nao* and two caravels set sail in search of a dream.

"Bring water and linens, quickly. I must stop the bleeding else she will die and the babe with her." Benjamin's voice was calm but firm as he issued orders for the servants, who scurried off to do his bidding.

Serafina and Ana stood outside the treating rooms at the front of their home. Both women were grave and pale as they watched the activity inside. "Come, Mother, we can do nothing here. You are shaking. Sit you and rest beneath the orange tree while I fetch a cooling draught of wine for you," Ana said, guiding Serafina into the sunny patio.

"Do not bother with the wine. I am not in need of refreshment, only company," the older woman replied. "If only your father had not sent to the apothecary for those herbs. Now José de Luna will know Benjamin treats a pregnant woman."

"That is scarce a rarity, Mother," Ana said, trying to sooth her agitation.

"But this is a Jewish woman who should have been on board ship with her family yesterday. If Luna decides to report what he knows to the familiars . . ." Serafina shuddered.

"If Father had not kept her here, she would have died on that awful, filthy boat with no physician to attend her. Even with his skills, the birth is going to be difficult," Ana said gently. "Would you expect my father to do otherwise and violate his oath to save lives?"

"Of course not," Serafina replied with a sigh. "We must find a way to smuggle her and the babe from Seville to Cadiz as soon as possible, though. She must leave Castile or face a terrible death."

"I can surely help by taking them to my estate. 'Twill be a simple matter to arrange passage on a safe ship to Fez." In the past years, Ana had grown into a resolute young woman.

Serafina nodded but said bitterly, "For a Jew, there is no safe passage to North Africa. The Muslim slavers take them from the ships, or worse yet, thieves from the slums slit their bellies open believing they have swallowed their gold to smuggle it from Castile."

"I, too, have heard such tales, but we can make safer arrangements. I only fear what may have befallen the girl's husband and parents by the time she arrives."

"*If* she arrives," Serafina echoed doubtfully. Just then a loud banging on the front gates was followed by a cry from without and the sounds of a scuffle. Serafina and Ana leaped to their feet and walked swiftly from the courtyard toward the entry.

"Yield in the name of the Holy Office of the Inquisition!" A man in a distinctive black robe with a white cross emblazoned on its front led a dozen armed civil militia into the house. "We seek Benjamin Torres," the familiar said to the two quaking women.

Fray Tomás de Torquemada felt every one of his seventy-two years that evening. He had ridden from Granada's mountain fastness across the river plain to Seville with his retinue of two hundred and fifty armed guards. He was saddlesore and exhausted. Yet it was far from a commonplace occurrence to have King Fernando's personal physician brought up on charges of relapsing into judaizing ways, hiding a Jewish woman and her newly delivered infant in his own home. The cursed brother, that crafty Isaac Torres, had escaped with his life and wealth, but the falsely converted Benjamin would not mock God thusly.

Torquemada knelt before the small alter in his quarters, made the sign of the cross, and clasped his hands tightly to pray. Always before interrogating a prisoner he went through the same ritual, praying for the extirpation of heresy and the destruction of all who clung to their vain belief in the Law of Moses. Except for a few chosen, such as himself, men with Jewish ancestors could not comprehend the beauty of the one true faith.

Often he feared for the king, whom he knew placed dynastic and political matters before his immortal soul. But Fernando could be ruled in this by the combined efforts of the queen and the Grand Inquisitor. He prayed fervently for almost an hour, then stood unsteadily. His knees ached so painfully that he had to allow the young friar who attended him to assist him in walking to the long dais where he would sit when Torres was brought before him.

Grunting as he sat down on the hard oak chair, Fray Tomás motioned for the friar to usher in the accused. He watched the tall man with graying blond hair and austerely chiseled features approach him. Benjamin's calm assurance evoked jealousy in the inquisitor, as did his physical appearance. For all Fray Tomás's fasting and secret flagellation, he could never seem to lose the slight corpulence that bloated his body. He, of a noble Castilian house, had the coarse features of a butcher, while this Jew possessed the lean elegance of a duke!

"You seem unmoved by the gravity of the charges brought against you, which are serious indeed, Don Benjamin," Torquemada said coldly.

"I assure you, Fray Tomás, I am most concerned, especially for my family who have been unjustly imprisoned with me. My wife and daughter had nothing to do with my treating a Jewish patient," Benjamin said, fighting to remain calm.

"You admit to breaking the law by succoring a Jewess after her expulsion, then." Tomás leaned forward in his chair.

Benjamin shifted the cumbersome manacles that threatened to drag down his thin shoulders. "I am a physician. A woman fell by the wayside, great with child and about to be delivered." He paused and a soft smile touched his lips. "Not altogether unlike the Holy Mother on her journey to Bethlehem. She, too, was a Jewess, Fray Tomás."

Torquemada stood up, furious anger compelling him to cry out, "That is blasphemy!"

"It certainly was not intended as such. The young woman is a mere mortal and yes, Jewish, but she fell too ill to be able to leave Castile with her family. As a physician I was bound by my oath to treat her—I ask about no man or woman's religion before doing this."

"You are a *converso*. To associate with Jews means backsliding into your old heresy," Torquemada thundered.

"I did nothing to violate my baptism, but I am guilty of offering shelter to a woman who would have died had I not cared for her and her child. Let the royal justice judge me for this if it be a criminal offense. The matter is not subject to jurisdiction of the Holy Office. And whether I am guilty or not of aiding a Jew illegally, my wife and daughter had nothing to do with my actions. You have no right to hold them."

"That is my decision to make," Torquemada said arrogantly, stroking his fleshy chin.

"You have bitten off much, Fray Tomás. I am still physician to King Fernando. My family and I cannot simply vanish beneath the dungeon gates of the Inquisition as so many thousands of others have."

Torquemada had always hated the tranquil assurance Torres exuded, but now he seized his opportunity to break the man. "Your royal appeal has been denied. You and your family," he paused to let the words sink in, "are under the complete jurisdiction of the Holy Office."

"On what charges?" Benjamin knew he was betraying fear for Serafina and Ana now. He fought to remain in control.

"You have attempted to corrupt a noblewoman from an Old Christian family, the daughter of one of my own Crossbearers here in Seville. Bernardo Valdés's youngest child, Doña Magdalena."

"She, too, was my patient. I am not to treat Jewish women, and now it seems I am not to treat gentile women either. If my credentials to practice medicine are in question, that, too, is a matter for secular courts, not the Holy Office," Benjamin argued. Serafina had warned him about Bernardo's spleen when he had befriended Magdalena. Pray God his wife and their Ana did not pay for his heedlessness. Bernardo Valdés was as ruthless as the man before him.

"There are other matters beside my foolish daughter's irresponsible behavior," Don Bernardo interrupted. He was pleased when Torres turned in surprise as he entered the room. "There is also the matter of *your* daughter's behavior—such as lighting candles on Friday evenings at sundown, abstaining from pork, and overmuch washing. Your wife, too, seems to purchase little pork for your household consumption."

"We do not keep the Jewish Sabbath, neither at my home nor at Ana's. Ask any of our Christian friends or our servants. As to eating pork, that is a medical matter. The heat of Andalusia engenders worms in it that cause a bleeding sickness in some. There is no rule in Christian instruction that enjoins us to eat particular meats, only that we eat none on Fridays or fast days. That we have observed."

"We have servants in your daughter's home who say otherwise," Torquemada said.

Benjamin turned from Bernardo to Tomás. "That is absurd! Ana is a good Christian. She has had her child baptized and will raise her as a Christian."

"Some trustworthy Old Christian family will . . . I doubt Ana Torres de Guzman will live to do so." As Benjamin paled visibly, the Grand Inquisitor felt a surge of triumph.

Now that the Jews had all left Castile, Magdalena was finally allowed to ride again. The roads were no longer filled with the heart-wrenching refugees and she was considered safe from any temptation that might disgrace her family. Only a few days ago her father had returned home and announced that she was no longer confined to the dreary interior of their rural estate. Unlike the city house, the crumbling old stone fortress had not yet been restored. Magdalena no longer cared about the ill repair of her surroundings, only that she be allowed to feel the wind in her hair as she set Blossom flying across the marshes.

As she returned home, sweat-soaked and weary, she noted a strange horse tethered near the door. It did not belong to one of the odious familiars of the confraternity, nor did she recognize it as one from her neighbor's stable. Such a magnificent black Barb would not go unremarked about the area.

Curious, she dismounted and approached the horse, but knew that in her present bedraggled, filthy state she dare not show herself before a visitor of rank. She would go upstairs and order a bath, but first . . . she must learn if the visitor was worthy of note or not. She slipped into the courtyard and listened at her father's study window.

"All has gone according to plan, then?" an unfamiliar voice asked.

"Better than even your informants could have arranged for me. My spies found him hiding a Jewess and her newborn infant in his own home! Coupled with that and the stories your servants told, the Grand Inquisitor was well satisfied, as were the king and queen. It was a risk for me, you must understand, involving Magdalena's name in this. I will have at least ten thousand ducats from the estate when all is done."

"You will receive your payment. Only be patient. Once Benjamin Torres and his wretched family are burned for judaizing, I will reward you."

Magdalena crumpled to the ground as the earth spun crazily around her, a small pitiful cry caught in her throat, drowned out by the scraping of chairs as the visitor and Don Bernardo rose and quit the library. She fought waves of nausea and blackness. "I must be calm. I have to find a way to save them," she whispered brokenly.

Serafina had always been kind to her, yet fearful because of her father. What had she done to this innocent family by merely associating with them? Had her friendship with Benjamin first brought him to the attention of the Holy Office? Did Benjamin think she had betrayed him?

Struggling to stand up, she clawed her way along the wall until her heartbeat slowed and her head cleared. Then she raced for her room. She had a small fortune in jewelry her frivolous mother had cast off, a careless gift for her daughter's debut at court. Could it be enough to bribe the guards into freeing the Torres family?

Magdalena rode through the twilight, heedless of the dangers lurking on the Seville road. Once in the city, she went to the home of her old friend, Lucia de Palma, only to learn the *auto de fe* was to be held at dawn. Benjamin, Serafina, and Ana were condemned along with a host of other New Christians. All would walk in the horrible procession to the Cathedral, where a mass would be celebrated along with a sermon of thundering denunciation. From there they would be taken to the outskirts of the city to the meadows of Tablada, traditional grounds for the burning of judaizers.

Magdalena swore Lucia to secrecy and then left the house before first light, headed for the Convent of San Pablo, whose grim gray cells housed those doomed to die on this day. Bribing a jailer proved easier than she had believed. No Dominicans were in the dungeons beneath the court, which was staffed by the city's watch. Although the Holy Office condemned men and women to die, often after horrible tortures, the Church itself was never allowed to execute heretics. Once tried in secret, accused by witnesses they were not allowed to see, and judged guilty by their Dominican Inquisitors, the apostates were turned over to the secular authorities to be burned.

The guard was a small, filthy fellow with narrow pale eyes that could freeze blood. God only knew what horrors he had witnessed while working in the dungeons. At first Magdalena feared he would refuse her, but the lure of a gold bracelet set with rubies quickly dazzled him. He sneaked her inside the convent and guided her along cold, dark passageways, leading ever deeper into the very bowels of the earth. At each twist of the labyrinth, a dim torch flickered in its iron wall sconce.

Magdalena tried not to look inside the rooms they passed. She had heard the stories of racks, iron boots, thumb screws, and water ladders. She had no wish to see those instruments from hell. This was hell. The sour odor of excrement and vomit mixed with the oily stench from the torches.

"There. That is the last abode of the one known as the royal physician," the guard said. He unbolted the door and it swung wide. "I will return in an hour's time when the friar has made his rounds. Be ready, else we are both bound for the same fate as your friend."

Steeling herself for what she might find within, she nodded and entered the dark cell with only a small candle she had brought for light and courage. The heavy door closed with a sepulchral clang and the bolt slid into place.

Magdalena accustomed her eyes to the dim light and called out in a broken whisper, "Benjamin?" Was he maimed beyond recognition by those fiends? Had they tortured him?

"Magdalena, child, is that you? You should never have come!" Benjamin's voice was strong as he materialized from the shadows in the far corner of the narrow cell.

"I only last evening learned what had happened! I have brought all my jewelry to bribe the guards. I have fast horses, but I have no plan. You and I must—"

"No, child, no. Your heart is good, but your hope is vain. The guards would never dare let me escape, not for a million ducats, which somehow I doubt you possess in any event." He was pale and unwashed, his hair a mat of tangles and his beard untrimmed, but he looked otherwise whole.

"What have they done to you?" she asked as he held her in a gentle embrace.

"Little enough but talk me into exhaustion."

"Can you not confess—do whatever it is they ask to gain your freedom?" she asked desperately.

93

"Magdalena, my guilt in judaizing, such as it is, is based on fact. I was hiding a Jewish woman and her babe, but that is only a part of the whole. Someone wants me and my family dead and has used spies to concoct tales of our breach of faith that have reached from Castile to Catalonia. Even my son Mateo has been taken. Your father's spies could not have done that."

"Oh, Benjamin, it *is* my fault! If I had not gone to your home so often—my father, accursed be his name for all eternity—must have set his familiars to follow me. I started this with my meddling."

He stroked her back. "Don Bernardo was only a catspaw. You are in no way to blame, Magdalena. As I was questioned by Don Bernardo and even the great Torquemada himself, I pieced together bits of information. Fray Tomas himself is not the least of my foes. He has long hated me, perhaps because of my closeness to the king, and my brother Isaac escaped as you know. That alone was enough to mark me and mine. At least my grandchildren will live, Ana's daughter and Mateo's son. For that Serafina and I thank God."

"You, your wife, your son, your daughter, even your daughter-in-law, all will die and yet you can thank God! I scarce believe in Him any longer and I care not whether he be Jesus or Jehovah!" she whispered tightly, tears burning her eyes as she squeezed them shut.

"Believe in God, Magdalena. It matters not if he is Christian or Jewish. He is still God, the same God for all people, I think." He smiled wistfully in the darkness as she stared up at his face.

"Isaiah said that over two thousand years ago. 'My house shall be a house of prayer for all people,'" she whispered.

"Yes, we did discuss Isaiah's world vision once. Perhaps I am judaizing after all. Be most careful you never say such to anyone else, child. I want you to stay alive for Aaron, not end up in this place."

"We can escape! Do not think to give up," she said with renewed conviction. "Only let me—"

He stayed her hand as she fumbled for the jewel pouch. "There is only one piece of jewelry that will serve useful ends—the ring I gave you."

Her fingers reached up and pulled the locket from beneath her cloak. "I have it hidden in here. I never take it off."

He smiled as he took the garish locket with its Christian symbol and held it in his palm. "Keep it safe for Aaron. Keep yourself safe for my son. Swear this as you love us both, daughter," he said with urgency in his voice.

"I swear, I swear," she whispered in a tear-choked voice.

Chapter Six

The Atlantic Ocean, September 21, 1492

"I like it not, I tell you. These stinking green weeds are the devil's trap to becalm us so we go mad with thirst and drink the ocean's salt until our bellies bloat and we die!" A hulking seaman spat as he looked out at the huge unbroken green, grassy-looking morass the ships were nearing. It seemed miles wide, growing thicker against the horizon.

"I have heard of this weed. It is a sign of land to the west, nothing to cause fear but rather to hearten us on," the admiral pronounced in a loud, clear voice that was calm and authoritative. Standing on the quarterdeck of the *Santa María*, his voice carried to the small cluster of grumbling men below on the maindeck. The sighting had just been made by a man high in the rigging.

For over five days they had seen clumps of the stuff called sargassum. Only mariners who sailed far out into the Atlantic encountered it. Except for the admiral, none of the men aboard the ships of the enterprise had sailed anywhere but south to the Canaries and thence to the coasts of Africa. Colon knew the weeds did not entrap ships, no matter what the myth.

"It does look intimidatingly thick, like a green porridge," Aaron muttered low, standing close to Colon's side so none but the admiral could hear.

Cristobal's lips quirked in the tiniest hint of a smile. "I assure you it is edible, but it will not eat us."

"Do not speak of food," Aaron said grimly.

"The water is calm. Look you how smoothly the bow slices through the sargassum. Surely you cannot suffer from this swift, gentle motion." Colon's faded blue eyes regarded the sun-bronzed face of his young companion.

"I fear I will never make a sailor," Aaron confessed ruefully. "My head still pounds like the siege cannons before Granada. That is sufficient to make a man suffer, even if he is no longer retching over the rail."

"You are as good a sailor as ever I was a soldier. Take heart," his friend said with fatherly toleration.

During the first leg of the voyage when the ship had sailed south to the Canary Islands to take on final supplies, Aaron had found to his shock and chagrin that he was seasick! A number of gentlemen aboard had been in even worse straits, being violently ill while he suffered, less visibly, from a continual headache. After stepping ashore on Gomera, the misery immediately departed, only to return once they sailed west into the Atlantic on the eighth day of September.

Several of the gentlemen were still in the grip of violent nausea and could hold down little food. All things considered, Aaron decided he had been fortunate at that. "I know you have been short-reckoning the leagues we have covered each day so as not to frighten the men with how far we sail west, but how long until we can stand on solid earth again? I promise to bear up," he added, forcing a smile.

Colon chuckled now. "At first you feared you would

die. Now you fear even more that you will not. That is common among young men when first they go to sea. As to how soon we reach landfall—with good fortune and faster winds," he paused as Aaron groaned, "it should be a fortnight, no more."

"Then let us hope we sail directly into the golden harbor of Cipangu."

"Would you rather not pause for respite on the small islands that dot the waters of the Indies first?" the admiral asked. "In truth, I know not if we can reach the land mass first. My charts are greatly at variance and the accounts of overland travelers do not give much detail but to say there are many islands, large and small."

"Perhaps I shall purchase a camel, or if fortune smiles on me, a fleet horse and ride home overland once we reach the mainland. It only took Marco Polo twenty years," Aaron added hopefully.

"I have need of your skills aboard *Santa Maria*, my young friend. There are few enough men I can trust. As marshal of the fleet, you must keep discipline among the crew."

"The estimable captain of *Pinta*, Martin Alonzo Pinzón gains adherents," Aaron said, scratching his bearded chin in consideration. "He is over-eager to reach the prize first and thence sail back to the Majesties and heap all the glory on himself."

Colon snorted in disgust. "*Pinta* is a far faster ship and he a good sailor, I give the devil his due. *Niña* can keep up with her, but *Santa María* is a wallowing giant, not their equal in Atlantic waters. We must endeavor to keep the *Pinta* with us. Perhaps Martin will not desert his brother, Vincente Yañez, aboard *Niña*. I trust Vincente far more than Martin, but I rely on you, Diego, to watch both Pinzón brothers closely."

Aaron grunted. "I will keep an eye on the Pinzóns."

Colon observed the weathered look of the young soldier, now bare-footed and bearded as were all the men while at sea. There were no facilities for the niceties of toilettes. Razors were reserved for landfall. On the slippery wet decks, bare feet gripped far more surely than boots. The court officials on board were aghast at such unseemly habits, but when the royal butler nearly washed overboard one night, he too grudgingly shed his elegant high-heeled slippers.

"The beard suits you well, even if the food does not," Cristobal said to Aaron, admiring the thick golden bristles on his face. "By the time we reach landfall you should have a handsome growth of whiskers."

"Do not even say it," Aaron replied, thinking of long weeks at sea. He stared out as the *Santa María* cut through the sargassum. Wanting to take his mind off that dismal prospect, he said, "I see some of our malcontents are gathering. I will go down and break up the useless fretting."

"I rely on you, Diego," the admiral said serenely.

As was the usual custom aboard all ships, prayers were said at day's end. The Pater Noster, the Ave Maria, and the Creed were spoken, then the Salve Regina was chanted. With his dinner of hard biscuit and a mouthful of salted anchovies sitting ill in his stomach, Aaron stood respectfully for the rote observance, not joining in. Here and there among the Castilians, Catalans, and Galicians of the crew a man remained quiet. The New Christians, although ostensibly converted, were uncomfortable with the ritual. There were no clergy on the voyage and the admiral, although fervent in his own devotions and strict about the custom of the men standing at attention morning and evening for the service, did not command participation of those with no heart to give it.

Aaron looked about the faces of the men, the grizzled common seamen with their red wool caps doffed respectfully, the coolly elegant royal officials mouthing words unconsciously, the Basque ship's master, Juan de

la Cosa, himself craftily watching the others. Then
Aaron's eyes caught those of Luis Torres, the Arabic
translator and scholar. Although sharing a surname,
they were not related, but both were *conversos. He too
wonders if we will find the legendary wealth of the East
and with it a place of freedom.* As if in answer, Luis' dark
brown eyes looked toward the promise of the setting sun
and Aaron's gaze followed.

"The ninth day of October and all we have are false
sightings of land, endless sea birds and clumps of
driftwood," the Basque boatswain said. Barrel chested
and oddly pale for a sailor, Chachu sat cross-legged on
the deck, stabbing a piece of salted mutton with his
knife. He gnawed the meat as he studied the clique of
men seated about him sharing the noonday repast. The
crew ate the day's main meal scattered about the deck
near the crude, wood-burning firebox amidships where
the cook fried the dried meat in olive oil and his helpers
dispensed biscuit, raisins, wine, and other stores. The
officers, the admiral, the master, the pilot, the marshal,
and various other gentlemen volunteers and royal ap-
pointees ate on the quarterdeck, well away from the
conversations of the sailors.

Chachu had a small group of Basque compatriots
gathered about him as well as several men from Palos.
One looked up at the admiral's cabin. "I say if we see no
land by day's end, we confront the Genoese."

Another, lounging against the railing, spat overboard
contemptuously. "Hah. What would that avail us? The
man has said he will sail on no matter how long it takes.
I say we make common cause with those Castilians from
Palos. If we join ranks, we will outnumber followers of
the Genoese. Then we will demand he turn back while
there is food and water left to see us to the Canaries."
He flashed his knife before plunging it meaningfully
into the pile of fried meat.

"I do not know," a youthful seaman said uneasily. "The admiral's marshal is—"

"But a Jew," Chachu interrupted. "Would you fear that yellow-haired boy?"

"Torres fought under the king in the Moorish wars. He is young, but dangerous," another seaman put in. "But he likes to walk a turn from the quarter to the foredeck each night. Perhaps an accident could be arranged. . . ."

The moon suddenly vanished behind the clouds and the ship pitched to starboard. Cursing, Aaron reached out toward the railing and felt cold steel as a knife slashed through his tunic, missing his back by a scant layer of cloth. He whirled, his own dagger instantly in his hand. His assailant had two advantages—the darkness and steady sea legs. Aaron could see by the man's clothes that he was a common seaman, but could not make out his face. The knife in the sailor's hand glowed evilly as he lunged with it. Fright lent him courage, but he was clumsy. As he came at Aaron, the young soldier simply ducked aside, letting the sailor's own momentum carry him forward. Aaron's knife found its target, the soft exposed expanse of throat. With a small, muffled gurgle, the assassin fell against Torres, nearly carrying them both overboard as the ship rolled again.

The moon reappeared, lighting the macabre scene. The man was not one of the Basques, but a sailor of Palos. So, the mutiny had spread. With a silent oath, he consigned the body to the sharks, then considered what to do as he walked aft. The men slept sprawled hither and yon across the ship's deck. He looked at the hatch cover the boatswain usually favored when not on watch. Chachu was not about.

Aaron made his way cautiously between the sleeping bodies, heading toward the ladder that led upward to the quarterdeck. A thin light flicked beneath the admir-

al's door. He rapped lightly and Colon's steward opened
to admit him. The room was small, crowded with charts
and papers piled on the crude wooden table. Cristobal
sat writing in his log book, looking careworn and weary.

"We have trouble brewing, I see," Cristobal said,
eyeing Aaron's blood-spattered tunic. "Are you unharmed?"

"I am fine, but we are one *gromet* fewer." Aaron sat as
the steward withdrew, closing the door. "We must lay
plans for the morrow."

October 10th dawned with golden brilliance. A young
gromet of the dawn watch sang in a clear sweet trill the
ritual morning salutation:

> *Blessed be the light of day*
> *and the Holy Cross we say;*
> *and the Lord of Veritie*
> *and the Holy Trinity.*
> *Blessed be th'immortal soul*
> *and the Lord who keeps it whole,*
> *blessed be the Light of Day*
> *and He who sends the night away.*

Colon paused at the door of his cabin, looking out
across the breaking waves. He could see the sails of the
Niña off starboard, close at hand, but as usual *Pinta* was
far ahead on the horizon. Turning his attention to the
men below, he noted a milling cluster gathered about
the five Basques—all in all, fifteen malcontents. Out of
a crew of thirty-nine, the odds seemed in his favor, but
the Genoese had been at sea most of his life and knew
how quickly loyalties could switch under the grinding
duress of isolation, fear, and even boredom. And there
had been much of all three during the past five weeks
since their departure from the Canaries.

The admiral looked across to where the ship's master,
Juan de la Cosa, stood. His compatriot, Chachu the

boatswain, was with the muttering seamen a distance away. Catching the master's eye, Colon signaled for Aaron to step from his cabin. The marshal was fully armed with sword and dagger, wearing leather armor and a steel helmet. He walked across the deck and leaned casually against the rail where the swivel gun, called a falconet, was mounted. Cosa's obsidian eyes grew round for an instant when he saw Torres, then narrowed, but it was enough to satisfy both men on the quarterdeck that the master was part of the conspiracy.

"The morning watch has been set. There are tasks enough for all to be busy now that the night's fast has been broken. Have you some reason for gathering, Boatswain?" Colon's calm words rang clearly, and the Genoese accent of his Castilian lent them a deceptive geniality. His pale blue eyes shifted from Chachu to Cosa meaningfully.

Finally, the master walked amidships to stand in front of the group led by Chachu. "We have sailed from September ninth, over a month out of the Canary Islands. This is the tenth of October, and we have journeyed farther west than any ships have ever done."

"Least those that lived to return and tell of it," a *gromet* muttered.

"The men want to turn back while there is still provision to reach the islands off Africa," Cosa continued.

"And a whisper of a southeast wind to carry us home," the boatswain finally chimed in. His surly look scanned the rest of the crew, most of whom were finishing the morning's light repast and preparing either to begin the chores of their watch or to find a shady spot out of the traffic and go to sleep. The royal officials, the Jewish scholar, and the ship's surgeon stood apart, beneath the shelter of the quarterdeck near the pilot who held the tiller steady against the wind. None of them was a part of this dispute, which they obviously felt was the responsibility of the admiral and his marshal to handle.

"There will be winds blowing from the southeast to carry us on a more northerly course home. We have provender enough for months yet and many heartening signs—island birds and fresh driftwood. We are nearing our goal. As I am the representative of their Majesties, King Fernando and Queen Ysabel, I mean to do what I have been commissioned to do. We sail on to the Indies." The admiral paused and looked about the men below him.

Now it was Chachu, not Cosa, who seemed to take charge, shoving his big muscular body ahead of Cosa's slight frame. "And if we like it not and want a conference with the captains of *Niña* and *Pinta?*"

"Yes, let us confer with the Pinzons, good men of Palos," one man shouted in a strident voice. Several other of the locals from the seaports of Andalusia joined in.

"As marshal of the fleet, I command all arms, dispensing them to the crew when needed . . . or using them against mutineers . . . when needed." Aaron spoke clearly as he turned the barrel of the small swivel gun attached to the rail. Its mouth, which could belch forth scrap iron in widely spread blasts at close range, was now pointed into the center of the group of Basques and their cohorts from Palos. "Have I your leave to demonstrate, admiral?" He looked at Colon, his face hardened and cold. Now, not even the arrogant boatswain mistook Diego Torres for a boy.

"I do not believe such an extreme measure is necessary, Marshal," Cristobal replied. "There will be no conference with the officers aboard *Niña* and *Pinta*. They, like all of you, have their orders. After the attempt on my marshal's life last night, I instructed him to take certain precautions." A soft murmur of shock rippled around the deck. "The next time anyone raises a hand against royal authority and this enterprise, I will not be so lenient. Don Diego has already dispensed justice to his attacker." Colon's piercing blue gaze riveted on the ship's master first, then on the boatswain. He paused, watching all of the milling, mumbling men.

"I say, let us stand with the admiral!" one seaman from Huelva cried.

Another two from Cadiz joined in, "Yes, yes, onward for gold and the Indies!" Soon others scattered about the deck took up the chorus, drowning out the dissenters. All of them began to disperse, each seaman going off to begin his duties or take his rest.

Aaron waited until everything was quiet, then swiveled the gun to face the open sea and locked it in place, pocketing the key. He walked over to the admiral and smiled grimly. "For now at least, we have weathered the storm."

"I know you will be doubly wary in the future, lest you indeed be swept overboard," Cristobal said with a worried smile. "I shall pray fervently that we sight land soon."

The admiral's prayers were answered. Just after ten in the dark of night on the eleventh day of October, Cristobal himself, looking from the small window of his cabin, saw a light flickering on the horizon. The king's butler, who had been sitting discussing how they might greet and convey messages and gifts to the Eastern rulers, agreed it might be land.

"It looks to be a candle or a torch, perhaps, being passed from one house to another. Summon the watch and have them signal the *Niña* and *Pinta*. Let us see if they can sight it as well," Colon commanded.

A sailor from the *Pinta* called out even before being signaled that they, too, had noted the light, but no further sign was seen through the midnight hour. The deck of the *Santa María* crackled with tension as every sailor, on watch or not, sat up with straining eyes on the western horizon. Then at two in the morning, a cry went up as land truly reappeared, far more clearly this time. The prearranged signal, a cannon shot, thundered from *Pinta*, once again far ahead of the other two ships. Martin Alonzo Pinzón, too, had sighted the dull white gleam of sand cliffs in the moonlight. Three small vessels saw both the end and the beginning of a dream.

Colon estimated the distance to be about six miles. As they neared the shore, the admiral ordered all ships to trim their sails and wait for daylight. The roar of breakers signaled shallows that might run the fleet aground. Best to hold off until they could see where they were. No one slept.

Aaron, on edge for days since the first whispers of mutiny, finally felt a respite. As the ships jogged south and west around the curve of the land mass, awaiting morning's light, he sat on his cramped berth beneath the quarterdeck writing in the diary he kept at his father's behest. Upon his return, it would be more treasured by Benjamin Torres than all the gold and pearls of the Indies. Aaron dated his entry October 12, 1492.

My Dearest Father,
    Land has been sighted. All the admiral's doubters are now rejoicing in his genius. When we go home, all his detractors across the Spains will sing his praises. As for me, I care only to return to the arms of my family, having served you by serving our Sovereigns. Surely this Enterprise will assure a place for the House of Torres alongside the most revered in the royal court. We land at dawn. Although we come in

peace, I have armaments to prepare as a
precaution. I will write more of the landing as
time allows me. Give my love to Mother, Ana,
Mateo, Rafaela, and the children.

As he signed his name with love, Aaron suddenly
found the vision of teary, luminous green eyes in a
small, heart-shaped face dancing in his mind. Preoccupied in recent weeks as the tensions of the voyage
mounted, Aaron had not had time to dwell on Magdalena Valdés or her motives for ingratiating herself with his
family. Still, often in the depths of troubled sleep, over
the long celibate months, she had come to him with the
siren's song of her sleek little body. Memories of the
sweet surcease he had found there haunted his dreams.
Shoving such thoughts aside, he closed the diary and
placed it beneath his bed with his writing instruments.
He would watch the sun rise on the Indies with the rest
of the fleet.

The admiral ordered the ship's boat hoisted over the
side and the royal standards to be brought forth. He was
dressed splendidly in a scarlet cloak and a deep green
brocade doublet, with dark woolen hose and fine black
kidskin boots. The large black velvet turbaned hat
increased his already imposing height. This morning
Cristobal Colon, son of a Genoese wool trader, looked
every inch the Admiral of the Ocean Sea.

Following him toward the ship's boat, Aaron smiled as
he recalled the shoddy, much-mended clothing his
friend had worn in years past as he went from court to
court as a supplicant.

The young marshal took his place in the boat behind
the admiral, having instructed two trustworthy men to
man the ship's lombard and falconet in the unlikely
event that the local populace proved hostile. The translator, royal inspector, and other functionaries took their

seats, and two sailors began rowing. From *Niña* and *Pinta* the Pinzóns did likewise with smaller complements of men.

"I shall be amazed if Martin Alonzo does not try to make this a race to see who lands first," Aaron murmured low for Cristobal's ears alone. He was rewarded with a smile.

"The royal secretary to record the landing rides in this boat," was all Colon said.

Aaron scanned the low, flat land mass which, after the night of circling off shore, they had ascertained to be a small island. The beaches were snow white and the vegetation wondrous. Palms swayed high against the azure dome of sky and lush flowers in brilliant fuchsias, golds, and lavenders dotted the dark primal greens of the forest. The waters of the shallow cove the ships had entered at daybreak were a luminous bluegreen color unlike any Aaron had ever seen off the coast of Castile or Catalonia.

"This is truly a whole new world," he murmured in awe as he watched the dense vegetation for signs of men or animals. Nothing stirred.

When they beached the boats, the Pinzóns showed remarkable restraint, following protocol as they waited for the admiral to step ashore first. Striding boldly through the shallow water, the Genoese traversed the firm, white sand twenty feet or so and then knelt with all reverence and touched the ground, making the sign of the cross and praying fervently and silently for a moment. Then his words rang out clearly. "I name this island San Salvador, after our Holy Redeemer without whose guidance we would never have found our way. I claim it under the temporal banner of my Sovereigns Fernando of Aragon and Ysabel of Castile."

He motioned then for all those poised in the boats to come ashore with banners unfurled. The huge flags of Aragon and Castile carried the initials F and Y emblazoned in green and gold. The royal officials, the ships' officers, and the seamen, as many as could fit in the boats, all knelt and touched the ground with great cries of joy and thanksgiving.

Aaron held back from joining the joyous melee, seeing a series of movements in the underbrush at the edge of the beach. He walked swiftly to Colon's side as the admiral supervised the erection of the large wooden cross he had brought for the first landing. Placing a hand on his commander's shoulder, he nodded to the brown-skinned men with round dark eyes and straight shaggy hair. Three of them stood partially visible in the bushes, watching the celebration on shore. Although adorned with feathers, shells, and gold and copper jewelry, they were completely naked. One carried a crude wooden spear, but none seemed hostile.

Colon opened his arms, sweeping back his blazing crimson cape as he signaled for them to approach. Luis Torres, the interpreter, stood on the admiral's left side, observing the natives, who seemed timid but curious as they approached the men on the beach.

After a few moments of sign language, an exchange of simple trinkets was made for cotton skeins worked in elaborate patterns, darts, and other implements, as well as small pieces of gold jewelry.

Standing on the admiral's right, Aaron observed Luis attempt to communicate by means of gestures and pointing, laughing silently at the waste of the *converso's* finely honed skills in Arabic, the international language of trade. Aaron said, "You do well enough with these simple people. Think you the Khan will speak Arabic?"

Luis shrugged philosophically. "I only hope I can learn this language and teach them Castilian before I must venture further."

Watching the people, mostly young men, who slowly emerged from the jungle, Aaron began to relax. They were not hostile. He had developed a sixth sense about

such things through years of war. Suddenly he felt
someone staring at him and the hairs on the back of his
neck prickled. He turned to find a strikingly handsome
young woman standing on an open stretch of beach,
watching his every move with huge, almond-shaped
eyes of dark liquid brown. Her hair was long, straight,
and lustrously black, her breasts high and pointed, with
dark nipples. She had golden skin, long legs, and a
slender build. Her face, although delicate, was strong
and attractive. She wore a large gold nose ring and
nothing else.

Chapter Seven

Pointing to her breast with one gracefully expressive hand, she said simply, "Aliyah."

He smiled and touched his palm to his chest. "Aaron."

Her eyes were alight with curiosity and open attraction as she gazed worshipfully at his tall, slim body clad in the formal clothing the admiral's orders had demanded. For an instant he recalled the marshes of the Guadalquiver and another young woman's adoring gaze. Then the cat-green eyes vanished, replaced by liquid brown ones.

While the native men examined the swords, armor, and the full cloth capes of the officers and gentlemen, Aliyah was fascinated by the marshal's blond beard and long golden hair. Reaching up, she ran her fingertips delicately through the curly locks that fell to his shoulders, then touched the much coarser bristling beard that had grown unattended on his jaw for weeks past.

Aaron had read that the black men of Africa had little body hair and those light-skinned men far to the East had even less. Looking about and gauging the age of the males with Aliyah, he surmised that these people had never seen bearded men, nor anyone with fair hair. Smiling, he reached out tentatively and touched her heavy tresses, which hung well below her slim waist. The raven hair was coarser than his beard and completely without curl or wave.

She seemed pleased by his examination and stepped closer, running her palm down his arm, then taking his hand in hers and placing it on her left breast. Juan de la Cosa, seeing the exchange, abandoned another, less comely wench and swaggered toward Aaron and Aliyah. "Look what our pretty marshal has discovered," he said leeringly. "She likes not men dark as her own kind, but favors your yellow hair. Still, I wonder how she will like your mutilated manhood once she sees it. It is obvious that these natives have yet all their natural equipment uncut." He put his hand on her right breast as he spoke and she slapped it away with haughty disdain. A swift torrent of words in her own language followed, obviously hostile.

Aaron bristled at the insult he had heard ever since childhood. In the close quarters on shipboard, those of Jewish ancestry were quickly marked as different, and much sly innuendo was bandied about concerning their circumcisions. Up until now, none of the seamen had dared such an impudent slur in the presence of the fleet's marshal, nearly a head taller than any man in the fleet except the admiral.

"These are the first women we all have seen in many weeks, Juan. Because this has caused your brains to drop between your thighs, I will allow you to escape with your life, but only if you keep the admiral's peace among these friendly people." He placed his hand on the hilt of his sword and allowed a mocking smile to spread slowly across his face. "Some men are forever jealous of those possessed of more imposing stature. Do not touch Ailyah."

Cosa flushed but backed off.

The admiral, seeing the confrontation over the most attractive of the four women with the natives, strode over to quash a possible outbreak of violence. "Luis has understood that this female is of some importance to their leader. I will have no quarrels over her nor win the enmity of these people."

"I will not entice her, Admiral," Aaron said as she continued to stand close to him, glaring at Cosa. "It was Juan's actions that sparked her anger."

Cosa glared at Torres but said nothing, knowing the look on Colon's face well by this time. It would serve him ill to protest.

"You will return to the ship for the night. I shall decide what to do and how best to communicate our wishes to their leader." Cristóbal dismissed Cosa, who turned and stomped toward the boats. Then the admiral fixed Aaron with an amused look. "She seems much taken with you, my young friend. Think you that you could teach her Castilian?" He paused and considered for a second. "From your learned father, you know languages as well as Luis does."

Aaron shrugged. "He has already tried Arabic, Hebrew, and Latin with no results. You yourself speak Castilian, Portuguese, and Genoese, the last of which I do not. These simple people comprehend no language common to any of us, I am certain. But they seem intelligent and swift to understand signs."

"You and Luis must ask their leader if he will meet with us tomorrow. I like not leaving us open to attack if we sleep on the beaches, even though they seem friendly enough. Besides, if they see us perform nature's functions, we may all too soon appear mere mortals to them," Colon said with the gentle irony he was wont to display at times. "Now they think we come from the skies, according to what Luis has ascertained."

"I will see what I can make Aliyah understand," Aaron said with a smile.

By the time dusk came and the landing party was ready to board the ships in the cove, Luis, Aaron, and Rigo Escobedo, the royal secretary, had proved most adept at sign language. The natives responded to their queries with simple, honest answers. While they attempted to communicate, Aaron felt Aliyah's eyes on him. Recalling his own words to Cosa about being so long without a woman that a man's reason might desert him, he steeled himself to act in an exemplary manner toward her. She was obviously a noblewoman of some import among the primitives, apparently from a distant island. He was not sorry to bid good even to their new-found friends and return to the *Santa María* for the night, as ignoring her lithesome body and blatant sexual invitations had grown increasingly difficult.

Once aboard, the admiral summoned the officers and other officials to his quarters to discuss what they had learned.

"They certainly like well enough the same trading trinkets used with the Africans," Martin Alonzo Pinzón said with satisfaction.

He and his brother, Vicente Yañez, also a veteran of the coastal trade, nodded his agreement. "For a few hawk's bells, we can obtain a piece of fine gold jewelry."

"Yes, but what we must learn is the source of the gold. Do they mine it or trade for it?" the ever practical Escobedo asked.

"Most vital of all, is the gold given out at the source of their government? How far are we from the great cities where Marco Polo saw the very roofs covered with it?" the admiral asked, his pale eyes aglow with visions of presenting his sovereigns' greetings at the throne of the Khan himself.

"The head man seems to be telling us that this is but a tiny island outpost of little value. The big island they call by a name I cannot pronounce, but it sounds like Cipangu. It is only a few days journey in the dugout boats," Luis interjected.

"They travel from island to island a great deal, I think," Aaron said speculatively. "From what I could gather from Aliyah, her home, where a very large village or city is situated, is due south and slightly east of here. I had her use pebbles to make a map of sorts. They travel across a long string of tiny atolls, using them to sleep at night and as food and water stations. Thus they journey to her brother's city. He is the great chief of the primitives."

"And you would meet him?" Colon asked.

Aaron nodded shrewdly, "If we could train these young people to understand Castilian and act as interpreters, we could learn where we are and where lies the mainland."

"The mainland and the gold," Martin interjected baldly.

Later that night as the moon rose, Aaron stood on the quarterdeck, gazing at the stars hung in silvery splendor over the black lushness of palms and dense foliage.

"You think deeply," Cristobal said, knowing his young friend had something on his mind.

"Now that you are proven right and we have found the outer islands of the Indies, how long do you intend to remain here to explore?" Aaron asked.

Colon joined him leaning on the railing. "I would sail for the mainland, but," he shrugged, "it is difficult to know how many small islands such as this we will encounter. If the accounts of travelers to Cathay I have read are true, there may be thousands. We could explore for many months."

Aaron grimaced at the prospect of more months at sea. "I will be skin and bones, Cristobal. In the still

115

waters of this cove, this is the first night and day I have been free of that infernal headache."

Colon's lips quirked a bit. "And you think travel by dugout preferable to travel by ship? It will be a difficult feat to return to Palos thus."

"Would that I could," the younger man sighed. "But that is not my purpose. If I remain with these primitives and let them guide me to the big island, I will have all those weeks, mayhap months, while you are making charts and exploring. I can learn their language and find out the sources of their gold, perhaps the key to the mainland's location, or the great island of Cipangu. If two or three of them would go with you, we could meet at the village of their great chief when you have finished your search."

"Is this a brave dedication, a terror of the seasickness, or the lovely Aliyah who makes you think of this plan?"

Now Aaron's lips quirked into a grin. "Perhaps a bit of all three."

"I will consider it," was the judicious reply.

October 15, 1492

My Dearest Father,

This land and its people are truly wonders, natural and unspoiled. The admiral has ordered me to remain with the Taino people, as the island primitives are called. I am to learn their ways, their language and their routes of travel about the islands of the Indies. Already we have journeyed by a marvelous boat, a long wooden tree hollowed out, like those on the African coast. Some of the larger Taino *canoas*, as these people call their dugouts, hold seventy people and can travel great distances. We have moved from island to island, and I find the respite on solid land each night greatly preferable to

116

sleeping on a pitching ship. The Tainos have a splendid device in which they sleep in comfort. They weave a cotton net and tie the two ends between trees, allowing a man to lie suspended on the *hamaca* so that the breezes may cool him and his body be spared the hard earth. A most marvelous invention!

I can scarce await the final leg of our journey to the great island where their overlord rules. I am given to understand, as much as I can communicate in their tongue and they in mine, that this island is divided among several overlords. I believe their main village is located on the north coast (although you know me to be no navigator!) I shall report on further wonders when we arrive.

Aaron paused as Aliyah walked quietly up to him and then sat with unconscious grace on the sand at his side. He had not made mention of her to his father, he thought ruefully, knowing his mother and sister would likely read all he wrote. Benjamin might understand, but Serafina and Ana must be protected.

She watched him carefully cork his ink bottle and wrap his writing supplies in the oiled skin pouch he guarded so carefully.

Aaron had not found it difficult to convey the significance of reading and writing to the Taino. They possessed rather sophisticated pictorial symbols with which they adorned their *canoas*, their pottery, even the walls of caves, leaving a historical record of their society. They were intrigued, however, that he could communicate so rapidly by means of his scratchings. He was learning their language a bit at a time. The soft vowel sounds were difficult for European ears to distinguish. So, often he communicated by signs when vocabulary failed.

Aliyah was very adept at sign language. Ever since they had begun their journey three days ago she had been his shadow, shooing away the guards sent to protect her and making overt sexual blandishments toward him that he could not ignore. Apparently, there were no rules governing chastity for Taino women. He had watched the other girls of their party bed with various of their own men, switching partners each night.

Only Aliyah held aloof from the activity, refusing other offers and playing cat and mouse with him. Desperate as he was for sexual release and attractive as he found her, Aaron was not at all certain he enjoyed being the mouse to her cat. Also, he was an officer of the fleet, and as such, a representative of the crown, and she was the daughter of a *cacique*, a headman of some importance.

Dusk on this third night began to envelope them in its balmy embrace and her nearness stirred him. If only they could communicate more clearly and he understood what lying with her might mean in terms of commitment.

Aliyah placed her hand on his chest and felt his heart thud. A slow smile played about her lips. After much coaxing, she had cajoled him to shed the strange hot cloth he wore above his waist, although he still insisted on the coverings for his lower body. Never would he relinquish the leather belt with its strange metal weapons that cut, but such was a warrior's prerogative. In time she was confident she could get him to wear only the sharp spears and abandon the rest of his foolish tight garments. Already the pale skin beneath that mysteriously furred chest grew darker as sun and wind touched it. How she longed to see the rest of his splendid body!

Her clever, soft fingers glided to the tight lacings at his waist and she began to untie them. Aaron froze and his hand shot up, closing over hers as he looked around the clearing to where other men and the handful of women sat at several small fires. Others lay stretched out on the soft sand. No one seemed to be paying any attention to Aliyah and him. The two older men who were the *cacique's* guards charged with protecting her were occupied eating the last of the roasted meat from the evening meal. Apparently, they had abandoned all attempts to watch over her. He stood up, pulling her with him. Then scooping up his dress cloak, now rather the worse for wear, he led her around a curve of the beach to a secluded spot and spread the cape on the sand.

"Now," he said with a smile, placing her hand at the lacings of his hose. She immediately comprehended and began to unfasten them as he unbuckled his sword belt and tossed it and his dirk onto the ground close at hand. Cupping a full, bronzed breast in each palm, he let his thumbs rub over the dark brown nipples. She arched into his caress and the tips of the large globes hardened and contracted.

Unfamiliarity with European clothing was all that kept her from stripping him with great haste. She uttered several words, expletives in her tongue, Aaron was certain, when the lacings knotted beneath her eager fingers. He helped her complete the task, then felt his breath leave him when she boldly reached inside his hose and freed his straining sex, caressing it with practiced hands.

About to lose control and spill his seed, Aaron took her skillful hands and removed them, then pulled her down to his cloak. He sat up and yanked off his boots and peeled down his hose. All the while Aliyah watched in fascination. The combination of frank sexual curiosity and childlike wonder was oddly familiar. The little Valdés witch had displayed much the same traits of eagerness and surprise, yet Magdalena's strange vulnerability and hesitance were absent in Aliyah. She reached out and pulled him toward her, letting her hands caress his body.

She stared in amazement at the difference in coloring of his skin. The sun had begun to bronze his upper body, while his lower half was starkly white in contrast. Always his body hair fascinated her. She traced the thick golden mat from his chest in its narrowed descent over his flat belly to where it blossomed thickly around his groin.

A smile twitched at his lips even as he fought the frissons of ecstasy her touch evoked. She handled his phallus, examining it as a Toledo steelmaker might a finely honed sword. Her eyes rose to meet his with an unspoken question. "Yes, I am different than your men," he said, then groaned as she stroked the hardened shaft. "Well, perhaps not all that different," he whispered raggedly, covering her soft flesh with his body.

He kissed her face and brow, traced his lips about her ear and temple, finding her hair amazingly fragrant. The Taino people were far cleaner than most Castilians, he observed as his mouth centered on hers for a deep, increasingly fierce kiss.

Aliyah had never had a lover such as the golden one from the sky, who worked such magic with his lips and hands. His body was wondrously different as well, with its patterns of crisp light furring. Even his planting stick, large and magnificent, stood smooth and proud, its tip uncovered without her touching it. He was truly magic!

Aaron watched her eyes open wide, then close in blissful surrender as her fingers curved around his shoulders and she pulled him close, her nails digging into the bunched muscles of his back. He felt her legs open wide for him, her hips arch in invitation. With an outrush of breath, he plunged into her wet warmth and felt her drawing him deeper into the vortex of passion.

He rode her fast and hard, oblivious of his surroundings, feeling only her fierce, joyous response as she wrapped her legs tightly about his hips and met each thrust.

Like a hot-blooded young stallion long held back from a mare in season, he quickly rode to a blinding climax. Then, as time and place returned, he feared he had disappointed her in his desperate need. Wounded green eyes flashed in his mind, filled with hurt puzzlement, but when he opened his eyes and gazed into Aliyah's brown ones, he saw an utter satiation that matched his own with its simple animal acceptance of a natural urge, well fulfilled.

They lay for a while, stroking and kissing lightly, comfortable without verbal communication, wrapped in the balmy night air. As he enjoyed his freedom from the sexual tension that had plagued him for weeks, his mind drifted and he remembered Magdalena's far different response to his passion. She was as experienced as Aliyah, yet far less honest about it, he thought angrily. Of course noblewomen of the court were always deceivers. *Why am I thinking of a foolish girl a world away when I have a far more satisfactory one right here?*

Aliyah sensed the tension that suddenly bloomed in him and recalled that he had cried out at the moment of his release. Some feminine intuition told her that the word "Magdalena" was a woman's name. She rolled up and began to kiss him, starting at the marvelous golden hair that grew from his face, then moved lower to his chest. Her lips and teeth worked on his hard male nipples until he groaned. She stroked his already hardened planting stick and smiled wickedly, but when he tried to roll atop her once more, she pushed him back onto the ground and straddled his narrow waist. Then she lowered herself onto him and they both let go of the past, at least for that night. . . .

* * *

"One more day and night in the *canoa* and we will arrive," Aaron murmured as he watched the men loading their supplies for the last leg of their island-hopping journey. Over the past fifteen days he had learned a great deal about the Tainos, especially their language. They would be good and loyal subjects of the Trastamaras, but only if the monarchs were wise enough to rule through their local leaders. The simplicity of their life in this rich island paradise was deceptive, for already he had learned they were skillful farmers, hunters, and fishermen. The tools and pottery they used hinted at a far more complex culture than he or the admiral had at first believed possible. Yet their lack of guile and abundance of childlike trust led him to fear what European avarice might wreak. He would have long and careful discussions with the *cacique* when they reached the big island.

Already he felt responsible for the Taino. Perhaps the lovely woman strolling sinuously up to him had something to do with this, he mused, wondering if they would be missed if they slipped off for a hour or so before embarkation.

Aliyah ran her hand along his stubbly jaw, feeling the prickly whiskers. "You need cut face again," she stated in Castilian. The first morning when he had shaved his beard off, he drew quite a crowd of amazed Tainos who watched as if it were a magic ritual of some sort. They insisted on feeling his smooth jaw when he had completed the greatly longed-for toilette. "I want watch." Her hand glided lower to the hair on his chest and she smiled as she felt his heartbeat accelerate.

Aaron smiled back and extracted his razor and the highly polished piece of steel which so fascinated her when he showed her her own reflection in it. "Lead me to the pool you spoke of and I will shave. You can watch," he said in Castilian. Aliyah understood.

They walked away from the low fires over which the

men roasted *hutias,* small rodent-like creatures which
were the first fresh meat he had tasted since crossing the
Atlantic. Aaron abandoned his qualms about dietary
restrictions, even in the face of his father's medical
opinions. The dark sweet flesh had tasted better than
fine beef to him! Dawn gilded the sky as the young
couple wended their way through the tangle of vines,
huge leafy plants and brilliant flowers, none of which he
or anyone else in the fleet could name.

At first he had wished another man from the fleet had
accompanied him, but the only one desirous of doing so
was Luis and he was under royal order to remain with
the admiral as translator in case they stumbled upon the
city of the Khan, an event Aaron thought more and
more unlikely. When all others refused, he insisted on
going alone. Since *Santa María* had no need of her
marshal while in the Indies, he could serve better
learning from the native peoples. Two brave Tainos
agreed to journey with the admiral and guide him at
length to their home island, where Aaron would be
waiting. Loneliness for another to speak his language
quickly passed as he became fascinated with the Taino
ways and language. His relationship with Aliyah was
also a decided cure for melancholy, he thought ruefully
as they approached the pool.

Women, even those of high rank such as Aliyah, were
not expected to be chaste. In fact, the onset of puberty
was celebrated as a time for boys and girls to begin
sexual experimentation quite openly. She had singled
him out from all the admiral's men on San Salvador and
did not regret it. He watched her rounded, golden-
brown buttocks swing enticingly as she led him to the
pool.

While he shaved, she watched in fascination, as
always insisting that the hair must all be carefully
gathered up, including that which he wiped from his
razor. Then she buried it in a hidden place so evil *zemis,*

as the Taino called their gods, could not use it to work mischief. Their religion was a fascinating puzzle to him, one he had not yet the language skills to fathom. They revered their family and village *zemis* and feared others, as well as the ghosts of dead mortals. He chuckled as he remembered how he had learned of that. The second time he and Aliyah made love, it was full dark. She had reached out and inserted her finger in his navel before she would let him touch her. Ghosts, it seemed, had no navels! This was a routine precaution taken before making love in the darkness.

Finishing his shave, he watched her bury the discarded whiskers while he laid out his full dress regalia. He had decided, hot and impractical or not, he would arrive to greet the headman looking impressive, as befitted a "man from the sky." The admiral's lessons in the deportment and dress of a leader had not been lost on him.

After a brief, playful interlude in the pool, he dressed and they returned to the beach. At once he could sense something was wrong. Women hid in the undergrowth and men stood in small groups, their crude lances and darts in hand, talking animatedly and pointing toward the opening of the cove where a large dugout rowed rapidly toward shore.

Aliyah exchanged words with one of her guards and turned to him in fright, speaking rapidly. He held her by her shoulders and said, "I cannot understand you. Talk slowly."

"Caribe come! The flesh-eaters," she said, pointing to the *canoa* about one hundred yards from them and closing rapidly.

The hair on the back of his neck prickled. These were the ancient enemies of the Tainos, who lived in the south. They took captives, not as slaves but to fatten for their stew pots! "We shall be meat for no Caribe," he growled, walking swiftly to the dugout where his possessions were stored. He extracted a light arbalest and a large quiver of fletched bolts.

"Go to the shelter of the jungle," he commanded Aliyah slowly in Castilian. When she paused with fear-filled eyes, he smiled. "I will be safe. Only watch from afar." Then he handed the open quiver to one of her guards, saying in the Taino language, "Hold arrows for me."

The man did as instructed, looking very dubious as he compared the four-foot-long arrows of the Caribes with the fifteen-inch bolts in Aaron's quiver. The Taino were spear throwers who could fight only at close range—when they fought at all. Aaron took the arbalest and placed the bow on the ground with the stock resting against the inside of his thigh. Then he braced his foot on the bow, reached down to grasp the bow-string, and pulled it upward until it fastened into the firing notch of the stock. He slipped a bolt into the groove atop the stock and then held the weapon aloft, sighting it in against the *canoa*, now barely eighty yards away. He squeezed the trigger lever and the bolt hissed free, flying toward the Caribes, overshooting the dugout by several yards. Cursing, he repeated the exercise as his quiver holder's eyes widened with amazement. The bolt flew true this time, knocking the first Caribe in the *canoa* backward against the fellow behind him. A third bolt felled another attacker. The paddlers stopped on command and the dugout began to turn in the water. Aaron took advantage of the easy targets presented when the Caribes shifted course, knocking half a dozen more into the water as he unleashed his powerful arbalest bolts with the deadly accuracy born of long and serious practice.

The Caribe rout was complete and they headed out to sea accompanied by the joyous shouts of Aaron's Taino friends. "Man from sky save us," one said in awe. Aliyah threw her arms about his neck as the others examined the magical crossbow and short arrows that traveled such great distances with unbelievable accuracy. During the siege of Granada, Aaron Torres had become famous for knocking Moorish guards from the citadel's walls from nearly three hundred yards with a heavy arbalest fitted with block and tackle.

"You truly a god," Aliyah said with pride infusing her whole body.

"Nay. I am but a man, all too good at killing," he replied, feeling oddly ambivalent. He was elated at saving his companions from their fierce predatory enemies, yet as always when the heat of battle ended, he felt saddened that he had never possessed his father's instincts to heal and preserve life. His only skill was in taking it.

With a sense of premonition he said, "Come, let us journey to your home. I grow eager to speak with your *cacique.*"

Chapter Eight

The Village of the Cacique *of Marien,*
December 22, 1492

Dearest Father,

So much has happened I scarce know where
to pick up my tale. Life among the Taino people
is remarkable indeed, with each day full of new
experiences. I have told you of their handsome
appearance, generosity and friendliness. During
the weeks since last I made an entry I have
become a fisherman apprenticed to my friend
Guacanaguri. They have a fantastical fish that
they actually leash-train to catch turtles, sharks
and other large fish. Had I not witnessed it
myself, I would not believe it either. The
creature has a long sucking snout which attaches
itself to the prey and holds fast. Then the
fisherman reels in his pet, who is fastened by
stout hemp lines, and dispatches the catch with
a spear. These marvelous creatures are captured

young and held in tidal pools where they
become accustomed to the leash and learn to
hunt, being rewarded with a piece of their prey
each time they are successful. This day I reeled
in the *cacique's* own *remora*, as that is what they
call them. Through its skill I caught a huge sea
turtle on which we all feast this night.

I will bring you one of their ceremonial pipes
and the aromatic, mildly narcotic powder they
inhale through it, which I have described earlier.
Some people, although not of this village, prefer
to roll the leaves and burn them, inhaling the
smoke directly into their nostrils, a most
disagreeable sight and smell. As to the medicinal
properties of this *tobacco*, I know not, but you
will doubtless find it interesting.

Aaron paused and looked across the room of their
large, gable-roofed *bohio*. As a residence for a *cacique's*
sister, it was much bigger than the *caneyes* of the lesser
classes, but made of cane poles, a wood-beamed ceiling,
and a thatched roof like theirs. A large, hearth-fired clay
pot, beautifully painted, sat in one corner next to the
twilled basket in which desiccated ancestral heads were
kept. He smiled to himself. There were many things he
could not write to his family for fear of shocking their
sensibilities, the Taino burial practices being among
them. The dead were prepared very reverently, but
before being interred with great ceremony in one of the
caves some distance from the village, the deceased was
decapitated. His or her head was lovingly shrunken and
dried, then placed in the basket. Only young children
who died escaped the basket. They were cremated and
their ashes kept in tiny urns beside the family's *zemis*, or
small idols. The *zemis*, too, were difficult to describe for
his family. They were really quite beautifully carved
male and female figures, all completely nude with

greatly exaggerated genitals and bellies. When he questioned Aliyah about this she had asked in all reasonableness, "Are not procreation and eating the most pleasurable gifts of the gods to humans?" The *zemis* merely reflected the philosophy of Taino life.

Another facet of their culture he could not share in his diary was the bizarre code of sexual morality. All positions of authority, including the royal line of *caciques*, were passed to the son of the dead ruler's eldest sister. Thus, maternity, not paternity determined inheritance. Chastity was not a value for women before they themselves chose a mate. That made the maternal inheritance rule imminently practical, he supposed, but his strict Jewish upbringing made the concept abhorrent. A man should know who his children were! Of course, considering the morality among the ruling classes in Castile, he doubted if many of the nobility could swear the children bearing their names were truly of their blood.

That disturbing thought brought memories of Magdalena Valdés rushing back to him. Did she carry his child? Such was possible, but since she was as free with her favors as any unwed Taino female, he could never be certain of his fatherhood. Forcing himself to dismiss the oddly painful and guilty thought, he looked at Aliyah. She, too, could be carrying his child. He had been received by her brother, the young *cacique* of Marien, as the savior of the trading expedition his sister had led. He was accorded every privilege of royalty, from the spacious *bohio* in which he lived to the privilege of having Aliyah share his bed. There were no conditions placed on this hospitality and the *cacique*'s sister certainly favored him, but Aaron often detected the wistful hope of Guacanagari that his guest would offer to marry Aliyah. His conscience smote him because he did not wish to do so. She was lovely, complaisant, and obviously worshipped him. Her brother, a man of honor and intelligence, entrusted him with all his wealth and placed everyone in the village of three thousand souls at his disposal.

What awaits me in Castile? Perhaps once I return and talk with my parents, I will come back here . . . to Aliyah. His love for her was the joyous uninhibited lustfulness of youth, but was it also the genuine companionship that created a permanent bond such as Benjamin and Serafina shared? He wished no less than that, but had often doubted he would find it. Ana certainly had been forced to settle for less.

"Your thoughts are troubled," Aliyah said, putting down her work. "Is it that my brother's gold hunters have been able to find so little for your admiral?"

He smiled at her and shook his head, replying in the Taino language, "No. I have seen the riches of this land, the people, the crops, the magnificence of mountains and rivers. Men can live and thrive in peace here. They need only tools and a will to work, not gold."

"Then you miss your family?" Aliyah watched his face grow even more pensive.

"Yes, my parents grow old and my sister is unhappily wed. My brother, like me, sojourns far from home. Yes, I miss them."

"But you have no wife," she said, her voice laced with uncertainty, although he had repeatedly told her he did not. "Will you go back to the sky when the admiral comes here?"

Her voice sounded both jealous and sad. Aaron felt the old guilt gnaw at him as he took her hand, pulling her up from the earthen floor. "I have told you we cross the waters. We do not sail to the sky. We are but men, not gods, Aliyah, all too mortal in our sins."

She waited patiently, knowing he did not want to answer her.

Sighing, he added. "Yes, Aliyah, I will have to return to Castile with Don Cristobal."

"Forever?" she asked with the beginning of a pout marring her full lips.

"Forever is a long time," he replied with a lazy smile, reaching out to her. "Let us not consider it until the admiral arrives here."

She came eagerly into his embrace.

Later, as evening fell, Aliyah prepared the staple food in their diet, *cassava* bread. Seated on a stool, she patiently scraped the outer skins from the *cassava* plant with a piece of sharp flint. The bitter roots, once peeled, squeezed, and shredded, were baked like unleavened bread, a food considerably more palatable than ship's biscuit. Outside their *bohio* the thick white meat of an iguana roasted slowly over the coals. With minimal hunting and fishing, the men of the Taino supplemented the carefully tended crops the women grew. Because of the year-round warmth, two planting seasons were possible. Nature yielded great bounty here.

Aaron lay in his *hamaca*, contemplating how it might be to live out his life among these people. Of course, he would first have to return to Seville and explain his choice to his family. His mother would be bereft, but somehow, he thought his father would understand. Aaron drifted off to sleep, dreaming of bringing his family here to see the marvels of the Indian islands. Then a russet-haired nymph intruded, standing beside Benjamin.

He was startled from his reverie when Aliyah's younger brother called his name excitedly. He swung from the *hamaca* and the disturbing dream faded as he faced the fourteen-year-old boy. Caonu was slim and fine-boned with the features of a choirboy, almost too delicate for a male. Only a heavy gold nose ring marred their perfection. "What has happened?"

"Your ad-mi-ral," the boy said, pronouncing the foreign title carefully, "he returns!" The youth's face split in a wide grin of pure joy. "His great *canoas* have been seen at the north of the river only a few miles from here. My brother Guacanagari prepares to greet him in person." Although he strove for dignity, it was all he could do not to hop up and down in excitement.

"The *cacique* does great honor to my admiral, Caonu," Aaron replied as he pulled on his tunic, hose, and boots, then buckled on his sword belt. Colon would be appalled at his marshal's newly acquired habits. He had taken to wearing only a small loincloth as a shield against the curiosity of the natives, who found his circumcision a thing of great wonder and puzzlement. Now European clothing seemed hot and constricting. Already he was sweaty as he left the *bohio* and strode into the central plaza with Aliyah at his side.

The plaza served as a gathering place for war councils, celebrations, and the rough and exhilarating ball sports the Taino played. Now several dozen highly ranked nobles were awaiting the *cacique*. Everyone was decked out in red body paint with feathers in their hair and heavy gold-copper alloyed jewelry adorning their arms and legs. Guacanagari wore a nose ring of pure gold, and about his neck the heavy pendant that symbolized his rank as the *cacique* of the province. At least twenty to thirty sub-chiefs from a hundred miles around bowed to the young leader's authority.

Guacanagari stepped onto an elaborately woven hemp litter, which was decorated with shells, bones, bits of gold and copper, and some of the tinkling hawk's bells the fleet had brought in trade. Half a dozen young men, chosen specially for the honor, lifted the wooden poles and bore their *cacique* aloft. He waved to Aaron. "Please, come with us to greet your admiral. You, who have learned our language so well, you may speak for me."

"You do me honor, Guacanagari," Aaron replied with a smile. "Many of your people have learned Castilian far better than I Taino."

"You are too modest, but come and let us see if my people who sojourned on your great *canoas* have learned as much of your speech as you have of ours."

Aliyah now came forward. "I will supervise the preparation of a great feast for your admiral."

Aaron took her hand and raised it to his lips. "He will be greatly pleased."

When the welcome party reached the cove, the *Santa María* and *Niña* bobbed in the water as a boat bearing the admiral made for shore.

Colon walked through the shallow surf with the dignity of command he always possessed, followed by Vicente Pinzón and a group of officers and seamen. Cristobal's face bore a look of amazement as he inspected Aaron, who had come ahead of the slowly moving litter bearers and the *cacique*. "You are growing darker than your Indians, my friend."

Aaron's teeth flashed whitely in his bronzed face. "I fear to offend your sensibilities, but all of me is as sun-kissed. I like the Taino's habits of dress."

"Then we must spirit you aboard ship before you become so dark that a Portuguese slaver will capture you when we return home."

Aaron's eyes swept the cove. "Where is Martin Alonzo and *Pinta?*" He noted Vicente's embarrassed flush even before Colon spoke.

"The captain of *Pinta* was separated from us on the twenty-first of November. We have no trace of her and fear the worst." The admiral's pale eyes were darkened slate blue with anger held in check. Obviously he felt the departure was deliberate, and it was in direct disobedience of orders. "We will speak more of this later. For now, you must tell me how your journey here was accomplished. Has the chief gold? Knows he of the great Khan on the mainland?"

Aaron shrugged, feeling helpless in the face of his friend's hopes—hopes he feared were bound to be

133

dashed. All the Majesties wanted was a route to swift riches—gold, pearls, spices, all the fabled wealth of the East. "These people know of no great mainland where the Khan resides, Cristobal," he began gently. "At least, in as much as I have been able to learn since coming to this, their home island. There is great wealth here—rich, fertile land to cultivate, exotic and wondrous fruits that grow wild on trees and bushes, water teaming with fish. There is some gold," he added when Colon's expression grew bleak. "I myself have seen men of Guacanagari's village return from gathering expeditions with it. They wash it from the rivers of the interior. What is here is not so great as what Polo described, but these are far outlying islands."

"Yes," Colon replied, rubbing his freshly shaven chin in consideration. "We charted hundreds of islands and followed one vast coastline far to the northeast of here. I hoped it to be part of the mainland, but all we found were more people who spoke the tongue of these people. They called the place Cuba. I named it Juana in honor of the Infanta. It may take years to chart the vastness of the Indies." The blue flame had returned to his eyes now.

Luis Torres, aboard the second boat with Juan de la Cosa and several others, quickly ran up to his compatriot. "Aaron! How happy I am to see you," he said in the Taino language.

"I see you have put your Taino guide to good use as a teacher," Aaron said, clapping his small, dark-haired friend on the back as he replied in the same tongue.

Luis smiled at the Taino who had journeyed with him. Analu was as short as the Spaniard, but of a far stockier, more muscular build. The native's square blunt-featured face bore a placid expression belying the keen intelligence that shone in his liquid brown eyes. "You, too, have learned our speech well," Analu replied in careful Castilian, smiling proudly as Aaron bowed politely to him.

"Analu has been a splendid teacher and pupil. He has all but mastered the rudiments of Castilian in little over two short months." Luis scanned the Taino entourage entering the open beach area. Laughing, he added, "I think your teacher far more comely than mine, you fortunate rascal. Where is the lovely Aliyah?"

"At the village. Wait until you see the feast in our honor—and the village. Mayhap three thousand souls. The streets are wide and straight, the houses clean and comfortable. The food—well, only wait," Aaron said to Luis and the admiral, who watched as the *cacique's* litter was ceremoniously lowered to the sand close by.

Walking over to stand by his new friend, Guacanagari, Aaron made the official introductions, acting as chief interpreter with Luis and Analu assisting him. Through them, the *cacique* and the admiral extended all courtesies to each other. There would be great feasting in the village this night.

Aaron awakened, hearing cries in Castilian and Taino echoing across the great plaza. "Shipwreck!" One of the two remaining vessels had run aground. How could such a thing have happened? "I must go with the others to help my admiral, Aliyah," he said as Caonu rushed into their *bohio* to describe the catastrophe which had befallen during the night. Already faint pink and gold hazed the eastern sky.

As he dressed, he felt her eyes on him. She did not speak, only waited unhappily for him to tell her what he would do. He walked over to where she lay on the raised sleeping platform, the bed where they so often had made love. Kneeling, he took her face between his hands and gazed into her eyes. Thick, shiny tears trickled from the corners. He wiped them away with the pads of his thumbs. "Please, do not cry. I must go to aid Cristobal. I do not know what his plans will be with this new misfortune."

"His plans will take you far from me, never to return," she said bitterly.

"I will return, Aliyah. This I swear by my God and the *zemis* of your ancestors."

She smiled weakly. "My *zemis* are strong, but they are not your gods. Your people have many—the Cristo your admiral speaks of is not the god of your family. By what god of the white men do you swear, Aaron?"

"I have told you enough of religious strife in the Spains to confuse you," he replied. "I am not certain that there is so much difference. You call Him by many names. Christians say He is Three in One—this Cristo, His Father, and the Holy Spirit. My ancestors call Him Jehovah, the Moors call Him Allah. Perhaps to each people He appears as their own. There is only one thing I do know. No one should be forced to convert from one belief to another. I mislike the strife across the ocean, Aliyah. Let Christian, Jew and Moor battle there. I will return here when my duty is done." Saying the words, Aaron suddenly realized that they were true and knew he would come back one day.

When they reached the beach, the wind was blowing lightly, but chaos reigned as if a great gale were roaring. The *Santa María* had run aground, bow down while the incoming surges of ocean waves smashed her repeatedly against the hard coral reef, punching holes in the wooden hull. The pumps had already been abandoned and the heavy main mast cut down to lighten the sinking vessel. The admiral was only buying time for the frantic crew to unload her supplies. Both ships' boats ferried back and forth with food, weapons, wine casks, and all the goods aboard the dying *nao*.

Aaron could see Colon's tall figure on the quarter-deck as he shouted orders to men who raced about, carrying trunks and barrels amidships where they were handed down to waiting boats. By now several of the Taino's larger dugouts had joined the rescue effort and were ferrying goods to the beach. Jumping aboard one *canoa*, Aaron took up a paddle and rowed with the Indian crew as if born to it.

Once aboard *Santa María* he rushed to the ladder and climbed to the badly listing quarterdeck. "How in all hell did this happen?" Immediately he suspected foul play and felt guilty for remaining in the village instead of returning to the ship.

Colon, barking orders to a *gromet*, turned to him and cried out over the din, "That dung heap Cosa fell asleep at his watch! The boy holding the tiller knew not we were aground until the bow was well sunk. Even so we could have saved her, but Cosa and his men disobeyed my direct orders to take the ship's boat out with anchor and cable and sink the anchor so we could then pull the *nao* off the reef. Instead, he and his Basques rowed straightway to *Niña!* Vicente refused to let them board. But by the time he ordered them back here and sent his own ship's boat to assist us, it was too late. The tides had done their work."

"I should have been here," Aaron said with an oath. "I would have threatened to blow Cosa and his Basques to hell if they disobeyed."

Colon shrugged in resignation. "Cosa was so terrified it would have meant naught. We would only have lost the ship's boat to the scrap iron shot from the swivel gun! I will deal with him later."

Adopting his commander's philosophical attitude, Aaron said with a grin, "You never liked this big *nao* anyway. We will do better without her. Let us get all stowed ashore and then treat with the mutinous cur."

By that evening all was safely on the beach, thanks in large measure to the assistance of the Tainos. "A rotten way to spend the Feast of our Lord's birth, eh?" one

Shirl Henke

gromet muttered to another as they hauled the last cask of wine ashore.

Aaron, overhearing, realized that he had forgotten it was indeed Christmas day. Bone-weary, he leaned against a stack of crates and let his thoughts travel across the ocean. What would his family be doing this day? No doubt attending mass at the cathedral with all other dutiful New Christians. Suddenly an image floated into his mind's eye, of Magdalena's deep russet hair veiled with white lace, kneeling beside his father. He shook his head to dispel it.

"Are we to attend the admiral aboard *Niña* now that all is completed here?" Luis asked, interrupting Aaron's musings.

"Guacanagari has done us much honor and we must rely on him to safeguard men and stores until we return. We are to request that he accompany us to the caravel and sup with the admiral," Aaron replied.

And so the young *cacique* sat at the head of a great *canoa* as it approached the *Niña*. Ever aware of the obligations of courtesy and of how much they owed Guacanagari, Colon had him brought aboard with full ceremonial honors befitting European royalty.

Night fell and the moon rose. After much feasting and reveling, rejoicing that all men and provisions had been saved, the Taino chief and his village elders made ready to leave the caravel. At a tacit signal, all withdrew from Guacanagari and Aaron, and the two tall men stood alone on the deck.

"You go far across the ocean now, to bring your great rulers word of us. I send many fine presents to show the friendship of the Taino. Also six of my men, to learn your ways and explain ours to your people. In return I ask only that you come back to me, my friend. You and your admiral." Tears filled Guacanagari's eyes as he spoke, for the Taino were an emotional people and quite unashamed of displaying either affection or sorrow.

138

Aaron felt his own throat tighten. "We will return. Have we not left many of our sailors, even a man of the royal court with you as our pledge?"

"I will guard your people well and help them search for more gold. They may journey with my men in gathering it high in the mountains."

Aaron's brow furrowed. "Better that they should do as your people do—first plant the seeds we have left with them, then once food is assured, let them search for gold." He hesitated, not certain how to phrase his caution. He met the young *cacique's* gaze squarely and said, "I give you warning. Those of my race often want more than they possess." He stumbled in his speech as there was no word in the Taino language for greed. "Do not let them take all the gold your people find. You need it to trade with other people to the west."

"We have all we need for pleasant life. The yellow metal is pretty, but so is the singing charm." He held up a small hawk's bell and let it tinkle, smiling. "We will watch over those who have been forced to stay behind because of the loss of your great ship. Have a swift journey across the great water. We will pray to the most powerful *zemis* in our temple and to the three gods your admiral has spoken of. You will return safely to us."

"I leave my love with you and Aliyah, my friend," Aaron said, embracing Guacanagari.

Colon stood on the quarterdeck above them, watching the *cacique* and his men depart in the *canoa*. A troubled expression crossed his face as Aaron climbed the ladder.

"You could remain on Española if you wish," the admiral said softly.

"I thank you for the consideration, but Cosa and his pack of cowardly curs need a marshal to watch them."

"Duty always, Diego?" Cristobal said with a sad smile. "I appreciate your loyalty. Truly this voyage home with no companion ships troubles me, even if Cosa and his

Basques were not aboard. We have much coastline of this vast island yet to chart as we head eastward and out into the Atlantic. Mayhap the *Pinta* will yet reappear."

"Then I know you will have need of a fleet's marshal," Aaron said grimly. He looked to the east and added, "Also, I would tell my family of this wondrous place."

The admiral nodded in understanding. "I have an old sailor's intuition, Diego. Both my sons—and yours as yet unborn—will one day call these islands home."

Chapter Nine

Palos, March 15, 1493

The crowd at the waterfront was rowdy, curious, and jubilant that the two caravels of their city had returned safely from the Indies. Separated at sea in a fierce gale, a miracle had brought *Niña* with the Genoese admiral and *Pinta* with their own Martin Alonzo Pinzon up the Rio Tinto on the very same tide! *Niña* had been held some weeks by the Portuguese king and *Pinta* had first landed in Galicia, on the far north coast of Castile, but both ships were now in home port.

When three men wearing black robes and white capes, bearing aloft the large green cross of the Inquisition, walked toward the *Niña*, the crowd quickly dispersed. A heavily armed retinue of a dozen horsemen stood guard at the river's edge while the Dominicans walked the narrow planking to the ship.

"Look you, they go after the Genoese and his Jews. Martin Alonzo Pinzón has already departed for his home in the country. They will not bother the crew of *Pinta*," one old sailor said, spitting through rotted teeth.

"Hah," scoffed a fat old washerwoman carrying a heavy basket of damp clothes, "What of his brother Vicente? He is aboard *Niña* with the foreigner."

Murmurs from the remnants of the welcoming crowd were low and nervous. No one liked seeing Inquisitors in Palos. Only the most bold remained lounging about the riverfront.

Aboard the *Niña*, Cristobal Colon, Admiral of the Ocean Sea, sat at the small wooden table in the captain's quarters, his log book and other letters scattered about him. He was red-eyed with exhaustion and his bones ached from the bitter cold of the storm-tossed Atlantic crossing. He looked levelly at the fat Dominican, Gabriel Osario, and said, "I have much to prepare while I await a summons before the Majesties in Barcelona. What possible reason can you have for boarding a royally commissioned vessel?"

Unused to such arrogance and calm in the face of his office, the Inquisitor said, "We have just heard you shelter heretics, strange Moorsmen from the Indies, aboard your ship."

Colon's eyes narrowed and he rubbed the quill he had been writing with against his cheek. "Who could possibly have told you this?"

Fray Jorge Gonzalo smiled serenely and crossed himself. "We had occasion to stop at a small country house just a short way from Palos. Your Captain Martin Alonzo Pinzon told us of these Indians, who are surely heretic. 'Twas his deathbed wish that we interrogate them."

"Deathbed wish? Captain Pinzon was ill and weary as am I, but surely he did not die?" the admiral asked steadily.

Fray Gabriel intoned, "Within the hour of our visit. We gave him the Holy Unction." When the admiral's face betrayed a hint of a smile, the Inquisitor sputtered, "Surely you do not rejoice in the death of a friend?"

"No, never would I rejoice in the death of a friend," Colon repeated with gravity. So the crafty troublemaker was dead. "You may see the men of the Indies I brought back with me, but as they are now the property of the Majesties, they are exempt from your power."

"Besides which, they speak no Castilian," Aaron added as he stood in the doorway. Having overheard that hated agents of Torquemada were aboard the caravel, he had hastened to Colon's quarters.

Fray Gabriel turned to the tall blond gentleman. "Who might you be?"

"My marshal," the admiral said, "Don Diego Torres." He gave Aaron a quelling look, then suggested, "Perhaps you might like to bring me one of those small tokens from Guacanagari. I will present the Holy Office with a symbol of good will."

The gold. They had brought a large chest of gold objects, masks, tools, and girdles, as a special gift from the *cacique* to the king and queen. Smiling ironically, Aaron quit the cabin and went below decks to the locked bin in the hold where the gold had been stored, along with the marshal's armament. A bribe for the Holy Office was a small enough sacrifice to keep the Taino visitors safe.

"Torres, a common enough name. He is not a New Christian, any relation to Benjamin Torres of Seville, is he, perchance?" Fray Gabriel asked Colon.

The hair on the back of the Genoese's neck prickled in warning as he looked at the oily, fat friar whose eyes glowed ferally. "No, Diego is from Cordoba, where my younger son and his mother reside. Why do you ask?"

Fray Jorge's yellow teeth were overlong and pointed when he smiled. "Our holy Inquisitor General, Fray Tomás, burned the whole family of Benjamin Torres last August. They were judaizers."

Shirl Henke

Quemadero, on the fields of Tablada,
March 15, 1493

Aaron fell to his knees on the flat hard rock of the vast desolate platform known as the Quemadero, the Burning Place. The immense field's rich grasses had been covered over with stones, now charred and blackened by the blood and bones of thousands of men and women over the past decade. Shortly after it had been erected to better accommodate Seville's autos de fe, Benjamin Torres had reached the agonizing decision to take his family away from their ancient faith. "All you accomplished was to place us in reach of the flames that leap on this hellish altar of hate," Aaron choked, seeing visions of the cruel fire consuming his gentle father, his frail mother, his sweet little Ana. He squeezed his eyes shut against the sting of tears, unable to comprehend the enormity of the monstrous tragedy. Even his brother and Mateo's Christian wife, so far away in Barcelona, were dead by the hand of the Inquisition. There was nowhere in all the Spains the minions of Torquemada could not reach.

"But here in Seville, I know who stood to gain, who sent his spies, who was responsible for whatever lies sent my family to this place—Bernardo Valdés and his treacherous daughter!" The hate consumed him, but it also gave him the strength to stand and to face the visions from the depths of hell—visions of his family, walking with their upper bodies naked through the streets of the city, the green candles of the Inquisition tied in their bound hands, dragged through this loathsome travesty to suffer a hideous death.

"Uncle Isaac, you were right to leave. There is nothing for the House of Torres in Castile. Like you, I too will depart, but there will be retribution . . . this I swear on the memory of my father, my mother . . ." Even the air stank of charred flesh as he drew in a ragged breath.

The stones were smooth now, scrubbed clean since the last auto de fe, as if the shamed heavens had tried to erase the foulness of what men did in their name.

"You can not lie abed this way forever, Magdalena! Faugh! You are pale and listless. Does nothing hold your interest? You do not even attempt to sneak out and ride any longer. Blossom grows fat from lack of exercise as you grow thin." Miralda placed her hands on her ample hips and glared down at the quiet girl. "Perverse creature. If you sicken and die, think what will happen to your poor old maid? Don Bernardo will cast me out without a crumb," she complained.

Magdalena's tangled russet hair obscured her face as she lay draped across the bed, still in her sleeping shift although it was nearly dusk. She had spent the day reading in her room. Unconsciously, her fingers clutched the locket she always wore. "Mayhap we should both take the veil, Miralda. That would ensure your future—if you followed me into a convent and became a nun."

Miralda snorted. "As if your father would dower his most marriageable daughter to the Church!"

"He will not wed me for his advantage," Magdalena gritted out. "Leave me now and attend your chores. I will arise when I will arise." God and all the Saints, how she despised her own father! For three days after Benjamin and his family died, she had lain immobilized with grief at the city house. Then she had forced herself to ride the short distance across town to the beautiful Torres palace. Her father had stood in the courtyard with agents of the Inquisition and several merchants. They were overseeing the stripping of every furnishing. All the accumulation of centuries of labor by the House of Torres, divided up by greedy men whose evil defied imagining.

"Now I languish here, confined to the country house as my punishment . . . and yet no word of Aaron," she murmured. What if he were lost at sea? The question had haunted her nightmares for months. Aaron, Benjamin's beloved son, was her only link with sanity, her only reason for surviving in a world devoid of love, reason, compassion. "I must wait for Aaron."

She recalled their bitter parting the previous summer. "He will hate me now," she thought miserably, but she had sworn an oath to his father, and beyond that, she loved him still. *I will convince him of my feelings—if only he returns to Castile.*

Magdalena arose and stripped off her shift, then tested the bath water her servant had poured much earlier. Scalding then, it was still warm now. She sank into the tub, all the while turning over ways to leave the valley and return to Seville. Perhaps some word of the Genoese and his fleet would be circulating. Surely by now they must be homeward bound from the Indies. Perhaps they had been summoned to the court now sitting in distant Barcelona.

If she could make peace with Bernardo, he might be willing to send her to the queen so that a marriage of political advantage could be arranged. Magdalena had no intention of accepting such a match, but it would be the means to find out where her lover was.

Aaron's eyes narrowed as he stood on the gallery looking into the dimly lit room. Bernardo Valdés's shabby old country estate had undergone some significant improvements since he had left Castile last summer. How much of the lavish furnishings had his father's money paid for, he wondered as he watched the whoreson Crossbearer's daughter lave her silky flesh in perfumed water. He had gone first to the city house of Valdés, only to find no one in residence but for a few servants. One informed him that the master and mistress were with the royal court in Barcelona, no doubt to greet the triumphant admiral.

He had thought first to race across Castile and Aragon in pursuit of Cristobal's procession. He could gain entry to the royal audience if he were part of the admiral's entourage. Then he might kill Bernardo Valdés.

Such an act would have been treacherous repayment for the man who had saved his life in Palos. Colon had given him stern orders about remaining in hiding, even offered him the sanctuary of his own home in Cordoba, where his mistress, Beatriz Harana, lived with Colon's two young sons. He had agreed to hide from the Holy Office until the admiral returned from his audience in Barcelona and thence to return to the Indies when the second voyage was outfitted.

Don Cristobal had not, however, wrung from him any promise against revenging himself on the Valdés family here in Seville.

"Perhaps Bernardo's beauteous familiar with the mahogany hair can provide me with some answers." In spite of the hate that burned his very soul, there was yet an inexplicable desire, a pull this small slip of a girl had on him. He felt the tightening in his loins and cursed himself for seventy kinds of a fool. Yet he could not tear his eyes from her as she lay in the tub, her head resting against the rim. He could see her thick, russet lashes flutter down, covering those cat-green eyes. In profile her face appeared stronger than he remembered it, more angular and aristocratic, less girlish. Then his gaze lowered, following her slim arched neck to the waterline where two impudently upthrust pink nipples barely broke the surface. She held a large gold locket clutched in one hand, nestled between the vale of her

Shirl Henke

breasts. He entered the room silently and knelt behind the tub as she dozed.

"Your dreams must be sweet, lady, for you to look at peace. Do you always bathe with your jewels on?" he whispered, pulling cruelly on the mass of curly hair that fell to the floor.

"Diego!" She tried to sit up, but he held her fast and muffled her surprised cry. Tears of pain burned her eyes as her slim neck arched over the edge of the tub.

He placed his knee on her hair, immobilizing her head. Then one hand slid down her throat and traveled to her breasts. Tweaking one nipple sharply, he whispered, "My name is Aaron, not Diego, witch."

"You must not use a Hebrew name," she said in a muffled voice. He did not loosen his grip on her head.

"Your concern is touching," he replied, his voice ice cold. He brushed one nipple, then the other, finding them eager to oblige his touch. They pebbled quickly and her heartbeat accelerated. So did his. "Tell me, does a familiar of the Holy Office usually respond so to the contaminating touch of a judaizer?"

"I have nothing to do with my father's evil!" she sobbed, hating her weakness yet knowing he would condemn her.

"Yes, your father, Don Bernardo, now such an important man at court. When does this evil man you abjure return to Seville?" he asked in a silky voice. His fingers slid to her throat in a palpable threat.

"He tells me naught of his plans," she replied in a pain-clogged voice.

"Surely you will be summoned to court? What a match that Satan's spawn can make with you as bait."

"I will not obey him. I am already pledged." She stiffened at his cold cynical chuckle.

"I wager you have pledged yourself many times—as you did with me, and with others too numerous to count

148

since I departed." Damning her, he left off handling her wet little body. Aaron stood and pulled her up beside him by her hair. The moment he did it, he realized his mistake. She fell against him full length, her arms holding fast to his shoulders while that soft, wet little body pressed to his. Her feet, still in the tub, began to slip and she clutched him tighter.

"There have been no others, Aaron." She buried her head against the rough leather of his jerkin and felt his heart thud furiously. "There is much that I would tell you. My father had another who helped him entrap Benjamin. I do not know his name—"

"*His* name, lady? I know *her* name. You wheedled your way into my father's affections. You spied within his home. You were my father's betrayer!" His voice choked.

Magdalena felt him shudder and held him tightly, shaking her head in denial as acid tears slipped from her eyes. "Did you see the penitential procession led by those hounds of hell who call themselves God's servants? Did you watch the burning in Tablada? My father, my mother, little Ana . . . Ana . . ." His voice broke and he shook.

"Oh, Aaron, I went to your father the night before he died—in the dungeons of San Pablo. I bribed a guard to let me in—"

"No, enough of your lies! You would only go to gloat." He felt her struggling furiously now as she raised her head to meet his accusing eyes. Her face was tear-streaked and her expression desperate.

"I loved your father as much as I despise my own. I would never have hurt Benjamin, never!" Her voice rose in hysteria.

Aaron stopped her cries with his mouth, letting all the agony and shock of the past day release itself through the cruelly punishing kiss. He ground his lips over hers, pinning her against him and lifting her from the tub. She was so small and frail, so soft. And she did not resist, but gave in to his rough passion.

Magdalena felt his pain, so akin to her own. *Oh, Aaron, we must heal each other!* She tasted her own blood but ignored it as he continued ravishing her mouth. So long, so many endless, lonely months, needing him, wanting him, and now she had him in her embrace.

I loved your father as much as I despise my own. Her impassioned words echoed in his mind. How he longed to believe her as she melted against him, her slim pale arms encircling him, her fingers entwined in his shaggy golden hair. His pain-drugged mind shut down and pure physical instinct overrode all thought. This woman, mistress of deceit, daughter of his worst enemy, had haunted his dreams ever since she had been a bedraggled girl in the marshes. Possessing her once had not appeased the hunger, only fed it so it grew greater.

He swept her into his arms, tossed her wet body onto the bed, then began to discard his jerkin, tunic, boots and hose with rough, desperate movements. She crouched in the middle of the bed covers, seeming to wait for him. When he stood before her, as naked as she, Magdalena reached out her hands and touched his sun-bronzed body in awe.

"You have been fair baked by the Indies' sun," she whispered. Running cunning little fingers through the sun-bleached hair of his chest, she asked, "'Twas the Indies you found, was it not?"

"Wherever, the sun burned me well enough," he murmured as his lips swooped down and plundered her mouth. He could taste her blood and knew he had hurt her. He should want to hurt her more, yet for some inexplicable reason he did not.

Magdalena felt him soften his hungry, desperate

caresses until they spoke more of love, less of punishment. Like him, she was filled with grief and loneliness. And now she knew the dark desire he had introduced her to when first he lay with her. Then she had felt unsatisfied, bereft when he was satiated. This time she intuited it would not end that way. Instinctively, she arched against him, luxuriating in the feel of his springy chest hair abrading her breasts and the insistent pressure of his male member against her belly.

Aaron cupped her buttocks and raised her against him. She continued to kiss him feverishly, as hungry as he. His tongue rimmed her lips, then darted inside when she gasped with pleasure. Slowly, as he let his lips and tongue brush, stroke, and caress her lovely little face, he knelt on the bed and lowered her until they lay side by side, arms and legs entwined. His mouth suckled one small breast, then the other as she writhed against him, lost in soft, panting moans, clutching him tightly.

His hand traveled down the silky curve of her hip and dipped to the furry mound between her thighs. "Open for me, Magdalena," he commanded hoarsely. She complied instantly. When his fingers slid over her swollen, wet nether lips she cried out and bucked with each stroke of his hand.

Her fiery need ignited his and he reached for one little hand and pulled it down between them. When he closed it around his aching shaft, a cry tore from his lips as she stroked him in rhythm with his caresses of her. The heat was as intense as the steel forges of Toledo. He rolled her atop him and let her impale herself on his aching sex. As he raised and lowered her slim hips, her hair fell like a burnished curtain about his face and chest. Aaron slid his hands up to her tiny waist, then reached out and grabbed great handfuls of the silky mantle and pulled her down for a molten kiss.

Magdalena felt the rhythm and the heat building

together. Now she knew the sensations, instinctively felt what she hungered for. Gliding on an arc of pure, golden bliss, she rode him over the crest as surge after surge of ecstatic contractions convulsed her quivering flesh. She felt Aaron's hands twist and tangle in her hair as he arched into her with one final plunge, swelling and spilling his seed in a long shuddering release.

Aaron felt her soft, tight sheath rippling in satiation about him and it carried him over the edge. He joined her in a spiraling world of color and light where there was, for a few brief moments, neither death nor hate, only the fiery perfection of two bodies replete in harmony.

Reality quickly intruded. Aaron felt the scratching of her locket against his chest. Raising his upper body and rolling her away, he leaned on one elbow and examined the gaudy piece of jewelry. "I repeat my earlier question, lady, do you always bathe with your jewelry?"

Magdalena, still awash in all the wondrous new sensations he had awakened in her, could not think clearly. Should she risk all and give him Benjamin's ring? If she did, would he listen to her explanation of how she came to possess it? Or would he think it a prize stolen when her father and the Holy Office appropriated the riches of the House of Torres? As her mind raced, she thought to distract him. Reaching out to stroke his dark bronzed chest, she said, "Truly the sun must be awesome in the Indies to burn you through your clothing."

"For all the wonders we found, the sun is yet the sun and it only colors a man's skin where he bares it." His eyes dropped to his groin and hers followed. She gasped and he chuckled mirthlessly. "There are some areas of my body I did not wish to burn."

"Only one that I can see. Did you live as do the people

of the Indies? Are they then so primitive they deport themselves free of all decency?" Magdalena was asking things she sensed she did not want answered.

His face tensed with anger. "After returning to the savagery of my homeland, I wonder who are the civilized and who the primitive. What think you, daughter of a Crossbearer? Is the obscenity of an auto de fe decent?" His grip on the fine bones of her wrist tightened and she winced in pain. He released her and rolled up on the side of the bed, reaching for his discarded hose and boots.

"No matter how I disclaim Bernardo Valdés's perfidy, you will never believe me, will you?" She let out a small choked laugh at the cruel irony. "I am banished here, locked away in the country while my parents revel at the court, for I am a most unnatural daughter. I tried to kill my father with a hay rake."

At those words, he turned in the midst of pulling on his second boot. A look of frank incredulity crossed his face, mingled with the tiniest hint of curiosity.

She swallowed hard and continued. "I told you that I visited your father the night . . . the night before he died. I had overheard my father and a stranger plotting to divide the riches of the Torres family after they had set a trap for Benjamin. I raced Blossom to the Convent of San Pablo. It was too late. He would not let me attempt to bribe the guards, and at dawn the next day . . ." Magdalena shook her head hopelessly. "I rode home and found Bernardo Valdés calmly berating a peasant who was not attending to his hay raking as he should. I seized the rake from the poor dullard and turned it on my father. He still bears the scars from the three gashes I placed on his right side," she said venomously. Then she looked up at his skeptical expression. "You do not believe me."

"Were you me, would you?" he asked, not unreasonably. "So, you are in exile and your father absents himself from his dangerous daughter. I will succeed where you have not, Magdalena."

"Aaron, please, he is dangerous! I would not see you in the hands of those madmen he consorts with—do not pursue him to court," she pleaded. Her hand reached out to grasp his arm.

"Never fear, Magdalena. I will not waste my life in a useless gesture most likely to fail." He paused and his eyes narrowed on her speculatively. "But your father will face the same fate as mine. The instruments of the Inquisition often devour their own." His voice had grown cold now, ice cold.

Magdalena studied his implacable, beautiful face as he finished dressing. Dare she tell him of his father's last request? She clutched the locket with one hand and held the bed linen to her body with the other. The decision was denied her when the pounding of horses' hooves and a cry from below interrupted them. Then Miralda's lumbering tread sounded on the stairs, calling ahead, "Doña Magdalena, hurry. 'Tis your father come with many important men of the Holy Office!"

Aaron gave her a look of pure loathing as he withdrew the dirk from his belt and held it at her throat. "Tell her you will be down anon—get rid of her or I'll kill you both!"

"Go and tell the cook to pour cool wine from the cellar cask into pitchers and set it before our visitors, along with the new cheeses hung in the well. Hurry. I will be along in but a moment!"

As Miralda's footfalls faded with her muttering, Aaron turned to Magdalena, the dirk gleaming dully in the dim light. "Well feigned. You almost kept me here long enough for the trap to spring closed."

"I did not—"

"Silence. You almost had me believing your lies." His low voice cut as deeply as a blade. Then, almost against

154

his will, his other hand took a long curling mass of russet hair, burnished almost black in the waning light, and held it up in his fist. He studied her face. "What is the hold you seem to have over me? Best beware, witch, lest the Holy Office burn you for the practice of necromancy!" He released her hair and with blurring speed his fist connected to her jaw, toppling her backward on the bed, unconscious.

Chapter Ten

Off the coast of Española, November 26, 1493

My Dearest Father:
   It seems strange to write these entries
knowing that you will never read them. Yet
somehow I sense your presence with me and
feel you would wish that I continue my accounts
of the wonders in the Indies. This is the link that
binds us together over time and distance,
reaching even beyond death.

   Aaron paused thoughtfully. Would a son of his ever
read what he wrote? Or write to him? "I grow fanciful
in my grief. Best attend to the matter at hand and record
what has transpired on this voyage," he murmured and
resumed writing.

   The admiral returned from his audience with
Fernando and Ysabel covered with great
triumph. In Castile and Aragon, all the way to

Catalonia and then back to Seville, crowds gathered to cheer the Genoese whom they had for so long scorned. On September 25th, after much disputing with Don Juan de Fonseca, the royal provisioner, we set sail from Cadiz with our fleet of seventeen ships. The gold and green banners of Castile flew alongside the new standard of the admiral, who has been granted, among other privileges, his own coat of arms. The admiral's flagship, the *María Galante*, is far more worthy than *Santa María*. She is two hundred tons, with spacious quarters for all officers.

For all the glory this voyage promises, I fear for my friend and commander. This enterprise has cost him dearly, for in the turbulant return across the Atlantic, the icy storms smote him with terrible pain in his joints that even the warm Andalusian sun cannot cure. In spite of the crippling sickness, Don Cristobal stood on the quarterdeck of his flagship, splendidly attired, waving to the crowds until we passed from the harbor and out into the open sea. By comparison, my slight seasickness is as nothing and 'twill be gone once I touch land.

This is indeed a Grand Fleet, including over fifteen hundred men of all classes—sailors, merchants, artisans, farmers, soldiers and, at the special request of Queen Ysabel, priests to convert the people of the Indies. Would that these Minions of Truth could leave the innocent Tainos to their *zemis*. Most of those hoping to build a new life on Española are gentlemen who have never known the deprivations of soldiering. Of the few who have, men such as Mosén Margarite, Francisco Roldan and Alonso Hojeda are brutal warriors and avaricious treasure seekers. I would prefer they not treat with the gentle Tainos.

I am also troubled by the admiral's youngest brother, Diego Colon, who accompanies us. Physically he resembles the admiral in that he is slim and possesses reddish hair, but there the resemblence ends. He was destined for a career in the Church, but rebelled and left Genoa to seek his fortune trading on Cristobal's triumph. He has none of his older brother's steady judgment or gentle sense of humor. I fear his ambition if he is left in command.

We have enough chaos already. Our decks are crowded with livestock as the holds are filled with seeds and foodstuffs. Pigs and chickens race about nervous horses and cattle. I long for the sight of our settlement. We have sailed from island to island for nearly a month, claiming all for God and monarch.

I know naught of navigation, but the genius of Don Cristobal awes me. Two times now he has brought the fleet across the vast Atlantic to the thousand islands of the Indies. We are but a day's sail from our departing point last January. Even I recognize the coastline of Española. The admiral says we should reach La Navidad, the fortress of our shipwrecked men, on the morrow. I wonder how they have fared in our absence? The Caribes are in evidence on many islands and even gave fight, killing one of our company. We found signs of human bones, even captive Tainos, whom the admiral freed.

These Caribes are far darker than the Taino with coarser hair, thicker and shorter of build. They are reasonably skilled with bow and arrow and with darts, but the greatest threat is from

the poison they employ on the tips of their
weapons. The pain from it is great, as I can
attest, having been grazed by an arrow.

Aaron put down his pen, thinking how fascinating
Benjamin would have found the poisonous herbs and
other items he had collected on the first voyage. If only
his sire had lived to see the curiosities. He forced the
thought aside and closed the log book. There would be
time to write more when his humor improved.

On November 26th, the marshal of the fleet found his
humor badly in want of improvement. When a *gromet*
signaled there were two men lying on the beach, two
ship's boats were put down at the mouth of the cove.
Aaron was the first to leap ashore, sword drawn, backed
by four crossbowmen, their arbalests ready to fire. The
men lying on the beach had made no response to their
cries of greeting. Now Aaron saw why. They had been
strangled with *bejuco* cord, a weapon Aaron had seen
used by Tainos as well as Caribes.

He prodded the body of Rigo Escobedo with his
sword. Although filthy and grotesque in death, he
looked to have suffered no other ailment, nor did the
gromet who lay beside him, but for one telling disfigure-
ment. Both men had their eyes plucked out. Taino
religion certified men as dead only when they no longer
possessed the power to see.

"Those savages!" Margarite swore a string of colorful
oaths. "Your Taino friends have turned on us!"

"I will not judge them, nor will you, for such is the
task of the admiral. These men have not long been dead,
for the heat makes bodies decay rapidly here." He
pointed to two young men more inclined to obey orders
than Mosén Margarite, who was full of himself and
possessed a foul Argonese temper. "Search the beaches
to the east and west for any signs of Indians, but do not

attack unless they clearly show hostile intent. You, Pedro, have seen Taino and Caribe and know the difference," he said to a quaking *gromet*. "Go with them."

Aaron knelt and further examined Escobedo. He instructed two sailors to bury the men and sent one boat back to the flagship to fetch a priest. "Let that fat, complaining Fray Buil bestir himself to say words over the dead," he muttered as his eyes scanned the jungle. What in hell had happened?

Within the hour they were back aboard *María Galante*, sailing toward La Navidad. The air aboard the flagship was tense with anxiety. What had begun as a pleasure jaunt and great adventure had become suddenly fraught with mysterious dangers.

"You think the Taino killed those men?" Colon asked incredulously.

Aaron shrugged, looking at Don Cristobal's brother Diego, who was pale and nervous already. "The Taino use this means of killing, but I have only seen them employ it to cut short the suffering of those already dying. Also, there are at least six *caciques* on the island. Guacanagari is but one of them."

"That does not signify that his men could not have strangled our men," Diego interjected, wanting to voice his opinion as his brother's second in command.

The three men were closeted in the admiral's more spacious quarters aboard the new flagship, sitting around an oak table. Aaron stood up and paced to the port window and looked out at the descending darkness. "I like it not that La Navidad does not return our cannon signal, but we will know the fate of the fortress come daylight. For now, all we can do is prepare for the worst. I trust my friend Guacanagari, but let us proceed with caution and take no rash action against the Taino, nor let ourselves fall prey to carelessness."

Dawn brought the worst fears of all into grim, merciless perspective. The fortress, so carefully built of timbers from the wrecked *Santa María*, was a burned-out shell. Skeletons lay obscenely sprawled in the golden light, scattered across the length of the beach. The destruction of La Navidad had taken place some time ago. Refuse littered the pristine sand, as if the men had lived like animals, wasting their provisions, planting no crops. A few were strangled, but many had been pierced by arrows or spears. Three, found near a poorly erected grass hut down the beach, had probably died of disease, if such could be judged from their remains.

"Forty men, sailors, soldiers, many of them gentlemen—all dead," Cristobal said in resignation. Standing next to him was Caonu, who had just arrived from Guacanagari's village, escorted by two wary soldiers. The trembling youth's face was strained and pale now, no longer joyous as his large dark eyes swept from his captors to Aaron, pleading for deliverence.

"How did this happen, my friend?" Aaron asked in the Taino language, his expression conveying a clear message to Hojeda and Margarite, who menaced the boy. Diego Colon, although standing back, also looked ready to prejudge based on the horrors surrounding them.

Caonu spoke rapidly and Aaron had to keep interjecting pleas for the frightened youth to slow down so he could follow the tale of debauchery and treachery that unfolded.

"What says the heathen?" Diego asked brusquely, interrupting the dialogue.

"Hold your peace, Diego. The marshal speaks the language and has spent some months living with them. Let him complete his task," Colon remonstrated. He had always been fond of his youngest brother, and had in fact named his elder son for him. But if Diego would command on Española while the admiral went to sea for further exploration, his brother must learn patience and whom to trust.

Colon ran one large, cruelly gnarled hand through his

thinning hair, no longer the bright fiery red of his youth, but now lightened with gray. Placing one arm about Diego's shoulders, he drew the younger man toward a clear stretch of beach, unmarred by the ugliness of death. "Go you back to the flagship and summon the captains of *Carrera* and *Primivera*. Send them with orders to search eastward and westward for a suitable site where we may build a new fortress. Let it not be too far from here, no more than a day's journey."

Diego digested the assignment, which he deemed to be worthy of his importance and nodded. "I will dispatch them at once, Cristobal."

Aaron turned from his conversation with Caonu and addressed the admiral. "I must go to the village and speak with Guacanagari."

"Is it safe to do so?" Cristobal asked bleakly, looking at the carnage about him.

"Yes, I believe so, although these fine *civilized* men comported themselves so abominably that I would not fault Guacanagari for killing us all!" He gestured to the bodies being gathered for burial.

"What, by the Blessed Virgin, happened?" Colon asked.

"The men split into factions. The gentlemen of the court expected the lowly seamen from the marshlands to obey them, which they would not. The assayer from Seville organized many of them to search for gold—which they did, not by prospecting in the streams as the Taino showed them, but by forcing Guacanagari's people to work in their stead." Aaron paused and shrugged. "As for the rest, Galicians, Cordobans, Basques, each small group took women from Guacanagari's village—some by force—and went off, deserting the fort and building these shacks. They drank, wenched, and had the Tainos do their bidding. Some of the more adventurous struck out with Guacanagari's people as guides and

162

trespassed into the *cacicazgos* of Caonabo and Behechio. Both are far less tolerant than young Guacanagari. Caonabo is half Carib! The *caciques* killed them, and I believe they were right. These men deserved to die," Aaron said grimly.

Don Cristobal Colon, brilliant navigator and chartmaker, visionary explorer, stood on the beach amid the wreckage. "I fear I am more at home at sea than on land. I thought these men could be trusted. I left Harana in charge, thinking we had taken all the troublemakers back to Castile with us." He looked at Aaron's grim face and met his gaze. "Perhaps we should send a company of heavily armed men with you."

"No. I would prefer to go alone. Guacanagari and his family trust you and trust me as your representative. If I return this trust, I think we can mend what these fools have wrought."

The admiral nodded. "Go with God, my young friend."

God, the Christian pantheon of saints, the Taino zemis, I will accept help from any and all, Aaron thought as he bade farewell to Colon and turned back to Caonu.

Ysabel, Española, February 2, 1494

The rude village was filled to overcrowding with pigs, chickens, sheep, cattle, even the few skittish horses that had survived the last bitter month. From the end of November to the opening of the new year, Colon and his grand fleet had struggled, beating a course eastward, against the wind, along the ruggedly beautiful coastline of Española. The admiral finally chose a level grassy plain with a small river not too far distant as the best choice for a new settlement, given the fact that both men and animals were sickening aboard ship. He named the new city Ysabel in honor of his patroness.

Aaron held his peace, but he thought it a singularly appropriate name for the unlikely site, feeling as he did about the unattractive and fanatical queen. The river was brackish and too far from the plain to be really convenient. The land was marshy and the climate, come the heat of summer, would be miasmic. But he had been otherwise occupied with peace-making missions between the colonists and the Tainos and had not been consulted.

Now, as he surveyed several thatched huts, greatly inferior in construction to those of Guacanagari's village, Aaron shook his head in disillusionment. Men idled about in the central plaza or sat drinking wine in front of their rude quarters. Dung littered the streets. Pigs squealed, chickens squawked, and sheep bleated in complaint, running hither and yon, heeded only when hunger bestirred the gold seekers to catch a prize and butcher it. Food was scarce and few crops had been planted. A combination of poor soil and poorer cultivation would yield meager harvests. Already the settlers had grown dependent on the Taino for *cassava* bread and yams as staples. Still many men sickened and died of fevers and other maladies.

A few stone buildings had been erected, an austere governor's residence for Don Cristobal, who according to his royal patents was the chief civil and military authority, and an arsenal. Although Colon had offered his fleet marshal command of the island's military, Aaron had declined, feeling that he better served both colonists and Tainos by living among the Indians and acting as a go-between. Few of the settlers had made any effort to learn the Taino language and most abused the generous Indians shamefully, trading cheap trinkets for vital food and gold.

Gold. Aaron looked at the harbor. A dozen ships were outfitted for the return voyage home. Over thirty thousand ducats in gold was aboard, along with exotic birds and other lesser booty. Even a few baskets of pearls had been obtained by trade with Tainos from outlying islands. Over three hundred of the disappointed colonists were returning, including many of the clergy who were as disillusioned with their meager success in converting the Indians as the *caballeros* were with their failure to find instant riches.

Yet riches were present, for those who had pluck and brains enough to gain them. Aaron's plan for vengeance swung on his ability to get rich. But beating and maiming Tainos to force them into giving up their small gold supplies was not the answer. A cold smile crossed his face as he recalled his conversation with a half-Caribe *cacique* from Higuey in the southeast. His people had found gold in the interior rivers. Someday soon, when he could gather enough from this richer yield, he could return to Seville and exact a fearsome penalty from Bernardo Valdés.

Francisco Roldan, big, bluff and hearty, strode up to Aaron, kicking a squawking chicken away with one booted foot. Throwing his meaty arm about the slimmer man's shoulders, he asked with genuine curiosity in his voice, "How do you manage to win more gold, even brazilwood, from the *caciques* by smiles than Margarite does with his sword?"

"You should know, my friend. You, too, are fast becoming as acclimated to Taino life as I," Aaron replied with a smile.

"Ah, but you have the favor of Guacanagari's lovely sister, an asset of priceless worth." Roldan's own prowess with the Taino women was legendary and his tastes notably catholic.

Aaron sighed and the smile left his face. "Unlike you, who have a 'wife' in each village from Marien to Xaragua, I am faithful to Aliyah."

"Faithful, yet unwed by either her laws or ours. Do I detect a hint of conscience in an adventurer such as you?" Roldan teased. "Have you a wench back in Seville—or worse yet, a lady who holds your heart captive?"

Aaron scoffed as the vision of cat-green eyes brimming with tears flashed into his mind. "Scarce that. I am pledged to no woman, nor would be until other matters are attended."

"Yet the fair Aliyah works her wiles on you and cajoles her brother to force the match."

"You have become far too adept at picking up Indian gossip," Aaron replied crossly.

Seeing that the joke had turned sour, the mercurial Francisco changed the subject. "You brought a good deal of booty in for our governor's treasure fleet. Think you the Majesties will be pleased?"

"Nothing will ever satisfy Fernando's greed," Aaron replied bluntly, for he had grown to like Roldan, a rough but honest soldier who treated the Tainos fairly. "As to his queen, when her priests go scurrying home without a soul baptized, I think she will be sore displeased. The admiral is. He hoped for mass conversions."

"I know you like him well," Roldan replied, looking about the busy harbor area where ship's boats busily loaded goods, "but Don Cristobal is a fool as an administrator. He should stay at sea, which is his own true element. On land he flops like a banked bonita, giving and countermanding orders, treating the Taino as allies one day, as enemies the next."

Aaron sighed. "He has chosen poor men to command, I agree. Margarite is a brutal butcher and Hojeda I would trust no sooner than I would pet a coiled adder. His brother Diego has little to recommend him either, but look you about us, Francisco. These men are not settlers. They do not adapt to the land. They will not become farmers or herdsmen and they are too arrogant to learn the Tainos' ways—all they do is bleed the *caciques* for food and gold."

"Soon there will be a rebellion," Roldan said softly. "You know it as I do. The question is, with your loyalties so divided, where will you stand?"

Aaron looked into the Castilian's shrewd brown eyes. "I do not know. There is an oath I must keep, sworn back in Seville. I would not see Guacanagari's people harmed. Nor do I wish the admiral's colony to fail and drag his dreams down with its demise."

"So that is why you stepped down as Colon's marshal. You could have had Margarite's job, but it would have meant spilling Taino blood. Even now he sets up forts across the interior mountains, from which our colonists will bleed the Tainos for yet more gold and food."

"Both can be obtained by honest barter—and by working alongside the Taino." Aaron studied Roldan. "I have heard about a powerful *cacique* in Xaragua, far to the southwest of here, who would defy the invaders. You will ally with him, will you not?"

"Let us pray to all the saints it comes not to that, but if it does, I will not ally with the *cacique* of Xaragua . . . I will *be* the *cacique* of Xaragua!" He threw back his head of thick brown curls and laughed.

Aliyah stroked Aaron's chest, then moved deft fingers up to his bristling jawline. "Will you cut the hair from your face? It burns my skin," she said with a pout, hefting her full breasts, one in each hand, to display whisker burns on the tender flesh.

Aaron rolled back on the platform bed inside the *bohio* and watched her as she posed artfully. She had grown shrewish and jealous since his return. Of course, in his absence she had resumed relations with several noblemen of Guacanagari's village.

With a sigh he said, "I will shave for you, Aliyah." *I seem to be cursed with faithless women,* he thought in irritation, wondering what had become of Magdalena Valdés so far across the ocean.

Valladolid, March 1494

"He is not so tall as the admiral, but has the same red hair. And Don Bartolome has not the crippling affliction, but is most robust," Estrella Valdés said breathlessly as she paced the carpeted floor of the quarters she shared with her daughter.

"I am surprised you did not look on his young nephews as prospects for dalliance as well," Magdalena said, rolling her eyes in disgust.

"You will show your mother some respect, Magdalena! They are but boys brought by Don Bartolome to be pages at the court. Don Cristobal's younger son is a babe of six and even the elder is a stripling of fourteen years." Estrella regarded her daughter consideringly, then mused aloud, "Of course, in a year or two he might have possibilities as a husband for you."

"All you ever think of is ridding yourself of me. I will wed none of your odious choices, Mother."

"You foolishly pine away for one long gone. His family is in disgrace and there is no possibility of your marrying him even if he were to return." Estrella shuddered, then continued with her scheming. "Your father will arrange a match if I do not. You might find some of his choices far more odious than mine." Ignoring Magdalena's angry scowl, she looked in the mirror of polished steel on the wall, studying her faded beauty, the loose skin beneath her chin, the fine lines webbing her eyes. "You are young and fresh. What power you could wield, stupid girl, if only you would cooperate!"

Magdalena's face became a hard mask. "I will not wed at your pleasure, nor will I sell myself as a leman to please you or that man you married." She could never again name Bernardo Valdés as father.

"You are a fool to hide yourself away and pine for that Jew! The king is taken with you."

Magdalena recalled Fernando's jet eyes following her last evening at the banquet honoring Don Cristobal's brother. Merciful Virgin, what had she done to deserve such unwanted attention! "I am not you, Mother. I want nothing to do with the king's favors. And less to do with the queen's wrath."

Ever a court game player, Estrella considered her daughter's words and found they had merit. "Ysabel minds not as much that Fernando sports with married women, but young maids of exceptional beauty . . . of those she is fierce jealous. Still—"

"The queen minds every infidelity of her lord," Magdalena interrupted. "But noblewomen who are wed and have the protection of a husband cannot be banished to a convent!" She had learned much in her scant weeks with the court. Until her mother's fading beauty had caused her fall from royal favor, she had been the king's mistress and thus had earned the enmity of the painfully plain queen. But Estrella had always been clever, managing to return to court on some pretext each time Ysabel sent her to Seville to tend her children. Now that she was unable to secure the advantages derived from being the royal whore she wanted to place her daughter in Fernando's bed and use Magdalena for her own selfish schemes.

"If you but use your brain, there is little danger of a convent," Estrella replied dismissively. "You will have to risk the queen's ire again tonight. I am certain his Majesty will ask you to dance at the ball. Forget your *marrano* love. Do not be a fool!"

Am I a fool? Magdalena thought that night as she kept step in a stately pavane. Her cloth-of-gold gown was cut low across her breasts and the squared neckline was lavishly sewn with pearls. She held the long train in her free hand, swinging it gracefully as she executed the intricate movements of the dance. It was pleasant to wear lovely clothes and have young noblemen attend her, such as the boy who fawningly held her hand at the moment. Half a dozen others waited at the sidelines of the polished stone floor, each eager to take his turn with Don Bernardo's lovely daughter.

Magdalena looked across the crowded room full of merry makers, glittering with rich furs, velvets, silks and jewels. The nephew of the Duke of Medina-Sidonia, Don Lorenzo Guzmán, began to walk deliberately toward her. She knew him only by sight, but his attention made her almost as uncomfortable as the king's. He was the widower of poor Ana Torres. After her cruel death, he had been exonerated of all blame in her supposed judaizing. Powerful family connections had weight, even with the Holy Office. She averted her eyes from his hawklike visage, praying he would pass her by.

Everywhere I go I am haunted by memories of the House of Torres, even at the royal court. Once she would have given anything to be the center of admiration, but that was when she had hopes Aaron would be one of those watching her, waiting his turn to dance and flirt with her. Instead, this tall, skinny man with malevolence in his cold pewter eyes stalked her.

"May I have the favor of this dance, beautiful lady?" Guzman looked at her with narrowed eyes, the lids heavy with passion as he inspected her body, pausing significantly at the swell of her breasts.

He was the nephew of one of the most powerful noblemen at court. Lorenzo could step before her other young swains and ask her to dance. None of them dared to protest and she saw no graceful way to refuse without creating a scene that would attract the king's attention. Magdalena nodded woodenly and let him take her hand.

"So somber. Can you not smile for me as you have for

those young pups?" Lorenzo again subjected her to a thorough perusal, knowing how nervous he made her and relishing her discomfiture. Bernardo's daughter had genuine possibilities as a mistress. He had always favored brunettes, but this one, with her cat's green eyes and russet hair, intrigued him. More than that, he knew from Bernardo's stupid wife that Magdalena had been smitten with Benjamin Torres' younger whelp, now vanished in the Indies. To take one last thing from the House of Torres would give him great pleasure.

Magdalena endured his teasing insinuations, replying with curt remarks barely a shade away from outright rudeness. Finally, she stopped at the end of the dance and said bluntly, "You seem to enjoy toying with me, Don Lorenzo. I am but a simple country girl lately come to court, not of my lady mother's stripe. I have no patience or skills for intrigue." *Or stomach for your hands on me!*

"Ah, but I have infinite patience . . . and skill, my lady." With that suggestive remark he pulled her hand to his lips and kissed it.

Magdalena started in horror at the touch of his wet lips on her flesh. Dear Mother of God, what web had she stepped into now?

"You are much bemused, my fair flame," King Fernando said as he dismissed Lorenzo with a wave of his elegant hand.

Seething inwardly, Guzmán replied, "As you wish, your majesty." He bowed to the king and then to Magdalena.

As they watched Lorenzo retreat, Fernando Trastamara reached for her hand and signaled the musicians to begin another pavane. "What do you think on?" he asked as he led her through the intricate steps of the dance.

"Nothing of import, your majesty. I do but daydream

of Seville," she said nervously, feeling the watery blue eyes of Queen Ysabel piercing her back like shards of glass.

"Seville. What could possibly be in Seville but heat and marshes? I prefer to journey no farther into Andalusia than the mountains of Granada."

"I understand the Moorish city is most beautiful," she replied.

"Moorish no longer. Now Christian, won at dear cost in battle, but let us speak not of wars. I would much enjoy showing you the great wonders of the Alhambra."

"My mother has spoken of its splendor, your majesty," she said, unable to resist mention of Doña Estrella, his former lover. At least with her red hair and green eyes, she was no get of this dark Argonese devil!

"Your mother was a woman of great beauty, but even in her prime she would pale by comparison with you," he murmured smoothly, escorting her from the dance floor toward a high-arched doorway. Beyond it was a courtyard filled with evergreens. "I grow warm from dancing and would have fresh spring air . . . and charming company." It was not a request.

Queen Ysabel sat on the dais across the crowded room, her eyes narrowed and her face flushed. She had dressed especially to please her husband in a splendid new gown of rich ruby velvet, trimmed in ermine, its slashed sleeves inset with pale rose satin. Her faded hair was hidden beneath an enormous turbaned headdress encrusted with rubies. Yet for all her pains to please him, he had left her side to cavort with that Valdés harlot, the daughter of a harlot.

Never, even as a young woman, had Ysabel's hair been that deep a red, that lustrous or thick, nor had her figure ever been slim, long-legged, and pliant. She cursed the girl, then realized her mortal sin of jealousy would have to be confessed. She studied the empty doorway to the courtyard where Fernando had taken the creature, a young unmarried girl whose father was a Crossbearer. Surely such a man of religion would be willing to dower his daughter suitably for entry into the Contemplative Second Order of Dominican nuns in Madrid. There she could spend her life under a vow of silence, fasting and praying for forgiveness of her sins. Ysabel smiled radiantly and nodded toward Don Pedro Gonzales de Mendoza, Cardinal of the Spains and Archbishop of Toledo. He would be pleased to handle the negotiations for the dowering, the queen was certain.

Chapter Eleven

"You cannot mean this?" Magdalena sank down onto the hard wooden bench. "A convent!" Her blood froze as she searched Bernardo Valdés's coldly furious expression.

Her father stood across the room from her, his face gray and taut. His grand schemes for this, his most marketable offspring, had all gone for naught. He drew himself up stiffly and laced his thick, beringed fingers across his paunch. "It is you who have brought us to this sorry pass. At least your mother knew how to be discreet! The queen saw you and the king slip into the courtyard. God's bones! There were hundreds of witnesses. Her majesty does not take well to public humiliation," he said grimly.

Magdalena's eyes blazed and she leaped up, wanting to claw his eyes out—cold, unfeeling, stupid man! "What was I to do when *his* majesty took my arm and led me to the door—slap his face and thrust him away from me? He gave me no choice! I have done everything I can to discourage him since you insisted on bringing me to court."

"If you had brains, or the cunning inherent in the more useful of your sex, you would never have discouraged the king. If you had plied him well, you could have made a discreet assignation for later that evening and her majesty would never have become so wroth."

Magdalena looked at Bernardo Valdés as if he were an insect. "I only regret I did not kill you that day in the stables," she said with quiet intensity.

Bernardo reddened in mortification. His eyes quickly scanned the room to see if any possible weapons were at hand. Nothing. His mouth twisted in a cruel parody of a smile. "I beat you bloody when last you tried such an unnatural act."

"You mean you had your groomsmen hold me while you vented your wrath," Magdalena said scornfully. "As to what is unnatural, selling your own daughter to be debauched and pawed for royal favor is unnatural. Benjamin Torres is the true father of my heart. You are but the Pandarus who may have sired me. Once I overheard my mother tell her cousin Lucia that she was uncertain who my father was. A young count was her lover at the time I was conceived. Then I cried. Now I pray nightly that it is true!"

Bernardo considered slapping her, but she was fierce-tempered and strong in spite of her slight size. Ignoring the slur, which he had long suspected was true, he said, "Now that you have disobeyed my instructions—and those of your mother—you will suffer the consequences."

"Tell me, will her majesty pay my dower to rid the court of me, or are you forced to bear that final burden?" Knowing Bernardo's greed, it was a small bit of revenge, all she could expect.

His deeply flushed face revealed the truth. "Entry into

the Dominican Convent in Madrid is an honor dearly bought. You have ever brought me grief. I am well rid of you." He turned to leave her quarters, then paused and fixed her with a malevolent glare. "Try none of your foolish escapades now. If you vex me enough, I could always denounce you to the Holy Office. You well know my influence with Fray Tomás," he finished on an oily smooth note, gloating to spite the red-haired bitch.

After he had slammed the heavy oak door, Magdalena sat numb with horror. A nun, cloistered away for the rest of her life to fast and pray. Never again would she know the freedom of racing Blossom across the Andalusian plains or feel the wind rippling her hair, never again smell the sweet fecund earth after spring rain . . . never again would she feel Aaron's lips on hers, his hard beautiful body covering her, caressing her. Never would he know how she loved him!

When Magdalena had come to court, she had done so in the very unlikely hopes of meeting Aaron Torres. Twelve of Admiral Colon's ships, laden with gold, spices and exotic Indians had returned to Castile and the men with them had been summoned at once to report to the king and queen. Of course, it would have been most dangerous for him to chance an encounter with the Holy Office after his family had been condemned, but she had prayed Aaron would return so covered in glory that the Majesties would pardon him. Nevertheless, she knew it was better that he had remained in the Indies with the Genoese. Now she would never see him again.

Tears burned her eyes, but she dashed them back. There must be a way. Her hands clenched the locket tightly, rubbing the gold exterior as if caressing her lover. Over the past months it had become an unconscious habit. Suddenly she looked down at it and her heartbeat, leaden with sorrow a moment before, speeded up with a fierce surge of hope.

"The admiral's brother!" she cried aloud in the empty room.

Bartolomé Colon had just passed an emotionally exhausting evening saying farewell to his brother's young sons. Diego, the young courtier, at fourteen was already becoming a politician, while little Fernando at six was a chubby child of endearing brightness. He had grown fond of them in the weeks he had spent in their company, escorting them from Cordoba to Valladolid. At the large and frightening court, he had become their surrogate father. After his years with the English and French courts, Bartolomé Colon had learned his lessons well. He did his best to teach his nephews how to survive as Prince Juan's pages.

How his heart ached to leave two lonely boys in this fearsome place of political intrigues. At least the young prince, who was slow and in frail health, was known to be kind, unlike his sire or his dame. Diego and Fernando had known so little of their father, and now their uncle was deserting them, too. But he had done as Cristobal had instructed and the Indies beckoned him. The dream, so long deferred, was about to be realized. Tomorrow he would begin his journey to Cadiz and thence to the new city of Ysabel on Española. He was to be Cristobal's *adelantado*, the second in command on the island.

Bartolomé walked across the courtyard. A light spring drizzle was falling, chill and uncomfortable. Cristobal's letter spoke of the balmy warmth of the Indies. He hastened his steps, pulling his heavy velvet cloak closer about his broad shoulders. Just as he reached the shelter of the portico that ringed the courtyard, a small figure darted from the shadow cast by a column. The hour was late and this part of the palace deserted. His dirk flashed into his hand with blurring speed. "Who goes?"

177

"Please, I mean you no harm, Don Bartolomé," a soft feminine voice beseeched.

He looked at the slight figure, clad in the rough clothes of a stableboy. "You are no lad," he said warily, looking about for others who might be hiding in the portico's colonnade.

"I come alone. I must speak with you on a matter of great urgency," Magdalena said.

Bartolomé replaced his dagger and inspected her in the faint light cast by a flickering torch some yards away. "You are dressed as a rude peasant boy, yet your speech betrays you as a noble lady," he said incredulously.

"I risked much to secure these clothes from a servant girl's brother, even more to slip from yon window and climb the trellis to waylay you." She gestured to a stone wall at the far corner of the courtyard, rising several stories above the rest of the palace.

"Those are the royal quarters," he said with dawning horror. "You could have broken your neck if you had slipped! Just who are you, my lady, and what do you want with me?"

Magdalena scoffed. "I have climbed oaks and palms back in Andalusia that made the descent child's play. As to who I am and what I seek, please, let us go somewhere safe to talk."

Every instinct honed in the French court led Bartolomé to be wary. "You must be one of the queen's ladies in waiting. I could end up on the block for this night's escapade."

"We will both come to a miserable end if we stand here arguing! At best we will get the lung fever from this accursed rain," she replied. "If I wanted to entice you, Don Bartolomé, I would have dressed more suitably," she added, pulling the thickset muscular man with her into a dark alcove that led to a winding, narrow set of stairs. "Come."

"I am doubtless a fool," he said glumly, allowing her to lead the way down the stairs to a deserted granary filled only with moldy bins of wheat and the mice that devoured it.

The room was barely illuminated by a small tallow candle carefully placed in a dish on the dirt floor. Two rude stools against one wall provided the only furnishing. He removed his damp cape and spread it across the splintering wooden slats of a grain bin, then took the candle and raised it to inspect Magdalena's face.

"You look familiar. I have seen you in the audience room."

"Your eye is good to remember one girl among hundreds in the queen's entourage, especially disguised as I am."

" 'Tis the hair," he said, noting the thick plait that had slipped from beneath her scratchy cap. "That dark color is like unto the wood brought from Africa and the Indies to make red dyes. Who are you, my lady?"

"Magdalena Valdés, daughter of Bernardo and Estrella Valdés of Seville," she replied desolately.

"The Count who is Crossbearer, who has the ear of Torquemada himself?" he asked, aghast.

"To my eternal shame, yes, but please, do not fear me for I am in desperate need of your help." Magdalena pulled her locket from its hiding place beneath the rough woolen tunic. "I have something to show you in strictest secrecy. Pray, please take a seat. I have filched a flagon of wine and some bread and cheese." For a moment her haunted face flashed a heart-stoppingly enchanting smile. "I am a most proficient thief," she said, extracting her booty from its hiding place in a leather pouch in the corner.

Bartolomé Colon sat down to listen and Magdalena began her long tale of treachery. When she had finished, he felt shaken to the core. He stood up, looking down at her pale, desperate face. "These are evil times in which we live. I would sooner return to Lisbon and make charts than continue in Castile or Aragon."

"But you would sooner yet journey to join your brother in the Indies," she argued hopefully.

"I know of this Diego Torres. He was my brother's marshal. They served together in the Moorish wars briefly. The *converso* saved Cristobal's life," he admitted grudgingly.

Magdalena shot up. "Then you owe it to Diego to bring his betrothed to him, lest the queen's jealousy consign me to perpetual imprisonment."

"Do you realize what it is you ask? If my part in aiding your escape from the queen is ever discovered, my whole family could be disgraced, even jailed or killed!"

"As was the House of Torres. Diego is the only one left alive and I have his pledge. He knows not what has befallen me," she said entreatingly.

Bartolomé shook his head. "You have showed me an expensive ring with a family crest. I know not if it indeed belongs to the House of Torres, nor can I be certain how you came by it." He studied her stricken face. Even dressed in stable boy's rags, she was lovely. Her green eyes glowed with tears.

"Know you what the Contemplative Dominicans are like? The convent outside of Madrid is isolated, the sisters are held behind stone walls as much in a dungeon as those poor wretches my father falsely accuses."

"Your father is no man to cross, my lady, least of all for a Genoese, a foreigner in a land not noted for its tolerance."

Turning from him she said, "My father has destroyed me then. If I cannot reach Diego, I will go to no convent."

The underlying steel in her voice sent a chill climbing his spine to raise the hairs on his nape. The girl made no idle threat. She would kill herself. He was certain of it. "So, you do not lie about the ring being given you by Benjamin Torres," he said quietly. Then a half-smile spread across his ruddy face, making him appear far more youthful than his forty years. "How are we to smuggle a noblewoman destined for a nunnery all the way from Valladolid to Cadiz, eh?"

Magdalena turned, wiping tears back with her fists, her face once more ablaze with hope. "I have thought of a plan. 'Twill seem I tried to escape and was set on by thieves. They will find the skirts that I use for riding, all smeared with blood—sheep's blood. I will take my jewelry and leave the empty cask lying by the bloody clothes. My father, and even the king, will be convinced that I am either dead or so dishonored they will not want to recover me. Once I am out of Fernando's favor, the queen will lose interest in me. It will work, Don Bartolomé, I know it!"

Cacicazgo of Marien, Summer 1494

Aaron stood in the center of the huge *bohio* that housed Guacanagari, his wives, and their children. The young *cacique* sat on a carved wooden chair that perfectly followed the contours of his body. He lounged back against the curve of the polished, gold-inlaid wood with a negligent ease that belied his inner feelings as he studied his friend.

"A child grows in Aliyah. I thought this would be a matter of rejoicing for you as well as for my people. We have come to think of you as one of us." Guacanagari's eyes were perplexed.

"I have shared your life here for many months, my friend, and there is much I have come to admire about the Taino." Aaron paused, combing his fingers through his shaggy golden hair, groping for words to explain

European values, perhaps to justify European prejudices. "Among my people—all peoples across the great
water—it is of greatest importance that a man know his
woman's children are of his blood." He looked at
Guacanagari to gauge his reaction.

Puzzled, the younger man replied, "Are not all children a gift from your God? That is what your holy men
tell us. We believe every baby should be loved."

Aaron felt trapped. "All children should be loved,
but . . ." He swore vividly in Castilian and tried again.
"It is good that your people accept children regardless
of their paternity."

"It is a sign of fertility in a woman. Such makes her a
good wife. A man knows when he weds a woman great
with child that she will bear him many children."
Guacanagari's position seemed imminently logical to
him.

"I must know that the child is mine, Guacanagari,"
Aaron said baldly, his blue eyes locking with the *cacique's* dark ones. "I am sorry, that is the way I have
been taught."

"Aliyah would be faithful to you after marriage oaths
were exchanged." He brightened. "My sister tells me
she has lain with you often, seldom with the others. So
the child is most likely yours. Always when men of your
race give a baby to one of my people, it is easy to discern
the mixed blood. We will wait and see when it is born.
Will that make you happy, my friend?" The earnest
entreaty in Guacanagari's voice was unmistakable.

"Yes," Aaron said, sighing in resignation that he tried
carefully to hide. "You are right. Half-white children of
the Taino do look different. I will take responsibility for
my own child. You have my word."

The child is most likely yours. Guacanagari's words
echoed in Aaron's mind that night as he reclined against
a palm tree near the door of his *bohio*, watching Aliyah

add hulled peanuts to the pepper pot bubbling over the fire. The large copper basin was filled with an aromatic mixture of wild duck, fish, yams, beans and the bitter spicy juices of the cassava root. As she stirred the stew with a wooden paddle, he watched her movements. She was still graceful, although her waist had thickened and her breasts, always full, had grown taut and heavier.

He knew that if the child had European features, he would wed her, but now that he was irretrievably confronted with the prospect, something in him rebelled. He had spent the better part of a year living and working among the Taino. The life was good, the people honest, kind and uncomplicated. They possessed none of the greed, cruelty, and fanaticism that had destroyed his family in Seville. He enjoyed Aliyah's passion, but he did not love her as his father had loved his mother. "The old world is dead to me. I will return only to exact revenge, not to build a life there."

Aaron knew that many men who had come with the fleet would never return to Castile. Men like Roldan married Taino women and became *caciques* in their own right, blending into the primitive world of lush jungle life, warm, unfettered, slow moving. But the Taino way of life would soon disappear. Already the officials from Ysabel came, building forts, enslaving Caribes and Tainos alike. They set quotas for gold each fortnight and when the beleaguered and frightened Tainos were unable to gather enough, they cut off their ears or sliced open their noses. When first this brutality touched Guacanagari's village, Aaron had gone to Ysabel to protest, ready to kill Margarite, but the commander was in the interior building forts. Diego Colon, Cristobal's youngest brother, was in charge of the government while the admiral was exploring. The haughty young man indignantly defended the governor's policy, saying the sovereigns must have the gold or all support for the colony would be withdrawn, including vital shipments of wheat, wine, clothing and weaponry, even medicines. Aaron had left Ysabel, barely escaping imprisonment for his outraged protest about the methods the soldiers used to obtain their booty.

Francisco Roldan did more than protest. He raised the standard of rebellion in Xaragua and drove out all intruders from Ysabel. The more cautious Guacanagari, as *cacique* in Marien, decided to wait upon the admiral's return, trusting him to be a just man who would stop the soldier's ravaging. Aaron had not been inclined to be so pacific. He had fought and killed several gold-hunting colonists who had attempted to force Tainos into slavery as miners. He wondered if his old friend Cristobal could undo the harm that was being done in his absence.

In the meanwhile, Aaron Torres learned to use the *bejuco* cord with silent, deadly efficiency. He also stockpiled bolts for his crossbows, but prayed that he would not be forced into open rebellion against the crown and its representative, Cristobal Colon. He valued their old friendship and wanted to keep open conversation between Guacanagari's people and the royal authority in Ysabel. Also, if his plan for vengeance against Bernardo Valdés was to be effected, he had to be able to return to Seville. As a hunted outlaw, this would not be possible.

Aliyah knelt by the fire, watching the expression on Aaron's face grow increasingly pensive. Ever since he had returned from across the waters he had seemed distant to her. She stood up and walked over to where he sat, then stretched out on the damp, mossy ground beside him. In spite of her well-advanced pregnancy, she was as sinuous and graceful as a sleek cat.

"What troubles you? Please speak these things so that I may share the burden."

He reached out and stroked her cheek. Her moods

were mercurial, ranging from petulance to pleading. "I think about the soldiers and others, all the men of my country who come here in ever increasing numbers to enslave and kill the Taino. We need protection for your people. Your brother waits on the admiral. I only wish he would return quickly."

"You have fought your own kind for us. Will you then become one with my people and turn your face away from the white men if the admiral will not help us?" she asked, visibly brightening at that idea.

He shook his head in perplexity. "I know not, Little Bird. I must journey across the great water again."

"To kill he who destroyed your family." She knew this well, for he had explained the tragedy that had befallen the House of Torres. "But after that you will once more return. Nothing remains for you in that place. Here you could be a great *cacique*. I am of royal blood. As my husband you could lead our people against the evil of the white men who make us dig in the earth for gold." She drew herself up with hauteur, as grand as a Castilian princess.

As Aaron had learned their language, he had found Aliyah was the word for a small, brightly plumed little bird that preened itself high in the tree tops of the jungle. "You do me great honor, Little Bird, but I have told you I must wait."

"But you will return to us," she insisted, placing her hand on his bare chest and stroking it. "Do you not still find me beautiful? I have had great bride prices offered for me by many fine nobles—*caciques* from Magua and Ciguayo, even as far away as Xaragua. Now that I am proven fertile, I may choose among many men." Her voice, at first wheedling, became strident as he made no response to her overtures but continued staring into the flames of the cook fire.

"I will do what I must do, Little Bird. You must do

what you think best," he said, rolling himself up in a smooth movement and stalking off across the plaza.

Luis Torres lay in his *hamaca,* sipping from a gourd filled with fermented papaya juice, reading an Arabic treatise on Aristotle, a treasure he had brought from Castile. The paper was moldy as were most of his books, but it was his favorite diversion. Hearing a commotion from the waterfront, he carefully placed the fragile volume on the earthen floor and swung out of the *hamaca.*

His Taino wife, Anacama, came running up to their hut, gesturing excitedly. "A ship has come from across the waters bearing the brother of the admiral!"

"So, at last the prodigal has come, all the way from France," Luis said, smiling broadly. Bartolomé was older and by all reports possessed far sounder judgment and far stiffer backbone than did his younger brother Diego.

Luis walked briskly toward the crowd gathered about the ships' boats at the harbor.

As the boat approached shore, Magdalena sat huddled in misery, hot, itchy and overcome with apprehension. *What will I do if he rejects me?* Looking at the wildly unkempt men gathered to greet them, she was appalled. "It is naught but a crude village of thatch huts with a small stone fortress at its center. I have seen far more impressive towns in the poorest marshes of Andalusia," she said in horror.

"My elder brother has always had a tendency toward exaggeration. It is a fault, I fear, of every visionary. I had hoped the settlement would be more substantial than this, but suspected it would be much as you see it. Like our Portuguese brethren, we Genoese are inclined to trade and industry. The Castilians are a warrior race who take ill to planting wheat and laying masonry.

Cristobal's letters to me decried the lack of discipline among the gentlemen adventurers whom he had recruited."

The smell of rotting fish and other offal filled her nostrils. The men crowding about the boats, staring at her, were scarcely less odoriferous. "Why do these men stare so? They look like savages themselves!"

"I am given to understand, Magdalena, that many of these men have not seen a lady since they left Cadiz in 1493. A few white females have sailed aboard the more recent supply vessels, but we have traveled with some of these women. I believe I can understand why the men view you differently," Bartolomé explained with gentle irony.

During the long tedious days aboard the heavily laden *nao*, Magdalena had stayed clear of both the seamen and the coarse women who accompanied them. A small handful of females were wives of soldiers, the rest common prostitutes. All were curious about the high-born lady who had come aboard in the pre-dawn darkness just before sailing. Wanting to leave no trail that her father could trace, Magdalena had boarded heavily cloaked, wearing a heavy net caul encasing her distinctive hair.

Now she was dressed to meet Aaron with as much care as possible, wearing her best green silk gown, covered by a gauze surcoat of palest green embroidered with gold thread.

As she fussed with the tight sleeves and then reached up to smooth her hair, Bartolomé said laughingly, "You look grand. Diego Torres will think you a vision."

"After weeks of bathing in salt water, I feel sticky and bedraggled. Do you think anyone here will write back that you accompanied a red-haired woman to Ysabel?" she asked worriedly.

Bartolomé replied with cynicism, "I doubt any of this

Shirl Henke

crew can write. Even if they do, we are far from your father's reach now. I can claim you as my sister," the big, red-haired man added genially.

"I must remember to affect a Genoese accent," she replied in what she hoped was a bantering tone. Bartolomé helped her from the boat and then scanned the motley crowd of colonists, looking for a familiar face. Surely the governor would come to greet three ships sailing into the harbor laden with such badly needed supplies.

"You have medicines, wine?" one man, a surgeon by the look of his bloody clothes, asked. "We die like flies with fevers and bloody bowels, those of us the primitives do not strangle in our sleep."

"Is there bread? Or wheat to make it? God's bones, I sicken on cassava cakes," another fellow said.

"I am Don Bartolomé Colon, the governor's brother. Where is Don Cristobal?" he asked of the most civilized looking man to venture through the press.

"I have heard much of you from your brother, Don Bartolomé. My name is Luis Torres, I am a scholar and was the fleet interpreter. Welcome to Ysabel, such as it is. I fear Don Cristobal is off in search of more lands to claim for the Majesties. Your younger brother, Diego, is left in charge. I am certain he will be along anon." Luis noted the way the beautiful lady studied him covertly as the other passengers disembarked amid loud shouts, shrieks of welcome and general chaos.

"Forgive my manners, Don Luis. This is Doña Magdalena Valdés, the betrothed of Diego Torres, my brother's fleet marshal. I do hope he is here to greet her."

Luis bowed gallantly over Magdalena's hand, an incongruous gesture for a man clad in a soiled white linen tunic that fell ungirdled to his knees. He wore muchmended hose and mud-covered boots, and his black curly hair was in sorry want of barbering. "Diego Torres' betrothed," he said in a strange voice.

"Are you related to him, sir? I know of no one in his family named Luis," Magdalena said in puzzlement.

Luis shrugged, glad of a momentary reprieve. Let that stripling Colon handle this dilemma for his brothers! "No, my lady. I have sailed with Diego, but we are not of the same family, although we do share a certain kinship, both being New Christians. I hail from Cordoba. Ah, here comes the acting governor now."

Diego Colon, dressed grandly in a flowing deep blue cloak, had come to greet the supply ships. The last person on earth he wished to see was his elder brother, whom Cristobal would doubtless place in charge during all future absences. He forced a smile on his sallow face and heartily embraced Bartolomé. "How come you from the royal court so soon? Were you not to see to our brother's children?"

"They are safely tucked away in Prince Juan's entourage as pages. I was dispatched by King Fernando with these supply ships our brother requested." He drew Magdalena nearer and introduced her to his brother.

She nodded politely as she sensed the tension exuding from Diego Colon. Something was amiss between the brothers.

Bartolomé looked about the rude shacks and half-constructed stone buildings on the plaza. "It would seem the food and medicine are badly needed."

"Yes, there has been much sickness in this pestilent climate," Diego quickly explained, ushering them away from the crowded beach toward a stark stone building on the square.

"There appears to be a marked lack of industry. So many men sit idly and I saw open fields bare of crops around the whole of the bay as we sailed in," Bartolomé countered.

Diego drew his thin body up so he stood a full two inches above his elder brother. "The men are an unskilled lot. Most who are not ill are either with our military commander setting up forts in the interior or off exploring with Cristobal." Wanting to change the subject from his possible malfeasance, Diego returned his attention to Magdalena, who was escorted by Luis Torres. "Why have you favored Ysabel with your presence, my lady?"

Bartolomé explained Magdalena's mission, giving her hand a reassuring squeeze.

"Diego Torres' betrothed?" his younger brother practically squeaked.

Magdalena turned to Luis and asked flatly, "Where is Diego? He is well, is he not?" Her heart constricted. So many had fallen ill.

Diego interrupted any possible reply from the scholar. "No, no, my brother's marshal flourishes, although he has quit his post since last we landed. He lives in a village of primitives—Indians, the colonists have taken to calling them."

"He lives among the savage people, like those Don Cristobal presented at court?" Magdalena asked incredulously.

"Well, yes. I will send a runner to summon him," Diego Colon said distractedly. "But first, let me offer you hospitality." They had reached the big stone governor's residence, where an Indian waited patiently, holding open the door for the acting governor and his guests.

Magdalena felt a premonition of disaster as Bartolomé took her arm and escorted her into the cool, dark interior.

Chapter Twelve

Aaron was hot, exhausted, and extremely irritated at the peremptory summons from Diego Colon. He wondered what new ill tidings there might be for the Taino. Since it was a hard day's journey for men afoot, he chanced riding one of the horses he had brought with him from Cadiz. Although of inferior bloodlines to his beloved Andaluz, the big bay was sturdy and sure-footed on the rough terrain of the twisting jungle paths and slippery mud.

He reined to a halt in front of the great hulking monstrosity of stone that was the governor's palace and slid from the bay. "God spare us an architect for this city named for a queen," he muttered wryly, wiping the sweat from his brow as he gazed toward the harbor. Several new caravels bobbed easily near the shoreline. Perhaps Colon wished him to mediate some altercation between these new arrivals and the Indians. Swearing beneath his breath, he strode toward the front entry and knocked. One of Diego Colon's Taino servants answered the door, clad in the loose cotton tunic the new government insisted all Indian women must wear while living in town. She ushered him toward the large audience room that took up the right side of the building, serving as a court of justice, public meeting place, and social hall.

"Diego, your summons said a matter of great urgency. What—" Aaron stood frozen in the doorway, ignoring the smug look on the acting governor's face. His eyes riveted on Magdalena Valdés. Dressed in a fine silk gown and gauze surcoat, she looked small and fragile, utterly out of place in this cold, masculine room. Her green eyes shone dark in her pale face. Did she tremble as she clutched the locket at her bosom?

"You! What in the name of all the angels of heaven do you here, lady?"

Magdalena stared at the savage standing before her. Sweet Mother of God, what had she done! This stranger was practically naked, wearing only a small cloth about his hips, with a wicked looking knife strapped to his side. His skin was bronzed as darkly as any of the Tainos she had seen in town, and his hair was long and shaggy. The shadow of a beard glistened on his jaw, which was clenched in amazement and fury. Cold blue eyes pierced her as he awaited a reply to his question.

Her throat constricted. She took a deep breath and said, "Hello, Diego." Before she could beg leave of the Colon brothers to talk in private with her "betrothed," Bartolomé interrupted.

"A passing strange way for a man to greet the lady he is to wed after she has crossed an ocean for him." The heavyset, red-haired man stood protectively next to Magdalena, dwarfing her.

"The lady I am to wed?" Aaron echoed in astonishment.

"We were given to understand that your father arranged the match," Diego Colon said, looking at Aaron's Taino clothing and sun-darkened body with disdain. He could scarce credit the sanity of such a beautiful woman as the Lady Magdalena, come to wed with this half-savage.

"My father was mayhap beguiled into friendship with this wench, but he arranged no betrothal between us, I assure you," Aaron gritted out, turning furiously to glare at Magdalena.

Bartolomé interposed himself between them. "I was told that you, like many other men here, kept a primitive female, but that is of no account now. You will honor your bond to this noble lady."

"There *is* no bond," Aaron almost shouted, eyeing the stranger who looked oddly familiar. "Who are you, her brother?"

"No, I am the admiral's brother, Bartolomé Colon, at your service, Sir Marshal," he answered with sarcasm. "Will you act the part of a gentleman or have you resided among the savages too long?"

Now it was Magdalena's turn to step between the two men, bristling at each other like two mastiffs. "Please, if I may speak with Diego alone for a moment," she said, placing her hand on Bartolomé's arm.

"I have nothing to say to you, Magdalena. What was between us in Seville is finished now. You, of all people, should understand why," he said with cold finality.

Her shock at his appearance and her fear about confronting him with his father's wishes dimmed as she stared into his icy eyes. He had used her and deserted her as if she were some Taino serving wench! "I understand that you took my honor in Seville and then left me."

"My lady, you gave freely what I took," he replied contemptuously.

She fought the urge to fly at him with her nails and instead said quietly, "Benjamin pledged you, Aaron."

The use of his given name caused his eyes to narrow. "My father was deceived by you, but not so far as to betroth us."

"He gave me this as a sign for you," Magdalena said, her anger evaporating into bitter hurt at his heartless rejection. She pulled the locket from her neck and opened it, then extracted the pomander and revealed its precious contents.

"How came you by that?" he asked with a strangled gasp, grabbing the ring from her fingers.

"Then you do not deny it is your father's signature ring?" Bartolomé said gravely.

Aaron looked at the ring in his palm. Its brilliant sapphire glowed like blue fire, the color of Torres eyes. "This is my father's ring," he said quietly, "but there are many ways she could have come to possess it." He slid it on his finger, then looked consideringly at the small pale woman before him. "Her father, Bernardo Valdés, was responsible for murdering my family. He turned them over to the Inquisition—for his share of Torres wealth. When I went home last year everyone was dead and all our property confiscated. She most like pilfered the ring from *her* father!"

Magdalena could hold back no longer. She slapped him as tears suddenly overflowed her eyes. "That is a monstrous lie! Benjamin gave me this ring the day after I met you at your home." She hesitated as he stood stone still, his hands clenched menacingly at his sides. Her cheeks flamed as she whispered, "He found my combs by your bed after you departed for Palos. He was going to force you to wed me before you sailed, but I begged him not to."

One golden eyebrow raised cynically. "And what prompted your change of heart after all this time has passed? Why is it you now cross the very ocean to wed me? Do you carry a Trastamara bastard in your belly and need a gullible father for it? I warrant King Fernando is fair out of archbishoprics with which to vest his bastards."

"You insult not only this lady but his majesty as well. You have lived too long with those savages and grow as primitive as they," Diego Colon said indignantly, but it was his elder brother who menaced Aaron by approaching him with hand on sword hilt.

"You will apologize to the Lady Magdalena, Don Diego, or I will slit your gullet, no matter if you did save Cristobal's life," Bartolomé said in a low deadly voice.

Looking at Bartolomé's hard face, he realized the man was as taken in by Magdalena as his father had been. *What is it about the wench?* He turned to her with a mock gallant gesture, bowing as he said, "My apologies, Doña Magdalena, I will not again insult you, but neither will I wed you . . . ever." He turned to Bartolomé and said, "Do your worst. I am not pledged to the woman and I will not be coerced into a marriage."

"And I will not force you," Magdalena said furiously, having regained her composure. The blatant cruelty of his words had left her numb for a moment. "Farewell, Diego Torres. I wish you well with your Indian woman."

With the blood pounding in his ears, Aaron walked stiffly and silently toward the door.

"One moment," Bartolomé said. "The ring is the lady's betrothal pledge. If you will not honor the pledge, you will not keep the ring." When Aaron turned, Bartolomé's drawn sword was at his throat. "Give the lady her ring or by the Blessed Mother, you will not depart Ysabel alive."

Muttering an oath, Aaron removed the ring and handed it to Bartolomé, for Magdalena would not approach him. "Keep it . . . for now," he said, again walking toward the door.

"You shall hear more of this matter when the admiral returns," Bartolomé called out at his retreating back.

Aaron did not break stride.

Magdalena accepted the ring from her champion with her head held high. "Please, do not press him. I will have none of him now." She turned to Diego Colon and said, "Only let me live here in Ysabel. You have many sick people and I am accounted a good nurse."

"This is a rough city, filled with unprincipled rogues and adventurers. Although there are some Indian women and a few white women from Castile . . . well," Diego Colon's face reddened. "You are the only lady in Ysabel. It is not safe for you to remain here without the protection of a husband."

Her grip on Bartolomé's arm tightened and she implored, "Please, you know what awaits me at court. Let me stay. I will be no trouble."

Bartolomé sighed, looking at her pale, proud face, silently cursing Diego Torres as seven kinds of a fool. "We will await Cristobal's return. Let him decide the right of it. He knows Torres well. In the meanwhile," he looked at his brother Diego's vacillating expression and said firmly, "the lady remains. There is no ship outfitted to make the return voyage anyway. We can do no less than offer Colon hospitality to her."

Magdalena went to her quarters, a simple but spacious room in the stone building, rudely furnished with a lumpy mattress of palm fibers, a small table, and a stool of rough dark wood. Throwing herself down across the bed, she let go of all the misery she had held back during the confrontation with Aaron. Shame and humiliation rushed over her in waves as fierce as any she had encountered in the ocean crossing. That he would mistrust her motives and be angry with her for coming in pursuit of him she had expected. He was proud and stubborn and such a man did not like to be forced into anything, much less marriage, at sword point.

Even his accusation that she came by Benjamin's ring through her father was forgivable. But to say she had come to him from Fernando Trastamara's bed! She shuddered and let out a fierce sob. That was beyond bearing. And worst of all, he preferred a Taino woman, one of those savages, to her. She could still feel his cold blue eyes mocking her, feel his surging fury and burning contempt. "Let him rot! A convent would be preferable to being wed to such a monster!" she spat out between clenched teeth, then gave way to another fit of weeping.

By evening, Magdalena had done with her storm of tears, soaked her ravaged face and performed an elaborate toilette to restore her spirits. If she was indeed the only lady on Española, she would look the part! When she entered the dining hall for the evening meal, Bartolomé and Diego Colon and six other gentlemen all rose to greet her effusively.

At court she had not enjoyed coquetry and was always nervous with the attention of devious and lecherous noblemen, but here the gallantry of the soldiers and adventurers was balm to her wounded spirit. That Diego Colon and the others wanted to court her was at first flattering. Then, as the simple meal wore on, she began to realize the problems such a contest might present. The rivals would soon be at one another with swords drawn. She could be forced to choose one of them to wed, and in truth, she wanted none of them.

The dark Argonese, Mosen Margarite, reminded her of the king with his cruel black eyes. But unlike Fernando Trastamara, Margarite had a face that was harsh and craggy like the hardened mercenary he was. No soft courtier, he wore his scars like badges of honor. His rapacity in dealing with Taino rebels in the interior already made people in Ysabel whisper his name and give him wide berth.

Alonso Hojeda was a cocky little Sevilliard who acted the part of a fop and a braggart, but beneath his lacy doublet sleeves and elegantly trimmed beard, he was

197

crafty and fiercely ambitious as only an impoverished hidalgo could be.

As for Diego Colon, Magdalena had taken an almost instant dislike to his opinionated arrogance. She fervently hoped the admiral possessed Bartolomé's temperament, not that of his younger brother.

"Please, Doña Magdalena, more wine?" Diego asked, motioning a Taino servant to pour before she could refuse. Already the room grew uncomfortably warm and her hair, bound by a lacy snood, felt like a great wool cloak clinging to her sticky back.

Taking a tiny sip of the bitter red liquid, she nodded her thanks to her petulant host. Diego was obviously put out with the untimely arrival of his elder brother, who had already taken over the duty of *adelantado,* issuing orders and making decisions in Cristobal's absence.

Alonso Hojeda eyed her as if she were a succulent partridge. His black button eyes danced as he said, "Your father is in high favor at court, I understand."

"Don Bernardo spends more time in Seville now than at court, sir," she replied noncommittally, loathing the very mention of Bernardo Valdés's name.

"Ah, yes, he is Crossbearer for Fray Tomás de Torquemada, is he not?" Mosen Margarite asked bluntly, full well knowing the answer.

At the mention of the Grand Inquisitor's name, several of the men grew very quiet, eyeing her warily, but Bartolomé came to her rescue, as always. "Doña Magdalena has been at court, high in the Majesties' favor herself before coming to Ysabel. She has no knowledge of her father's activities."

"Still, the House of Valdés is on the ascendency," Don Alonso said, further testing the water to frighten off Magdalena's more timid suitors.

Wanting to leave the unpleasant subject of Bernardo Valdés, Bartolomé turned to Diego and asked, "How goes the construction of the arsenal and the irrigation canal?"

Diego scowled for an instant, then quickly covered his face with a smile. "Well enough. Some of the common men assigned to dig the canal from the river fell ill, and we have been forced to call on those of higher rank to work at the task, but we progress."

"You have many shirkers in this settlement, fine gentlemen who will do no work they cannot accomplish on horseback," Bartolomé said in disgust, pointedly eyeing Hojeda and Margarite.

"We need more Tainos to do menial tasks. White men forced to dig and chop sicken and die in this climate," Don Mosen replied coldly. As commander of the interior forts he was a man of some power. The Argonese had easily manipulated Diego Colon but already could forsee trouble in dealing with Bartolomé. "I would take a force into the interior once more and finish with those rebel leaders, thus providing us with suitable labor to complete the construction of the city—Indian slaves."

Magdalena looked at Margarite. "Don Diego mentioned earlier that there is much unrest across the island since the gold seekers invaded the interior. Perhaps it is against them you should lead an expedition."

Margarite chuckled indulgently. "You sound like that *marrano* Torres—or his companion in Xaragua, Roldan, who is in open rebellion against royal authority —although I know such was not the intention of a gentle lady."

Magdalena bristled but held her temper. "Gentle, perhaps, but not stupid, Don Mosen," she replied sweetly.

Bartolomé interjected, "I would withhold judgment about Roldan and Torres, but I must confess that Torres intrigues me." He cast a look at Magdalena, trying to reassure her. "He knows the Taino language and has maintained the trust of one of the most powerful *caciques*—I believe you call them—on Española. This Guacanagari fellow has the admiral's complete trust. He has been a loyal ally and I would keep him so. I think we should visit his village in peace and ask Diego Torres to help us control the men of Castile and Aragon who run loose doing ill."

"Absurd! He has become a primitive, no more than a savage himself," Diego said to his brother.

Margarite scowled but said nothing. He would bide his time and hope the Colon brothers completely lost control of Española. Bartolomé and Cristobal allied with Torres' savages would serve all the better. He could then sail home and gain King Fernando's ear. The Genoeses' downfall would mean his rise.

Magdalena wanted never again to hear Aaron's name. "If you will excuse me, gentlemen, I fear I have a headache and must leave your company. The heat of this place makes Andalusia seem as cool as Burgos."

"I apologize for distressing you, my lady, with our frightening talk of savages and politics," Diego said, hastening to help her rise from the heavy chair, but it was Bartolomé who took her arm proprietarily. He had become a surrogate uncle or elder brother, always protecting her.

"I will escort you to your quarters, Doña Magdalena," he said solicitously.

When they were alone in the dimly lit hallway, Magdalena turned to Bartolomé. "Do you really plan to ask Diego Torres to help you pacify the primitives of the interior?"

He shrugged. "From what I have learned, the man is a good friend of Cristobal's ally, Guacanagari. We need his help, Magdalena." He paused and a sad, gentle smile touched his rough face. "In spite of his cruel words, you love him still, do you not?"

Magdalena felt hot words of denial catch in her throat and when she looked into his shrewd, pale blue eyes, she knew protest was useless. "It matters not what I feel, Bartolomé. Diego, or Aaron, as he prefers to be called, has made his feelings on our match abundantly plain."

"After all the rigors and risks of escaping the court and a convent, I thought you more of a fighter, Magdalena." His eyes crinkled at the corners when her expression became angry. "Now, rest easy. I will not drag him bound before you. Only give the matter time."

"Aye, time. Something that may quickly run out. I am not a sheltered, convent-reared girl, Bartolomé. Life has dealt me more than a few blows. I know there will be dissention among the men over me. Mayhap I must return to Seville and hope her majesty will forget me and let drop the convent threat if I do not again attend court."

"You cannot hide yourself in the country, Magdalena. The queen is as famous for her memory as your father is for his ambition. You must needs be a bride of Christ or a bride of some mortal man—and soon if you would choose him yourself."

Magdalena nodded in resignation. Bartolomé was right, she thought, bidding him good-night at the door to her room. Once inside, she had taken only one step toward her bed when she felt the steely grip of a strong arm about her arms and waist while the other hand clamped over her mouth. Even before he spoke, Magdalena knew Aaron's touch.

He whispered low. "Now, my pretty fluttering bird, return my father's ring and I will allow you to spend many nights to come with your adoring gaggle of ganders below. How practiced at flirting you have become—or were ever so and did but hide it from me."

She tried to shake her head, but the cruel grip of his calloused fingers held her immobile.

"I will release you, but you must not scream else I will be forced to deal with you as I did in Seville. Besides, think of how it will look when all your suitors find you thus compromised. Will you be quiet?"

This time he allowed her to nod, then eased his hand from her mouth, although his tight grip about her body did not loosen. She had no breath to cry out. His hand wandered across her shoulder and bosom, bared by the low, square-cut neckline of her gown. Frissons of passion tingled through her traitorous body. When he chuckled low, she knew he felt the tautening of her nipples through the sheer layers of silk. But her own shame was mollified by the unmistakable proof of his desire, pressing ever harder into her back.

"Now, let me remove my ring from the ugly bauble which holds it and I will leave you to sleep in peace," he whispered silkily. His hand opened the locket and extracted the pomander.

She stiffened in outrage. "You have no right!"

"This is my father's ring. As the only surviving son of Benjamin Torres, who else should have it? A scheming girl who stole it from a man she had foully murdered?"

"That is a monstrous lie! I loved Benjamin. Never would I have harmed him." She felt the wracking sobs steal up and fought to suppress them.

Aaron could sense how she struggled to control her rage. Good God, could she possibly be telling the truth? He had every reason to doubt, none to believe—but for that instinct deep in his gut that had plagued him ever since he first touched her. Seville seemed a lifetime ago. Unwillingly, he gentled his hold and turned her to face him.

The moonlight silvered her pale skin to a pearly sheen, light and delicate against his darkly bronzed body. Tears trailed silently down her cheeks, but she made no sound and would not meet his eyes. "What am

I to do with you, Magdalena?" he whispered in perplexity.

Her eyes, lustrous with the tears, opened wide and clashed with his as she tilted her chin up proudly. "Obviously not wed me. Benjamin was mistaken in that. Take his ring and go, Aaron."

"So, you cry off. Men like Margarite, even that milksop Diego Colon, will become rich and return to Castile covered in glory. With new suitors, you no longer need me."

"I want no man," she gritted, pushing him away ineffectually. His bare chest was hard as Toledo steel. "Better the convent."

He touched her temple and traced a path down her lovely cheekbone to the pulse that leaped in her throat. "You are too passionate and full of life for the cold walls of a convent. Whence came such a notion?"

"From the queen," she said, suddenly overcome with the desire to wound him as he had her. "When I caught King Fernando's eye, she misliked it as much as I did. I was to be dowered to the Dominican sisters. I enlisted Bartolomé's aid to escape to the Indies. Even marriage to you was preferable to cold stone walls in Madrid! But now I have changed my mind. The cloister looks more promising!"

To her mortification, instead of growing angry, he began to chuckle. "Ah, lady, you are ever leaping from one boiling kettle to another. Watch you do not burn that lovely little rump," he said, holding her closely to him by lifting her buttocks in his hands.

She wriggled to get free of his disturbing touch. "Let me go, else I *will* scream—your neck and my reputation be damned!"

"Consorting with Fernando Trastamara has already sealed your reputation in the Spains. Beware lest you also lose it in Española." With that he lifted her in his arms and his mouth descended in a searing exploration. His tongue rimmed her lips, until she opened them, then it darted inside and retreated. His own lips ground against hers fiercely. All breath, all reason deserted her as she spiraled downward in the whirlpool of passion. Her body turned to hot liquid, pouring itself into his as her hands held his bare shoulders and her nails sank into his muscles.

As quickly as it began, it ended. Aaron broke free of her with a muffled oath and shoved her, dazed and panting, against the door, like a rabbit run to ground and then merely wounded by a cruelly playful predator. Before she could gather her wits, he vanished out the large open window and melted into the dense black shadows along the wall. In a moment she heard the pounding of hoofbeats and knew he had escaped, taking with him his father's ring.

She sank onto the bed, numb and dry-eyed now. "'Twas his to take. I can do no more, Benjamin," she whispered on the silent night air.

Now that it was emptied of its treasure, Magdalena could not bear the ugly weight of the locket. She prayed Bartolomé would not suspect that Aaron had reclaimed the ring.

The next morning, vowing to find a place in the new colony, she dressed in the coolest gown she owned, copying the fashion of the women of the settlement who wore neither surcoats nor under-tunics, merely simple loose gowns of linen or cotton. The heat of Española left her bereft of vanity. She braided her long thick hair into a fat plait and tied it with a bit of ribbon, her only ornament. Slipping from the governor's residence, she headed for the hospital to talk with the physician in charge. Diego Álvarez Chanca was reputed to be reclusive but a man of some learning.

The hospital turned out to be no more than a rude

thatched hovel, scarcely better than a moderately pros-
perous peasant's cottage in Andalusia. She eyed it from
across the plaza, which was crowded with large numbers of people. A Galician fisherman hawked fresh crabs
and lobsters, caught at dawn that day. Smelling them in
the intense heat, Magdalena doubted the veracity of his
claim. Two Tainos, brown skin gleaming with sweat,
bartered in sign language with a merchant from Huelva
to obtain several strings of beads in return for a copper
arm band.

One dealer in cheap red cotton cloth had a Taino
female enthralled with his product and was quoting her
a price for it with graphic gestures. A scraggly whore
from the Barcelona waterfront advertised her wares,
sauntering from one group of lounging soldiers to
another. Several Indian women sat impassively behind
piles of yams and papayas, willing to take cheap trinkets
in return for the food. Pigs squealed and chickens
squawked, running wild across the crowded plaza,
adding both noise and excrement to the chaotic and
aromatic scene.

The smell of cassava bread, the coarse dry cakes made
of shredded manioc root, assailed her nostrils. She
disliked its acid taste and crumbly consistency, but it
was the substitute for wheat bread on Española. Magdalena dodged a pair of hounds in furious pursuit of a
fluttering chicken and moved closer to watch a woman
shove cassava cakes into the hot coals with a crude
wooden paddle.

A pair of soldiers, roughly dressed in loose linen
tunics and leather hose walked up to her. One, with
matted dark hair of some unidentifiable color, seized
her braid roughly and pulled her into his arms. She
nearly gagged at the foulness of his breath. His companion smiled, revealing the stumps of rotted brown teeth
in a badly pock-marked face.

"What have we here, Yañez, a new arrival from

Castile? Look you at the hair. They say the queen has red hair like this," her captor said to his friend.

Yañez weaved slightly to the left and then took another pull at the wineskin he was holding in a dirt-encrusted paw. "Let us ask her price for servicing us both—but let her get no grand ideas. She is no queen."

"But I am of her court, you mangy cur. Release me lest the admiral's brother cut off your filthy hands. You could not heft that wineskin with bloody stumps."

Yañez took a step backward, his wine-fogged brain dimly registering the lisping accent of an educated noblewoman, but her captor would not so easily relinquish his prize.

"She is but a whore as are all who come on the ships from Cadiz and Palos," he reassured his friend, running one hand crudely across her breast.

Magdalena reacted with instinctive loathing, kicking at his shin with her pointy-toed slipper. When he loosened his hold with an oath of surprise, she shoved him off balance and reached frantically to her girdle for her dagger.

Yañez, by now clear of his stupor, saw the blade flash and backed off, but his compatriot Alfredo again attempted to seize her, snarling, "Can you not disarm a small wench?"

She whirled and slashed out with her weapon. Alfredo's blood oozed through the filth of what had once been a white linen tunic sleeve. This galvanized Yañez who wrapped one arm about her, pinning her arms to her sides and immobilizing her knife hand for an instant. In that instant she kicked back at his legs and thrashed, throwing him off balance so they both fell to the dusty red earth in a heap with her on top. Alfredo was on her just as Yañez loosed his hold, but again she wielded her knife, this time opening a slash across his chest before he disarmed her.

By now a crowd had gathered to watch the sport.

Several of the settlement whores cheered her on while two Palos sailors made bets on which of Margarite's soldiers would have her first.

Suddenly a cry went up from the edge of the crowd and Bartolomé Colon came thundering through the press, knocking aside men and women alike. His sword was drawn but the look on his florid face could have killed without its aid.

Alfredo leaped away from Magdalena, holding his bloody arm against his slashed chest, trembling with a mixture of fury and fear. Magdalena rolled away from Yañez's foul stench, struggling for breath as Bartolomé called for two of the guards from the governor's house to throw the men in jail.

"Doña Magdalena, your sense of adventure will be your undoing. You were to wait for me. I warned you of how rough this place is."

As he assisted her up, the two soldiers were hauled off at sword point. She spared them not another glance, but looked down at her ruined gown, now wrinkled, torn, and covered with dust and blood. As she made a vain attempt to smooth it and then her wildly tangled hair, which had come unplaited, a stranger's voice caused her to raise her head with a snap.

"It would seem, Bartolomé, that I can leave neither of my brothers in charge of Ysabel while I am away, lest there be a riot over a comely wench."

Magdalena stared at the tall, thin man with graying red hair and piercing blue eyes, alight with mirth. The admiral had returned.

Chapter Thirteen

Magdalena stood outside the door to the audience chamber, her nerves stretched to the breaking point. She had bathed, washed her hair and brushed it dry, then dressed it with a beautiful pearl snood. She had chosen a rather old-fashioned gown of brown silk with a high neckline, showing only a frilly ruffle of white linen under-tunic at the throat. She hoped Bartolomé would think she wore her locket and the missing ring beneath it.

She had rehearsed her speech for the admiral, begging his permission to remain on Española. Magdalena wanted to speak of Aaron not at all, but feared Bartolomé might already have berated her lover to his old commander. If Cristobal Colon was a loyal friend of his marshal, he might quickly decide to evict her from his domain—back to Seville and the convent. Taking a deep breath for courage, she tapped on the door, and that strong clear voice commanded her to enter.

Unlike the heavy-boned, solid Bartolomé, his elder brother was slim and almost frail looking but for his piercing pale blue eyes and a firm expression about his generous mouth. The crippling sickness had gnarled his hands and caused his tall, straight back to stoop a bit, but he was yet one of the most imposing men Magdalena had ever met. "Good afternoon, Admiral," she said as he smiled and gestured for her to enter.

Cristobal noted the way her eyes scanned the large room and locked for an instant with those of her champion, Bartolomé. "Good day to you, Doña Magdalena. You look much improved since first we met this morning. I trust you have recovered from that, ah . . . encounter?"

Magdalena felt her cheeks heat with a blush. *Such a way to meet the man who holds my fate in his hands!* "I am well, thank you, Admiral Colon."

"You will find Doña Magdalena a most resourceful young woman, Cristobal," Bartolomé said drily.

"I would that she not risk her life among the rough and dangerous soldiers and other even more unsavory residents of Ysabel," he replied with a gently reproving look at Magdalena.

"I was attempting to go to Dr. Chanca's hospital across the plaza. I understand there is much illness here and I have some skills caring for the sick."

Cristobal looked at her with frank puzzlement and a bit of distress mirrored on his face. "Surely, Doña Magdalena, as a lady of the court, you cannot wish to do such menial and dangerous work? Bartolomé has spent the better part of the past hour avoiding an explanation of precisely why you are here. This is scarcely Seville."

"It is preferable to the convent of the Dominican sisters in Madrid, Admiral," Magdalena replied forthrightly. "I am much in debt to your brother for his kindness and now I must beg your indulgence, too." She began the tale of her disastrous sojourn with the court, ending with her father's agreement to seal her up in that heinous convent, but she omitted any mention of her betrothal to the admiral's marshal. "I never wish to return to Castile or to see my father again as long as I live," she finished.

As she had unfolded the story of immorality and jealousy, Magdalena had paced back and forth by the long open windows facing the plaza. When she finished speaking, Bartolomé offered her a goblet of wine and pulled a heavy wooden chair out for her to have a seat. She accepted both with thanks, her eyes quickly moving back to the tall, thin man staring intently at her with a troubled expression on his face.

"I can see why you wished to leave Valladolid, even to flee the Spains, but surely there was some refuge better than this wildly improbable venture. Have you no kinsman who could arrange a marriage for you?"

Magdalena let her eyes drop, her mind racing. *Please, Bartolomé, do not tell him!* Then she met the admiral's earnest gaze and said, "I have no other family—at least, none who would dare defy Bernardo Valdés. You see, my father is a Crossbearer for the Holy Office in Seville."

Colon's fingers tapped on the rough wooden table. "A most dangerous foe with whom to cross swords," he murmured with a meaningful look at Bartolomé, who had the good grace to redden.

"There is a simple remedy for all our problems," Bartolomé began very carefully.

"Yes, there is," Magdalena interjected. "I will cause no trouble. I grew up on my parents' country estates outside Seville. I am used to hard work. I can tend sick people, sick animals. I will be a good colonist for Ysabel, Admiral." Her eyes were huge and entreating.

"You are a beautiful young woman of the nobility—your very presence in a place such as this is trouble,

Doña Magdalena," Colon rebuked gently. "You had a bitter taste of the problem already this morning, and you have been in Ysabel only three days. I am given to understand from my youngest brother that every gentleman at table last even was exceedingly smitten—including Diego himself. There will be fighting among my men. I cannot allow this. You must choose to wed one of them, or I will be forced to send you back to Seville, no matter how painful the decision is for me," the admiral said quietly.

Magdalena looked at his careworn but stern face and knew he meant his words. "But I do not love . . . that is none . . . oh, forgive me, for I am most flattered by all the gentlemen who have shown me such kindness, but I do not wish to wed any of them, not even your brother Diego."

"Perhaps you should follow your heart, Magdalena," Bartolomé prompted. "In spite of his mule-headed stubbornness, you love him still, do you not?"

Magdalena's eyes darkened with pain. She shook her head as a lump tightened in her throat so that she could not speak.

Cristobal looked from the distressed young woman seated before him to Bartolomé. "Who is this man whom the lady would wed?" he asked his brother in a tone of voice that demanded an end to the earlier evasion.

"Magdalena was betrothed to your marshal, Diego Torres. She carries the crest ring of his father's house. I brought her here to wed Torres, but when we summoned the young fool, he refused." Bartolomé paused for a moment, hating to hurt Magdalena further, but knowing he must speak. "Torres lives among the Taino."

"I know. I sent him with them when first we made landfall on San Salvador nearly two years ago." Then

211

understanding struck the admiral. He looked to Bartolomé for confirmation. "Surely he cannot hold to a Taino female and deny his obligation to a Castilian noblewoman after all she has risked—"

"After all she has risked, he denies even the betrothal!" Bartolomé interrupted angrily. "Did those Indians of his work some necromancy on him to cause him to behave so?"

Cristobal rubbed his temple with his palm, then said, "This is not what I would expect of Diego Torres." He looked down at Magdalena uncertainly. "In all the time I spent with him aboard ship, never did he mention this betrothal."

Magdalena's shoulders slumped as she admitted in a quiet voice. "The pledge was made by his father Benjamin on Diego's behalf, just before he sailed with you on your first voyage here." She blushed in complete humiliation, recalling the painful scene with Benjamin and the even more hateful way his son had repudiated her in front of Bartolomé and Diego Colon.

"The young whelp seduced her in his father's home. When Benjamin Torres found out the truth, he would have ridden with Magdalena to Palos and had them wed before the voyage, but the lady refused to force him. The elder Torres made the pledge. Show the Admiral the ring, Magdalena," Bartolomé commanded softly.

Magdalena stood up and looked from Bartolomé to Cristobal, then said calmly, "I cannot do so. Last even when I returned to my room, he lay waiting for me and took it from me."

Bartolomé's hand clenched on his sword hilt and he swore.

"'Twas his ring. He has refused to believe that Benjamin pledged him. I would not force him to wed me," she said, turning to stare out the window, her back rigidly straight.

"And I would not have him dishonor you. How dare he invade the governor's residence and your room!" Bartolomé said in outrage.

"You have verified that this ring belonged to the House of Torres?" Cristobal asked Bartolomé.

"Yes. I examined it well enough. Why else would he come to reclaim it at such risk? He would have taken it when first the lady showed it to him, but I made him return it at sword's point," Bartolomé added grimly.

A hint of a smile tugged at Cristobal's lips as he considered his arrogant young marshal being forced to return the ring. Diego Torres would mislike being forced to do anything. Then his expression became grave. "You say your father is a Crossbearer in Seville. . . ."

She turned and the absolute coldness of her eyes stunned both men. "Yes, Bernardo Valdés betrayed Benjamin Torres to the Inquisition. He has sold his soul for wealth and power. I would that he were dead."

"And Diego blames you for the sins of your father. I begin to understand," the Admiral said, nodding slowly as he decided on a course of action.

Three days later Aaron paced across the floor, uncomfortable in the hot, tight clothing he had donned to meet with the admiral. Resting his hand lightly on the hilt of his sword, he looked down at the sapphire ring on his finger, then his eyes met Colon's, blue on blue, both gazes intense. "I will not wed her," he stated flatly.

"Nor I him!" Magdalena said, standing up with a furious swish of her skirts.

Colon looked from Aaron to Magdalena. "Then, Doña Magdalena, choose another. Any man of gentle birth and good breeding among the residents of Ysabel. I know many would be honored to wed you. You have but to select one and I will see to the rest." He waited, feeling the tension crackling between the two young people before him. Whatever his feelings for Magdalena Valdés, Diego Torres did desire her and she him. By the Blessed Virgin, the fire fair leaped between them, like the sparks that swept a ship's rigging before the lightning came!

Magdalena felt the admiral's eyes on her. The man was compassionate but convinced of his course. Aaron's hard, dark gaze scorched her with his fury. What was she to do? Wed poor, weak Diego Colon? Or Mosen Margarite? Or Alonzo Hojeda? Better to return and accept the cold cell of the convent! She walked a few steps and then stopped short. Her fists clenched, hidden in the folds of her skirts. She whirled and faced the admiral and his arrogant marshal. "I have chosen. I will have Diego . . . Torres! I will swear any oath you care to devise that Benjamin gave that ring to me in pledge of betrothal to his son," she said, pointing to the sapphire crest on Aaron's finger. She faced his steely glare levelly and did not flinch beneath his withering contempt.

"You may have bewitched my father, but I warn you, Magdalena, I am not so gentle a man as he was," Aaron said, biting off each word.

Aaron paced like a caged lion before Cristobal and Bartolomé after Magdalena had been asked to leave the room. "What you ask, in addition to what you have already ordered, is too much," he said tightly.

"Such onerous duty—to be wed to a beautiful and wealthy noblewoman who adores you. You are much put upon, Torres," Bartolomé said angrily.

Cristobal waved his brother aside, motioning him to take a seat and cool his ire. "I understand your concern for the *cacique's* sister and her child, but you yourself have said there is no dishonor among these people if a woman bears a child without a husband. Guacanagari will not blame you for wedding one of your own kind. If you are concerned for the Taino, then you can best serve them by taking the post just vacated by Margarite."

"Margarite has set sail to Castile with Fray Buil and a host of other troublemakers. They will report ill to the Majesties about how the Colon family misgoverns Española," Bartolomé interjected.

"Mosen Margarite has the king's ear, and Fray Buil will doubtless report to the queen that the Taino refuse conversion and are warlike," Cristobal said wearily.

"That is absurd. We are better off without Margarite and Buil. Fray Pane is truly interested in learning Taino ways and will do more good without that pious ass Buil," Aaron replied.

"Yet that pious ass, as you so aptly describe him, has powerful friends at court. Both he and Margarite are my bitter enemies. I have received some troubling dispatches from the Majesties already, questioning how I keep order on Española. The king asks why we have sent so little gold back." The Admiral looked at Aaron with earnest entreaty. "I always favored you to be my commandant."

Bartolomé stood up and leveled his most intimidating glare on Aaron. "We fully expect a royal investigator to set sail from Cadiz any time."

"I would have us at peace, prosperously trading with the Taino, when the next caravels arrive. Those *caciques* who will not accept the governance of the king and queen must be vanquished and Guacanagari's people must be protected. You are the man both Taino and colonists most respect, Aaron. I ask you to become commandant and to marry the Lady Magdalena." The admiral waited, piercing Aaron with his pale blue eyes.

Aaron scowled as he turned and met the stare. "As in all matters, you leave me little choice. I assume my bride and I are to reside here in Ysabel. When is the marriage to take place?"

"You will take my quarters," Bartolomé said. "It is a small building with a stout mahogany frame and cane walls which will afford comfort through the warmer season. By the time the rains come, if we have the colonists in hand doing their tasks, a stone house should be completed for each of us," Bartolomé said with a challenge in his voice. "In the meantime, I can reside here with my brothers.

"As to the marriage," Cristobal added, more delicately, "I think it best to summon Fray Pane and have him perform it quickly, to ally possible conflicts with others of the lady's suitors."

A chilly smile slashed Aaron's mouth. "You have considered all options. We will wed and bed ere this night is done. Then I am bound to Magdalena for life, but still I must see Guacanagari and Aliyah, Cristobal. You needs must trust me outside Ysabel if I am to be your commandant."

"I trust your word, Aaron. But you must realize the very reasons necessitating the marriage also call for your appearance with your wife here in the settlement before you make a return visit to your old home among the Taino," Cristobal said gravely.

Aaron's smile broadened but still did not reach his eyes. "So, in but a week, Magdalena has managed to wreak as much havoc among the men of Ysabel as she did the men of Seville."

"She is headstrong, beautiful and, yes," Cristobal agreed, grudgingly, "prone to accidents."

"Such as?" Aaron prompted.

"She wished to help Dr. Chanca at the hospital and while crossing the plaza was set upon by two drunken soldiers," Bartolomé interposed. "It was no fault of the lady's."

Aaron threw back his head and laughed mirthlessly. "When first I met her, two worthless pups from the marshlands of the Guadalquiver were attacking her. I was forced to kill them," he added grimly. "Mayhap I should have let them have her!"

"I understand she gave good account of herself with her dagger before Bartolomé, here, came charging to her rescue," Cristobal said, recalling the bedraggled but fiery girl and the two cowering, blood-spattered men still languishing in the settlement's jail. A faint smile crossed his face in spite of himself. His intuition, always strong when he was sailing, now seemed especially positive here on land. The match between these two was right.

Fray Ramon Pane, of the Jeronymite Order, was a simple, scholarly man, fascinated by Indian culture and, perhaps because of his empathy with them, a failure at the task of converting the Tainos from their *zemis* to the Christian God. He was conveniently at hand to perform the marriage between Aaron and Magdalena, which the nervous little priest immediately sensed was in accord with the admiral's wishes, not the participants'. Only Cristobal and Bartolomé Colon were present for the brief ceremony. The ink was scarce dry on the contracts when he was dismissed. Puzzled, he departed the governor's residence to resume his studies of primitive religious and social customs among Ysabel's Taino residents.

The admiral gave the pale-faced bride a fatherly salute on the forehead and then bade her return to her room while he spoke for a moment with her grim-faced new husband.

Magdalena looked at Aaron, so forbidding and formal, as if a stranger had taken his place inside the much beloved, laughing golden man she had so long loved. *He hates me and yet I love him.* She forced a tremulous smile for the Admiral and Bartolomé, then quit the hall to await her new husband's pleasure in her lonely room.

Once inside the door, she crumpled against its massive wooden surface for support, willing herself not to cry. "You have made your bargain," she whispered to herself, "now you must live with it." But would Aaron Torres live with her? Or would he turn his back on her and flee to the interior as others, such as Francisco Roldan, had done? As she dwelled on the dismal choices, Magdalena was torn, not wanting to live out a travesty of a marriage with a man who held her in contempt, yet desperate to hold on to him. "I must be his wife in deed or my father can yet wall me up in a convent," she rationalized. Her heart cried out, *You would have him truly love you. Naught else matters.*

She walked over to the much-battered leather trunk that had crossed the wide Atlantic with her. Kneeling on the rough stone floor, heedless of her lovely pale-gold gown, she opened it and dug among the meager treasures she had been able to smuggle from Castile. Her hands lingered on a volume of Latin poetry, a beloved gift from Benjamin, then ran quickly through a pile of silk and brocade cloaks and gowns, linen under-tunics and lace hair coverings. She dug deeply to the bottom of the chest and extracted a carefully rolled and sealed document. Written in Benjamin's own hand, it attested to her innocence, innocence she had given so foolishly and wantonly to his son. This could prove to Aaron that she was not like her mother. He had believed from the first that she was cheap and tainted. Here lay proof of his misjudgment.

Turning it over in her hands, Magdalena pondered what to do. He had refused to believe how she had come by the signet ring. He had even accused her of witchery in deceiving his father. Well might a man as proud and stubborn as Aaron Torres throw this back at her and accuse her again of deceiving Benjamin into writing it. Yet longing so desperately as she did to win his love and trust, Magdalena knew she had to try to convince him that she belonged to him and no other. Nor in truth could she ever consider letting another man touch her as he had.

Shuddering, she remembered King Fernando's loathsome hands, roughly pawing her, his voice chuckling and coaxing when she pleaded with him to dismiss her. Even earnest suitors such as Diego Colon, men who offered marriage, had been unthinkable alternatives to her. "I will have Aaron or I will have none, damn him!" She stood up and carried the document to the small table near the window to await her husband.

Magdalena heard the door latch lift with a slight creak in the damp evening air. Aaron stepped inside the room without the courtesy of a knock or a word of greeting. He inspected his new bride of scarce an hour, noting the lovely gown of gold tissue and her hair, that curling red-black mass, the color of sweet dark cherries in the Andalusian spring. That world was lost forever to him, yet here stood its embodiment, all the witching soft allure, the corruption of it. He tried to fix on his hatred of her father, her family name, everything he had vowed to destroy. Still he desired her. And damned her for it.

"Gather what you would have the servants take to our new home. The admiral's *adelantado*, Bartolomé, has graciously given us his house—and a private feast to celebrate the consummation of our marriage. It would seem appearances are all. We are to make peace among your squabbling suitors by acting the loving bridal couple on the morrow. Think you we can manage, lady?" He stood by the door, across the room from her.

"'Twill serve naught if you are afraid to come near me, Aaron," she whispered, trying to break through the invisible barriers separating them. Her words were spoken lightly, yet she quailed inside.

"You are single-minded, Magdalena. I will give you

my admiration for that. You have pursued me since that encounter on the marshes—nay, even before that, at the royal court when we were both but children. Why? Why me?" he asked as he strode across the room and stood facing her, smelling her sweet orange-blossom perfume. "Once my family was wealthy and powerful, but now . . ." His voice trailed off in perplexity.

"Perhaps it is quite simple, Aaron," Magdalena said, her voice ragged and breathy. She raised one small hand and placed it on his doublet, working up her courage to speak.

The words died in her throat when he said, "Your pursuit of me is as bold and unnatural as Aliyah's. At least she had the customs of her people as an excuse."

"Your mistress, so beloved that you became a naked savage for her?" Magdalena asked, stung bitterly. Every sailor had women in primitive lands far from home. There was no reason to expect Aaron to be different from other men, yet some self-punishing instinct forced her to continue her questioning. "You say I am an unnatural woman like her. What virtue does she possess that I do not, since you seem to prefer her? Is she beautiful?"

He could sense her jealousy, and his own anger at her scheming and manipulation of his life led him to smile coldly and say, "In her way, Aliyah is as beautiful as you, although at present she is not so lithesome, being great with child."

Magdalena felt her blood freeze. "She carries your child?"

He shrugged in feigned indifference. "I will not know for certain until it is born. She took two Taino lovers while I was away."

Rage began to thaw her frozen blood, now pounding hotly through her veins. "You still live with a woman who betrayed you while you were away—who carries a child and you know not if it is even yours?" she cried furiously.

"You, Magdalena, are a poor one to disparage Aliyah. Her people do not value chastity in women as do ours." He saw her hands curl into claws and imprisoned both slim wrists just as she would have raised them to his face. "You do not like reminders of whom you were spawned by, do you?"

She struggled against his hold on her and cursed him as she had heard stable boys do to mules and oxen in the streets of Seville.

He took her wrists and wrenched them behind her back, gripping them with one hand while he pulled her tightly against his body and held her fast. "Perhaps that is the answer to my riddle. Were you so disgraced at court with your whoring that no nobleman of worth would take you? Did you deceive Bartolomé as a means to escape some diseased old lecher?"

"Any man—diseased, old, ugly as a toad, smelly as a goat—any man would be less repellent than you," she shrieked, kicking at him with her soft brocade slippers and struggling mightily not to betray herself with tears. Tears! He was worth not a one. "I will kill you and be widowed. That will satisfy the admiral's accursed propriety!"

"I think not. I am still fond of my life, although this past year causes me to wonder upon the reason."

"Then send me back to Seville—I will go gladly to the convent!"

He scoffed. "That fairy tale again. Leave off your tales of woe. I am not Bartolomé, nor that conceited stripling Diego."

She ceased her struggles. "You do not believe the queen banished me?" she asked in amazement. "The utter density of a man forced to do something against his will is staggering. I had always believed you passing bright. I would not lie, Aaron. Only send me back to court. Queen Ysabel will relieve you of any further burden!"

"Now you finally realize that I will not be ruled by guile and cry off. It is too late to repent of your bargain, Magdalena. The admiral would never allow you to sail and you have lost all other opportunities by remaining here to ensnare me. Well," he gritted out, "if I am saddled with a wife, I will act the husband."

With that he swooped down and kissed her, holding her in a bone-breaking grip as he savaged her mouth.

Marseilles, France, Summer 1494

Isaac Torres sat behind the huge slab of polished walnut that served him as desk and table, oblivious of the lavish appointments of the vast room. He crumpled the letter, grinding the waxed seal upon it to powder. The seal had borne the crest of Los Reyes Católicos, as they were now designated. With a furious oath he threw the letter against a heavy tapestry hanging on the far wall, rose from his seat, and began to pace the room.

Just then Ruth entered, carrying Olivia, Ana's small daughter, whom they had paid a fortune to have smuggled from Seville while her father Lorenzo was at court. The child's curly golden hair was tousled and she looked wide-eyed with wonder to see her beloved Great Uncle Isaac in such an angry humor. Ruth turned and handed Olivia to a servant, shushing the child with a gentle kiss and a promise of sweets later. Then she closed the door and turned to her husband. "What distresses you so? Have we word of Mateo's son? Our agent in Barcelona has not reported in many weeks," she said worriedly.

Isaac sat down in one of two large chairs positioned on either side of a small brass table in one corner of the room. He motioned for her to come join him, and she did so, sinking into the chair opposite him as he spoke.

"We have no word, good or ill, of my brother's grandson, but this—this perfidy!" He glared at the crumpled letter on the floor, his blue eyes glowing with rage and calculation. "I must find a way to put that Trastamara bastard's greed to my use."

"It is from the King of Aragon?" Ruth asked, her face turning waxen. "Can he harm us here? I thought we were safe."

He reached out and patted her hand. "We are as safe as Jews ever are. No, as long as we have wealth enough, we will be undisturbed in King Charles's turbulent land. He and our previous sovereign are always at each other's throats."

"Then why does King Fernando send to you?" Her voice was still weak with fear.

Isaac stood up and once more began to pace, smashing a meaty fist into his other palm. "He wishes his just share of my brother's estates! It seems the Holy Office and its minions have been cheating him. King Fernando would have fair accounting," he said with steely sarcasm.

Ruth's hand stole to her throat, where she was certain her heart had leaped. "How can he do such a monstrous thing?"

"Ha!" Isaac sneered at the crumbled wax lying on his desk. "I have heard from several of our friends who fled, some in Naples, others here in France. The Trastamara is upset with Torquemada's instrument of death—it cheats him of his share of the wealth! But," he added, running his stubby strong fingers through his hair, "this can work for us. I can tell him where every maravedi Benjamin owned was laid—for a price."

He looked at Ruth. "You have worried overmuch about Aaron, so far off in the Indies with the Genoese. I—I did not tell you, but I received a letter from him through my agents a month past. I wished not to disturb

Shirl Henke

you. He is well," Isaac added quickly when she paled, "but he plans to gather wealth enough in the Indies to return and kill Bernardo Valdés."

Ruth gasped, "No! He will be killed!"

"I have sent word to him that I would see to Valdés." A smile of cold satisfaction spread across Isaac Torres' face as he once more sat down beside his wife. "Now, it would seem the wily Argonese will aid me in fulfilling that pledge." He reached for his writing instrument and began to work furiously as Ruth watched with a troubled expression on her face.

Chapter Fourteen

Ysabel, Española, Summer 1494

Magdalena stared at the large raised platform that served as a bed in their new quarters. The mattress was plump, filled with soft cotton, and of a size to accommodate two people easily. Her gaze swept to her husband. After his brutal kiss at the governor's palace, he had given her but a few moments in which to gather her scattered belongings. She had quickly thrust the sealed document from Benjamin beneath a cloak and thrown it into her chest. Later she would conceal it more carefully. *Mayhap I should destroy it.* Yet some instinct —a faint flicker of hope—led her to keep it for the present even if she did not share it with this blind, arrogant stranger she had wed.

All around her Taino servants carried in her furnishings and placed them at Aaron's direction in the small quarters Bartolomé had originally appropriated as his own. The wooden house had several windows and was surrounded by palm trees and luxuriant frangipani, giving it an aura of isolation even though it was at the edge of Ysabel. A lone candle flickered against the onrush of sunset. Insects hummed and a songbird in the distant jungle gave out with a low sweet trill.

"That will be fine for now, Analu, my thanks," Aaron said in the Taino tongue, dismissing the servants. Smiling at the bridal couple, they quickly departed. He turned to her. "Do you find the accommodations to your liking? 'Tis not the Alhambra, nor the Alcazar."

"The house is suitable enough. 'Tis the company that lacks," she replied tartly, walking over to the small table, where a modest feast of cold roasted duck, cassava bread and lush fruits awaited them. She took a slice of sweet melon, but it tasted like ashes in her mouth.

"No appetite?" Aaron asked, coming up behind her so closely she could feel his breath on her neck as he spoke. He inhaled her fragrance and felt the tension between them in a way he had felt with no other woman, not even Aliyah.

Magdalena flinched as he ran his fingers lightly up her arm. "You have brought me here and kept your word to the admiral. We need go no further," she pleaded, knowing it was in vain.

"Ah, but I think we do. If I am to have a wife by fiat she will be a wife in fact," he said softly, turning her to face him. "Do not lie to us both by saying you do not desire me, Magdalena."

Her thick russet lashes fluttered low, shielding her dark green eyes. "No, Aaron, I will not say that I do not desire you, only that I do not wish it to be this way."

"You, not I, made up the game, my lady. Now, you must play," he said as he raised her hair away from her slender white neck and kissed her throat softly. His mouth moved with wet warm insistence up to her earlobe. He licked, bit, and then deserted it to brush softly over her eyelids and then move to her lips. All he did to hold her during the exploration was to tangle his hands in the curls tumbling down her back.

Slowly, against her will, Magdalena's hands crept up his arms to his shoulders. She leaned into him as he rimmed her lips with his tongue. She moaned, or mayhap he did; she could not tell as the kiss deepened to a hungry hard pressure that was both bruising and exquisite. His arms now enfolded her as tightly as hers did him. Both lost all sense of time and place, swaying like two closely planted palms stirred by a gentle ocean breeze. Finally, he broke off the kiss and scooped her into his arms with a breathless oath. She clung to him as he stalked to the bed and stood her once more on very unsteady legs.

"Take off the gown. I might tear it in my haste, and I will not be able to afford to replace it for some time," he said hoarsely as he began to unfasten his doublet with swift, rough movements.

For a moment, she stood frozen in indecision, watching him bare his splendid bronzed body with the cunning pattern of dark gold hair on his chest. Muscle and sinew flexed on his lean, hard frame as he pulled off his boots and began to unlace his hose. Then the treacherous heat that had been building inside her, turning her will to wax, sent a leaping flame searing through her. With a deep, unsteady breath she fumbled at the intricate fastenings of her gown and began to slide it from her shoulders.

Aaron finished removing his clothes and then stood watching her. The gold tissue crumpled in a glistening heap on the wooden floor as Magdalena stepped free of it, now clad only in a soft, sheer linen under-tunic. She kicked her tiny soft slippers free and then, sensing the heat of his eyes on her, she paused and looked up at him.

Again, that look of wounded vulnerability that always haunted his dreams filled her face. Her eyes were the color of moss in the depths of the jungle.

Silently he reached for the folds of the under-tunic and pulled it over her head as she lifted her arms like an obedient child to assist him. Her pale flesh left him breathless. "So, you already adapt to the heat of Española and wear no undergarments. Soon you will be naked as one of the Tainos. Watch you do not turn brown."

"Would that please you?" The question seemed to ask itself before she could quash it. *I will not be jealous of his Indian love!*

"Little in my life pleases me these last few years," he said evasively as he reached for her. He smothered an oath of sheer animal pleasure as his hands followed the curves of her breast down to span her tiny waist, then lower to whisper around the gentle swell of her slim hips and rounded buttocks. "You are perfect, damn you," he said angrily, pulling her into his arms.

Magdalena went willingly, sensing some small victory in his betrayal of desire. He, too, was a prisoner of this strange and powerful force that kept drawing them together across religious barriers and storm-tossed oceans. *This was fated to be,* she thought with resignation as she opened her mouth for his kiss. His tongue plunged in with hot, slick strokes that perfectly emulated what would come later. Knowing now what to expect, Magdalena gave herself over to the mindless drug of passion.

They sank onto the edge of the bed, then fell backward onto the soft, wide mattress covered with rich, cool silks. Aaron rolled on top of her and continued the kiss, while his hands roamed about her breasts with maddening deftness, cupping, caressing, then softly tweaking her pebbled nipples until she arched, searching for those little pinches of pleasure. When he raised himself over her and began to suckle and tongue each breast in turn, the scalding heat of his mouth caused her to cry aloud shamelessly.

Aaron watched her toss her head from side to side with her eyes tightly closed, her mouth open, panting, wanting. She arched against him, her mound rubbing against the aching hardness of his staff. He could feel her nails scouring his back; he could sense the desperation that drove her, just as it drove him. He rolled onto his back, pulling her with him to drape her soft, small body over his. They were buried in a cloud of russet fire as her hair curtained them. He held her hips in his hands and whispered hoarsely, "Raise yourself up, Magdalena."

She obeyed and his mouth again blistered her small, perfectly rounded breasts as they hung suspended like ripe, sweet melons for him to taste. As he moved to and fro from one to the other, she let out small whimpering moans. Then he reached up and spanned her waist with long slim fingers, lifting her up and back to seat her on his upthrust staff. Her thighs parted instinctively, hungrily, and she sank slowly downward into a burning bliss.

His ragged cry blended with hers as he filled her, probing her incredibly tight, moist sheath. She felt as virginally small as she had over a year ago in Seville, as if she had had no man but him. The fleeting thought infused him with a surge of intense pleasure. He guided her gently at first, plumbing the hot slippery depths of her body with a gradually increasing tempo.

Alive with indescribable hunger, Magdalena followed his lead, riding harder and faster, wanting to scream out her pleasure and her need. Then he rolled on top of her, never breaking the swift, even rhythm of their ecstatic joining. His mouth came down over hers in a fierce sealing kiss. She could feel his hands framing her head as she opened for his invading tongue, twining it with her own. His fingertips massaged her scalp as he tangled his hands in her hair.

They strove on, lost in a fiery haze of need, sweating until their bodies glided against each other, her silken skin abraded by his curly, crisp hair. Magdalena reveled in the welter of sensations denied her for so long, now so beautifully restored.

My husband! Did she cry the words aloud as the final convulsive surge of release seized her? Aaron had his mouth buried against her throat as he stroked against her in his own swelling, blinding explosion, adding to her release, prolonging it until they both collapsed, breathless, spent, satiated.

Magdalena welcomed the weight of his body on hers and held him tightly, unwilling to let the moment of such perfect unity end, even though she knew it must. Gradually, as his breathing returned to normal, she could feel him withdraw and roll away. She knew it was not only a physical loss. His words underlined her cruel intuition.

"Now it is done. You are my wife. Neither your father, our sovereign, nor the Church can undo what we have consummated." He spoke low and rapidly, as if it were a long rehearsed speech that he must deliver, a way of purging his blood of the fever she had ignited. He stared unseeing at the crude mahogany beams and thatched vines of the ceiling, unwilling to look into her pain-filled eyes. *I will not be victim to her witchery!* The thought hammered through his brain, yet he felt cowardly as she turned from him in silence and curled into a small protective ball, like an injured kitten.

Guilt and anger warred in him as he reached down and yanked the sheer bedclothes over them. Then, inexplicably, he felt compelled to move his body protectively around hers and pull her back against his chest, burying his face in the soft sweet cloud of her hair.

They lay very still for several moments, each afraid to breathe. Sleep finally claimed them.

Aaron awakened as the first rays of dawn filtered hazy gold through the dense foliage at the window. Disengaging himself from the soft warmth of Magdalena's body, he studied her as she slept. *So delicate and vulnerable-looking,* he thought bitterly. Guilt gnawed at him as he recalled the fierce hunger of their marriage consummation. He had gentled his touch for her, wooing his enemy, responding to her artful air of innocence. She was Bernardo Valdés's daughter and the woman who had insinuated herself into his father's affections. When the admiral had forced him to wed her, Aaron had promised her retribution for pursuing him to Española. Instead he had fallen under her spell once more. The years stretched ahead bleakly as his mind conjured up the hellish nightmare of a marriage in which he could not resist taking his wife, yet must suffer pangs of wrenching self-loathing each time he did so.

Disentangling his hand from the dark mahogany strands of her hair, Aaron rolled quietly from the bed. She was a Valdés and he had sworn to destroy her house as hers had destroyed his. "A marriage made in hell," he muttered softly as he opened his small leather chest and extracted a breachclout and leather sandals. He must get away from here and think this tangle through to some solution. Going to Guacanagari's village to explain about his marriage would put distance between him and his wife, something he sorely needed.

Magdalena stirred, feeling the absence of Aaron's protective warmth. She heard him rise from the bed, muttering some oath beneath his breath. Slowly she rolled over and surreptitiously watched him walk across

231

the room. His lean, muscular body was splendid. He moved with sinuous grace, oblivious of his nakedness. Although the darkly bronzed color of his skin had at first shocked her, Magdalena now found it far more appealing than the pallor so carefully cultivated by European gentlemen, who thought the sun's touch poisonous. For a dreamy moment she simply feasted on the sight of his chiseled profile, the curl of his long shaggy golden hair as he leaned over his trunk to extract some clothing. The satiety of the previous night's lovemaking had left her feeling oddly at peace. Then, as he began to don the scandalous Taino breechclout, the mood shattered.

"Where are you going?" she blurted out before thinking, her voice accusatory.

He turned and looked at her tousled loveliness. She sat amid the bed clothes with her hair tumbling about her breasts like dark fire, her eyes looking wounded. "Where does it appear I go? My friend and the admiral's best ally on Española, Guacanagari, must be informed of Cristobal's return. We are well rid of Diego Colon as acting governor!"

"And you must explain to your friend and his sister that you have wed a woman from across the ocean," she said, half-hopeful, half-resentful.

Aaron met her eyes steadily, standing with his legs braced wide apart in the center of the room. His long hair and nearly naked body made him appear savage, larger than life, menacing. His expression was tight and grim.

"I have been considering what we should do about this marriage. We are bound to it. Your father cannot set it aside. The specter of the convent—if ever such did loom—can no longer menace you. You may return to Seville with the protection of my name, if you wish. As of now I have little of worldly wealth, but soon—"

"No!" she interrupted, then stopped before she utterly humiliated herself by telling him she did not wish to leave him, that she loved him. "You merely wish to be quit of me so you can return to your savage. As you said, my husband, we are both of us bound by this marriage. I will not meekly leave you to your pleasures."

His eyebrows rose sardonically. "You would be free to find pleasures of your own in Castile. Perhaps the king would take you back?" He could see the blow struck home as she flinched at his cruelty. No matter how he felt about Magdalena, he knew well the reputation Fernando Trastamara had as a coarse and brutal lover. Sighing, he walked to the bed and sat down beside her. "I am sorry. It seems I am either saying evil things to wound you, or I am lustfully attacking you. We have no middle ground in this marriage. The best way to deal with it is to live separately."

"We cannot do that unless I conveniently return home, or you break your word to the admiral and return to the Tainos to live. She, not I, is the witch, Aaron, who holds such sway over you. You return to her to see if she has borne your child. Do not deny it!"

"That, among other things, does concern me, but our marriage has ended any means of giving the child my name."

"Then you are in love with her and want her babe, even if it is not yours. She has a hold on you that the admiral, the king, no one can break," she said bitterly.

He shook his head at her willful misunderstanding. "Do not underestimate yourself, wife," he said softly, then rose and turned to the door.

"Aaron, come back! How dare you leave me humiliated on the morn after our wedding!"

"Sob on Bartolomé's shoulder. He is ever good at consoling your spoiled child's tears," he said as he walked out the door.

She felt the sting of those tears burn her eyes and

blinked them back with an oath. Then a slow, catlike smile tilted the corners of her lips. "Ah, yes, husband, I *will* tell Bartolomé."

Aliyah lay exhausted, yet utterly replete, as the women attending her bathed her body and anointed her with fragrant oils. She could hear the lusty cry of her son. Aaron's son!

"He is splendid, your glory," her young cousin said as she watched Aliyah's older sister bathe the newborn.

"He shares his father's magical eyes. He will grow to be a great chief," Mahia added as she handed the babe back to her sister.

Aliyah smiled beneath her elder sister's praise, putting the infant to her breast. "He is as hungry as his sire." She felt the sweet fierce pull on her nipple and thought of Aaron. How proud he would be! She studied the babe's sculpted European features. His hair was inky black but there was no doubt at all that he was Aaron Torres' child.

"You endured the birthing well," Mahia said. "That is always a good sign. You will be able to bear many fine healthy children. Now Guacanagari can arrange a profitable marriage for you with a great chieftan. Perhaps Behechio."

"No!" Aliyah's eyes flashed defiantly at Mahia. "I will wed only Aaron. He will become a powerful chieftan among our people. With the fearful weapons he brought with him from across the sea he can defeat all our enemies."

Mahia shrugged at her spoiled younger sister. "Always Guacanagari has given you your way, but he cannot force the Golden One to wed you."

"He will not have to force Aaron." Aliyah's voice was petulant, but she was too pleased with herself to entertain anger with her foolish sister. "I have learned much about how the men from across the sea think. Aaron, like the rest of them, will prize a male as firstborn. He can plainly see this is his son." She touched the babe's face as if to prove her point.

"The men from across the sea have many strange notions. They also prize virginity in a bride." Mahia's voice was laced with scorn for such a ridiculous idea. How could a man know if his wife would be barren or not if she bore no children before he wed her? "I do not understand why you want the Golden One. His planting stick must be much like any other's, no matter what color his skin."

A sensuous smile curved Aliyah's lips. "Ah, but you have never seen his planting stick . . . and I have."

Mahia snorted in disgust, but said nothing.

Aliyah handed her the babe, who had fallen soundly asleep. "Take and show him to our brother while I rest."

"Will you name him now?"

"Aaron's people have their own custom. The father names his children. I will wait until he returns."

When Mahia had departed, Aliyah reclined on the huge raised bed. She was sore and tired and her breasts ached as they filled with milk for the child, but she was triumphant. The birth had not been difficult, but she would tell Aaron differently. He had expressed grave concern about her pregnancy and the impending birth ordeal. She smiled. Mahia was right about some foolish notions of white men. But if he thought birthing a great danger, then all the better. She would convince him his son had nearly killed her coming into the world! "Ah, yes, Aaron, you will wed me and you will become a great war chief. You will crush all the other chieftans between Marien and Xaragua—and I shall stand by your side as your queen!"

Late that evening, as several slaves served Aliyah an elaborate meal, Guacanagari arrived at her *bohio*. At once she knew he brought bad news. Dismissing the slaves, she turned to him and asked, "What has happened?" His grave expression, so at variance with his joy earlier in the day, frightened her. "Aaron is well, is he not?"

"Aaron is well. He is here. I have shown him his son and he is well pleased by the babe."

His reticence baffled her. "If he is returned, why has he not come to me?"

Guacanagari felt a great wave of anguish for his young sister. She had so hoped to wed Aaron, and he, too, had wished the match which now was fated not to be. "He felt it better if I spoke with you first. The admiral has returned and commanded Aaron to wed a white woman from his homeland. She awaits him in their village by the sea."

All color drained from Aliyah's face as she stared in disbelief at her brother. Then a killing rage infused her. "How dare he do this to me! Who is this woman that he scorns a royal princess to wed her?"

"He told me he did not wish the marriage, but his admiral commanded it, just as I can command my nobles to wed where it suits me. Under his law he may have only one wife."

She forced her fury under control and said, "He is happy with the child and knows it is his."

"He wishes to keep the boy." Guacanagari looked at her uncertainly. Such was not unusual once a babe was weaned.

"I will think on it, but for now the child is mine. I will name him Navaro."

Guacanagari considered this. "Navaro was a fierce war chief who defeated our enemies many generations ago. The boy must be a great warrior to live up to such a name. We do not fight now but have learned to live in peace. Perhaps—"

"Peace!" Aliyah saw the surprise her outburst caused her brother and quickly let the rest of her words die on her lips. *Peace is for weaklings such as you!* "I have the right to name my child, do I not, Guacanagari?"

He nodded. "I will tell Aaron of the name. Do you wish to speak with him now?"

"I grow weary tonight. Bid him come to me in the morning." After her brother had departed, Aliyah considered her plans, allowing her anger to cool and her mind to calculate. So, he did not like the white wife he was forced to wed. And he did want his splendid son. She clapped her hands, summoning a slave from outside her *bohio*. "Bring the child to me. My milk is come and I would feed him."

As she nursed Navaro, Aliyah made a vow, crooning low in his tiny ear. "You will be a great warrior. And the means by which I rid Aaron of his pale-skinned wife and claim him for myself!"

"This is madness. We do not even speak their language, and we know nothing of their customs. Some outlying sentry will probably kill me with his poison-tipped spear and carry you off as his slave. You should have remained in Ysabel," Bartolomé complained as he ducked a low-hanging vine.

The trail they followed into the hills beyond the coast was narrow and twisting, slippery from a sudden rain squall that had just blown inland. The jungle trees loomed high above them. Tall palms interlaced with dense stands of mahogany, silk-cotton, and ebony. Brilliantly colored parrots screeched when the small party of riders disturbed them and a bird that sounded for all the world like a Spanish nightingale sang sweetly in the distance.

"Nonsense," Magdalena chided Colon patiently. "Luis is with us and he is fluent in their tongue. More probably a poisonous snake may prove our undoing," she said with a shiver as she looked at the lushly beautiful jungle.

"The Tainos do not use poison as the Caribes do," Luis said, overhearing their conversation. "I would not fear snakes overmuch, but do beware these." He pointed to a small tree of considerable beauty with waxy green leaves shimmering with fresh rain. "Even the rainwater off the leaves causes a painful rash and the fruit if eaten is always fatal. The natives call it the *manchineel.*"

Bartolomé grunted in distaste. "For all its beauty this place is treacherous."

"Yet look at the flowers, Bartolomé," Magdalena said in awe. "They grow in the trees, climbing on vines thick as ropes. Every color, shape, fragrance. It is truly paradise."

"I pray then for the angel with his flaming sword to bar us from traveling further into paradise," Colon replied in mock piety.

"Soon we shall be at the village," Luis said, looking at Magdalena's rapt expression. At once her face lost its pleasure-filled awe and sobered.

"We crest a hill soon. Is it beyond that?" she asked warily. Her throat constricted, and the furious anger and stricken pride that had goaded her into following Aaron now began to desert her. How would he accept her latest defiance of his will?

Luis Torres nodded. "You can see the village and fields from the top of the ridge. It is a magnificent sight."

When Magdalena beheld the orderly rows of large cane houses, with wide clean streets stretching between them and a huge central plaza in the center of the settlement, she said in amazement, "It is truly a city. Thousands must reside here."

"Look you at the fields beyond," Bartolomé said in wonder. "Would that our meager crops thrived so well as those below us. The soil is as black and rich as that about Ysabel is rocky and poor."

"Any settlement of colonists must first possess the will to work," Luis reminded the admiral's *adelantado*.

"Nevertheless, I have been considering asking my brother to search out a new site for our principal settlement, a location with a better harbor and richer land."

As the men discussed the possible relocation of the colony, Magdalena rehearsed in her mind how she would face Aaron and his mistress. She had stormed into the governor's house yesterday, beseeching Bartolomé's assistance. She told him that Aaron had gone to make peace with Guacanagari and with Aliyah in light of his marriage, but that she feared the woman's hold on him. Together they had faced the dubious admiral with a scheme to follow Aaron, bringing gifts and assurances that Magdalena's marriage with their adopted friend did not pose any threat to the friendship between Colon and Guacanagari.

"She will but slip away and risk the jungle alone if I do not accompany her," Bartolomé had said with a sigh to Cristobal, who had agreed to the diplomatic mission with grave reservations.

While they rode through the hot, steamy forest, they were bitten by insects and baked by the sun, but Magdalena had held to her resolve. Now as the small party of a dozen riders entered the fertile valley and approached the impressive village, she was overcome with doubt. *Do I really want to see if she is as beautiful as I have heard?*

Momentarily, she was distracted as she saw the Tainos gathering apprehensively to watch their advance. The Indians had never seen horses before the colonists of the second voyage had brought them, and they greatly feared the beasts. For her part, Magdalena was as appalled at the savages as they at her astride her big gray mount. Unlike the natives who lived and worked in Ysabel, those of the interior were as naked as their mothers bore them!

The admiral had insisted on simple cotton tunics for the Taino women in Ysabel. Even the men wore at least a scandalous breechclout, if not a cloak or some other decent covering. But these brown-skinned people, men and women as well as children, were completely nude. Some of them were painted with brilliant red and black dyes in odd markings. Many of the women seemed to favor white paints. All wore brilliant parrot feathers in their hair and a wide variety of jewelry made of fish bones, shells, various metals and, now, the trading beads and hawk's bells brought from Castile.

Magdalena eyed them uneasily as they spoke rapidly and pointed at her, singling her out from her male escorts. They seemed curious but were too terrified of the horse to approach. Luis dismounted, leaving his horse with Bartolomé, and engaged in conversation with several young boys who then raced into the village.

"Are we welcome or not?" Magdalena asked nervously.

Luis smiled in reassurance. "These people have always been friendly and honest. They will be our staunchest allies against any Indians who would refuse allegiance to the monarchs. All we need do in return is keep faith and not abuse them."

"You mean slit their noses and cut off their ears if they do not bring sufficient gold to satisfy us?" Bartolomé asked, knowing of the gold quotas Hojeda and Margarite had tried to impose earlier.

Magdalena gasped in horror. "That has been done?"

"Yes, and it earns us more enemies daily," Luis said. "As yet Aaron has kept Guacanagari's people from

feeling any more Toledo steel, but I know not how long
the peace can last if we do not mend our ways."

"That is why he is to resume his duties for my brother.
He is a trained soldier and can hold the avaricious
'gentlemen' goldseekers in check," Bartolomé replied.

"We must dismount now. 'Twould be poor return for
their hospitality to terrify them by riding our horses into
the village. See the enclosure of canes Aaron has built
yonder? We will leave them in there with his horses until
we are ready to depart. I am afraid we must act as our
own grooms," he added ruefully as they reined in
beside a fenced area outside the village. Several horses,
including the bay Aaron had ridden, grazed peacefully
in its confines.

After the horses were tended, the numbers of Tainos
swelled around the visitors as they walked into the
village. On foot, Magdalena felt far more vulnerable.
The natives stared in wonder at her hair and her
clothing. How strange it was to feel uncomfortable
because she was dressed while those who were naked
gawked in casual curiosity!

"'Tis fearful hot. Go slowly, Magdalena, lest you
overtax yourself," Bartolomé cautioned, observing her
flushed face and shortness of breath.

"She is not faint from heat but faint at the prospect of
confronting her husband, whom she has disobeyed,"
Aaron said, moving into their path. He had materialized
suddenly from behind a large building, dressed in the
minimal scrap of cotton that some of the armed men
wore. He scowled at his wife. "By all the saints, what do
you here?"

"The *adelantado* and I have come with the admiral's
gifts to present them to his friend Guacanagari," she
said with feigned sweetness, ignoring his black frown.
"Will you present me as your wife—or have you told
him of our marriage?"

His eyes were dark as seawater, "Oh, I have told

Guacanagari of you, my lady. He was a bit disappointed at my rash act—considering that his sister has presented me with a son in my brief absence."

Magdalena felt as if she would never breathe again. Only the numbed pain kept her from running across the jungle trails back to Ysabel.

"Who has come from the admiral?" a tall handsome young man asked as he approached Aaron.

From the way the people parted for him, Magdalena knew at once he must be Guacanagari, the *cacique*.

Luis presented Bartolomé, the admiral's brother and Magdalena, Aaron's new wife. The young *cacique* bowed to Bartolomé and then assessed her with keen black eyes and spoke in his soft melodious tongue to Aaron.

Grimacing, Aaron translated for her. "Guacanagari is most gracious. He says you are very beautiful, a fit mate for me," he replied in a tone heavy with irony.

Luis, Bartolomé, and Guacanagari walked apart, engaging in a conversation, discreetly leaving Aaron and Magdalena to settle their differences alone.

"You are mad! With Aliyah just delivered of her first child, I do not wish to parade my fine lady wife in front of her or Guacanagari."

"Yes, 'tis a pity that 'your fine lady wife' did not choose to meekly sit and repine in Ysabel, while you strutted about here receiving the plaudits of these savages for your virility. And you dare call Fernando Trastamara a lecher!" She lashed out with all her humiliation and suppressed pain transmuted into sheer rage.

His face, taut with anger before, now became rigid. "I will give you a good taste of how savages live! You have come after me, now you will live with me—and I choose to live here."

"The admiral commanded you live in Ysabel," she said, stamping her foot furiously.

"The admiral commanded me to strengthen the ties between him and Guacanagari's people. I will do so in my own way. But now, I will escort you to your new abode." He reached for her wrist and took it in a steel-hard grip, yanking her behind him as he strode toward the center of the huge village.

Magdalena stumbled after him, grateful for her leather riding boots. Even though they were miserably hot and itchy, they offered more protection from the rocky earth than her cloth slippers would have.

Aaron stopped in front of a thatched-roofed cane hut of medium proportions near the large sunken courtyard at the center of the village. "'Tis not as spacious as the *bohio* I shared with Aliyah, but as befits my new status as your husband," he shrugged, "'twill serve." He pulled her inside.

After the blazing sun, Magdalena blinked to accustom her eyes to the dimmer light. In truth, it was much like the cane house they inhabited in Ysabel, except the construction was a bit sturdier, but she would never admit that to this arrogant lout. The hut was spartanly furnished. A strangely shaped chair with a curving back and claw feet sat in one corner, a *hamaca* was strung between two support posts in the center of the room, and several pieces of pottery were placed neatly in a corner. Only Aaron's weapons and a saddlebag filled with his personal effects attested to the fact he lived here.

"Even less luxury than Ysabel afforded, I fear. You will find sleeping in a *hamaca* very interesting," he said with an icy smile.

Just looking at the wretched hemp netting made her insect-bitten skin cry for mercy, but she said nothing. Surely men and women did not make love in those awful contraptions! Magdalena would have cut out her tongue before she asked. Changing the subject, she inquired, "What of the much-praised Taino hospitality?

Are we to be fed—or are you punishing me by excluding me from the feast for the *adelantado?*"

"There will be food aplenty . . . and in time you will learn to help cook it."

She stiffened angrily. "I am not one of your Indian women. I am nobly born."

"Aliyah is the sister of a great *cacique.* A royal princess by European standards. Yet she tended a cookfire for me. I fear I was forced into a poor bargain with you to wife, my lady."

"At this moment, no one could wish you wed to your savage mistress more than I!" she spat.

"You continue to refer to these people as savages. They may be primitive in the ways of weaponry and plain cruelty so familiar to the white race, but they have a beautiful way of life. Never again will you call them savages. Do you understand me?" His steely blue eyes bored into her furious green ones.

"You do this in revenge! Because I have forced you to wed me, you would make a peasant of me. Do your worst, Don Diego Torres," she said scornfully, "for I was raised on horseback in a miserable crumbling estate on the marshes of the Guadalquiver. I can do anything your fine royal princess of the Tainos can!"

Chapter Fifteen

Magdalena quickly was compelled to eat her words—and a few other items even more difficult to choke down. There was indeed a great feast that evening in honor of the admiral's *adelantado*. All the highest ranking nobility of the vast village met at the long, high-roofed *bohio* belonging to Guacanagari.

Magdalena, having brought little clothing, was at a loss as they dressed for the occasion. She watched Aaron don a scanty loincloth and wrap an intricately wrought girdle about his slim hips. The workmanship was beautiful, she grudgingly admitted to herself. The fine cotton threads were worked with colorful shells, beads, and gold jewelry.

When he looked up and caught her observing the girdle, he flushed beneath his bronzed skin and said gruffly, "Aliyah made this for me as a gift. I must wear it for ceremonial occasions." With that he casually selected several brilliant red parrot feathers and worked them artfully into his hair. "You look like a yellow-haired Taino," she said accusingly. "Would you truly turn your back on civilization and join these people?"

His eyes met hers with an icy blue stare. "I did not turn my back on civilization until it turned on me. My whole family is either dead or in exile. Should I love the lofty ideals of European 'civilization' for that?"

Magdalena forced herself not to flinch beneath the bitter sting of his words. "And for the sins of the fathers, the children shall be punished. You will always see me as the Crossbearer's daughter and hate me for what Bernardo Valdés did."

He did not reply to that, only instructed her, "Get dressed. We will be late. I hear the drums summoning the honored guests."

"I have naught but a white linen under-tunic and a loose brown velvet gown."

He scoffed aloud. "God's bones! Velvet in this heat. You are more foolish than those soldiers behind the stockades who are sweating in their leather armor. Wear the under-tunic alone. 'Twill serve."

Recalling her humiliating introduction to the admiral when she dressed so scandalously on the plaza at Ysabel, she flushed. "In Seville I would be thought a woman of the streets to go dressed in such a fashion."

"Had you stayed in Seville, this all would have been spared you," he replied without the slightest sympathy.

By the time Aaron and Magdalena arrived at the *bohio* of Guacanagari, she felt her heart hammering within her breast. *'Tis a miracle no one can see it vibrate through this sheer cloth!* she thought with mortification as she followed Aaron into the large, crowded room. Guacanagari reclined on a low wooden couch which was elaborately carved and covered with soft cotton cushions. Several other men of obvious rank had similar seats, as did a number of women. As guest of honor,

Bartolomé was seated at Guacanagari's right hand and Luis Torres just behind him.

While Aaron led her to a couch set aside for them, Magdalena felt the hot, hateful glare from a pair of narrowed obsidian eyes, glowing like coals. Instinctively, she knew the woman was Aliyah. Magdalena's heart sank as she surreptitiously studied her rival's flowing ebony hair draped across her body like black satin. She wore brilliant yellow feathers worked all through her hair and a heavy tangle of beads about her throat. Her only concession to modesty was the long skirt woven cunningly of native grasses that clung to her hips and fell to midcalf. Her skin was a dusky golden hue, no darker than Aaron's. Her breasts were large and milk-filled, but otherwise she was marvelously recovered from birthing a child a scant three days ago. She was lushly curved, yet her belly was as flat as any virgin's. She had borne Aaron's child and suckled it. Magdalena felt faint as she forced herself to remain calm and recline on the couch as if this were an everyday occurrence.

She met Aliyah's fiery glare boldly. *I will not cower. I am his wife!* Aliyah's face was round, the planes of it austere and handsome rather than pretty. Her nose was broad and slightly flat but small, her lips pouty and generous. Her eyes were her most arresting feature—so dark a brown they looked night black. Cat-green eyes returned the killing stare. Magdalena forced herself to smooth her linen tunic out and then casually, possessively, glide her hand up to Aaron's shoulder. "Small wonder she is taken with you. 'Tis your yellow hair she covets. All the feathers she sports in hers must have made bald half the parrots on Española," she said snidely.

He chuckled mirthlessly. "Never fear. We will doubtless have them served up as one course in our feast."

"Parrots? They eat parrots?" She hoped her voice did not break.

He leaned near her and said quietly, "Do not disgrace me. Whatever food is placed before you is a special tribute given first to Guacanagari and shared only by those of highest rank. There will be dogs, iguanas, and *hutias* roasted . . . then other things. You must sample all of them as if you were at a banquet with the queen." His eyes challenged her as he threw back her words. "You told me to do my worst. This feast is the pleasant part. Enjoy tonight, Magdalena—if you have the heart."

His smug condescension indicated that he did not believe she possessed the courage. *You will see otherwise, husband!* But dogs? Reptiles? She repressed a shudder and raised her chin as Guacanagari clapped his hands and all the brilliantly arrayed revelers settled back to feast.

Slaves, supervised by lower-class servants, began to carry in the food in endless bowls. Each delicacy was first served to Guacanagari, then when he had signaled his approval, more was served to the assemblage. To her surprise, Magdalena found the firm white meat of the iguana to be quite tasty. Even the dark sweetish *hutia* was palatable, as were the ever-present fruits, cassava bread, and yams. When the grayish chunks of stewed meat, which she assumed was made from the small, barkless dogs indigenous to Española, was served, Magdalena even managed to force a few bites of it down under Aaron's scrutiny. "'Twould not be so terrible if I knew not what I ate," she managed to say with admirable calm.

Then came the greatest treat, for everyone began to make oohing and aahing sounds of delight when a large, hearth-fired tureen was placed before Guacanagari. His slaves dipped a gourd spoon into it and brought forth a strange, whitish substance, which he ate with great relish. Immediately a platter filled with big lobsters and whole roasted fresh river fish was served.

"The seafood course is always considered the greatest delicacy," Aaron said matter of factly.

When a slave bowed before them with the serving gourd filled with the noisome white matter, Magdalena nearly gagged. Close up, the smell was overpoweringly fishy—and raw! She inspected the small, round, grayish-green lumps with great suspicion, then recoiled and placed her hand over her mouth lest she emit a shriek. Fish eyes, *raw* fish eyes stared at her from a bizarre jumble in the heaping spoon! She watched Aaron take a hearty helping. If Magdalena had not been so horror-stricken, she might have noticed how swiftly he swallowed the delicacy.

As the slave readied a mercifully smaller portion for her, she glanced frantically across the room to Bartolomé, who was manfully gulping down the treat. Guacanagari beamed at the *adelantado*. Aliyah smiled malevolently at her red-haired nemesis. *You savage witch!* Magdalena took a deep breath before the spoon neared her lips, then held it and swallowed the slimy mass with the speed of a lizard snatching a fly with his forked tongue.

Seizing her water goblet, she gulped down several huge slugs before she dared exhale. "Blessed Virgin, what I would give for a flagon of good red wine," she muttered beneath her breath, meeting Aliyah's hostile stare with a triumphant smirk.

"The Taino people do not use spirits, only the *tobaco*, a mild stimulant that is burned. The smoke, when inhaled up the nostrils, brings on effects somewhat similar to strong drink," Aaron replied, admiring her grit in spite of himself. The first time he had been forced to partake of fish eyes, he had excused himself soon after, to go wretch quietly in the jungle.

"I detest the evil stink of their stimulants. Good wine is preferable to sour smoke that surely rots the brain," she replied, trying desperately to bring her rebellious stomach under control by discussing anything else but what was in it.

"You and Bartolomé will favor the next course—nuts soaked in honey."

Recognizing the agreeable looking sweet, she let out a long sigh of relief.

Magdalena had hoped the feast was a trial that, once overcome, would give her acceptance in Taino society. Early the next morning, at dawn's light, she was disabused of the notion when Aaron awakened her, pulling the sheer cotton insect netting from her body. "I am going fishing with Caonu," he said as he reached for a long-handled spear with sharp fishbone prongs attached to one end. "You are to learn the skills practiced by noblewomen here."

She rolled over with a moan. "I can imagine well their *skills*, plucking the eyes from innocent fish," she said with a shudder.

"Scarcely that. They weave beautiful twilled baskets and paint cunning designs on pottery. Dress quickly and I will escort you to Guacanagari's *bohio*."

Magdalena did not ask if Aliyah would be present, but with each step nearer the *cacique's* residence, she dreaded another confrontation. *She might be holding Aaron's child, suckling his son in front of me*, she thought in silent anguish. Then she looked at his harsh profile, so cleanly chiseled in the golden light of morn. *I, too, may bear you a son, Aaron.* Would he welcome him or reject him for his Valdés blood? She would know in time if they continued to make love as they had on their wedding night. Holding the thought of a golden-haired babe close to her heart, she steeled herself to face Aliyah.

Aaron, too, worried silently about how the two women would deal together. If he were wise, he would send his wife back to Ysabel with Bartolomé and Luis on the morrow. Then he looked at her haughty, beautiful face and the inbred pride that carried her each step toward Guacanagari's *bohio*. No, he would lesson her well here in the interior before letting her return to the comforts of Castilian civilization.

Lorenzo Guzman watched the settlement of Ysabel draw nearer as the caravel floated in on the tide. God's bones, what a bleak piece of offal! A Palos tavern looked like the Alhambra compared to this dismal sinkhole. To think he had been banished here, possibly for the rest of his life, never again to see the glittering courts of Castile and Aragon! He drew himself up from his slumped posture against the rail. He would face that arrogant Genoese wool merchant's spawn like the nephew of a duke.

Bitterly he recalled his last interview with Medina-Sidonia. The duke had been trembling with fright, his skin like damp parchment, as he informed Lorenzo that Torquemada and his Holy Office had secured a full confession from Bernardo Valdés, who was scheduled to burn in the next auto de fe in Seville.

"All incited by a letter written by an accused Jew," he had cried fiercely to his uncle. "Who would believe Isaac Torres, fled into exile, a traitor to the crowns of Castile and Aragon?"

"Apparently King Fernando did," Medina-Sidonia had replied tightly. "It seems his former minister gave a most thorough accounting of where every last maravedi of Benjamin Torres had been sequestered. The royal portion and that due the Church were far short. When Valdés's country estate was searched, several highly incriminating pieces of jewelry were found, as well as documents regarding transfers of gold."

Then Lorenzo, too, had begun to tremble as he asked, "My name was not—"

"Yes, it was in the records of that idiot Valdés," the duke had hissed. "To keep the honor—and the very line—of the House of Medina-Sidonia safe, I had them destroyed before the Inquisitors saw them. Valdés alone stands accused . . . for now. I have risked everything pleading your case before the king. He and I are in accord. We would see you gone from court. Your own wife was accused by the Holy Office, and your daughter mysteriously vanished after Ana's death at the stake. This family can endure no more dishonor. You will leave for the Indies!"

" 'Tis no fault of mine that you and that treacherous judaizing *converso* Benjamin Torres arranged my marriage with his daughter," Lorenzo said with fists clenched at his sides.

"You coveted too much. Not only your father-in-law's wealth, but that of his elder son in Barcelona. That was your undoing. I know not how long I can keep the familiars in Catalonia from your trail. If you leave now, we will all be better served by it." The old man's voice was steely with finality.

And so Lorenzo had been banished in disgrace. All the wealth he had secured from Torres' estates had been claimed either by that greedy Trastamara king who set in motion the hellish inquiry, or by the Inquisition itself. He was near penury. Only a pittance from his uncle had allowed him to book passage for the new colony as a gentleman.

As the *gromets* lowered the ship's boat into the water, he straightened his cloak and looked at the jungle and jagged mountains rising in the steamy distant haze. *If only there is indeed gold here for the taking.*

Magdalena looked down at her hands, the tender palms and fingertips bloody, crisscrossed with a thousand tiny cuts from her futile and clumsy attempts at working the sharp-edged cane strips into the tightly woven patterned baskets. She succeeded no better with basketry than she had with painting pottery. After several pieces of fine hearth-fired clay lay shattered around her feet, Mahia, Guacanagari's elder sister, pronounced her hopeless. At least that is what Magdalena deduced. In her two weeks with the Taino, she had mastered only bits of the language, but the disgust of Aliyah's sister was plain.

"I was ever pricking my fingers with embroidery needles, too," she said, forcing a sweet smile as she bowed and left the Taino gentlewomen to their art. She held her long, hot plait of hair away from her neck and felt the sweat trickle down her back. How wonderful it would be to ride, she thought with a smirk. The haughty Taino royalty remained terrified of horses. "Stupid savages," she muttered, heading purposefully through the crowded streets to the edge of town and Aaron's corral.

He would be furious, of course, but he was sore displeased with her anyway, so what did it matter? Only in the dark of night, on their sleeping platform, did he reach out for her in tenderness. But that was passion, not love, she reminded herself as she opened the heavy cane gate and grabbed a hackamore for her mount. Quickly, she captured her flea-bitten old horse and in moments was galloping bareback across the valley. The breeze cooled her sweaty body, but she could not enjoy the stolen freedom. Her relationship with her husband intruded.

By now, Aliyah had recovered fully from the birth of Navaro. Each time Magdalena saw the beautiful black-haired child with his sculpted European features and Aaron's piercing blue eyes, she wanted to sob. When the noblewomen gathered, Aliyah carried the boy with her, taking every opportunity to nurse him in front of

Magdalena. "She grows slimmer and more desirable. If I become pregnant and grow fat, he will return to her."

The hot, sultry air swallowed up her anguished words as she rode blindly past carefully tended fields of manioc, yams, and peanuts. The golden-brown skins of the women laboring in them glistened with perspiration as they worked the long, fire-hardened points of their planting sticks in the soft black earth. They wore no clothing in the heat and kept their hair tied on their heads with cunning clasps made of twilled cane. She pulled at the heavy linen that clung to her sweat drenched body, cursing the jungle, Española, and her husband.

As if she had conjured him, Aaron rode up beside her, reached over, and took the hackamore from her hands, reining in the heaving old gray with a gentle steady pull. "What in the name of Michael and all his angels are you doing riding in the heat of the day, unescorted?" he gritted between clenched teeth. "You will either kill the horse with heat stroke or break your neck."

"For the last you would doubtless be grateful. Then you could wed Aliyah and claim your son!"

"I plan nothing so drastic as your death to claim Navaro," he replied tersely.

Her eyes were suddenly shiny with tears as she fought to control her runaway emotions. "Do you deny going to visit them each day? I saw you playing with the boy yesterday in Guacanagari's *bohio*."

"He is my son, Magdalena. I wish to claim him and raise him as my own. There is no dishonor in that. In Cordoba the admiral had a son by his mistress. Young Fernando is being raised at court with Diego, Colon's legal heir. It is my responsibility to provide for Navaro," Aaron said, irritated by his own feelings of guilt.

"And what of your responsibility to Aliyah?" The instant she tossed the words at him, she wanted to call them back. *You do not want to know!*

He fixed her with his cool blue eyes, eyes mirrored in that tiny, swarthy infant's face, and said, "Aliyah is beyond my reach now. You have seen to that. Guacanagari will arrange a fine marriage for her with a *cacique* of high rank. Even now he searches for one she will accept. *You* are my responsibility, Magdalena, not Aliyah."

"A poor trade indeed here on Española. I know Aliyah and all the Taino women have told you how inept I am at their domestic skills—as I was at ladies' work back in Seville." She threw back her head and looked at him defiantly. His words about her scheming and his being bound to her by duty stung bitterly.

Aaron studied the proud contours of her beautiful Castilian face. "You were ever cosseted and spoiled back in Seville. Española is different." He looked across the broad fertile valley bounded by the sparkling river. Across the fields the women were planting. "The admiral has complained that hidalgos will do no work that cannot be accomplished on horseback. You seem to prove his claim."

"I merely rode to get away from—" She stopped, realizing that she was going to blurt out that she fled the village where his mistress and child tormented her. "I needed exercise," she evaded lamely.

A slow smile slashed his mouth. "And so you shall have it, my fine spoiled lady. Come," he commanded, pulling on the reins of the gray. "I will introduce you to Tanei."

They rode toward a large field where several dozen women worked beneath the scrutiny of one older Taino woman who directed their planting, issuing occasional terse orders and taking the sharpened planting stick to show a young girl the correct way to use it.

"This is a maize field—a marvelous grain that does not grow in Europe," Aaron explained as he swung down from his horse.

Puzzled and wary, Magdalena followed suit, watching the old woman approach Aaron with a broad smile wreathing her face. Her rotund body was clad in a knee-length grass skirt, a sign of marriage and social rank. She bowed slightly to Aaron and they began to chat in rapid Taino phrases that Magdalena could not begin to understand. Then he gestured to her and pulled her near him as if to present her to Tanei. By now the old woman's smile had been replaced by a look of uneasiness, perhaps even grave discomfort, which she strove to conceal.

Another exchange between Tanei and Aaron followed, after which he turned to Magdalena and said, "She is head woman for all the planting in this valley. Since you seem unable to do the skilled chores performed indoors by noblewomen, and you wished exercise, Tanei will teach you how to grow maize and other foods. The Taino are very inventive at agriculture, doing many things the Moors in Granada did, such as using soil enrichers and irrigating."

Magdalena's jaw dropped in shock. "You mean I am to—to muck in the mud with crude wooden implements!"

He smirked. "The first time I met you, you were mucking about in the mud of a marsh—quite covered with it, in fact. Now that you are a grown woman, not a child, you will learn to work instead of play in the mud."

Her plait of hair swung with a solid thunk, slapping one shoulder, as she shook her head vehemently. "I will do no such thing!" She stared at the row of clay pots standing nearby. The odor emanating from them was gagging. They were filled with a nasty grayish liquid.

"That is their soil enricher, made from urine and wood ash. To it they often add dung. It works wonders to make crops grow," he said as if discussing the latest style of lace cuffs with an Argonese couturier.

Magdalena felt her bile rising, but then she studied his

face and that of the distraught head woman. *He expects me to fail—or to beg and cry.* "As I said before, Don Aaron, do your worst!" She turned to the very unhappy Tanei and bowed, then stalked over to where a pile of the sharply pointed sticks lay. Picking one up, she asked in broken Taino, "Show me, please?" She gestured from her implement to the other workers.

Shrugging in perplexity at the strange customs of the men from the sky, Tanei guided her through the long, straight rows of newly planted maize to where two naked Taino women toiled.

Magdalena set to work, not deigning to look at her husband's expression. She heard him ride away, the rotten villain, taking her gray with him.

By evening she was sunburned, sweat-soaked, and painfully insect-bitten. Her back felt as if it would snap if she stooped but one more time. She was covered from head to foot with muddy, soil-enriched earth. By midday she had been so encumbered by her long, hot under-tunic that she had scandalously pulled the back of the skirt up between her legs and tied it into her girdle. Then she rolled the long sleeves well above her elbows. The mosquitoes feasted and the sun blistered, but Magdalena doggedly persisted, even pouring the loathsome contents of the urns along the furrows in a thin trickle that spilled onto her bare feet and squished between her toes. As she had with the fish eyes at that first banquet, she breathed through her mouth, never her nose. As a child she had frequently been forced to drink down Miralda's noisesome home remedies, and the trick had served her queasy stomach well. But even those horrid concoctions had not stunk as vilely as did the dung-filled soil enrichers. Now she was proud of simply holding down her morning meal!

Aaron rode back to the village, puzzling over his rash act. "Always she drives me to do things I later regret," he muttered sourly to his bay gelding, Rubio, feeling certain that long before nightfall she would come limping into their *bohio*, muddy and defeated. Keeping her here was a disaster. He would simply have to face returning to Ysabel and fulfilling his promise to the admiral. Much as he disliked the prospect of commanding the ill-disciplined, motley lot of adventurers who had come to Española to get rich, he knew he could accomplish the most good for Guacanagarí's people if he did so.

What should I do about my son? The thought tormented him. He had approached his friend the *cacique* about it, and Guacanagarí agreed to try and persuade Aliyah to give him the child once he was weaned. Of course, that left the next problem unsolved. How would Magdalena treat his half-caste son when he introduced him into their home? He supposed he could always hire a Taino servant as a nurse.

All of this destroyed, or at least greatly postponed, his plans to sail to Seville and exact his revenge on Bernardo Valdés. He was a man pulled in two directions, bound to his enemy's daughter in wedlock, bound to Española by his son. He cursed the fates that had led him to this sorry tangle.

Aliyah watched Aaron dismount and begin to rub down his big red beast and a gray one that she knew his wife rode. She had waited at his horse pen for over an hour with Navaro. At last Aaron was alone. To speak with him she would brave nearing those fearful great snorting creatures. She decided to wait until he finished his task and closed the gate. When he began to walk toward the village, she stepped from behind a copse of flowering shrubbery.

"Aaron, you are deep in thought. Does she who rides that great beast worry you?"

Pulled from his preoccupied thoughts by Aliyah's purring voice, Aaron smiled at her, his smile deepening as he caught sight of the infant in her arms. Her rich chocolate eyes were darkened in calculation, and she sauntered toward him with blatant sexual invitation, letting her large, milk-laden breasts sway seductively. "I have asked you not to discuss Magdalena," he replied, not wanting to reveal the reasons for his deep thoughts about her and their son either. "You have brought the babe far from the village, Aliyah."

She stopped directly in his path and placed one hand on his bare chest. "Your son is in no danger. See how content he is? Would you like to hold him?"

Aaron eagerly took the sleeping infant in his arms. Since Navaro's birth, he had become quite adept at handling such a fragile miracle. Each time he gazed on his son, he was newly amazed at the perfection of each tiny feature in the dark little face. *I do but act the vain father, for he is made so like me!* He smiled as he touched the delicate nose and finely formed lips with his fingertips, then bent to kiss them. When he brushed his lips across the babe's thick black lashes, Navaro opened his eyes. Torres blue in brilliance, they stared with the intent fascination of newborns into his father's face.

"I have done well with him, have I not, Aaron?" she asked proudly, relishing the bond that grew daily between him and his son.

"Yes, Aliyah, you have done well." He still remembered the shock of first seeing his son when Guacanagari told him the news, then watching the tiny rosebud mouth suckle at Aliyah's breast the following morning. *What am I to do?* He stroked Navaro's cap of soft black hair.

Watching the interplay between father and son, Aliyah broke in, saying, "Guacanagari has received a very high bride price for me from Behechio, great *cacique* of Xaragua." She studied his profile from beneath sooty lashes as they strolled.

He stopped and faced her. "Will you agree to the marriage?"

She shrugged coyly, still studying him covertly. "Will you be jealous if I go to him?"

"Once," he began with a sigh, "when I was younger and more foolish, I was jealous of your other lovers. But now . . . no. I only wish you happiness." *And I want my son.* He said nothing more, waiting for her to speak of her reason for lying in wait for him. A songbird warbled in the silk-cotton trees high above them and the steamy noontide heat intensified the heavy perfume from the flowers.

"I do not wish to go to Xaragua. It is many days' journey." She could read nothing on his face, which was turned down to Navaro, again asleep in his arms. "But Behechio is very handsome and rich."

"Then perhaps you should accept his offer." He looked at her crestfallen expression and stopped on the path. "Aliyah, I am already wed. I cannot claim you. It is not the custom of my people to allow a man more than one wife. And you, as the sister of a great *cacique*, should be first wife, not second," he said placatingly.

She nodded in agreement. "But if I go to Xaragua, when will you play with Navaro? He will miss you—or do you not care because of the pale-skinned children your white woman may give you?"

"I have spoken to you and asked Guacanagari to intercede with you, Aliyah. You know I want this child. I love Navaro and would not be separated from him. Let me keep him. As wife of a great *cacique*, you will bear him sons and Navaro will not have the place of honor there which he has here."

"The red-haired one," she said venomously, "your wife, she will treat my son worse than my husband would. I have seen the looks of hatred she casts at him."

He smiled bitterly. "You misread her, Aliyah. She is jealous of you, but she does not hate the boy." He was not at all certain if the latter were true. "It matters not what Magdalena feels. I will find a good Taino nurse to raise him. He will grow up here protected by the love of his uncle and all his Taino family, as well as by mine." He looked at her earnestly now. "Please, I know it is a hard thing I ask, but one many of your people have done in the past. Will you give me Navaro to raise?"

She studied him. "He will not be weaned for several months yet." She took advantage of his entreaty to step nearer and rub her breasts against his chest as she reclaimed the babe from his arms. "I will think on it," she said softly.

Aaron felt empty. All the lusty affection he had once held for this woman who bore his son was inexplicably gone. He did not wish to hurt her, but he had learned that she was childish and vain, subject to great emotional outbursts. He must be careful not to antagonize her and at the same time he must not encourage her sexuality. He gently placed his hands about her shoulders, cupping them and planting a chaste kiss on her forehead. Then he stood away, struggling not to look at Navaro again. "I must return to the village, for I am pledged to go with Caonu to hunt *hutia* this afternoon."

"You care nothing for hunting! You only fear the wrath of that one with the ugly red hair," she said petulantly.

He laughed. "I fear naught from Magdalena. At this moment she is doubtless soaking her sore feet in cool water in our *bohio*." He proceeded to tell her of Magdalena's introduction to Tanei and maize planting. Her laughter echoed down the path as they entered the village. Good. His ploy had worked. Aliyah was not angry with him. He prayed that the proposed match with Behechio went well, for then she might be willing to leave Navaro behind with him.

Chapter Sixteen

When Aaron returned from hunting, it was nearing dusk. He and Caonu had taken nearly a dozen *hutias*. The young Taino was growing increasingly proficient with the arbalest as Aaron was with stalking skills. He was weary but felt the hunt had been an excellent means of purging himself of the tensions the women in his life had caused. Now a refreshing swim and he would feel infinitely better.

Fully expecting to find a chastened, if cross, Magdalena in their *bohio*, he was surprised to see the big open room empty. No dinner bubbled in the cook pots, nor had any fire been laid outside for the roasting of yams or fresh meat. He swore beneath his breath, cursing the vagaries of spoiled Castilian noblewomen.

"Where in this lovely creation is—" His breath left his body as he beheld the long line of women from the fields dispersing to the various small *caneyes*. Magdalena walked with Tanei. At least he *thought* it was Magdalena. Her hair was tied atop her head and she was nearly naked! The modest linen under-tunic that covered her pale skin from neck to ankle had been drastically altered. The sleeves were ripped off at the armholes and the skirt was swaddled between her thighs, baring an enticing length of slim, shapely legs.

He stalked up to the pair of women, who stood in the wide dirt street communicating animatedly by means of Magdalena's broken bits of Taino and a great deal of sign language. Before he could open his mouth, the old woman turned to him with a broad smile on her wizened features.

"Your woman, she is a good worker. The white dress is foolishness. Better to wear no clothes, but she has learned much today. In time she will grow stronger and her skin will darken as yours has. She is a good Taino." With that startlingly fulsome praise, Tanei bowed and walked serenely away.

Magdalena turned to face Aaron's fierce scowl. His face looked like the *huracan* she had heard Don Cristobal describe. Mustering every ounce of pride she had left, she forced the wilted, aching, itchy misery that was her body to stand straight before him and defiantly placed her mud-and-excrement encased hands on the equally filthy cloth bunched about her hips. "You wrinkle your nose?"

"You look like a harlot crawled from the sewers of the Malaga waterfront," he ground out in low, whiplashing tones.

"You knew the nature of the work you assigned me—even the composition of the soil enrichers. Do you not like smelling it so close? See you how it smells when worked into your skin," she said as she rubbed both grimy hands roughly and thoroughly across his bare arms. Then she embraced him, her sweat-soaked, reeking body rubbing the under-tunic's coating on his chest and loincloth.

Shirl Henke

Before he could untangle himself, Aaron was covered with the awful muck. "By the twenty-four balls of the twelve apostles! You have covered me with shit!"

Magdalena's eyes widened in amazement. "Wherever did you hear such an oath?" she gasped.

Aaron smirked. "I learned that and many another worse from the sailors of their Most Catholic Majesties' ships *Santa María* and *Niña*," he said, shoving her away and trying desperately to breathe without gagging.

"Most certainly not from the admiral," she replied righteously, striding boldly past him to enter the *bohio*. She ignored him and began to wash her hands in a basin of tepid water. Before she could even pick up a towel on which to dry herself after a bath, she had to get this filth free from at least one part of her body!

He leaned on the door frame, watching her with a peculiar mixture of emotions—intense irritation combined with an inexplicable surge of desire—and admiration. Aliyah's sweet-smelling body, pressed so intimately to his this morning had aroused no passion. This excrement-coated little vixen made his pulse leap. "You are right, the admiral does not indulge in the vices common to sailors—and soldiers. I learned a few choice epithets from the Moors, too, during the war. You, *my lady*, incite my penchant for blasphemy in at least two religions!"

"Best beware, if not for your benighted soul, then for your position. I am certain the admiral would reprimand you," she snapped, still scrubbing furiously at her hands.

"The admiral would more certainly reprimand you for appearing in public with arms and legs bared. You are, as you have ever reminded me, a Castilian noblewoman, *my lady*," he said with contemptuous irony in his voice.

She swiveled from her kneeling position in front of

he basin and flung the filthy water directly into his face.
'In a village of naked people, with you yourself clad
nly in that—that codpiece and your sun-darkened
kin, you dare to tell me I should cover myself to slave in
sewer!" She was shrieking as he advanced on her. He
eftly dodged the basin as she heaved it at him, ignoring
he noise as the fired clay shattered on the door frame.
haking droplets of the foul water from his face and
air, he seized her and tossed her up over his shoulder.

"Now we both stink so badly I scarce can tell where
ne of us ends and the other begins, but do not wriggle
hat shapely bottom overmuch or I will paddle it until it
rows as red as your hair." He scooped up the large
rying cloth and his leather saddlebag, then strode
oward the door. Magdalena clawed and shrieked as
uriously as an enraged parrot.

Aaron gave her rump a hard stinging swat and she
ubsided to mere guttural curses. "For a fine-born lady,
ou have heard an oath or two yourself, wife," he said
rimly as he walked toward the river.

Realizing that she was creating great amusement for
he Tainos and that her already screaming muscles
ched even more abominably with each kick and wrig-
le, Magdalena subsided as Aaron walked from the
illage. Soon he reached the river, the most public and
ommon place where the villagers bathed. He did not
top but continued upstream, following the twists and
urns of the water into higher elevations. The jungle
losed about them in emerald splendor, the soft hues of
wilight muting the brilliance of flowers from vivid
rimsons and golds to delicate pinks and yellows.

Finally he turned off the trail and stepped between the
arge, fanlike leaves of a copse of dense low bushes, then
topped and put Magdalena down. Even before she
urned, she heard the splash of the waterfall from a
ocky ledge jutting out over the enchantingly lovely,

secluded pool. The beauty of the silvery spray and aqua water, surrounded by whispering palms and flowering shrubs, robbed her of speech.

"'Tis a small tributary of the river below. An underground spring feeds its waters into the main body at the foot of the mountain," he said as he tossed his bags onto the mossy ground beside the drying cloth.

"Did you find it or do others know of this enchantment?" she asked in awe.

He smiled, feeling oddly warmed by her pleasure and the disparity between the pristine beauty of the setting and the filth-covered condition of the intruders. "I was brought here when first I arrived at the village. At that time public bathing with, er, women and girl children watching me made me most uncomfortable. Guacanagari and his brother first showed me this place."

"The women and girls, indeed! You puffed-up hypocrite," she said, bristling as she surveyed his scanty loincloth.

A slow smile spread across his face. "Perhaps *puffed up* is appropriate, wife, but I do not want you stinking as you do now. Disrobe and bathe. I only pray you do no pollute the drinking water so far below with your foulness."

She turned and looked at his excrement-smeared skin. The left side of his head, which had rubbed against her hip while he carried her, attested to how her clothes had marked his jaw and clotted its debris in his long, curling hair. "You are no cleaner than I am now." It was her turn to smirk.

"Then God help the fishes," he said with an oath. He quickly stripped off his loincloth and weapons, then looked at Magdalena with impatience.

She was struggling with the tight knot that tied her skirts. He stalked across the clearing, snatching up the knife from his belt on the ground, and said tersely, "Let it go. 'Tis ruined beyond washing anyway." When she continued to tug at the garment he yanked her hands free and she let out a small involuntary hiss of pain.

"You are bleeding," he exclaimed in puzzlement as he grabbed one small hand and inspected it. Blood of the Martyrs, her fingertips were crisscrossed with tiny cuts and her palms laced with broken blisters! The acidic soil enrichers must have burned like fire, yet she had worked in them all day. "You will sicken with a disease of the blood from rubbing filth in this broken skin," he said, his voice cross with concern. "Let me cut the tunic away, Magdalena," he added more gently.

Slowly she let her stinging hands drop and he quickly cut the noisome garment from her and threw it in the bushes. "Now I have one less piece of clothing. Soon I will work as the Taino women do," she said as she turned and began to unfasten the *bejuco* ties holding her braid atop her head.

He watched her, noting the way she winced perceptibly with every movement. Her feet were almost as cut and blistered as her hands. Every muscle in her body must have been taxed beyond his capacity to imagine. Raised to be a soldier since boyhood, Aaron had long known physical hardship, but this delicate woman could never have imagined this hellish kind of toil.

Once she finished unplaiting her hair, Magdalena felt his eyes on her and looked up to meet the level blue gaze. Instead of the scorching, smirking arrogance she expected, he appeared contrite—perhaps even ashamed? More likely he pitied her! She turned on her heel and dove into the water, swimming to the center of the pool before she surfaced. The smell was almost gone already when she shook her head free of sparkling droplets. *Blessed Virgin, thank you!*

"You gave me a fright," Aaron said as one long arm

snaked out and seized her around her slim waist, pulling her to him as he treaded water. "Few ladies of the cour' learn to swim."

"More is the pity for you, then, that I was raised in the marshes swimming with peasant girls, else you might have been free of an unwanted wife," she said, kicking off and crossing the pool with strong, smooth strokes.

He chuckled and began to swim for the shore where his bag lay. The sound of his rich laughter did queer things to her heart, making it leap and beat erratically in her breast. Then, when he walked dripping from the water and knelt with unconscious grace before a low shrub, the heat in her cheeks began to move lower thrumming through her racing blood. He broke off a handful of the spiky green branches from the plant and returned to the water with them.

"This will cleanse the stench from us," he said coaxing her near by offering her a piece of the aromatic plant. "'Tis called fruit soap by the sailors. I can barely pronounce the Taino word for it myself, but it means sweet smell in their language."

When she reached for it, his hand closed firmly yet gently about her wrist and he pulled her into the shallow water near the falls. "Stand up and let me show you how to apply it," he commanded, himself rising to stand knee-deep in the silvery aqua water.

Magdalena complied and he began to work the pulpy mass between his palms until he had a creamy white liquid which he then began to rub over her arms, then up to her throat and about her face. "Close your eyes. It stings." She obeyed, swaying in the warm night air. Unconsciously, her arm reached out and held to his shoulder as he worked the lather downward, reaching her breasts, which he washed with exquisite care. Her eyes flew open as she felt the raw frisson of pleasure that tightened her firm young nipples until they ached.

Aaron suppressed the groan of desire that struggled

to burst from deep in his throat and said hoarsely, "Here, take this piece and lather me as I do you." His hands moved lower and he slid them about her slim hips, gliding around her to cup and massage her buttocks.

Magdalena worked the creamy white soap onto his shoulders and across his chest. When she began to cleanse his shaggy gold hair, he turned her around and worked the soap into her masses of dark russet curls, then moved down her slim back, her legs, even to her small feet, lifting them one at a time from the shallow water. Taking more of the plant from the rocky ledge by the side of the falls, he handed her some leaves and turned his back. At the unspoken command she soaped his broad back, her fingers caressing the old scars, now so familiar on his hard, splendid body. When he turned again to face her, she reddened, feeling his straining staff push gently against her belly.

"Wash it, Magdalena," he whispered as he began to lather her belly and then moved to the curls at the juncture of her thighs. He felt her quiver. The breathy little moan she emitted felt sweet and warm against his cheek.

Magdalena felt the world begin to spin, and her body seemed to whirl out of control. Always Aaron's touch had this effect on her. She quickly grasped his staff in her small hands, wanting to evoke a similar feeling of powerlessness in him. When she massaged the hard pulsing rod with slick soap, he gasped and muttered what sounded like an oath in the Taino tongue.

They stood quietly for a moment, gently caressing as they bathed, both inundated with such intense feelings they could scarcely breathe. Then one soapy lock of her hair plopped against his chest, breaking the spell. He ceased his delicate stroking on her soft nether lips and scooped her into his arms, carrying her beneath the waterfall. "Let us rinse off. We are bathed cleaner than a

Jewish rabbi before Yom Kippur," he said as he set her on her feet in the falls.

The cool water splashed everywhere, like silky music stinging them softly as they ran their hands over each other, partly to wipe away the soap, mostly to feel the heat from the other's flesh. Their laughter blended with the gentle patter of the falls as they clung and kissed beneath its purifying blessing.

Aliyah, who had seen them bypass the village's public bathing place, followed the lovers to their secluded Eden and watched as they bathed and laughed, cavorting so sensuously in the water. She remembered a distant atoll where he had done the same thing with her in a secluded pool, always careful of his privacy when coupling with a woman. A jealous rage built in her as she watched Aaron pull the pale, skinny foreigner deeper behind the curtain of water and sink slowly to the earth with her in his arms. She turned and ran from the hateful sight, unable to bear seeing Magdalena claim her golden lover. How easily he had refused the enticement of her lush curves this very morning, only to fly to his shapeless, ugly, red-haired wife!

Aaron gently lay Magdalena back on the soft moss behind the falls. As he caressed her skin, now free of the lubricating soap, he could feel all the insect bites and abrasions she had endured. The sun had painfully reddened her face, arms and legs. He leaned down and kissed her eyelids, murmuring, "Lie here and wait but a moment. I have medicines in my pack to soothe your sore skin." Gently touching her cheek with a featherlike caress, he stood up and walked around the falls, circling the pool to fetch the cloth and his saddlebag.

Magdalena lay bemused, the flame inside her raging far more fiercely than any in her burned skin. He was back in a moment, kneeling at her side to dry her with a cloth. Then as she toweled at her hair, he opened a small vial of sweet-smelling oil which he began to work gently into her skin, stroking her nose, cheeks, arms, and lower legs, paying particular attention to the little weals from insect bites. Lastly, kissing her palms and fingertips, he worked the oil into her small, delicate hands.

"I am sorry, Magdalena. I did not intend for you to stay out all day doing such menial and difficult labor. I am ever wanting to break your high-spirited Castilian pride, but at the same time I know well that if ever I succeeded, I would regret it." He paused and looked into her eyes, filled with wonder, luminous in the twilight.

A small smile wobbled on her lips. "Then 'tis a good thing I am possessed of such a mighty reserve of stubborn pride, is it not?" She reached up and pulled him into her arms.

Aaron kissed her slowly, as if to drain the sweet heat from her mouth, deepening the kiss as he tangled his hands in her glorious mane of hair. Then he moved down her body with wet silky caresses, stopping to suckle and tease the pale pink nipples of her proudly upthrust breasts. When she arched her back to meet his mouth, he felt a primitive thrill. Magdalena always made him feel, at least while they made love, that she had never felt another man's touch.

His questing hands moved lower, followed by his hot moist lips, brushing firmly across her belly onto the mound of curls below. Then he parted her thighs and nuzzled the delicate flesh of her sex. He could feel her trembling yet resisting. He ignored her shocked protest as he persisted, holding her hips prisoner with his strong hands. Magdalena surrendered with a moan of ecstasy, and he continued to stroke, lick, and kiss, using his mouth to make her limp and mindless with pleasure.

She was aflame, writhing, no longer in resistance but in utter abandon as he probed and lapped her in this shocking, incredible new way. She should stop him. This was unnatural. This was glorious. Soon her hands had left off pushing at his shoulders to tangle in his shaggy gold hair, urging him onward until she felt the most exquisite, intense release she had ever experienced. Her hips arched up toward the starry sky, then fell back to earth like the soft lapping waters that caressed the edges of the pool.

Aaron lifted his head and looked at his wife's dazed, replete face. For all she had been with other men, he felt equally certain that none had ever made love to her this way. Even Magdalena could not act that well! He watched her luminous green eyes open as she stared up at him in awe. Still shaking, she touched his cheek with great tenderness and then looked away, her thick russet lashes shielding her emotions from him. As she sat up, her body was sheened silver in the moonlight that filtered through their waterfall curtain. The night air was balmy and perfumed, sweetened even more with the rich musk of sex.

Magdalena watched his face. She was satiated by the incredible pleasure he had given her, yet embarrassed and vulnerable because of the way he had done so. Finally she found her voice. "Where . . . where did you learn of that?" The moment she asked the question she feared the answer—the hedonistic Taino women were doubtless highly inventive in the art of love.

His low, rich chuckle did nothing to dispel her fears until he answered, "In Granada. I was ever a good student of Arabic. On several occasions I was sent into the city before the siege, posing as a Jewish scholar loyal to their cause. While spying for the Trastamaras, I visited Boabdil's court, and the various pleasure houses of that decadent and beautiful city." He ran his hand along her thigh and up to her breast softly. "The Moors are very attuned to the needs and pleasures of the human body."

She almost blurted out another question. *Have you done this with Aliyah?* She stopped herself. It was foolish

272

to seek answers best left unknown. She looked at his splendid body as he reclined on his side. His shaft remained rigid, his whole frame filled with sexual tension. Magdalena took a deep breath for courage and reached out to touch him, running her fingertips from his face down to the golden fur on his chest, tracing its narrowed descent across his taut belly. She paused in mock playfulness and whispered, "This Moorish way of loving . . . can a woman do for a man . . ." Her courage deserted her.

Aaron reached for her hand and wrapped it around his aching phallus. "Yes, she can," he managed to reply hoarsely as he felt the white hot jolt of pleasure her touch brought. "'Tis a way of making love that is very ancient. Not only the Moors know its secret."

"Teach me," she said softly, almost as if it were a supplication. She leaned over him as he guided her, slowly, gently, to taste of him. Magdalena felt increasingly bold when he gasped and arched at the slight grazing by her lips and tongue. Then he attempted to instruct her in roughened, breathless phrases, but she no longer needed instruction, and he was no longer capable of giving it. She took the sleek velvety heat of him into her mouth. His response communicated the same feeling of powerless surrender that she had felt when he held her in thrall. Slowly she savored him, pleasured by giving him the same ecstasy he had given her. When he stiffened and swelled, crying out incoherently, she felt a thrill of power that was almost intoxicating. Then he trembled and exploded, achieving the same earth-shattering release she had.

Aaron lay spent. Always there was this brief moment of deep peace that hovered about him after making love with this woman, only this woman, *his* woman, his wife. He pulled her up into his arms, not wanting to think on it or the reasons why it was so. He stroked her hair and held her close.

She nestled against him and murmured against his chest, "'Tis not unnatural at all. At first I thought it must be . . . but it is so good." She hesitated, then turned her face up to his, searching for a kiss. "Do we taste of each other?" she asked boldly.

"Let us see," he replied to her ingenuous plea for a kiss. He drew her close and claimed her mouth for a long, savoring kiss, not of passion, but of exceeding gentleness.

"Yes," was her simple answer to her own question. With that her lips curved in a slight smile and she snuggled in his arms and slept.

They returned to the village at dawn's first light, she clad in the long swath of cotton cloth they had dried on last evening, he again in a simple loincloth. Many people were stirring when they walked the wide streets, for this day was to be a special religious festival. Magdalena was curious about what would transpire. Her attitude toward these generous and gentle people was gradually undergoing a transformation. Always possessed of a lively and inquiring mind, she had honed it in the all-too-brief months of friendship with Benjamin Torres. Wanting to grow closer to her husband and please him, she too sought to understand the Tainos who had taken him to their hearts.

No longer were they simply naked savages to her, even though she chaffed beneath the double standards Aaron placed on her. The women of the village were sexually promiscuous and went about completely naked until they were wed. Yet he had always condemned her for what he unjustly considered her impurity and was furious when she did but bare her arms and legs.

She smiled and nodded as they passed by people busily at work outside their houses. Aaron was jealous! No man but him should see her unclothed. That gladdened her heart, especially after his tenderness last night. He had been penitent about sending her to work in the fields. Half his anger had been guilt, the other frightened possessiveness. Surely that meant he was beginning to return her feelings for him. *It may take me a great while, my husband, but I vowed to make you love me and I shall!*

Around noon the drums began to beat in a slow, steady cadence. Everyone of rank in the village was freshly bathed and dressed in their finest ceremonial garb, bedecked with feathers in their hair, wearing many fine pieces of gold and copper jewelry as well as necklaces and girdles of intricate beauty.

"What do we do?" Magdalena asked Aaron nervously as she watched the streets fill with solemn Tainos queuing up to enter the temple next to Guacanagari's *bohio*.

"I have told you that it might be best if you remained here," he replied cautiously. "This is a feast to honor their *zemis*, and as such may upset your religious sensibilities."

She looked at him warily. "They are not going to serve me fish eyes or some such delicacy?"

He smiled. "No, nothing like that. Only cassava bread, specially blessed."

"Then I shall go. I tire of those puling priests in Ysabel decrying the heathenish religion of the Tainos when they will not even come to the village and learn what the Tainos *do* believe. How can we teach them of our faith if we do not even know of theirs?"

"Fray Ramon is learning their language and customs. In time I think he might have more success—if they do not convert him first," he said with a smile.

"Fray Ramon is a good man, if over-bookish, but I do not think he alone can accomplish much. The admiral petitions constantly for more priests and none are sent.

Shirl Henke

There is no harm in my learning more of Taino religion in the meanwhile." She looked at him to see how he responded.

"I doubt you are in any danger of being converted to *zemi* worship!" Then his face lost its smile and he walked over to her, caressing her long, burnished hair. "If you go, there is some unpleasantness I would warn you of—not so bad as the fish eyes, but . . ." He stopped and extracted two small gourd spoons from a pot in the corner and handed her one. "It is customary before this high festival to purge oneself at the door of the temple, as a purification."

She looked confused. "I thought you said their daily bathing was their means of honoring the temple of the human body. What else would they need do—fast, mayhap?"

"In a manner of speaking." Only when he attempted to explain to an outsider did Aaron realize how assimilated into Taino culture he had become. Not that he worshiped the *zemis*, but he did accept their way of seeing God and felt no need to convert them. He looked at her puzzled expression. "This," he held up the small spoon, "is used thusly at the temple door." He inserted the spoon to the back of his throat without pressing down. "You must purge yourself by vomiting."

She paled. "I would as leave fast, but . . ." She shrugged philosophically. "'Twill be most interesting. Guacanagari is the priest as well as the *cacique*, is he not?"

"Yes. He will lead the procession," Aaron replied.

Then Aliyah will be with him. "I will go with you and I promise not to disgrace myself or you. After the fish eyes, this will be but a simple matter—like eating green apples in early spring," she added mischievously.

At times like this, Aaron felt himself falling more deeply under her spell. He forgot that her father was Bernardo Valdés, forgot that she may have been involved in his family's tragedy. She was not his enemy, but his wife. "Let us go. See you do as I show you," he said sternly.

The procession was long and slow moving as nearly one thousand people—all those free people of sufficient rank, from artisans to the royal family—marched to the beat of the drum. Guacanagari, his brother, his wives, and his sisters led the procession. All the women of the royal family bore great baskets of cassava bread on their heads. Aliyah carried hers with regal grace while holding Navaro easily on one hip. Magdalena watched as Aaron's eyes fastened on his son. *He wants the child. I must accept that.* But she knew she would never accept her husband's continuing a relationship with Aliyah!

Steeling herself when they reached the large urns situated at each side of the wide door, she did as Aaron instructed quickly and then took a sip of water gratefully from a temple servant. The cane and thatch edifice was enormous, nearly fifty yards long and twenty wide. People huddled inside, squatting on their heels with the ease of those born to spend hours in such an uncomfortable position. Magdalena copied the others and sat close to Aaron, praying the ceremony would not take long.

Soon quiet spread as the women bearing the bread carried it into the center of the temple and placed the baskets around the large *zemi* of Guacanagari and a cluster of others.

As if on some prearranged signal, all began to sing. The chant was slow and resonant, coming from so many earnest voices raised in union. Aaron remained respectful but silent. Not knowing enough Taino to even understand the words, she did likewise, realizing with a sudden insight how a fifteen-year-old boy forced into a new faith must have felt when first brought to the cathedral in Seville. Since birth Aaron had been a Jew, an outsider in Castile, then a *converso*, unfamiliar and

Shirl Henke

confused by the Christian faith. This for him was no new experience. But for Magdalena it was. She, too, bowed her head and maintained a respectful silence.

Then, as if sensing her curiosity, Aaron whispered that the song was one beseeching good health and a bountiful harvest for all people of Guacanagari's *cacicazgo*. When it ended, Guacanagari stood up and began to pray over the bread set before the *zemis*. "He blesses it for all the people to partake. It will give them sustenance in the coming year," Aaron whispered to her.

When he had finished, the women of the royal family began to distribute the cassava bread, breaking it carefully into small pieces so that the head of each household could come forth and take one piece for his family to share once returned to their homes. Even field laborers and slaves were permitted to partake of the blessed bread.

The similarity to the Holy Communion was not lost on Magdalena, who turned questioning eyes to Aaron as he explained the practice. "The blessings of bread is as old as civilization in places all across the world—Christians and Jews, Moors, even those peoples of the Indies mainland Marco Polo wrote of—all have some custom similar to this. I warned you it might be troublesome for your single-minded conscience," he said softly as the Tainos again began to chant reverently, filing out of the temple as each received his blessed cassava bread.

Magdalena's smile was sincere when her eyes met Aaron's. "I am not troubled at all," she said quietly. *Benjamin, you were right, so right about so many things, my friend. . . .*

Chapter Seventeen

"Guacanagari has need of me—as Cristobal's representative. He has received a messenger from Caonabo, an old enemy who wishes to discuss matters of importance with the *cacique* of Marien," Aaron said as he entered their *bohio* and began to gather his arbalest and several quivers of bolts from their pegs on the walls.

"Matters of importance—such as war?" Magdalena asked with dread, letting the stirring paddle drop unattended into the pepper pot bubbling over the low fire.

Aaron shrugged. "It is possible. Caonabo is the *cacique* who ordered the gold seekers of Navidad killed— that is, those who did not hack each other to pieces in their lust and greed."

"But surely Guacanagari will not join him in warring on the admiral and the colonists of Ysabel?" Magdalena felt suddenly vulnerable, isolated so far from white civilization.

Shirl Henke

"Guacanagari has always been a loyal friend of ours, but men like Margarite and Hojeda sorely try his patience with their cruelties. The Colóns have been unable to control them. Guacanagari does not trust Caonabo. I will see what that crafty old fox is up to and then report back to Cristobal."

Magdalena placed her hand hesitantly on his arm as he strode past her. When he stopped, she asked, "What shall I do?"

He smiled. "You will be quite safe here. In fact, safer here than in Ysabel. Only wait. We should return by dark. Caonabo has deigned to journey all the way from the Vega just to treat with Guacanagari."

With that he was gone. Magdalena knelt dejectedly by the cookpot. In the weeks they had spent with the Tainos, she had developed some little skills as a cook, even if basketry still eluded her as much as embroidery had. "Wonderful! I have finally steeped a whole pot of stew overnight and now he will probably not return in time to eat of it before it is burned. Oh, how I long for someone who speaks Castilian," she murmured to herself. She knew the only person who spoke her language now that Guacanagari and his advisors had gone was Aliyah. "Rather would I cut out my tongue than converse with that one," she said glumly.

Again she recalled how beautiful young Navaro was and how much his swarthy little face had already grown to resemble his sire's. The startling blue eyes were always the Torres stamp, even if the boy's hair was coal black and his skin tawny. *If only I could give Aaron a son.* But she knew that would not end her husband's sense of responsibility or love for his firstborn. Her ambivalence about Navaro troubled her more with each passing day. Could she take the child of Aaron's mistress and love it as her own? For their tenuous relationship to grow into a true marriage bond, that is what she would have to do.

"Sitting here pitying myself will settle naught," she

said with a dejected sigh. After she grated the last of the manioc roots and pressed them into flat cakes, she would bake them and then dry them. Picking up the sharp-edged *tipiti*, she began the laborious chore, carefully saving the juice from the plant for the pepper pot.

By the time the last of the dark, crisp cakes of cassava bread had been set out to cool, Magdalena felt she had accomplished a good day's work, but in spite of her aching back, it was only mid-afternoon. Rubbing the small of her back, she looked at the pile of dirty linen clothes and decided to wash them. For once, Aaron's scandalous loincloths appealed to her—they meant far less washing now that she was the family laundress. If anyone in Seville had told Magdalena Valdés that she would one day find herself living among a tribe of primitives, cooking and scrubbing like a peasant woman, she would have laughed at the absurdity of the idea. She swore at her absent husband as she gathered up her pile of wash and began to trudge to the river.

The flat, rocky stretch of shallows at the south side of the village was where the Taino women did their laundry, since there were lots of smooth stones on which to scrub the coarse cotton cloths they occasionally wore or used for bed covers and for drying their bodies. She stopped by the edge of the jungle and gathered some fresh fruit soap. Each time she did so now, she remembered the time Aaron had introduced her to the marvelous plant and the way they had made love by the waterfall afterward.

Just thinking of it heated her cheeks far more than the hot afternoon sun ever could. "I grow as brown as a Taino," she said in dismay, then wondered if Aaron found the golden color of her skin, with its light dusting of freckles, unattractive. She certainly preferred his sinewy bronzed appearance to the pale, white-faced courtiers who languished in the shade of Ysabel's houses, sweating in their heavy doublets, hose, and boots. Covered from head to toe in layers of clothing, they mostly stank and seldom bathed. A small smile twitched at her lips when she recalled Miralda's scolding about her obsession for daily bathing. "Would she accuse the heathen Tainos of judaizing?"

Sweating even in her sheer under-tunic, Magdalena worked a rich lather into her laundry, piece by piece, then rinsed each item and lay it out to dry on a larger rounded rock that jutted from the knee-deep water. Numerous Taino women laughed and chattered about her as they, too, attended to similar chores. She smiled and returned the gestures of friendship, wishing she understood more of their language. Two young women sat at the edge of the river unabashedly nursing their babies as the late afternoon shadows grew longer across the water.

Out of the corner of her eye, Magdalena saw Aliyah draw near carrying Navaro. As she sat down with the nursing mothers, all the women around the riverside grew very quiet, their dark eyes moving uneasily from the *cacique*'s haughty sister to the white woman. Magdalena quickly decided the best course was to ignore Aaron's mistress. She turned her back and continued to scrub her clothes.

Aliyah watched the fire-haired woman's slim golden arms twist and squeeze one of her foolish white garments. Giving Navaro to her cousin, she rose and slowly walked into the shallow water.

Magdalena saw the shadow of her nemesis fall across her but ignored the woman standing behind her.

"A pity you must work like a slave girl to wash so much cloth, but if my body were skinny and white like the underbelly of a fish, perhaps I, too, would wish to cover it in ugly long garments," Aliyah said in serviceable Castilian.

"If I were cursed with fat thighs and sagging breasts, I would certainly not display them for all to see as you

282

do," Magdalena said, looking with contempt at the overly lush curves of the Taino woman.

Aliyah's eyes darkened and narrowed, but she drew herself up proudly, thrusting her large breasts out tauntingly. "My body is a woman's body, one that gives a man pleasure . . . and suckles his children. You are flat as a starved slave boy!"

"My husband has left your bed, Aliyah. My *starved body* must please him well enough, for he makes love to me every night," Magdalena replied with a triumphant glitter in her green eyes as she stood up to face her larger rival.

Aliyah could still see Aaron and this hateful foreigner beneath the waterfall, kneeling on the soft ground in a bone-melting embrace. "He will not stay long with you. Aaron will quickly tire of your passionless child's body. I have given him a fine strong son. You—who say he lays each night with you—are barren. You cannot give him children. I can!"

The pain of Aaron's rejection, their forced marriage, and now the terrible divisiveness of his love for his half-caste son—all Magdalena's bottled up insecurities caused a red rage to well up inside her. With a snarled oath she took the water-logged tunic in both hands and swung it like a cudgel at Aliyah, smacking the taller woman full in the face. The proud Taino fell backward with a shriek and a loud splash, landing on her rump in the soft sand beneath a foot of water. Instantly she was up, fingers drawn into claws, raking at Magdalena's face.

The red-haired woman grabbed a fistful of flying ebony hair and yanked with all her strength, using Aliyah's momentum to unbalance her and send her flying once more, this time headfirst into the river. As Aliyah rolled over, coughing and cursing, Magdalena was on her, gouging and clawing. The Taino was heavier-boned and larger, but Magdalena was wily and fast. Sheer fury fueled her now. Beyond any reason, they each grabbed fistfuls of the other's hair, rolling in the shallow water in a frenzy of kicking. Aliyah ripped Magdalena's tunic, baring one breast, and then yanked the long-sleeved garment down about her right arm. The long skirts rucked up about her hips as Magdalena kicked and struggled until she finally emerged on top of her opponent.

The Taino women were aghast, frozen in horror as the two combatants exchanged hostile words in the strange language of their man and then the wife attacked the mistress. Aliyah was the sister of Guacanagari, but Magdalena was wife to Guacanagari's honored guest. What were they to do?

Magdalena held Aliyah beneath the water, attempting to drown the flailing woman. Suddenly there was a commotion behind them and the sound of a furious male voice. Strong arms fastened about Magdalena from behind and Aaron lifted her from Aliyah's submerged body. The Taino came up sputtering and screeching and lunged for the woman in his arms. By this time Guacanagari had arrived at the battle ground and restrained his sister. Both women continued screaming threats at each other and trying to break free so they could resume the fray.

Guacanagari remonstrated with Aliyah in the sibilant Taino language, gently holding the furious woman whose eyes were black with hate. Struggling to catch her breath, she spoke rapidly to her brother, then to Aaron in Taino, now ignoring Magdalena. Then she called out several words to Aaron and he froze for a moment. Without another word he tossed Magdalena over his shoulder and strode toward their *bohio*. One of the onlookers unobtrusively gathered Magdalena's laundry together. On the morrow she would return it. Somehow the Taino knew this would not be an opportune time to visit their *bohio*!

When Aaron reached the door, he set his wife roughly

on the ground. "Why by the Keys of St. Peter did you attack a member of the royal family? That is a crime punishable by death!"

"Then you would be well rid of me, would you not? She came after me, deliberately taunting me, spoiling for a fight, thinking her great fat body could easily overpower my *pale skinny* one. Now she knows not to assume fat is a substitute for muscle! I would have drowned her, and damn the consequences!"

He looked at her wet, tangled hair and half-naked body. "Aliyah did manage to strip you all but naked," he said, observing her shiver in the cool twilight air.

"I care not. 'Tis she who has the bruises from my fingers about her throat!"

"She insulted you with a few childish taunts about your smaller breasts and pale skin, so you tried to choke and drown her. What of your much-vaunted Christian charity?" he asked bitterly. "Could you not turn the other cheek, my lady? 'Twould have served much better."

"I should let her hound and humiliate me? You would never bear such an insult from any man. Women have pride, too, my fine lord, in case you did not know it," she snapped.

His eyes were glacial now. "Castilian courtesans have a great excess of it, 'twould seem."

Magdalena seethed with jealousy and hurt. "So, we come back to the heart of the matter—your mistress can flaunt her lovers and that is no stain on her. But you think me a harlot although none but you has ever touched me. You did not wish to wed a tainted Valdés. Nothing will ever be right between us, Aaron. Bernardo, damn his soul to hell, will ever keep us apart."

"Your father . . . and my son," Aaron replied, his voice as broken as hers now. "Guacanagari told me on the way back this afternoon that Aliyah had agreed to give Navaro to me. Now she has changed her mind. The boy goes with her to Xaragua." He turned and stalked off into the gathering darkness.

Magdalena felt as if a great weight were crushing life and breath from her. So that was what those final hateful words were that Aliyah had called out to Aaron. *And he blames me, as always.*

Aaron did not return to their bed that night, but went down to the pen where he kept the horses. He took Rubio and rode down the river in the silver moonlight. Magdalena lay staring at the night sky for sleepless hours, then rose and dressed with the first light of dawn. If it took abasing her vaunted Castilian pride to gain her husband his son, she would do so. If only she could sway the *cacique* and he his sister.

Dressing in her last clean under-tunic, she brushed her hair until it shone and let it fall in thick, rich curls about her shoulders. She donned her leather slippers and even the copper necklace that had been a gift from Guacanagari. "I must bring a gift, something worthy," she mused aloud. Then her eyes fastened on the foolish velvet gown she had brought. The long heavy garment now seemed ludicrous to her, but perhaps . . . She set to work with a small dagger, unfastening the seams of the wide skirt with its long full train. When she had completed her task, she had a roughly cut cloak of some handsome proportions, fit, she hoped, for a king.

Carefully folding the rich brown velvet in her arms, she walked purposefully to the *bohio* of Guacanagari. When one of his wives smiled uncertainly at her, Magdalena took all her courage in hand and held out her peace offering, saying Guacanagari's name.

The woman quickly understood and bowed, offering Magdalena a stool in front of the bubbling pepper pot, then vanished inside the huge *bohio*. In a moment Guacanagari strode out and looked at the young woman huddled so forlornly on the small stool, clutching her treasure. She stood at once and offered the heavy velvet to the *cacique*, unfolding the cloak with a flourish. When he stepped nearer, she boldly showed him how it would fit, much as that worn by his friend, the admiral.

Guacanagari spoke in halting Castilian, "This is a great honor, wife of Aaron. What may I give you in return?"

She swallowed and said, "A far greater treasure—my husband's son."

His face became troubled and he sighed. "Aliyah is very bitter. She hoped to wed Aaron when Navaro was born with his blue eyes."

"Then I came and spoiled her plans. I am sorry, but I have loved Aaron for many, many years. I would love his son as my own. Navaro would want for nothing. This I swear to you." She held her breath, suddenly seeing the small dark child with her husband's face. She knew even as she spoke the words that she truly meant them. Navaro was Aaron's child. She did love him, just for that!

"If I could make Aliyah give over the boy, I would, but there are laws among my people. A woman may keep any children born to her before she weds. No man—or other woman—may claim them, for they are hers alone. Last night I tried to talk with her on the matter so dear to my friend's heart. But she would not listen." He began to fold the cloak and give it back to Magdalena.

Tears filled her eyes, but she dashed them back, shaking her head and saying, "Please, keep the cloak. It is fit for a good and wise *cacique*. I would have you wear it and remember me with fondness, not as one who brought such unhappiness to your village."

"You love Aaron well," he said softly, studying the small, delicate woman from across the great waters.

"I only pray that some day he may come to be as wise as you are," she said simply. "May I ask that you do not speak of my request to anyone?"

"Least of all to your husband?" He nodded and bowed.

Magdalena did the same and departed in the cool golden light of morn.

The pestilence in Ysabel had grown worse in their absence. As soon as they neared the settlement, the stench of death pervaded the air. The flat meadows near the bay were churned up by hundreds of fresh graves. More soil had been turned to bury men than to plant crops.

"The whites die of fever and bloody flux, the Tainos of our diseases, smallpox and measles. How well we deal together already," Aaron muttered in disgust.

"The Indians do seem to suffer fatally from ailments that would but disfigure a person in Castile."

"My father would doubtless have had some learned Jewish or Moorish physician's opinion on why that is so," Aaron replied sadly, then added with contempt, "But I do know why the colonists fare so poorly here. They refuse to adapt, going about covered head to foot in heavy clothes, refusing to eat native foods, insisting on red wine and pork in this heat. Small wonder their guts are eaten away. Even I am physician enough to understand that!"

Magdalena bit her lips in vexation at his obdurate attitude. When *she* went about with her arms and legs bared, he was roundly furious, but with the barriers between them once more so bitterly in place, she forbore to comment. Changing the subject she asked, "How went the meeting with Caonabo? You never did tell me."

Aaron's eyes glowed with grudging admiration. "God above, you should have seen the wily old devil! His face seems as old as the islands, yet he possesses the body of a lean young warrior. He can hold a *bohio* full of *caciques* spellbound with his entrancing speeches, and those glittering black eyes—they seem to cut through to a man's very soul. He knew from his spies that I spoke his language fluently, so when I appeared at the meeting he made no attempt to enlist Guacanagari as an ally against the Colóns."

"What was his pretense for the meeting then?"

"His men offered lavish gifts to Guacanagari in honor of Aliyah's marriage to Behechio. A sort of subtle bribe, I suppose, although you know well how generous the Taino people always are. A few meaningless pleasantries were exchanged, and Caonabo departed for the Vega with his entourage."

"Will he cause trouble?" Magdalena asked apprehensively, looking at the sick men lying about the filthy, cluttered streets of Ysabel. "There are so many more of them than us."

Aaron scoffed. "One shot from the admiral's lombard aboard *Niña* and they will all flee into the jungles. The accuracy and distance of my lightweight crossbow terrifies them. With our weaponry and armor, not to mention horses, we could kill every Taino on Española in a matter of a few months. But I intend to see that does not happen. Even the troublemakers like that half-Caribe Caonabo would live in peace if the colonists would treat fairly with them."

"But surely Guacanagari will remain the admiral's friend," Magdalena said earnestly.

"Yes, he will. He may be too loyal, though," Aaron replied darkly. "If the Colons cannot keep control of these damnable young nobles bent on enslaving the Tainos, Guacanagari's people will suffer first and most from the greed of men like Hojeda, that frilly little weasel."

After stabling their mounts and refreshing themselves, Aaron and Magdalena dressed to greet the Colóns and report on their time in the interior. The young Taino girl who worked as Magdalena's maid had hung out all her mistress's remaining gowns lest they rot stored in the damp heat of her trunk. Considering the depletion of her wardrobe, Magdalena was most grateful as she chose a lovely light-blue brocade. Now her white linen under-tunic shone in almost dazzling contrast next to her golden-hued skin. Even the blue dress, one she had never considered particularly flattering, made her look vibrantly healthy.

The rainy season was upon them, and the leaden skies gave way to a steady drizzle. Her hair, always wiry with curls, now stood out, crackling as if the lightning bolts in the sky were drawn to the russet masses. She struggled to plait it with a string of pearls and then placed a veil over it. Still, curly wisps escaped at her nape and about her face.

Aaron watched her fuss with her hair and felt that old familiar ache in his loins. He cursed the tight hose that revealed far more than a loose loincloth would have, but he must look the proper soldier for the governor. "Are you ready? Cristobal awaits me and I am certain Bartolomé is pacing the floor in concern over your well-being."

"Then let us go reassure them both," she replied sweetly, reaching for a dark velvet cape to ward off the worst of the rain.

As he placed it about her shoulders, he asked absently, "Where is that foolish brown velvet gown you took to the village? I see it not with your others hanging on the walls."

"It rotted in the moist air. I threw it away," she answered quickly, praying Guacanagari would not chose to wear his treasure at some ceremonial occasion where Aaron could recognize it.

By the time they reached the governor's residence, the rain squall had stopped. Weather patterns in the Indies were as different from those of Andalusia as Andalusia was from the Pyrenees. Magdalena felt damp and tired, yet eager to greet her old friend Bartolomé and his stern elder brother. If only they approved of her shocking transformation. Although nowhere near as dark as Aaron, her skin was far from the milky pallor favored by ladies of the court. Dutifully, Aaron helped her from the small thatch litter four Taino servants carried. Swinging her onto the stones that led up to the wide stairs of the official residence, Aaron assisted her in keeping the mud from her dainty cloth slippers.

As soon as they were ushered inside, the Admiral and his *adelantado* both rushed into the wide hall outside the audience chamber.

Bartolomé's face split in a wide grin of delighted amazement. "Taino life seems to agree with you, my lady," he said, gallantly kissing her hand, then turning to his brother, he added, "Does she not look splendid, Cristobal?"

The governor smiled warmly, seeing the bloom of health on Magdalena's beautiful face. "Yes, Doña Magdalena, it would seem marriage and adventures in the Taino village agree well with you." He turned to Aaron and read contradictory feelings in the depths of his young friend's eyes. "I trust you have much to report about our friend Guacanagari."

"And Caonabo," Aaron added, seeing that the mention of the name brought a great wariness to Cristobal's face.

"We have much to discuss, but before we do, there is a gentleman who has been inquiring about you since he landed a fortnight ago and found you were here. A kinsman." Colon's eyes flashed a warning as he added. "Lorenzo Guzman, your brother-in-law, I believe."

Aaron's face became a stone mask, gray and taut with loathing. "He was wed to Ana. When the Inquisition took her, he did nothing to stop them."

"Few men can stand against the Holy Office of Fray Tomás, Diego," Lorenzo said with a languidness that belied the tension within him. *How can he yet be alive?*

As if reading his mind, Aaron smiled a cold, sharkish

grin and said, "I see you are surprised to find me alive and well, Lorenzo. I, too, was surprised to find you alive and well when I returned to Seville last year. Your wife and my parents, my brother and his wife Rafaela—all were burned by Torquemada and his minions. How did you alone escape?" Filled with disgust, his eyes bored into Lorenzo's. He was sure that the Duke of Medina-Sidonia had intervened in behalf of his nephew.

"I am from an Old Christian family. No one accused me," Lorenzo replied in a doleful voice.

"So was Rafaela. She was devoutly Christian, yet she died with Mateo," Aaron replied bitterly.

Lorenzo's face darkened, and he fought to retain a facade of pious sorrow in front of the governor. "Perhaps my family was simply more influential. I knew naught of your brother and his wife so far away in Aragon."

"If your family is so influential, surely you could have saved Ana. And what of your daughter Olivia?" Aaron asked, even though he knew the child was safe with his uncle Isaac.

"Ana confessed before I could rescue her." He looked to the governor for help. "Please, this is all too painful. Olivia has been abducted by your Jewish family in France, as you probably already know. I was quite beside myself when I was unable to secure her return. That is why I decided to come to the Indies and seek a new life."

"I can see how you suffer her loss," Aaron said with bitter irony.

Just then Lorenzo's eyes moved from the fearsome Diego Torres to examine his wife, whom everyone in Ysabel praised for her beauty. He started to make a graceful courtier's bow, but his knees nearly buckled when he saw her step forward and remove her veil, shaking droplets of rain from her russet hair. "Mag—

Magdalena Valdés, lady, is it you? We thought you dead since last spring, set upon and murdered by brigands."

Magdalena smiled coldly at the man she had instinctively disliked from the first time she had met him at court. "As you can plainly discern, I am quite alive and married to Don A—Diego Torres. 'Twas for our betrothal that I left the court under such . . . a misunderstanding."

Lorenzo's eyes were slitted, their gray depths murky with suspicion. "You and Diego Torres betrothed? Odd, your parents never spoke of it. But then after the great tragedy . . ." He paused and looked about the assembly with a horrified expression. "Of course, you did not know. I am afraid, Doña Magdalena, that I must be the bearer of most calamitous news." He turned to Cristobal. "Governor, might we all retire to your audience chamber and allow the lady a seat?" he said, moving to take Magdalena's arm.

With a swift, proprietary gesture Aaron pulled her against him and escorted her into the big room where first he had confronted his betrothed wife. The governor led the way and his *adelantado* followed with Lorenzo. Aaron's arm about her was warm and steady as he whispered low. "Be prepared for anything from that cur."

"I will. There is no more left me in Seville than there is for you, Diego," she said, using his Christian name very carefully. Since Fray Buil and his cohorts had sailed back to Castile, leaving only the faithful Fray Pane to save Taino souls, the threat of reports to the Inquisition had gone, but now Magdalena was frightened. The House of Guzman was a powerful one with the royal ear. If Lorenzo had escaped the Holy Office while everyone else allied to the House of Torres had been destroyed, might he have ties to Torquemada? Something about his oily courtier's manner and those cold gray eyes made the hairs on her nape prickle in warning. What was it about him that had always caused her to instinctively loathe him?

Aaron sensed Magdalena's uneasiness and knew she feared for him. Best let Lorenzo Guzman be the one to fear Aaron Torres, he thought grimly as they were all seated. His icy blue eyes pierced the tall foppish courtier, who did not meet his stare but turned his attention to Magdalena.

With grave solicitude he said, "I fear I have the worst sort of news—I know not how to phrase it."

"Try straightforwardly," Aaron suggested bluntly, still standing with his arm about his wife's shoulders.

Lorenzo cleared his throat and said, "Your father, Don Bernardo, is dead." When that elicited no reaction other than an intense stare, he continued warily, "He was found, er, owing money to the crown and the Holy Office. It seems the king felt . . . well, you know your father was Crossbearer in Seville," he said with a very nervous glance at Aaron's cold, set face.

"Yes, I know what Bernardo Valdés was," she replied coldly. "Pray continue."

A look of great consternation passed over Lorenzo's face as he looked first to the governor, then the *adelantado* for some hint as to how to proceed.

"Did the lady's father run afoul of the king's justice?" Cristobal asked, only half-surprised. Although he was clever, Valdés was a knave.

"The king received information from one of his former ministers," Lorenzo continued, this time not meeting Aaron's face even for an instant. "Isaac Torres, in exile in France, reported that your father had not given honest accounting of the confiscated estates of Benjamin Torres. Both the royal treasury and the coffers of the Inquisition were cheated. Don Bernardo stood accused, and the Holy Office questioned him."

"And, of course, he was found guilty," Magdalena

said in a brittle voice. *Oh, Benjamin, how well the forces of darkness devour themselves, even as you said they would.*

Aaron could feel the tension in Magdalena, but also an awful calm, almost as if she rejoiced in her father's death. *I am a most unnatural daughter. I tried to kill my father with a hay rake.* Her words echoed in his brain and he almost believed them.

"Tell me, Don Lorenzo, did the *king's justice*," she paused to emphasize the irony of the words, "claim others of my family?"

Now Aaron could feel her fear—not for her mother, he suspected, but for her sisters.

"No. Only your father suffered death. Of course, your mother was forced to retire from court and went to live with your sister Maria and her husband."

"A fate worse than death for that lady," Magdalena said tartly. "Did the authorities burn Don Bernardo?"

Lorenzo felt himself go hot, then ice cold as he looked from the cooly self-possessed woman to her hard, dangerous husband. What coil had he stepped into by coming to this accursed place of exile? It seemed not only the damnable Torres whelp but even Bernardo's own daughter rejoiced in his death! "Yes, I am afraid he perished on the Field of Tablada."

Isaac, I know not whether to bless or curse you, you master manipulator, playing God. You have robbed me of my revenge, yet done the deed just as I would have done it.

Magdalena looked at her husband, now reading *his* thoughts.

Chapter Eighteen

"If we are to keep Guacanagari as an ally and prevent a general uprising, this is the very sort of thing we must stop!" Aaron said, furious anger in his voice as he looked down the stone steps of the governor's palace into the plaza. He turned from the governor to where Alonso Hojeda stood preening like a peacock with two Tainos lying beaten and bloodied in the mud at his feet.

The little man stood poised on the balls of his feet, his hand resting casually on the hilt of his sword as his keen hazel eyes moved between the hesitant Governor and his incensed military commander, Torres. "They stole from my men. An example must be set lest all of the heathen savages take to such practices." He stared at Torres boldly, knowing he lived among the Tainos as one of them.

"The Tainos do not steal," Aaron said, moving menacingly down one stone step. He, too, had his hand on his sword.

"When *Santa María* was wrecked, Guacanagari's people brought all the ship's stores ashore and not so much as a lace point was missing," Cristobal said calmly, placing a restraining hand on Aaron's shoulder. "How do you know these men took the clothing from your soldiers?" he asked Hojeda.

"We were crossing a river—"

"And the Tainos, of course, were carrying your soldiers, who cannot swim, on their shoulders," Aaron interjected, deriding the slothful and stupid colonists who followed a glory-seeker such as Alonso Hojeda.

"Tainos are no more than beasts of burden," Hojeda replied with contempt. "I say the penalty is just. Cut off the hand that steals, for they did run with two baskets filled with fine linen tunics."

"Two basketsful of underwear scarce seem worth a maiming," the governor said with distaste. "Perhaps there has been some misunderstanding. These people have had the opportunity to steal things of far greater value and have not done so." He turned to Aaron. "Question them and see what story they tell."

Aaron moved past Alonso with arrogant dismissal of the little man. He knelt in the mud and requested one of the women in the gathering crowd to bring a flagon of water. Once he had offered a cooling drink to the elder Taino, he questioned him, then the younger, briefly. When he rose, his face was dark with fury. "These men, along with a dozen other Tainos and their women, were forced to journey with Hojeda's gold seekers. When one tried to escape the drudgery of working the streams for bits of gold, his nose was slit. Another had an ear slashed. All the soldiers drew lots and took the Taino women—against their will. These young men were carrying light loads of clothing. When separated downriver from the others, they dumped the worthless cargo in the jungle and tried to escape to their home village to warn the *cacique* of the arrival of these fine representatives of the crown."

"That is a lie," Hojeda said baldly. "In Seville I have killed men for such an insult!"

"This is *not* Seville. I am governor here and I say clemency is only just. We must have the Taino people help us to survive and our colony to flourish. We will not achieve those ends by making them beasts of burden—nor by raping their women. I put you on notice, Don Alonso, as I did Commander Margarite before he returned to Cadiz, that I will tolerate no further abuse of these people. They make willing servants if paid honestly and treated with Christian kindness, but they are not ours to enslave." The governor motioned to Aaron. "Free them, if you please, Commander Torres."

"Jew and Genoese, how well you deal together," Hojeda said, spitting in the mud at Aaron's feet. He turned and stalked away, parting the crowd as if swinging a scythe.

"You have made a vicious enemy, my friend," Aaron said to Cristobal.

Colon smiled wearily. "'Twill not be my first—or my last, I fear. See to our fellows here, then come to my office. We must discuss the news from your Taino spies in Caonabo's camp."

My Dearest Father,

Since our return to Ysabel many things grow increasingly difficult to bear. My son Navaro's dark blue eyes mark him as a Torres, yet I cannot claim him. I ache for the loss of my son whom I had to leave behind. How hard it must have been for you to send Mateo all the way to Barcelona. Uncle Isaac's last letter just reached

me. I pray that soon Mateo's son Alejandro will
be reunited with his family in France. Then, if
only Navaro could be here with me, at least the
children of our House would be safe.

God, using your brother as His instrument, has
wrought justice on Bernardo Valdés. I do not
think you exalt in the vengeance as I do. Please
forgive me that I am glad of his burning.
Strangely, Magdalena seems to share my sense of
justice in the death of her father. She truly did
hate him, but did she tell me the truth about her
friendship with you? It would seem she loved
you and mother well. But I fear to read too
much into the situation, for I still do not trust
her. She weaves a spell of witchery that frightens
me. If only I had some way of knowing, some
sign from you that you truly wished me to wed
her.

Aaron put down the quill and ran his fingers through
his hair. Over the past year he had faithfully continued
making his journal entries to Benjamin. He seemed
compelled to do so, as if there were some mysterious
reason for committing the unfolding tale of his life to
paper. "Perhaps someday I shall grow wise and know
the reason for it." he murmured sleepily. The hour was
late and he wrote by a flickering tallow candle, sitting in one corner of their *bohio* on a carved chair
while Magdalena slept on the high bed across the
room.

Magdalena. His wife. He could not even look at her as
she slept without wanting to awaken her with fierce,
passionate kisses. All too often he did just that, making
love to her like a man possessed. He wondered if his
parents had ever shared such an overpowering physical
bond. Certainly he and Magdalena had little else to

cement their relationship. Even if Benjamin forgave her her hated Valdés blood and amoral past, Aaron could not.

How many lovers, Magdalena? How many men were there at court? In Seville? The thought tormented him increasingly, even when he was forced to dismiss any idea of her possible complicity in the deaths of his family. But unlike Aliyah, whose blandishments he was able to resist, he could never leave his wife. "Is it only *because* she is my wife?" he whispered on the heavy night air. Outside a steady rain fell, beating a soft tattoo on the roof. The night held no answers for him. He carefully closed his diary and replaced it in his saddle bag, then snuffed out the candle and walked toward the bed in darkness.

Bartolomé Colon paced nervously in his brother's private library, a small room filled with Latin and Castilian books as well as rolls upon rolls of charts and sundry navigational instruments. Cristobal sat, calmly testing the thread and weight on a marine quadrant while he let Bartolomé vent his nervous energy.

"I am much concerned with Torres' news from Guacanagari. If Caonabo can convince other *caciques* to join him, it augers ill for our colony, but if he can ally himself with the likes of unscrupulous liars such as Hojeda or Roldan, then our position is even less tenable. They have the same weapons and skills we do!" Bartolomé looked at Cristobal.

Already intent on his quest for the mainland and heartily sick of bickering Castilian noblemen, the governor, who far preferred to be the admiral, sighed and laid down his instruments. "Alonso Hojeda is too vicious for any Taino chieftain to ally with him. All he can do is incite them to rebellion against all white men."

"Then he must be stopped! Hojeda is openly insubordinate to you as governor of Española and the representative of the Majesties in the Indies. He speaks treason, Cristobal!"

The elder Colon's eyes were sad as he replied, "Yes, against Jews and Genoese. For how many years have I lived in Seville and Cordoba? Followed the royal court? I am as loyal to the sovereigns who supported my enterprise as was Diego Torres, who fought their ancient enemies at Granada."

"Yes, and look you at his reward! His whole family killed or exiled by those same sovereigns. New Christians, Jews, and Genoese, we are all outsiders to men like these Castilian peacocks—to all the people of the Spains, but the king and queen gave you charge of these colonial possessions, Genoese or no. If you would keep the Colon family as the governors of the Indies, you must put down rebellion. Begin with Hojeda—and what of that rogue Roldan?"

Overhearing Bartolomé's impassioned speech from the doorway, Aaron stepped inside and said, "Let Behechio, the *cacique* of Xaragua, beware of Francisco, who will one day rule that distant penninsula. We would be unwise to venture so far to the south and west as to beard the lion Roldan in his lair. There is too much sickness here. We cannot spread ourselves so thin."

"You know this fellow?" Bartolomé asked skeptically.

Aaron smiled. "Quite well. Roldan can be treated with, perhaps even bribed into submitting to royal authority if left alone." He sat down at the big table across from the governor, as did the now intrigued Bartolomé. "It is Caonabo allying with other *caciques* of the interior that we must fear—the provinces of Ciguayo, Magua, and Maguana are far closer to Ysabel than Xaragua. If Hojeda continues what Margarite began, then all of those *caciques* will follow Caonabo. Even without modern weapons they can exact a fearful toll by surprise attack and the use of fire. And they will turn first on our one loyal friend."

"Guacanagari," Cristobal said quietly. "Yes, he has been true to the Majesties. Without his aid we would likely all have perished at the shipwreck of *Santa María*."

Bartolomé asked Aaron, "Do you have a plan to deal with Caonabo before he can unite the other *caciques* of the interior?"

"Yes, and it begins with stopping Hojeda and others like him from roaming at will, raping and pillaging from the Tainos. Once we make the interior peaceful and secure, we can ally with Guacanagari and face Caonabo. He will have far less backing if every gold-mad Castilian nobleman on Española is not riding about hill and valley with sword and arbalest ready to kill Indians." Aaron paused and smiled grimly, recalling Magdalena's lesson in the hard, dirty work of agriculture. "We begin by putting every able-bodied man in Ysabel to work."

"So many are sick," Cristobal said unhappily.

Aaron scoffed. "I will speak with Dr. Chanca about why they suffer. They must learn to eat cassava, fresh fish, and yams, and drink clean water. Enough of swilling wine and eating rancid pork. This is a new land. We must adapt to it or we perish. If you allow me the power to act, I will give you more healthy men fit to work than are willing to do so."

Bartolomé raised his eyebrows sardonically. "The will to do manual labor is scarce secondary to the health to do it."

"Will you lend me your official power as agent of the crown?" Aaron asked both brothers.

Bartolomé nodded, his hand on his sword hilt, but Cristobal seemed troubled. Always calm and decisive in the worst crisis at sea, he looked tired and frail to Aaron.

He wants to chart new lands, to be aboard ship, not fighting petty political battles, Aaron realized sadly.

Sighing, Cristobal stood up. The pain in his joints, a constant misery since his return to Palos in 1493, now constantly racked his body. The tall, thin man stood straight and walked across to the window by sheer dint of will. Turning, he said, "We must do what we must do, Diego. You are commandant under Bartolomé here. What is your plan?"

"Hojeda is still in Ysabel, gathering a coterie of worthless noblemen to journey to the interior and find gold. Let me deal with him first."

"He has influence at court. His patron is the Duke of Medina-Celi. Tread lightly, Diego." Cristobal cautioned, as fearful for his young *converso* friend as for himself.

While the men planned and argued, Magdalena accomplished what she had so long intended, a visit to Dr. Chanca's hospital. The wizened old doctor was delighted with her medical skills and strong stomach, once he overcame his male prejudice about females—especially noblewomen—treating illness. She spent the day brewing bark infusions to spoon between fevered lips and making poultices to draw poison from injuries.

"You have the touch, my lady," the doctor said. "I myself have observed the Taino's use of certain plants and other natural herbs that seem to cure their ailments, but alas, the language barrier prevents me from learning much yet."

Magdalena smiled as she sponged a feverish man who had cut his foot on sharp rocks while fishing. "I lived among Guacanagari's people with my husband for nearly a month. Although my skills in the language are poor, his are great. He was able to show me much, and many of the village healers taught me more. They learn our language with far more skill than we theirs, I fear."

"To our loss," Chanca muttered, moving to the next

pallet to check the man doubled over with cramps from the flux. "I would be willing to try some of that bark infusion you have aboil outside," he said, looking up at Magdalena, who nodded and hurried out to get the bitter liquid.

By evening's end, when she walked through the open doorway of the big cane building, Magdalena was every bit as tired as she had been after her day of planting maize with Tanei. But unlike that disastrous misadventure, this work had purpose. She could scarcely wait to return home and dig out the Latin medical treatises Benjamin had given her—and some Arabic ones she knew Aaron possessed. He could translate for her. That was, she amended unhappily, if he did not again forbid her going to the hospital.

Now that he had hired a Taino girl to wash their laundry and prepare meals, Magdalena had nothing to do. Even with all the frivolous distractions for idle noblewomen at court, she had always detested what she considered boredom. "He must let me continue my work here. Blessed Virgin, he wants me gone from his presence enough," she muttered bitterly to herself as she threw her cloak about her shoulders and headed down the street. Her guard, one of Luis Torres' friends named Analu, followed closely as she wended her way through the noisome streets of Ysabel.

As she neared the *bohio*, Magdalena was suddenly accosted by the nattily dressed Alonso Hojeda. His velvet doublet with scarlet slashing on the sleeves and his heavy sword seemed too big for his thin, wiry frame. His eyes gleamed with keen feral intelligence as he placed his surprisingly strong hand on her arm.

"Good evening, Doña Magdalena," he said with a courtly bow at variance with his rude seizure of her arm.

"Good evening, Don Alonso," she replied frostily,

trying to pull away. Analu stepped up to him, menacing the intruder, but she waved him back. In spite of the Taino's muscular strength, the smaller nobleman's weapons were far superior to Analu's simple spear.

Don Alonso eyed her with malevolent assessment. "Why by all that is holy would a lady from court wed Aaron Torres?"

"Do you know my husband?" she asked calmly, trying to decide what to do. Surely Hojeda did not consider himself a scorned suitor after but one dinner table encounter!

His face hardened. "The new *commandant*," he stressed Aaron's title contemptuously, "and I are well acquainted, yes. He would take a gentleman from Andalusia and have him muck about with common masons and farmers, digging irrigation ditches and planting wheat!"

A smile curved her lips as she recalled how Aaron had sent her to Tanei. "I, too, have served as a field worker. Ysabel has an excess of nobility and far too few hands to till the soil, I fear."

"Pah! We are here to get rich—gold, pearls, spices, the riches of the Indies—that is what brought us here, not to become colonizers of this hell, God deliver me back to Castile!"

"I prefer to live and work here, even though there be no gold. If you do not, only take ship," she gestured to the cove where several caravels bobbed with sails furled, "and return to Castile now." She tried to walk past him but his hand again held her arm.

"Not until I have my gold," he snarled.

"What have I to do with that?" she asked, not liking the turn of this entire conversation. She slid her free arm inside her cloak for her dagger, but before either of them could act, another voice interrupted.

"Hojeda, you little maggot crawled from the ass of a

rotted pig, release my wife and draw your sword."
Aaron strode from the shadows between two houses.

With a muttered oath, the Castilian flung Magdalena
away and faced his much taller opponent, drawing his
sword. If Magdalena had ever thought him small or
weak, she soon found appearances deceptive, for Alonso
Hojeda was lightning quick, crafty, and a highly skilled
swordsman. The two men clashed furiously and the
ringing of steel echoed across the evening air.

Soon a crowd gathered, many partisans of Hojeda, a
few loyal to the governor and his commandant. Magdalena stood with Analu and a small group of frightened
Taino men and women, her dagger clenched in her fist,
ready to do battle with anyone who menaced Aaron.

"You are too good with the sword to waste your skills
maiming defenseless Tainos for gold they do not possess," Aaron said as he parried a thrust and returned the
attack to Hojeda, nicking his expensive doublet sleeve.

"You are too busy consorting with those savages to
know about the gold," Hojeda replied, renewing the
attack in spite of several freely bleeding cuts on his arm
and chest.

"There is no golden treasure in the interior—only
death," Aaron said as he thrust wickedly, nearly removing one heavy sleeve and badly slashing Hojeda's left
arm. "The same death I should give you for touching my
wife."

"You were going to force me to dig like a peasant! I
was but attempting to plead with the noble lady of the
court to stop your madness," the little Castilian said,
now badly winded and knowing he was going to lose the
match. Damn the accursed *marrano's* longer arms!

Aaron administered a series of painful strokes, cutting, slashing, almost disarming Hojeda, who was
forced to realize how badly he had been bested and that
the victor did but toy with him before the kill. The little

cockscomb did have courage, Aaron admitted grudgingly, even though he was furious because Hojeda had
accosted Magdalena.

Just then the crowd, cheering and betting on the
contest, parted, and the imposing presence of the
governor filled the small circle where the men fought.
"You appear to be losing, Alonso. I would recommend you cry off. And you, Diego, are to do likewise."
The old steel was returned to Cristobal's voice. Bartolomé and several guards from the governor's palace
stood behind their leader.

Both men slowly lowered their swords. Aaron was
soaked with sweat, Alonso with blood, but fierce pride
still glowed in his eyes. He turned to the governor. "I
will not be a peasant and dig ditches!"

"Then mayhap I can offer you a task more to your
liking," Bartolomé said. "Disband your private force of
gold hunters and follow us. There is to be a real battle
between our army and the forces of Caonabo on the
Vega. Guacanagari and his warriors join us. Will you?"

Aaron's hand rested lightly on his sword hilt as he
absorbed this bit of news. "Has it come to that?" he
asked quietly.

"Yes. Guacanagari's runner just reached us this afternoon. What you prophesied has come true," Cristobal
replied.

"And we need all the able-bodied men we can get,"
Bartolomé said, eyeing Hojeda sternly.

The shrewd gleam in Hojeda's eyes betrayed his
delight at the prospect of a fight in which he might fare
better. "I will join you to fight Tainos," he said, looking
from the Colons to Torres to gauge his reaction.

"You will fight *with* Guacanagari's Tainos. Against
Caonabo's army. Keep that fixed in your arrogant little
head," Aaron said in cold menace.

After Hojeda bowed to the governor and then to

Magdalena, he walked off, head high and stride firm, even though his once grand clothes were in shreds and his body covered with superficial wounds.

"I mislike having my back to him in the thick of a melee," Aaron muttered to Bartolomé.

"I agree. He will be assigned a place of honor near me, away from all his fellows from Seville," Bartolomé replied with a grim smile.

With the fight ended, the crowd broke apart and dispersed. The Colons and the guards departed after a few brief courtesies to Magdalena and promises to meet with Aaron at dawn.

Aaron's eyes were icy as he glared at his wife. "Were you going to skewer Don Alonso as you did those two ruffians in the plaza?" he asked, looking at the dagger she still clutched unconsciously in her hand.

Red-faced, she replaced it in its sheath, hidden beneath her cloak. "Only if Hojeda endangered you," she replied as she walked toward their house.

"Best beware endangering yourself, you little fool! I have told you not to be about in this city without me. You were at that hospital again without my permission, were you not?"

"If Dr. Chanca can use my skills, why would you refuse to let me help?" she argued, hating the pleading sound that had crept into her voice.

You might be injured or take a fever! He refused to let her see his fear for her, his weakness, so he answered harshly, "You will remain in our home where you cannot incite more mayhem. Bartolomé and I must both leave Ysabel. There will be no rescuers to save that beautiful skin while we journey to the interior."

"What am I to do? Sit and wither? There is no useful task for me in Ysabel but plying my healing skills. Benjamin gave me instruction—even books. You have seen me read them. He thought me a good pupil."

The anguish of his relationship with her and the loss of his father caused him to seize her wrist in a cruel grip and whisper curtly, "You are not a student dabbling at healing back in Seville. You chose to follow me to this dangerous place. Now sit home and wither! 'Twas your choice. Mayhap you are breeding. A babe would give you plenty to occupy your time. Fit work for a wife."

She flinched as if he had struck her, but did not break stride as he virtually dragged her into their house. "If I am not breeding, 'tis not your fault, I know. You have not stinted in performing your husbandly duty. As in all else, I am inferior—add barrenness to my other sins, Aaron! You have a son you cannot claim. Perhaps 'twould be best if I returned to Seville. Then Aliyah would doubtless give you Navaro, and you would be quit of your troublesome wife." She turned and walked to the window, fighting with every fiber of her being not to give way to the womanish weakness of tears.

"You cannot return to Seville," he said curtly. "The authorities have confiscated all your father's estates. The Holy Office might well decide to question your involvement with him. They could have you burned."

"Then you would be free," she said with a tear-clogged voice.

"Do not be foolish!" Aaron cursed himself for falling so under her spell. She was spoiled and perverse, stubborn in her refusal to be an ornament. Of course the fact that he once scorned her because he thought she was such did not enter his mind at the moment. All logic and reason fled as he took her in his arms and she turned to face him with tears glistening in her bright green eyes.

Muttering a particularly vile expletive, he took her face in his hand and tilted it up for a savage, hungry kiss. Her arms tightened about his shoulders as she returned it. They both tasted the salt of her tears in their mouths as they sank onto the raised bed beside the open window.

The dawn stillness was broken by screeching parrots, then the gentle rustling of the lush jungle vegetation as a long line of naked Tainos padded over the thick, soft carpet of damp leaves and moss, headed up a steep and twisting path. The men and women walked single file, moving sinuously as a snake, resolute in their purpose and unfaltering in their steps. Then their leader reached the end of the jungle's shelter.

A sharp promontory jutted out over a large lake, deep and silent as death. Its waters were black, overshadowed by the steep mountains that surrounded it, hiding it from the eyes of the white invaders.

Caonabo waited by the very edge of the straight drop-off as all his people filed onto the barren, rocky shelf high above the lake. One step farther and he would plunge to his death hundreds of feet below in the icy dark waters. Their medicine man said *zemis* with great power slept in the fathomless depths. It was wise never to disturb them . . . until now. Now everything was changed. Nothing the *zemis* might do would surpass the evils that the white men had already visited upon them. *Let the Old Ones awaken*, he thought. His obsidian eyes glowed in a wizened face, old as time itself. His body, in odd contrast, was yet lean and vigorous although he was well past his middle years.

The *cacique* waited until each person was standing in a semi-circle about him on the cliff's edge. Then he took the golden necklace with its heavy, flat, oblong medallion, the symbol of his royal office, and removed it. Lifting it high over his head, he let the dawning rays of the sun catch its radiant glow and reflect on all the faces assembled about him. Every eye was fixed on him.

"This is the god of our enemies!" Caonabo cried. "Gold!" He paused, looking at all his nobles, their wives and children, all richly arrayed with their best jewelry. "They seek this great god gold in every place they go. When they find him, there they remain. If he hides in the rocks or the earth, they discover him. If we swallow him, they rip open our bowels and drag him out."

A soft murmur rose from the assembly, like the keening of a *huracán* wind near its eye. They waited for Caonabo to speak again. His glittering eyes held them spellbound. "Let us cast him into the waters below for the *zemis* to hold as prisoner. When he is no longer with us, the white men will forget us." His face twisted by hate, Caonabo smiled a cold, lethal smile as he threw the priceless symbol of his office into the inky depths below. "Once disturbed, the *zemis* will remember the white men. Awaken them from their slumber!"

With that he began tearing off his armbands and nose plug, then the girdle at his waist, throwing them all into the lake. All the men and women in turn did likewise, removing every piece of gold jewelry and adornment from their persons and solemnly casting them into the black waters, which now seemed to come alive, rippling, rippling in ever widening circles. Just then the sun rose atop the peak directly across from the lake and everyone on the promontory was cast in blood-red light.

Chapter Nineteen

Magdalena stood in the plaza watching the long lines of the governor's army form into some semblance of order. It had been chaos when men, horses, and dogs began arriving at dawn. All the noblemen under Colon's command were mounted as befitted their status, outfitted in leather jerkins, knee pads, and boots that served admirably as armor against Taino darts, spears, and arrows. Their own arms were far more sophisticated and deadly—steel swords that could disembowel a man with a single stroke and long powerful lances with which a man riding full tilt could impale his target clean through from belly to backbone.

Most fearful of all were the dogs, large brown-and-black beasts, half as high as the horses with powerful jaws and long yellow teeth.

Infantrymen stood by cannons set on small carts hitched to strong horses, others held packs of the baying, slobbering hounds on tight chains, while the rest carried arbalests with short, deadly bolts that had a range of seventy yards, knives, and wildly inaccurate muskets whose noise upon discharge was of greater value in frightening the Indians than in killing them. A few drummer boys were set to lead the way when given the signal to move ahead.

Horses skittered, men swore, and dogs yelped as the governor, his *adelantado* and the commandant all mounted. Magdalena tried to catch Aaron's attention, but he was busily engaged in issuing orders to unruly young noblemen and surly infantrymen to form their lines. A hound took a swipe at his booted foot in the stirrup and he gave it a sharp cuff, then upbraided its holder to tighten his leash chain.

They had said their farewells, she supposed, last night after making love long and hungrily. "That is all we can do to truly communicate," she murmured, bereft. Aaron had bade her stay abed when he rose in the darkness to arm himself and leave. She had felt his warmth depart from beside her body at once and lay awake, not knowing what to say to him, afraid to confess her love and have it rejected, yet afraid, too, that he might be injured or killed in battle without peace being made between them.

Thus, after he left, she had dressed with clumsy, nervous fingers and rushed out into the dim morning light. The rain had finally stopped and the golden sun cast soft shadows across the narrow, cluttered streets as she picked her way through the mud and offal toward the plaza. But now Aaron was in the middle of a throng of rough soldiers bristling with arms, holding slavering, vicious dogs. She was too late. *Oh, please God, Blessed Mother, all the Saints, bring him safely back to me!*

As the governor gave the signal with a wave of his arm, the cavalcade began to move, headed inland to their rendezvous with Guacanagari and his warriors. While watching them depart, Magdalena did not notice the cool gray eyes of Lorenzo Guzman studying her assessingly. Then, feeling a prickle at the nape of her neck, she turned and met his stare. He was dressed in ridiculous courtiers' garb much as Hojeda had affected yesterday. In the wilting jungle heat, he looked sweaty and mean, not in the least courtly or dashing. She would have smiled at the ludicrousness of his appearance, but something about the man had always unsettled her, from the first time she had danced with him at the court in Valladolid. He was a dispicable lecher who made her skin crawl.

Yet there was something more, something about the arrogant fop that had been nagging at her ever since their meeting in Ysabel. His solicitude for her father's demise rang false in her ears, but all politicians were devious and hypocritical. He eyed her lustfully, but that, too, she had grown used to. No, Lorenzo Guzman was dangerous. She knew it. But she did not know exactly why.

With a shiver, she turned with Analu, her faithful escort, and headed to Dr. Chanca's hospital. While they were away, neither Aaron nor the Colons could prevent her from doing as her conscience urged her. As she walked, she considered the enmity between Aaron and Lorenzo. Although brothers-in-law, they had always disliked each other. Aaron had not approved of the match between his gentle sister and the worldly nephew of a duke. When Lorenzo proved faithless and uncaring to Ana, Aaron had vowed to punish him. She feared he still harbored such plans and only bided his time. Of course, now that the vengeance against Bernardo Valdés had been taken from his hands by Isaac, Aaron could turn full attention to Guzman upon his return from the interior. *If only he does return.*

Lorenzo Guzman watched Torres' beautiful redhead walk to the hospital. What passion there must be beneath that soft, loose-fitting under-tunic! How he would love to strip her silken curves free of all clothing. Was her skin sun-kissed all over, as it was on her face and hands? She had fire, as unlike the frigid little milksop he had married as a fleet Arabian was to a plowman's nag.

Taking her away from Torres would be sweet revenge, too. After all that had happened to his splendid plans to destroy the House of Torres and gain its wealth, he was cast out, virtually penniless in this ghastly jungle, while his old foe's son was in league with the Genoese trash who governed here. He had barely escaped being forced to risk life and health fighting a horde of savages with poisonous weapons! Only the plea that his horse had gone lame on the ocean crossing had saved him from being impressed on this expedition!

Tonight he would dine with the acting governor and his council. Young Diego Colon was a fool, better suited to a monastery than a governor's palace, even one in this backwater. That too would serve his ends. Diego was easily impressed and would be useful. Already he had prevailed on the infatuated young Colon to invite the lovely Doña Magdalena to join them for their evening meal. She had hated her father and that troubled him. Of course, if she abandoned life at court to follow a penniless *marrano* to this hell, she was no true daughter of Bernardo Valdés. Still, he wished to learn more about her. He had ever been good at wheedling secrets from ladies and felt certain that with enough time and her husband absent, he could win her over. Smiling, he sauntered off to rest, now that all his foes were gone from Ysabel. He would have Enrique, his body servant, hang out his best brocade doublet and fine woolen hose for the governor's banquet tonight.

After a long day feeding and attending sick men and women, Magdalena was in an ill humor indeed to bathe and dress for Diego Colon's foolish dinner. But he was acting governor, Cristobal and Bartolomé's beloved younger brother, and he was infatuated with her. Sighing, she stepped into her small wooden tub and lay back, letting the warm, fresh water soak away the stench of dysentery and death.

There had been so many Tainos in the hospital this day. They died of simple maladies that she and her countrymen were impervious to. If the curse of disease combined with the decimation of warfare, she could foresee a day when Española would have no Taino people left. Just as the Spains had no Jews left. . . . The water felt suddenly chill as she stepped out and began to dry herself.

The long banquet table in the audience chamber of the governor's palace had been set as lavishly as circumstances in Española allowed, with a simple linen tablecloth and pewter table service. Fat white candles of good quality lit the room as the gentlemen of the ruling council stood about with wine goblets in their hands, chatting amiably while Taino servants carried in trays laden with roasted pork and spicy mutton, fresh melons and other exotic fruits, as well as the ever present yams and large loaves of real white bread. A feast indeed for Ysabel! Nodding at Don Gonzolo and Don Bernal, Magdalena entered the room and immediately was set upon by Diego Colon, acting the solicitous host for his sole female guest. Taking her arm gallantly, his face wreathed in smiles, he escorted her across the room to the small group of gentlemen. Lorenzo Guzman stood with another man, one she had not yet met.

"Allow me to present Don Peralonso Guerra, formerly of the royal court, a dear friend of Don Lorenzo and his uncle the duke."

As Diego completed the introductions, Magdalena smiled and offered her hand to both Lorenzo and his minion. Peralonso was shorter than his friend, thickset with thinning tan hair, obviously an older hanger-on from the duke's entourage, banished to the Indies to watch over Medina-Sidonia's nephew. She fought the desire to flinch or wipe her hand on her skirts after they saluted her by kissing it.

"I cannot believe such beauty was present in Valladolid when last I was at court with Lorenzo here. Why did I not see you?" Peralonso asked with oily charm.

"The court was crowded. I seldom attended the royal functions. Such frivolities interest me little," Magdalena replied.

Diego chuckled disparagingly. "I fear the lovely lady is more interested in tending sick colonists, even Indians, than in dancing at balls."

"Yes, well since your husband has lived among the savages for so long, I suppose he wants you to aid them with the medical skills for which his family was famous," Lorenzo said.

"I studied briefly with Benjamin Torres before his death and it is my wish to use what small skill I possess to help Guacanagari's people, who are our allies against those in the interior," Magdalena retorted as smoothly as she could.

"I assume Don Diego Torres has not yet placed his approval on your activities?" Diego asked, knowing full well the whole story of her fight with Aaron about her hospital work.

She smiled serenely at him. "When a husband is away, he often finds his wife will do as she pleases." *Let this shallow boy try to stop me!*

By this time the other council members had clustered about them, and Magdalena was plied with wine and compliments on her gown, hair, even the color of her eyes. Somehow, when the seating was arranged for the meal, she found herself beside Lorenzo Guzman, much to her dismay. Of all the men present, old Gasparo Morales and the fat, jolly Nicolas de Palmas were the only two she could abide and they were at the far end of the table.

Everyone discussed the upcoming campaign against Caonabo and his allies. To Magdalena it seemed as if the men felt the Indians less than human, fit only to be butchered or enslaved. Recalling her own harsh condemnation of Guacanagari's people as savage, her cheeks burned with shame. "We are supposedly people of the Christian faith, sent by the crown not only to claim lands, but to save souls. Yet it seems that you," she directed her eyes for a telling moment to Lorenzo and the pompous Bernal, "see Tainos as beings without souls, whom we may exploit as if they were cattle. Is this not in conflict with what our Church teaches?"

Several councilmen squirmed uncomfortably, but Diego Colon, smiling indulgently as if treating with a dim-witted child, replied, "The Church wants us to baptize them, yes, but only if they will accept peaceful ways. Most of those in the interior are cannibals and as such, may be enslaved with the full sanction of the Holy See. But this is a bloody subject, unfit for the tender sensibilities of a lady," he added, patting her hand.

"Yes, let us do discuss something less unsettling," Lorenzo chimed in with a feral smile that did not touch his icy gray eyes.

For the duration of the meal they discussed the news from the royal court—dynastic marriage plans for Fernando and Ysabel's children, the ongoing maneuvering between Charles VIII of France and their clever Argonese king, even the settlement of the boundary dispute between the Majesties and João II of Portugal. By the terms of a treaty negotiated by the Pope, the Atlantic was cut in twain, north to south, and all lands of the Indies were divided between the two kingdoms.

"'Twould seem the Portuguese are doomed to failure. Our sovereigns' admiral has claimed all the islands of the Indies for them. What can lie in the middle of the south Atlantic but empty water?" Don Gasparo said with a chuckle.

318

"King João was given his chance to fund the enterprise by Admiral Colon. He foolishly missed his opportunity by declining. Perhaps the Lord works in ways none of us yet understands," Magdalena said with a smile. "Even the Genoese are favored by Him." She loved baiting the haughty Castilians such as Don Gonzolo and Don Bernal, both of whom detested the Colons. She strongly suspected Lorenzo shared their feelings. One look at the way he was glaring at the oblivious, beaming Diego Colon assured Magdalena that her judgment was correct. Again a prickle of apprehension made her shiver in spite of the humid night air.

Pleading a headache, which was not far from the truth, Magdalena decided to take a turn outside in the fresh air. Nicolas de Palmas strolled across the stone patio behind the palace with her for a few moments. Once they were outdoors, her mood lifted, as if escaping the cold eyes of Lorenzo Guzman made it easier to breathe. However, the very corpulent older man huffed and puffed as he kept pace with her in the sticky humidity. Like most Castilians, he insisted on wearing heavy clothing in the heat. As he tugged at the high gathered collar of the satin tunic beneath his velvet doublet, Magdalena took pity on him.

"Please, you are eager to rejoin the political discussion inside. I will retire upstairs and attend to my hair, which is quite wilted, then rejoin you and the other gentlemen in the audience chamber."

Gratefully, de Palmas waddled off, after being assured her headache was all but gone. Magdalena found a young servant girl who showed her to the room she had occupied when first she came to Ysabel. As she used the chamber pot and fussed with her hair, then bathed her hands and face with a cool cloth, she considered all that had happened to her in the past few months. Never would she return to Seville, but that no longer concerned her. "I would live in a Taino *bohio* for the rest of my life if only Aaron loved me," she whispered sadly. If only she could give him a son in place of the one he lost to Aliyah's spite.

Deep in thought, Magdalena did not rush back to the audience hall, but wandered through the shrubbery at the edge of the patio, delaying her return to the odious and boring party. She paused behind a clump of pink *poui* trees, deep in the shadows. Soft male voices murmured, the sound carrying across the courtyard with startling clarity. A sudden chill of premonition seized her as she strained to see who the two men were.

"You are right about the Torres woman. She is beautiful, but so razor-tongued that I would not want her in my bed. I can buy all the willing female flesh I desire back in Seville. When will your uncle send you the funds he has promised? God's balls, I am stranded here for no crime of my own! 'Tis you who was banished and must win your fortune here. I am for home—if you will give me what you owe."

"You will receive your payment. Only be patient. The duke's anger has cooled and he will soon send me funds."

Magdalena felt as if the breath had been squeezed from her. She struggled to overcome the same dizziness she had experienced outside Bernardo Valdés' study that day in Seville when the same man had spoken the same words in the same harsh Castilian lisp: *You will receive your payment. Only be patient.* Lorenzo Guzman was her father's co-conspirator!

Slowly, not daring to breathe, she moved farther into the darkness, watching each step lest she make a sound that might echo across the courtyard.

Diego Colon's face blanched with shock; then the patronizing courtliness she had always found so annoying asserted itself. He faced her across the round table where he broke his fast upon rising. The room was small and rather dark, well suited to the occasion, for no one could overhear their conversation although many might speculate about what had brought Doña Magdalena Valdés de Torres to visit the acting governor at such a scandalous hour.

"Surely you cannot expect me to give credence to such a wild accusation, my lady. You speak of treason here—the very crimes for which your poor father, may God forgive him, was executed."

Magdalena looked at the weak, vacillating young man across from her. He had none of Cristobal's visionary drive, nor Bartolomé's blunt decisiveness. Neither did he possess their gentle sense of humor or their tolerance. To Diego she was but a hysterical female, overwrought and frightened in the wilderness because her husband was away. She had rehearsed her speech to Diego carefully, knowing how difficult it would be to have him believe her, much less act on her charges. "Don Diego, my father stole from the crown and the Holy Office. He took much more than his Crossbearer's share from the wealth of my husband's house. He deserved to die. But he was only one man working in Seville to entrap Benjamin Torres. Being Benjamin's son-in-law, Lorenzo was the one with every opportunity to set servants spying on Ana—and only he had connections in Barcelona who could spy upon and betray Mateo and Rafaela. All the wealth of Rafaela Torres' family—a vast merchant fleet—was also confiscated when the family was taken. I overheard Lorenzo Guzman plot this with my father. If my father was guilty of treason, then so is Don Lorenzo! He must be held for royal justice."

Diego was torn between wanting to console the white-faced, desperate woman and wanting to shake her until her pretty white teeth loosened. By the staff of St. Peter, how could he silence her hysterical accusations?

"My dear, you say you overheard the conversation back in Seville—over two years ago. You never saw Don Lorenzo with your father. You met him at the court and here in Ysabel and did not recognize him. Now, after overhearing a conversation in the garden, you come to me and ask that I imprison the nephew of the Duke of Medina-Sidonia." He shrugged helplessly, then extended his hand across the table and took her white clenched fists and patted them. "You must miss your husband. Er . . ." His face reddened and he hesitated, then worked up his courage and asked, "Might you be with child? Often in women this causes them to imagine all sorts of—"

"I am neither with child nor imagining anything!" Magdalena stood up, fury boiling through her veins. "I realize to whom the exalted Don Lorenzo is related and the power of that ducal house. Doubtless 'twas the reason he was exiled here rather than sent to the dungeons beneath St. Paul's Convent as Benjamin Torres and his family—and Bernardo Valdés—were. But he *is* guilty and I will see justice done."

With that she turned to leave. Diego Colon's face mottled even ruddier than his fair complexion usually allowed. He stood up, both fright and anger evident in his voice as he called after her, "So, you think to wait until my high and mighty brothers return, conquering heroes who will believe your absurd tales! I rather think, having spent years about royal courts across Europe, they will be a bit more cautious than to imprison a duke's nephew on the word of the woman whose own father and husband's family have been burned for crimes against Church and Crown."

Magdalena did not even pause to bid the jealous idiot good-day. What a fool she had been to come to him with the tale. He was so impressed with nobility that he was blind to all else—and he was bitterly envious of his elder brothers. "I will have to wait until Aaron and the

Colons return," she whispered to herself with a shudder, wondering how she could avoid any accidental meetings with Lorenzo Guzman in the following days. Magdalena knew that if she looked into that cruel, haughty face with its cold gray eyes, she would surely give away her loathing and terror. *Small wonder I was so apprehensive when first we met!*

Don Lorenzo nodded at the guard leaning in a slouched position in front of the governor's palace. The Castilian straightened a bit in deference to his rank. *Crude colonial rabble.* How he hated being consigned to abide among such! A caravel had arrived that morning. Perhaps there was word from his uncle that he could return to Castile, or at least some funds to pacify Peralonso. He walked down the long, cool hallway of the palace as if it were his own residence, then turned into the audience chamber. Diego Colon was hearing several complaints from local farmers and tradespeople, even a handful of Indians. Upon seeing the nobleman, the acting governor at once stood up and motioned for all those waiting on his judgment to take seats. He strode across the hall to the duke's nephew, a nervous smile in place.

"Good day, Don Lorenzo. Please, this is no place for a gentleman. These poor folk can wait while we have a draught of wine. I have just received the mail from home and your uncle sends a letter to you."

"I had hoped he would do so," Guzman said in delight as they strolled across the hall into the Colons' private quarters. Diego summoned a Taino servant and instructed him to bring fruit and wine to the library.

"Please forgive the clutter. My eldest brother's charts and navigational instruments are his life's work. No one is to disturb them. The servants regard him as if he were a god." Diego motioned for Lorenzo to take a seat on a high-backed mahogany chair of crude but sturdy workmanship.

Lorenzo smiled thinly. "Ah, yes, they call him the man from heaven, do they not?"

Diego flushed. "Precisely so."

As the servant brought the food and wine and then departed, Lorenzo noted the apparent nervousness of Colon. Something was amiss, but what? He took a sip of the foul warm wine and eyed the oddly colored tropical fruit lying in neat slices on the plate. He did not even know what half the foods he consumed in Española were! "I believe you said my uncle posted me a message?" he prompted.

Colon began to dig through the large leather pouch in one corner of the room. After a moment's search, he extracted a rolled missive with the wax seal of the House of Medina-Sidonia on it. Handing it to Guzman, he cleared his throat and said, "There is a matter, Don Lorenzo, that I fear you should be apprised of . . ." He floundered to a halt.

Guzman, about to take his coveted missive from Castile and depart, looked up warily at the inept acting governor. His brows rose in irritation and impatience. "Yes?"

"Doña Magdalena came to me early this morning with an absurd and fanciful tale. A young woman of noble blood, suffering the ill effects of a long sea voyage to this alien land, and then the shock of family disgrace and the death of her father—well, I am certain you will be tolerant of her sad outburst."

By this time, Guzman's face had turned the color of ash and his hand crumpled the wax seal on the letter. "What did she say?" His voice was cold, precise, brittle with terror.

Colon, too absorbed in his own discomfiture to notice Guzman's reaction, continued fluttering his hands across the papers on Cristobal's desk. "Well, she thinks you to be the man who aided her father in his activities against your father-in-law, Benjamin Torres, and his family. I know it is ridiculous. She admits she had never seen you until she was at court in Valladolid last spring.

"Then why did she accuse me of such a heinous crime?" Lorenzo's voice was strained with fear and fury.

"It seems she overheard her father and another man speaking of betraying the Torres family to the Inquisition. 'Twas over two years ago, at her country estate outside Seville," Diego said apologetically.

Lorenzo forced a laugh. "As you most certainly know, the charge is absurd. I have met Don Bernardo and his wife at court, even in Seville many years earlier when I was but a green boy. As to ever visiting their country estate . . ." He shrugged in perplexity. Then, leaning forward, he affixed Diego with his most chilling stare and said, "I do assume you will attempt everything in your power to keep this horrendous gossip from spreading through Ysabel."

"Of course, Don Lorenzo. I sent her home with stern admonitions to keep quiet about this. As soon as her husband and her champion Bartolomé return, I am certain they will take her in hand and calm her fanciful imagination. I myself will look in on her every evening when she returns from the hospital. She is best kept busy nursing feverish colonists and Indians who speak no Castilian, eh?"

As he arose, Lorenzo nodded in agreement, then asked casually, "Those caravels in the harbor, are any for Castile in the next days? My old friend Don Peralonso wishes to return to his patron, the duke."

"The *Galiante* should be departing within a week, as soon as she is outfitted, but sometimes there are delays —careening to scrape the hull, reprovisioning, the usual matters—that and finding able-bodied seamen enough to man her. So many fall ill in this pestilential climate."

Lorenzo nodded, attempting to maintain his facade of

calm in front of the Genoese fool. "I shall send to learn from the *Galiente's* master when she will be ready."

Guzman forced himself to walk calmly from the stone palace to where his horse was being held by a groom. He mounted and rode to the wretched cane and thatch hovel that passed for his residence in Ysabel. Once inside, he unrolled the letter with trembling hands and read its contents, then crumpled it with a curse and threw it across the rough-planked floor.

"I assume that means I must be patient yet a while longer," Peralonso said from the doorway, one brow arched in disgust. "I heard the latest ship from Cadiz had just come in this morning."

"We are in grave trouble, Peralonso. My uncle sends not one *maravedi*. We are to remain in exile and make our own fortunes. Hah! 'Tis but his way of assuring that we never return!"

"We? You speak as if I had aught to do with your banishment," Guerra said tightly. "I have only been an adventurer seeking gold in this supposed land of glittering wealth. What an ill-conceived jest the Colons have perpetrated upon crafty old Fernando!"

"Forget the king, forget your supposed innocence! If I stand accused of killing his father, Diego Torres will slit your gullet as swiftly as he does mine."

Guerra sat down on a small stool and looked up at the sweating, trembling younger man. "You had best explain."

When Guzman finished the tale of Magdalena's discovery, he looked at the ashen Peralonso Guerra.

"Torres is dangerous and high in favor with the governor. When they return, you will be fed to the hounds—if you are fortunate enough not to be returned to the gentle mercies of Torquemada!" Guerra rasped.

"And you with me. As my uncle's retainer and my

companion, think you that you may escape my fate? We are in this together, Peralonso."

"We are trapped here. What can we do? The girl—if we kill her before Torres returns . . ." Guerra's eyes lit up as he looked at Guzman.

"Simply doing away with her will serve naught. She has babbled all to that young fool Colon. If she is killed, he will sooner or later blunder into confessing her story to his brothers."

"What are we to do? Flee into the jungles and live as the savages do?"

Guzman began to stroke his goatee as he paced, a slow ruthless smile now hardening across his face. "These past weeks here in Ysabel, I have reacquainted myself with a boyhood companion from Seville, Alonso Hojeda."

"He has gone with the Colons to fight savages, which from what I have heard of him, is his most favored sport," Guerra said in disgust.

"No, there you are mistaken. His most favored sport is getting rich. He only remains with the admiral until he learns where the gold, silver, pearls—whatever the Indies may in time give up—are located. Then he will outfit his own ships with backing from Medina-Celi. He was forced into fighting here to maintain his honor, but he has ever been busy learning which way blow the winds of chance. He has put me in contact with another soldier and gold seeker, one Francisco Roldan."

Now Guerra's eyes narrowed in calculation. "The one in the south who rules independent of the Colons?"

"The same. Also the one who seized two caravels off the coast of Xaragua. He may be our means of escape from Española—and, perhaps our means of securing our fortunes, too. It is said he lives far better in the south than do the miserable wretches here in Ysabel."

"I have heard rumors about gold aplenty to the

south. . . ." Peralonso replied, then added, "but I still believe we should kill Torres' woman lest she slander us one day back at court."

Lorenzo's eyes were cold as the storm-tossed North Atlantic when he said flatly, "No. I will not kill the bitch. At least not yet. Ever since I saw her at court I have fancied her. You will go to a man named Jesús María who is in service to Hojeda. He speaks the Taino language and will secure us Indian guides so we may reach Xaragua and Roldan. I will take care of Doña Magdalena."

When she bade Dr. Chanca good evening and began her walk home, Magdalena was so weary she could scarce place one foot before the other. After a week working at the hospital, her already battered spirits were cast down even more. Three colonists and a Taino baby had died that day, the men of the flux, but the baby of simple measles. The child's mother and whole family were ill as well. Some of them had left Ysabel, desperately ill, to try and reach Guacanagari's village. If they succeeded, it would mean more death, for those with the disease seemed somehow to carry it with them to others. She shuddered to think of the decimation that could result. The sick Tainos should be stopped, but she knew going to Diego Colon would be useless. With so many of the able-bodied men off in the interior, he would never consent to send anyone to his brother's allies, even with a warning.

"Perhaps I can go myself. I think I know the way. If only I can convince Analu to go with me," she murmured to herself as she turned toward her house. The faithful servant had gone ahead to tell the serving girl to prepare a meal. Now that she worked each day at the hospital, she was beginning to be accorded genuine respect by the colonists. In truth, so many lay ill, there were few strong enough to molest her.

As the twilight deepened, she walked between two deserted huts whose former occupants were with the army in the interior. Suddenly a pair of strong arms seized her and a gloved hand clamped brutally over her mouth.

"Now, my little russet-haired bitch, let us see how you can spin tales for me!" Lorenzo Guzman's purring voice was the last thing she heard before she felt a crashing blow to her head and everything went black.

Chapter Twenty

"We are to meet Guacanagari and his warriors at th[e] ridge overlooking the interior plains," Aaron informe[d] Cristobal and Bartolomé as he reined in his mou[nt] beside them. He had just returned from a conferenc[e] with Caonu.

"Is that not too near the hostile *caciques*?" Bartolom[é] asked with a worried frown.

Aaron shook his head, combing wet gold hair bac[k] from his forehead. He was drenched with sweat in th[e] hot leather armor. "Once this conflict is finished, I vo[w] never to don more than a linen shirt again, should I li[ve] to be ninety! Caonabo is massing his forces at th[e] southern end of the valley. Guacanagari's spies hav[e] brought word of this. It will be another day before a[n]other rebel *cacique* arrives.

"Then if we dispose of Caonabo first, all the better[,"] Cristobal said, adjusting his seat on his skittering hors[e.] "I am most eager to see this battle done."

Bartolomé laughed. "You are eager to set foot on a ship's deck once more and leave behind all land-locked strife for the thrill of discovery."

"Nonetheless, the governor is right," Aaron agreed. If we defeat Caonabo quickly, it may well deter his allies. Even Behechio from Xaragua has considered an alliance with his rebellious fellow *caciques* against Guacanagari and us."

"Does not that rascal Roldan have a sizeable following of insurrectionists in Xaragua?" Bartolomé asked.

A worried look crossed Aaron's face as he ducked beneath a low-hanging limb on the narrowing trail. "Roldan has the loyalty of some of the Taino villages on the peninsula. Since those two caravels of men from Castile mutinied and joined forces with him, he can certainly challenge the *cacique*."

"Perhaps they will kill each other and save us further trouble," Bartolomé said sourly.

Thinking of Aliyah and Navaro, now on their way to Xaragua where she was to wed Behechio, Aaron was frankly troubled but kept his own council about his former mistress and his son. For now the fighting would be on the broad, fertile valley spreading below them. He prayed that Behechio would not be so foolish as to join the fight against his new brother-in-law, Guacanagari. Once he had done his duty by serving the governor, Aaron would consider what to do about Navaro.

"How soon will Guacanagari's men arrive?" Cristobal asked.

Aaron scanned the heavily forested mountain that fringed the northern perimeter of the plain. "They are already here. As soon as all our men with their horses and dogs descend to the valley floor, our Taino allies will show themselves—but only at a distance. You know how they fear large animals."

"Cowardly curs, they are no better than dogs them-

selves," Hojeda said as he pulled abreast of the Color
and Torres.

The governor's glacial blue eyes pierced Alonz
Hojeda in rebuke. "Guacanagari is our friend. Withou
him and his people we would never have survived th
shipwreck. He is brave and steadfast. I will have n
slander made against him."

Aaron looked at the arrogant little Castilian with ope
contempt. "Have you ever been trapped in a *huraca*
with naught but a wooden paddle and a dugout? Th
Tainos traverse thousands of miles across these island
facing storms so incredible they would send even th
Portuguese fleeing for dry land."

Hojeda returned Torres' hostility, saying, "I will n
turn my back on those savages who profess to be ou
allies any more than I will on those who are openly ou
enemies."

"Just so you use your bolts and your blade against th
warriors of Caonabo," Cristobal said with a decide
chill in his voice. "Come, let us lead our men to th
ground below. We will await Guacanagari's men there
With that he raised his arm and Bartolomé called ou
for all the soldiers to follow.

Aaron spent the rest of the afternoon moving betwee
the two armed camps of mutually suspicious allie
deciding on strategies for the deployment
Guacanagari's foot soldiers with their spears and dar
and on positioning the much more heavily arme
Castilians with their cannons, arbalests, and sword
The dogs worried him the most. Even if he could kee
the undisciplined soldiers' attention on shooting
Caonabo's men, how could they keep those accurse
hounds from turning on their Taino allies?. The dog
had been trained to kill Indians, any Indians, in th
most brutal and vicious ways. The best use
Guacanagari's men was to send them into the jung
that edged the plain and have them report on Caonabo

moves, then watch for the arrival of his allies from the interior, and possibly even Behechio. Yet if he did so, Guacanagari would feel his warrior's honor had been slighted. Finally Aaron came up with a plan.

When he approached Guacanagari and his men, standing in a small clearing half way up the steep valley wall, he asked the *cacique* and his brother Caonu to walk away from the others. The three men conversed in the Taino language, drawing diagrams in the muddy black soil with sharp sticks as they agreed upon troop movements.

"You must send twenty of your best men to the south to watch the trails leading into the valley. Here, here . . ." Aaron marked all the possible places from which Behechio might come.

Guacanagari's face was grave. "My heart is heavy that the husband of my sister would spill the blood of his own family. But you are right. We must guard against the chance that he may surprise us and join the others."

"It is a long way from Xaragua. Perhaps he will not come," Aaron said hopefully.

Guacanagari shrugged fatalistically. "What will be, will be. One of the admiral's soldiers, Roldan, makes war on Behechio. If Caonabo can win a great victory here, Behechio hopes to have his newly triumphant allies come to his aid in Xaragua."

Aaron shook his head at the senseless warfare. Before the white men came, the Taino *caciques* lived mostly in peace, occasionally feuding among themselves but more often joining together to repel Caribe attackers. Now this would be a blood bath with these simple people killing one another. *What our crossbows and wounds do not destroy, our diseases will,* he thought sadly.

"Where will the rest of my warriors stand and fight?" Guacanagari asked with a shrewdness belied by his youthful face.

Shirl Henke

Putting his misgivings aside, Aaron laid out his idea. "The admiral wishes for your warriors to sweep down from here when Caonabo attacks." He drew another diagram in the mud, showing a simple flanking maneuver from the east. He planned to position all the men with dogs on the west flank.

Guacanagari nodded. "We will charge when you give the signal."

Aaron prayed the battle would end quickly before the slaughter got out of hand and Guacanagari's people were as much at risk as Caonabo's.

That evening, with sentries posted, Aaron, Cristobal, Bartolomé and several other of the officers sat about a smouldering campfire. The air was oppressively heavy with humidity and a pall hung over the rich agricultural valley. To the south, east, and west of them, the beautifully cultivated fields of the Vega were spread like an intricately woven design in a Moorish carpet. Irrigation ditches brought water from the mountains to the lush black soil, which grew manioc, beans, yams, and maize.

"'Tis a shame to destroy these fields with a battle," Cristobal said.

"Aye, Ysabel could use the foodstuffs," Bartolomé agreed.

"So could the Tainos who planted them," Aaron said softly. "For the sake of all our bellies, let us attempt to keep the pillage at a minimum." Aaron's eyes locked with Alonso Hojeda's meaningfully.

"I do but wish to capture that old fox Caonabo. What a trophy to bring before the Majesties at court!" the little man said boldly.

Bartolomé laughed mirthlessly. "If you can bring that one down alive, you have my leave to sail across the Atlantic with him and welcome!"

Cristobal and Aaron exchanged uneasy looks. They knew how unfavorable had been the reports from the

334

royal court since Margarite and Buil had returned to slander the Colons' rule on Española. What would Hojeda say about the Genoese if he arrived at court with the leader of a Taino rebellion in chains?

"Do not think it that simple a matter to capture Caonabo. He is as wily a survivor as are you, Alonso," Aaron said with deceptive geniality.

"Then we will be well met," Hojeda replied.

"Mayhap you will kill each other," Bartolomé interjected with no hint of regret in his voice.

"We all need rest for the morrow," Cristobal said, soothing frayed tempers with his calm authority. "Let us to bed, gentlemen."

Aaron lay awake as the camp quieted, staring at the rising moon which hung low in the sky, obscured by a reddish cloud. Blood on the moon was an ill omen the night before a battle. Finally, sleep claimed him.

Roldan looked at the disheveled men and their captive, amazed that they had successfully crossed the whole of Española and found his stronghold in the mountains of Xaragua, even with Hojeda's Indian slave guiding them. "Take the woman and give her to my wives," he said in Taino to two of the Indians standing beside him.

When they approached Magdalena, Guzman protested. "She is mine, Don Francisco."

Roldan shook his head in mock reproof. "In truth, she belongs to Diego Torres, but that is neither here nor there. I have no desire for the lady. My wives will bathe and feed her. She looks sore abused and exhausted."

Magdalena struggled to stand up straight, meeting the brigand's dark brown eyes steadily. His expression was unreadable, but he and Aaron had once been friends. Perhaps he might help her against Guzman. Unable to suppress her resentment at being discussed as if she were a child or an imbecile, she said hotly, "I am most grateful for the hospitality, Don Francisco. After I rid myself of a week's trail mire, I would much appreciate it if you would rid me of the mire of these vermin." She shoved her tangled filthy hair over her shoulder and glared at Lorenzo and Peralonso.

Roldan threw back his big shaggy head and laughed. "Torres certainly has a handful with you. Perhaps these *vermin* did him a favor by spiriting such a shrewish wench away."

"My husband will follow them here and flay them alive, even as the Moors did their captives in the wars!" *If only I believed he cared enough for me to do it.*

When Lorenzo moved closer and raised his hand to strike her, the big renegade stepped down from the wooden platform on which he had been standing. He was of a height with Guzman, but far heavier. "I would not do that if I were you," he said very softly. Then he motioned to the two Taino servants, who escorted Magdalena toward a *bohio*. She could hear Roldan saying, "Hojeda speaks well of you, Don Lorenzo, but I mislike your kidnapping Torres' wife. She will bring trouble. Why did you do it?"

After that she lost the thread of their conversation as she was ushered into a large cane house across the way. Muddy, mosquito-bitten, and exhausted, she felt ready to collapse, but pride held her body erect as three curious Taino women inspected their captive. One older woman rapidly exchanged a few words in their language with the men, then shooed them out and clapped her hands; issuing terse orders. From her knowledge of Taino speech, Magdalena understood that Roldan was a man of his word—at least as far as the bath went.

As she soaked in the cooling water of the small stream, two of Roldan's women used the sudsy soap plant to lather her hair and skin, chattering and marveling about the colors of both. Magdalena closed her eyes, recalling the horrors of their breakneck ride through the jungle. She had been tied to a horse while they rode and trussed up like a roasting fowl each night while they slept on the damp earth. Praise to the Blessed Mother, they had not raped her! Lorenzo and Peralonso had argued over her the first night, and finally Lorenzo had decided no one would use her until they were safely in Roldan's stronghold. Each, fearing the other might kill him while he took her, abided by the decision.

What will happen to me now in this deadly wilderness? Magdalena squeezed back the tears, realizing that she must survive by her wits. When the menace from Caonabo was past, would Aaron search for her? He would have no idea where Lorenzo had taken her, unless she could convince Roldan to send him word. She was at the mercy of a soldier in rebellion against the governor and a courtier guilty of treason against the crown—and she knew not if her husband would rescue her from either of them.

The two young women who bathed her helped her dress in a soft length of cotton cloth dyed a pale shade of orange that complemented her dark russet hair. She twisted the cloth this way and that, until she was as decently covered as was possible, with the ankle-length gown draped over one shoulder, baring the other. The servants untangled her hair with a fish-bone comb and helped her fasten the makeshift cloth wrap with several bone pins. Then they offered her a beautifully wrought necklace of sea shells and two splendid gold arm bands.

With so much of her skin bared and her hair flowing loosely down her back, she looked like an exotic Indian princess. She was to dine with her "host," Francisco Roldan, and her loathsome abductors. As she was escorted across the village, Magdalena studied Roldan's fortress, estimating that nearly one thousand souls lived within its walls. It was made of heavy cane frames and thatch, which was soaked nightly with water to protect it from any attacker who might try to burn it. The people were of the same Taino stock as those in Guacanagari's village, along with a liberal sprinkling of Castilians who had muntinied and sailed their ships into Roldan's empire rather than submit to the Colon family's authority in Ysabel.

"Even if I could get out of this stockade, I would need a horse. If I found the horses and could steal one, which way back to Ysabel?" she murmured beneath her breath. Then her guards motioned for her to enter Roldan's *bohio*.

When she adjusted her eyes to the dim torchlight, Magdalena's heart leaped into her throat. There, stretched sinuously as a cat on a pallet by the low banquet table, was Aliyah. The raven-haired beauty inspected her rival with hate gleaming in her ebony eyes.

The carnage was even worse than the noise, and the din of the battle was causing his head to throb. All around Aaron cannons belched forth flames and gouged great ragged holes in the muddy black earth. The screams of the maimed and dying blended with the feral growls and high yiping barks of the huge hounds that gave chase to the haplessly retreating Tainos. He tried to stop the butchery of the surrendering Indians, but for each one he could reach, others were caught by the Spanish hell-hounds. Dogs brought them down and devoured their naked flesh as they lay steeped in their own gore.

The mounted Castilians slashed their way through a living wall of Indians. As the Tainos fell, the sharp hooves of the big horses trampled the vanquished beneath their feet. At first as he directed the charge of each group—cavalry, infantry, the firing of the cannoneers, Aaron had prayed Caonabo would call retreat, but he did not. Poisonous darts and a few half-spent arrows whizzed by him as he led his soldiers, keeping a wall of the most disciplined men between Guacanagari's warriors and the Castilian's dogs.

This was not a battle but a slaughter, the likes of which he had never witnessed in two years of warfare on the plains of Andalusia. The Moors were as well versed in the arts of death as the Castilians. But the attacking Tainos were not and would not yield. They threw wall after wall of warriors across the flat, open fields into the jaws of death. Only a handful could even get close enough to make effective use of their spears.

Guacanagari's men were engaged at the east side of the plain with a large host of Caonabo's men. These warriors closed on one another with spears and clubs, fighting fiercely, almost evenly matched. Aaron scanned the chaos, looking for his tall young friend. He wanted to join the fray, but feared that if he deserted his post, the soldiers would loose their hounds on all the Tainos, friend and foe alike. He held his position, trying desperately to get the attention of Bartolomé who, sword in hand, was in the thick of the fight.

The governor, crippled and barely able to sit his horse, watched from the high ground at the rear, issuing calm orders now and again, but far less in command on land than on sea. *If this were a huracan, Cristobal, you would be right at home and damn the danger.*

A flash of steel caught Aaron's eye as Hojeda swung his big sword and beheaded a fleeing Taino, then turned his horse east toward the battle between the two Indian forces. Aaron gave pursuit, cutting the little soldier off just as he reached the retreating forces of Caonabo. His big bay shouldered Hojeda's smaller brown gelding as Aaron yelled over the din, "Return to your men. You cannot distinguish Guacanagari's men from Caonabo's!"

"I *distinguish* the old bastard himself—there!" Hojeda cried, pointing to an older man issuing commands. "We have met on several occasions." Pulling his horse away from Aaron's, Hojeda dug wickedly sharp rowels into the poor beast's side and bolted after Caonabo, who was finally retreating, surrounded by a small group of special warrior guards.

Seeing that Hojeda was indeed in pursuit of appropriate quarry, Aaron turned to what remained of the old man's forces. The roar of cannons had ceased, the hiss of arbalest bolts grew silent. Only feral cries of jubilation by Castilians dispatching dying Tainos and the frantic barking of the hounds continued—that and the moans and anguished pleadings of the vanquished.

Aaron stood guard with a small core of hand-picked men between Guacanagari's now victorious forces and the rest of the colonial soldiers. When one hound, dragging his blood-soaked chain, loped past him headed toward the friendly Tainos, Aaron cleanly sliced off its head with one powerful blow.

Cristobal Colon, Admiral of the Ocean Sea, Governor of Española, looked down on the grisly scene unfolded before him and felt as old and weary as time. "This is not Cathay, yet it was a place of peace and beauty, a paradise of innocents untouched by greed and hate. Now look what we have wrought," he whispered brokenly.

"They will never rise against a Castilian again, Excellency," one of the captains said to him.

Aaron rode up the hill and reined in beside his leader, sensing the same desolation in Colon that he felt. "No, the organized rebellion of *caciques* is crushed. Those we have not killed on the field of battle will fall more slowly to starvation and our diseases."

"What would you have me do, Diego? Let Caonabo and the others have Española? Pack up all our settlers and sail away?" He looked out across the plain, his eyes dulled in misery.

Aaron sighed. "No, Cristobal. You are not to blame. And if we had not opposed Caonabo and his allies, they

would have attacked Guacanagari's village and killed
every Taino in Marien, then massed to attack us."

"They were so childlike in their generosity and trust
before we came among them," Cristobal said softly.

"We cannot restore what is lost, but we can try to
prevent the spread of what caused this loss of innocence," Aaron replied. "We must work with the *caciques* to keep order and protect their people from
being enslaved by colonists who force them to search
for gold."

"Easier said than done, Torres," Bartolomé said as he
rode up. "As an outsider yourself, you see how well we
Genoese Colons are obeyed by the Castilians. Already
we have word from the royal council itself that letters of
commission have been granted to others—Castilians—
to explore the waters of the Indies. Fernando wants his
tribute. If we send nothing back, we will be replaced."

Knowing the truth of court politics, Aaron looked at
Cristobal and asked, "What will you do?"

The explorer looked off into the distance, as if seeing
beyond the mountains to alien lands far away. Then,
dragging himself back to the ugly scene about them, he
said in a weary voice, "First we will send the king and
queen what tribute we can—the hostile captives from
the interior to be sold in Seville as slaves, then what
precious little gold we have at hand and other goods,
cotton cloth, herbs and spices . . ." His voice trailed off.

"You must return to the Majesties' court and plead for
loyal soldiers who will follow your orders. Stop the lies
of Margarite and Buil and the others who are poisoning
the royal ear," Bartolomé said with fervor.

Aaron looked about him. Would some Castilian or
Argonese bureaucrat be any worse in dealing with the
Tainos? In settling disputes between the greedy colo-
nists? He honestly was not certain any longer. Still,
Cristóbal and Bartolomé were known quantities. Some

faceless nobleman might be infinitely worse. "Perhaps you might convince the king and queen to send more honest settlers and recall all the useless gold-hungry nobles who refuse to act peacefully."

The elder Colon studied Aaron's face intently, as if knowing his friend's doubts and fears. Some of his old resolution returned as he finally replied, "It will take a good while to ready the ships and set things in order in Ysabel, but then I will sail to Castile."

"Readying ships will prove far easier than setting things in order back in Ysabel," Bartolomé said sourly.

Cristóbal looked from his brother to his commandant. "You are the two men I most trust in all the Indies. You must keep a close watch on Alonso Hojeda lest he decide to strike out again gold hunting in the interior."

"Or strike out to ally with your old friend Roldan," Bartolomé added, with a meaningful stare at Aaron.

Aaron sighed. "Francisco has ever been a trial to me. I do not expect him to heed Hojeda's vanity and march an army from Xaragua to Ysabel, but I know that as long as Roldan defies your authority, it looks ill to the powers at court. Perhaps I can convince him to make peace. After we return to the settlement I will send word to him and see which way the wind blows in distant Xaragua."

Bartolomé clapped Aaron on the back while Cristóbal smiled quietly and said, "I trust your diplomacy, Diego."

Hojeda, true to his word, brought Caonabo back, tied to a horse. He paraded the haughty old *cacique* before the camp the night after the battle, saying he would sail with the slaves and personally present the old chief to the queen. Mayhap her old confessor, Torquemada, could save his soul.

Aaron bid Cristobal and Bartolomé farewell at dawn the next day, explaining that he would return to Ysabel after accompanying Guacanagari and his warriors back to their village. They, too, had a sizeable party of slaves from among the vanquished. Yet in a Taino village, even enemy captives would fare better than among whites. Aaron had not the heart to watch the defeated Tainos being herded onto the pitching deck of caravels and sent to their doom in cold northern climes.

"Your heart is troubled," Guacanagari said to Aaron as they walked along the narrow, tortuous path, their men following behind at a discreet distance. "Aliyah has gone to Behechio to wed. She will not be in the village."

Not wishing to discuss Aliyah any more than he wished to discuss the complex issue of slavery, Aaron brought up another concern of his. "I will miss Navaro," he said with regret.

"Perhaps when she carries Behechio's child, she will agree to give over yours," Guacanagari said very carefully. "Your wife would welcome Navaro into your home, I think."

Aaron's eyes fastened on his friend. In spite of Guacanagari's dusky complexion, Aaron detected a blush. "Magdalena's jealousy sparked the fight that led to my losing the boy. What do you know of her feelings for Navaro?"

Guacanagari said nothing for a moment, neither slowing his step, nor looking at Aaron. He appeared to ponder, then said, "Aliyah taunted your wife most cruelly, my friend. She, too, was jealous, boasting of how she had your son and your skinny pale wife was barren and useless. That was why Magdalena attacked her. I only found this out when my sister left for her marriage. I overheard her telling one of her cousins what she said to Magdalena in your tongue that day." He let Aaron digest this; then after they walked a little farther, he asked, "Have you ever considered why your wife is jealous? If I mistake it not, she is even more jealous than Aliyah."

Familiar irritating feelings of guilt washed over Aaron once again. And again his wife was the cause. "I cannot explain it, but ever since we were children in our homeland far across the ocean, she has pursued me. She entranced my father into pledging me to a marriage with her." He smiled ruefully at Guacanagari. "That is the first time I have ever admitted the truth of her claim on me. She had my father's ring, but I denied what it meant. I think even then I knew what he had done, but I was too bitter and proud to admit it—too filled with hate for *her* father. But that is all over now. Bernardo Valdés is dead, and the House of Torres is avenged. Magdalena is alone, thousands of miles from home, wed to a man who has not used her at all kindly."

"She has pursued you so far, for so long. Does it not mean she loves you?" Guacanagari prompted.

"Yes, I suppose it does," Aaron admitted. "Perhaps her family, the past, the whole world back there no longer matter."

"Do you love her?"

The words hung suspended between them as the jungle noises seemed suddenly magnified. Parrots fluttered and screeched, small animals made light brushing noises beneath the dense foliage and the low murmur of a stream running down the mountainside seemed to call out to him. *Do you love her?*

Aaron finally spoke. "She bewitches me, like one of your *zemi* goddesses. I desire her, I feel alive when I am with her, whether we make love or whether we argue . . . is that love, Guacanagari?"

The young *cacique* shrugged in puzzlement. "For the men from the sky, perhaps it is. I do not know, for your ways are not our ways. What to us is simple, you make difficult. We plant enough food to eat. You must store it in great wooden bins. We fight only if someone offends our family's honor. You fight for gold and land. Every Taino family offers prayers to their family *zemis* and is blessed. No one tells them to pray otherwise. You have many gods and all of them seem angry with one another, each demanding that you worship only him

and stop other white men from praying to their god."
He stopped walking and gave a signal for the warriors
behind them to sit and rest. Then he strolled to the
banks of the stream, which had now wended its way
nearer the trail.

Aaron followed him and the two men sat apart from
the others. "You are right. We do make life very difficult
at times. Perhaps that is why I have enjoyed the time I
spent learning your ways so much."

"Yet you remain a white man. Your heart is not
among us," Guacanagari said gently.

"My heart is not truly among the white people here,
either," Aaron replied. "I belong nowhere, neither here
nor in Ysabel, certainly not in the land of my birth. My
uncle and what remains of my family are in a cold and
distant country. I would not live in France either."

"Would you live with your wife? Is Magdalena not the
one to make you a home?"

Aaron remembered how it had felt, both in
Guacanagari's village and in Ysabel, when he entered
their simple dwellings and saw her russet head bent
over simple household tasks, or how she would open
her arms to him when he claimed her in bed at
night . . . the nights, filled with passion . . . and with
love. Suddenly he felt the need to see her face once
again. Did he love Magdalena?

Guacanagari read Aaron's expression for a while,
then said, "I promised her I would not speak of this
thing . . . but now I am going to assert my royal right to
change my mind, for you are both like children stumbling in the darkness. Perhaps I possess a small torch to
light your way to each other. Before Magdalena left our
village with you, she came to call on me, very early in
the morning . . ."

When Guacanagari had finished telling the tale of the
brown velvet cloak and Magdalena's desperate attempt
to regain Navaro for his father, he looked at his friend.

Shirl Henke

A small, wistful smile touched Aaron's lips. "So, that is what truly became of her finest court gown. She would love Navaro as her own. Now I know that. Like me, my wife has learned much from the Taino people. We are both grateful."

"Good," Guacanagari said with a grunt as he rose and motioned for the entourage to follow him. "Then let us make haste so you may return to your wife and tell her that you have been a very big fool."

Chapter Twenty-One

On his long trek back to Ysabel, Aaron had much time
to ponder what he would say to Magdalena. Out of
deference to the Tainos, he had left his mount with the
Colons, who would return it to the settlement. He ran
along the rough, twisting pathways, now so familiar to
him, observing afoot all the splendors of this paradise
that were so often trampled by men on horseback. The
warm, fecund smell of the rain-washed earth, its lush
emerald vegetation, the brilliance of birds and flowers
—all bathed his senses with new wonder.

Magdalena had appreciated the beauty of Española,
not complaining of the heat or insects, or shrinking
from joining the rhythm of life on the island. As he
dog-trotted, sure and strong as any Taino runner, he
realized that she had adapted here as much as he had.
He could still see her kneeling in wonder before a bed of
crimson flowers, smelling and touching their delicate

beauty with childlike awe. A smile touched his lips as he recalled her courage in swallowing—and keeping down—the delicacy of the fish eyes. Even the religious observances of the Tainos had meaning in her eyes.

"I have always condemned her for the sins of her parents—even when she was but an innocent child in the marshes of Andalusia, surely then still untouched by any man." There was an inherent goodness in Magdalena that transcended the taint of Estrella and Bernardo Valdés, no matter what corruption they had surrounded her with at home or at the court. Benjamin had sensed it immediately, and his father had always been a meticulously shrewd judge of character.

"But I have been a fool!" How many men had a woman pursue them across the ocean, all for a love she had borne him since she was a girl? And love it must be, for she knew he owned naught but his sword and horse after his family's wealth had been confiscated. She could have wed a duke or a count—or accepted lavish royal favors from that Trastamara bastard as her mother had.

He considered her story about Ysabel banishing her to a convent, not so preposterous really if he believed that she had rebuffed the lecherous old king. Fernando always sought with feckless abandon what was denied him. The spiteful queen would have had to be blind not to sense Magdalena's vulnerability and the effect it had on her philandering royal consort. Just recalling his taunts to her about being the king's paramour made him cringe now for his cruelty and blindness. Whatever lover or lovers she may have had before he seduced her into his bed in Seville, they had not been taken with the calculation of Estrella Valdés. Anyway, that was all behind them now. It did not matter.

Vowing to begin again with his wife, Aaron stopped at the edge of the settlement and surveyed its squalor. Bartolomé had attempted to persuade his brother to move the colony to a more suitable site, and Cristobal had agreed that along the southern coasts of Española he had found more felicitous harbors where they might relocate. This place was a sinkhole, the river too far away, the soil too rocky, the harbor too exposed for it ever to grow into a true port city. Of course, if the Colons did not receive more royal backing, and suitable settlers willing to obey the law and work to build the island, no place would serve.

"I shall take Magdalena away from here before she falls victim to a fever or noxious disease nursing these contentious people. We will build our own life." Smiling, he thought of a russet-haired girl riding her horse breakneck across the marshes outside Seville, sweaty and windblown with her fat plait of hair flying behind her like a horses' tail. Something inside him softened as he imagined a small replica of Magdalena, riding across Española on a fine pony given her by her father.

When he approached their home, the place was oddly quiet. Analu came running from inside the house with a frightened look on his face. He fell to his knees at Aaron's feet and the white man's chest squeezed tight with dread. "Where is my lady?"

"Gone. I know not where. The second night after you and the governor left, she did not return from the hospital. I went in search of her and the medicine man told me she had departed as usual."

"That was a week ago!" Aaron's face was chalky with fear. He yanked the servant to his feet. "Did you go to the governor's brother, Don Diego?"

"Yes, but he refused to see me for three days. Then when I cried out to him on the streets while he was riding one of your great beasts, he told me he knew nothing of the lady." Analu hesitated, feeling the steel imprint of Aaron's fingers digging into his arm. The lady had been very sad at their parting. "Several ships sailed away while you were gone, one that second day . . . I

searched everywhere, even sending a runner to
Guacanagari's people. She has vanished.''

A ship sailed away that day. Surely she had not given
up, left him? With chilling clarity all his words of scorn
and rejection, his suggestions that she return to the
court, everything came rushing back to him. He had left
her feeling responsible for Aliyah's spiteful decision to
keep Navaro. *Why could she not have told me she tried to
regain my son?* Feeling a wave of nausea sweeping over
him, Aaron pushed past the distraught servant and
entered their home.

His eyes quickly scanned the orderly room. Would
she have left a note? Surely she would have taken her
few possessions—she treasured the books from his
father. Nothing seemed to be missing. Like a crazed
man, he began to toss clothing on the floor, throwing
things from her chests. All her gowns, her cloak, even
the books, her jewel cask—everything was here. What
could she have used to purchase passage on a ship?
What would she have worn? Then his fingertips brushed
a rolled parchment buried at the bottom of the second
chest, the smaller one she kept her books in to prevent
their mildewing in the damp jungle air.

As he extracted it, a strange sense of forboding
washed over him, for he recognized the seal on it—the
one his father had used for medical documents. Trembling, he unrolled it, instantly recognizing Benjamin
Torres' strong, sweeping penmanship. His eyes flew
down the page, reading the clinical details describing
precisely how his wife had lost her maidenhead. The
date registered in his spinning head—scant months
before he seduced that oddly vulnerable, eagerly innocent girl who had fled his quarters in tears after her
initiation into womanhood. And he, callous fool, had
been the one who first touched her! The *only* one who
had ever touched her. And now she was gone.

"Magdalena, oh Magdalena, my wife, what have I

done to you? Have I driven you to flee?" He sat on the floor, head buried in his hands with the parchment lying beside him, its edges limp in the dampness.

"What will you do? Perhaps now that the governor has returned he can speak with his young brother. . . ." Analu's voice cut into Aaron's trance.

Quickly standing up, Aaron rolled the parchment carefully and reverently replaced it in Magdalena's chest.

"Straighten up this mess. I will go to the governor and see what can be learned," he commanded the Taino. Then he grabbed a pair of his hose, boots for riding, and a loose tunic. Shedding the loincloth he had worn while journeying with the Indians, he dressed rapidly. His armor and sword would be awaiting him at the palace, and his horse would be stabled and cared for with the rest of the Colon's mounts.

"When did the soldiers return?" he asked Analu.

"Late last night. They had many captives who will be sent across the waters to be sold as slaves . . . or to die." There was an odd fatalism in the Taino's voice.

Aaron nodded and departed for his interview with Cristobal. Diego Colon had better know something about where Magdalena had gone!

When he reached the palace and retrieved his sword, he was informed that everyone was at the waterfront, seeing to the loading of the caravels bound for home, laden with slaves and booty. Sickened by the very scene he had hoped to avoid, yet desperate to find word of Magdalena, he traversed the short distance to the harbor where a great crowd had gathered.

The scene was chaos, with mounted soldiers brandishing the flat of their swords against the backs of chained Indians, many of whom were injured and stumbling, terrified to be so close to the horses. They climbed aboard the ship's boats, eager to be away from the cursing, milling throngs of mounted white men.

Hojeda rode back and forth, yelling orders to the men loading slaves into the boats.

Aaron searched the crowd for the tall figure of Cristobal. Looking bent and exhausted, the governor stood off to one side on a small hill, Bartolomé and Diego Colon at his side. As soon as Aaron climbed to where they stood, Hojeda turned his horse and cleared a path through the crowd until he reached them. Swinging down, he swaggered up to Torres, a gloating smile on his face. "Did you witness the great Caonabo enter the boats? I told you I would sail with him in chains."

"Sail to hell for all I care, Alonso." He turned to Cristobal. "Magdalena has vanished! My servant said she did not return from the hospital that evening after we departed for the Vega." He looked at Diego Colon, who seemed to blanch and step back suddenly. "Do you know what has happened to her?" Aaron took a menacing step toward the youngest Colon.

Cristobal put his hand firmly on Aaron's chest to stay him as Bartolomé's eyes narrowed on Diego. "You seem to have had conversation with the lady. What did she say? Speak, man!"

Diego shook his head as if in disbelief. "We had a dinner the evening you departed. Don Lorenzo and various members of the council and Doña Magdalena attended. The next morning she came to me with an insane tale—accusing Lorenzo Guzman, the Duke of Medina-Sidonia's nephew, of treason. Of course I could give no credence to it," he added defensively, eyeing Aaron as he moved closer to his brothers.

"Where is the great Don Lorenzo now?" Aaron asked tightly, his fingers on his sword hilt.

"I—I do not know. He and his companion, Guerra, rode off in search of gold, I presumed," Diego finished lamely.

"What did Magdalena say about treason? Explain it.

Every syllable. The lady lived at court. She was no fool when it came to political intrigues," Bartolomé said. Now he looked every bit as menacing as Aaron.

Diego took a gulp of air and recounted Magdalena's story. By the time he had finished, he was sweating and more than a bit frightened. "Surely you do not think—"

"That Lorenzo Guzman took her?" Alonso Hojeda interrupted. "Just so. He was banished by his uncle for some greedy machinations with the Holy Office. If she discovered such, he would surely have wished to silence her before her champions returned."

Aaron's heart turned to ice, not beating as he asked Hojeda, "How came you to know aught of my former brother-in-law?" He stepped between the Castilian and his horse.

"We were acquainted at court briefly," Alonso said smoothly. "Lorenzo is a bitter man. One night when first he arrived here, he lapped enough wine to drown all the maggots in his wretched guts. Then the fawning court jackal told me all."

"Have you any idea where he might flee if he feared discovery?" Aaron asked in a low deadly voice. He itched to place his fingers about that sinewy little throat and snap it!

"I mentioned a friend of yours," Hojeda said tauntingly. "Roldan. I even told Guzman of how the rascal has carved out his own domain in Xaragua. Perhaps he has gone to Roldan and taken your lady with him."

"That is across the island! Days of hard riding. Why would he do something so dangerous . . . the ships!" Bartolomé answered his own question.

"Two caravels, afloat in Roldan's waters off the peninsula," Aaron said. "Yes, that is what he would hope for if he found no passage from Española in Ysabel." He turned to the shrinking, pale figure of Diego Colon and said quietly, "I owe Cristobal my life and Magdalena owes Bartolomé hers. For that I will not kill you! But pray, Don Diego, pray very hard that my wife is alive and unharmed when I reach Roldan."

With the threat hanging in the sultry air, Aaron turned and seized a surprised Alonso Hojeda by his leather-armored breastplate, lifting him off the ground. "You, too, are involved in this. I know Lorenzo Guzman would not set out blindly. He needed someone to guide him and doubtless greetings to pass along to Francisco. You are as treacherous as Guzman." He threw Hojeda to Bartolomé, whose stout, muscled body caught the little man easily.

"I will see to it Don Alonso does not sail on this tide—or any other until you return with Magdalena," Bartolomé said grimly.

"Can you be certain your old comrade Roldan will not kill you on sight if you trespass in Xaragua?" Cristobal asked Aaron. "Take some of the soldiers whom you led in battle with you."

"No, I can find my way to the *cacicazgo* more swiftly if I take some Tainos who know Roldan." Aaron saw the pain and helplessness in Cristobal's face. "We have all made mistakes, my friend. I have wronged my wife and now I must atone—or die trying. You must restore order and give justice to the Taino people."

Aliyah looked at her rival with thinly veiled hate. She did nothing to disguise the gloating look on her face. Rising in one lithe, sinuous movement, she eyed Magdalena with contempt. "Still you must cover your skinny body to hide its ugliness." She caressed her own large breasts with bold and sensuous impudence, looking from Magdalena to Roldan, who was taking in the confrontation with obvious relish.

He chuckled at the Taino woman in her voluptuous nakedness. In violation of the custom of married females, she wore no skirt. "Perhaps a man prefers a bit of mystery to enchant his imagination when he looks on a woman's body, Aliyah," he said as his eyes raked Magdalena's soft curves, artfully draped in the sheer cotton cloth. "Although your assets are considerable," he added with a swift glance at the golden, naked woman standing across from him, "I find it intriguing to play the old games of court once more."

With that, he walked over to where Magdalena stood and took her hand, raising it for a gallant kiss. "You act as if we were still in Castile," she said, ignoring the seething Aliyah and looking about the large, lavishly appointed *bohio*. The walls were hung with several tapestries of far superior quality to anything in the governor's palace in Ysabel, yet the room was furnished with only the low wooden stools and oddly shaped chairs carved of whole tree trunks that she had seen in Guacanagari's village. Modern weapons hung on the walls beside traditional Taino spears.

Roldan flashed a grin as he escorted her to a seat by a long, low trestle table laden with roasted meats, cassava bread, and lush melons and fruits. Goblets of red wine graced the table, which was set with Castilian pewter plates and Taino clay bowls. "As you can see, I have borrowed the best from both worlds. This, Doña Magdalena, is *my* royal court."

"But the tapestries, the pewter—"

His rich laughter interrupted her. "I, er, said I borrowed it—perhaps I should have used a different word. I stole the best from two worlds—the *cacicazgo* from Behechio, along with his lovely bride," he flourished a hand at Aliyah's pouting face, "and the European furnishings and fine wine from several caravels whose crews I persuaded to pledge allegiance to me instead of to the Colons in Ysabel."

"But that is piracy, sir!" The minute Magdalena blurted out the words, she could have swallowed her tongue. She must make this volatile man her ally, not antagonize him.

Shirl Henke

But far from being angered, Roldan, the curly-headed giant with the roguish grin, seemed delighted with her spirit. "Piracy, humm." He scratched his head and appeared to consider her words. "Yes, I do believe that would be how the admiral would look upon it." He chuckled again. "He did so want those supplies, but a Genoese has nothing on a good Castilian when it comes to piracy—on land or sea!"

Magdalena arranged her scanty skirt carefully to conceal as much as possible of her legs, all the while ignoring the hostility radiating from across the table where Aliyah reclined. Roldan sat at the head, negligently at ease in a loose white tunic and hose, his feet encased in soft kid slippers and his neck and arms dripping with elaborate Taino jewelry, most obvious of which was the heavy gold medallion, the badge of royal chieftainship. Had he killed Behechio? She shivered, not wanting to know.

Roldan raised his goblet in a toast. "I heard my old comrade Torres had wed a noblewoman of great beauty. The tales of you were not exaggerated, my lady."

"You and my husband were friends once." A flicker of hope flared. Thus far Lorenzo and his minion Guerra had not yet arrived for dinner. If she could only convince Roldan to protect her. . . .

"Diego Torres—or do I recall he preferred being called Aaron?"

"When out of earshot of the Inquisition, he prefers his birth name," Magdalena answered.

Roldan smiled in appreciation. "Wit and beauty. Most rare, most rare. As you may gather, Doña Magdalena, there is no Holy Office in Xaragua, nor likely ever to be. Your husband and I made the last crossing together on *María Galante* and served a turn in Ysabel together. I liked him well, even though he was the admiral's man."

She tasted the wine slowly and peered at him over the

356

rim of her goblet. "And now, do you still call him friend?"

"We agreed about Colon's ineptitude as a governor. We disagreed over what to do about it. He is too loyal." Francisco studied her for a moment. "Alas, I fear you, too, are loyal."

"To the governor in Ysabel or to my husband?" she inquired guilelessly and again was rewarded with his booming laugh.

"God's balls! I like you well," he replied.

Lorenzo Guzman stood in the doorway, overhearing the last of the exchange. He paused as fury mottled his pale complexion, but the flickering torchlight hid it when he cleared his throat and walked up to where Roldan and Magdalena sat. "Please, Don Francisco, remember that this woman is my captive. She will try her wiles on you as she has on me, but she is in league with the governor."

Roldan gestured with the leg bone from a roasted *hutia* for Lorenzo and Peralonso to be seated; then he gnawed on his "septer," chewed, and swallowed. Wiping his mouth with the back of his sleeve, he smiled mirthlessly at the two elegant courtiers. "I am a rough, unlettered fellow who served in the Moorish wars, Don Lorenzo, but I have been to court and know a trick or two. No one deceives me, and here I am *cacique*. I do as I wish." His brown eyes glared with dark brilliance as he tossed the bone to one of the small, barkless dogs always underfoot in the Taino villages.

Guzman felt a frisson of fear and silently cursed his ill fortune for coming to this wilderness run by a madman. "My warning about the beautiful Magdalena was not intended to insult you, Don Francisco," he said smoothly.

"Alonso Hojeda commends you to me, saying we have common grievances against the Colon family. What I need are fighting men, Don Lorenzo," Roldan said, looking at the foppishly attired courtier dubiously.

Lorenzo's eyes were the color of the plate from which he delicately speared a piece of meat with his dirk. His long, angular face was not handsome, but in the flickering torchlight, it was haughty and contained. "I have not had the chance to test my blade against the Moors, but in Seville, I was accounted a passing good swordsman. I understand you have ships and men who can sail them back to Cadiz."

Roldan shrugged. "I have ships, but what profit is it to me to send them off? The royal customs collectors at any port in Castile will confiscate my booty. Only those ships sent by the Colons sail with royal approval."

Now Lorenzo smiled, catlike and cunning. "As the nephew of Medina-Sidonia, I believe I could have some influence on the customs collectors."

Roldan betrayed mild interest. "So you desire to return home and need the means. Perhaps we can do business, perhaps not. What of the woman? Taking Torres' wife was lunacy."

"He has no idea I took her, nor where I have fled," Lorenzo said dismissively.

"You are a fool. Every Taino *cacique* on Española talks with the others. 'Twill not take overlong for one of them to receive word of a russet-haired beauty and inform Guacanagari's good friend."

"Then kill her!" cried Aliyah. "She will bring death and destruction down on us all. Kill her and throw her body into the sea!"

Magdalena paled, but before she could respond, Roldan said, "I see no profit in that either. Nor will I have jealous women's bickering. Doña Magdalena is Torres' wife. I will hold her until he comes for her." He paused and searched Magdalena's desolate face. "*If* he comes for her. What a fascinating test of mettle—you against Torres," he said to Guzman, grinning like a shark.

Guzman paled, but rallied. "The man was forced to wed the wench. He did not want her in Ysabel. He will not risk coming here for her. She is mine and I see no reason—"

"You are quite correct, Guzman. You see no reason, none at all. Here you sit at my table, in my fortress, under the weapons of my soldiers. You fled in desperation. Now you will await my pleasure." He turned to Magdalena. "And right now, my pleasure is to see if Torres comes to claim his woman."

"He will not come," Aliyah said bitterly. "My son lies grievous ill with the white man's sickness. Already Aaron hates her for causing him to lose Navaro. He will never want to see her again if the boy dies."

"Navaro is ill?" Magdalena turned from Aliyah to Roldan. "I have nursed many people with fevers—Tainos and white men. I could help. Please—"

"No!" Aliyah stood up, glaring at Magdalena. "She would kill my son out of jealousy. Do not let her near him."

"The babe scarce looked ill this morning. Go attend him yourself if you think him in any danger," Roldan commanded Aliyah, dismissing her with a wave of his hand. Then, observing Magdalena, he said, "Do not distress yourself. The babe is not truly taken with the pox as she would have you believe. She is filled with hate for your husband and for you."

"As is Don Lorenzo here. 'Twas he who conspired to murder his own wife and all her family, just to obtain their wealth," Magdalena said, casting a loathing, contemptuous glance at Guzman. "Please do not let him touch me." She searched his unreadable expression.

"I will do as I have said. No one will touch you until Torres and Guzman settle their ancient feud. I think your husband will come, my lady. Were you mine, I would." He watched her cheeks heat, then resumed eating, motioning for the others to do likewise.

"Is there much sickness in your compound?" Magdalena asked as she bit into a slice of papaya.

"Some, although more among the Indians than the whites," Roldan replied. "Nothing so fearsome as what I hear goes on in Ysabel."

"I worked with Dr. Chanca in Ysabel. I would be happy to lend my nursing skills here, if you would let me." She held her breath. This might mean freedom to learn the village, to make friends, to escape!

"I do not want her subjected to such danger. 'Tis not the place for a lady," Lorenzo protested.

Roldan shook his head in mock disbelief. "Still you try to command. Old habits die hard, Guzman. 'Twas not your place to abduct a lady and drag her here, but now that she *is* here, if she wishes to help with my people who are sick, I will allow it."

Aliyah watched dispassionately as the child died. It was a girl, about the same age and size as Navaro, stricken with the strange pox that caused high fever and an ugly red rash and killed so many of her people. She let the weeping mother wrap the babe in a swaddling of cotton, as was the custom. Then with a feigned compassion, she placed her hand on the woman's shoulder and said, "I will take her to the fires. Only rest. You yourself are ill."

The woman, sick and dispirited, looked suspiciously at her chieftain's wife. The *cacique* Behechio had been driven from the village by the one called Roldan, who had lived in the coastal mountains for over a year. With a small band of followers, some Tainos, some bearded ones, Roldan had challenged Behechio on the day after his wedding with Aliyah. When the white man won, the royal woman allied herself with him, becoming his mistress, bestowing on him Behechio's medallion. "Why do you wish to see my daughter burned?"

"Does your *zemi* need her ashes?" Aliyah asked, already knowing that the burial jars in this hut were filled with the cremated ashes of three other of the woman's young children. She had lost three sons and her husband. Now the fever raged within her. What mattered anything else? "Take her," she said, handing the small, tightly wrapped bundle to the mysterious princess from Marien.

As darkness fell that night, Aliyah nursed Navaro one last time so that he would not be hungry and make a cry in the night to awaken anyone. Then, with his curious blue eyes studying her, eyes that were Aaron's, Aliyah slipped from the compound with him hidden in a blanket she carried across one hip. The night air was sickeningly pungent from burial fires. Many children had died this day. Tomorrow there would be one more, she thought with a slight, cruel smile twisting the corners of her lips as she watched the sky's eerie orange glow. Darkness enveloped her as she entered the jungle, leaving the wailing of mourners behind.

"Vanara, are you here?" she hissed as she adjusted her eyes to the blackness.

A plump older woman appeared from behind a palm. "Yes, my princess, I am ready." She emerged carrying a heavy girdle filled with all the possessions she would take on this journey. She was afraid to go, but even more afraid to remain and disobey the sister of her *cacique*, her cousin Aliyah.

Together the two women walked through the darkness until the moon rose. Navaro stirred, then dozed once again.

"It is a very hard thing you do, your glory," Vanara said.

Aliyah's face was all harsh planes and angles in the stark moonlight. "It is what I must do. Navaro will have

361

a good life. The man I met from Roldan's great boat promised me."

That man paced the beach, frightened to be in thi rebel territory. What madness had possessed him t wait for her? His ship had been driven to this cove t seek shelter during a storm, not knowing they ha ventured into a rebel stronghold. Roldan had allowe them to leave after exacting tribute in the form c almost half the brazilwood they had cut. When he me the white *cacique*, he also met the mysterious Aliya and her blue-eyed babe. She spoke Castilian fluently an told him the most incredible tale.

Suddenly he heard a rustling in the bushes and hi blood froze. He eyed the ship's boat, beached on th glistening white sand, waves lapping gently at its side Should he run? Then two Taino woman entered th clearing and crossed the sand. He breathed more freel when he saw the child. No men were with them.

"I have brought him," the beautiful Taino announce "You have said how handsome he is." She held a sleep Navaro up for inspection.

Pedro de Las Casas looked at the boy's features. Eve in the moonlight he could see the stamp of the whit father on the babe's face. "You are certain his fathe does not want him? He is a splendid boy," he sai quietly, his hand ruffling the thick black cap of hair.

"No, his father will not take him. I am forced to liv with that brutal man who will kill him. You promised t take him across the water—to where he will be taugh white ways. When he grows, tell him his father did n love him. His mother did, but she could not keep him. With that, Aliyah stroked her son's back and held hi tightly for a moment, then, with a deep shudderin breath, she thrust him into Varana's arms. "She will g with him. She can feed him and care for him."

Las Casas looked at the wet nurse who held the chil

After a moment's debate, he sighed and said, "Come with me. I will take the boy to Castile."

Aliyah stood on the beach, a small figure in the gleaming moonlight, watching the boat grow smaller as the men rowed it toward a waiting ship. In it sat Varana, holding Navaro. She watched them climb aboard the gently bobbing caravel silhouetted on the silvery horizon. A thin chilling wail of protest from the babe echoed across the water and reached her. Aliyah turned her back and walked into the jungle.

Chapter Twenty-Two

"I have sent Lorenzo and Peralonso with several of my men to inspect the caravels in the bay," Roldan said with a hint of a smile playing about his lips. He looked at Magdalena to gauge her reaction.

"I am most grateful you have prevented Guzman from threatening me, Don Francisco," she replied evenly as she took a seat at the table to break her fast.

He flashed a toothy grin. "But you mistrust my own motives in eliminating the competition for your favor?"

She looked at him with clear green eyes. "My favors, as you call them, belong only to my husband, but I am here at your mercy and well know I may be given to anyone you choose." She had sensed that as much as Roldan loved playing cat and mouse with the scheming Guzman and his ilk, he admired forthrightness.

"I will give you to no one but your husband, my lady," he said simply, studying her reaction. "Why is it that you doubt he will come for you? Do not deny it. I can sense it."

"You are most perceptive." Her face flamed as she considered confessing the nature and circumstances of her marriage to her enigmatic husband. "Let me just say Aaron was forced by the admiral to wed me. He will feel himself well quit of a wife he did not choose, but he may come to kill Lorenzo in revenge."

"I know of the fate of his family," Francisco said softly. He reclined on the low couch beside the table, studying the morning sky of blazing gold and brilliant azure through the doorway of the hut. "We knew each other briefly during the siege of Granada, but became better acquainted during the voyage across the Atlantic. 'Twas my first ocean crossing, his second." Then he grinned, his mood lightening. "Of course we had little time for talk. The fleet's marshal was a very busy man—between losing his meals over the railing during rough weather and soothing his pounding head, even when the sea was smooth as glass."

Magdalena's eyes widened in amazement. "Aaron, seasick?" she asked incredulously.

"He hid it from the men fair well with the admiral's connivance, but those who knew him during the war could see how carefully he nursed his aching head. We all did that after a night's carousing with a large jug of wine. The symptoms of both maladies, I am given to understand, are quite the same," Roldan added innocently.

Magdalena let loose a burble of laughter. Blessed Virgin, alone in this deadly wilderness, her life and her honor hanging by a thread, and she could not but see humor in the suffering of the man who had brought her to this pass! Had her situation unhinged her mind? She saw Roldan eye her curiously, then join her in a hearty roar of laughter.

Magdalena swiped tears of mirth from her eyes and choked out, "'Tis passing difficult to imagine my arrogant lord, that fearful white Taino warrior, puking and holding his drumming head aboard ship! I myself found the voyage overall boring but loved the rare occasions when I could go above decks and walk in the salt wind." Again the laughter seized her. "Small wonder he is so loyal to Don Cristobal for keeping his secret."

Roldan slapped his knee and they laughed together.

That is how Aaron found them as he stood in the door of the *cacique's bohio*. "What a pleasantly domestic scene. I nearly break the legs of my horse riding through jungles and across mountains to save my lady wife, only to find her so handsomely amused," Aaron said with a black scowl. "Pray share the joke with me?"

Magdalena's head jerked up when Aaron began to speak, but before she could utter a word, Roldan said, "You are here sooner than I thought possible. That horse must have wings like those of the Greeks to bring you to Xaragua so quickly."

Aaron looked at Magdalena, clad in a scandalous yet enticing wrap of sheer cotton. "You seem quite unharmed. I thought you abducted and feared you dead." Against his will, his blood stirred at the sight of her soft curves and shimmering mantle of loose russet hair.

Magdalena stood up, suppressing the urge to run into his arms. Again, he was angry with her. "After all I have been through over you, my lord husband, a few days hard ride should be as nothing. Your old comrade here rescued me from Lorenzo Guzman. You owe Don Francisco your thanks, if you care that I am unharmed—or believe me!"

Aaron had the good grace to flush as he approached her and reached out to place his fingertips gently beneath her proudly uptilted chin. He could feel the pulse in her throat racing. "I care, green-eyed witch, I care very much," he said quietly as he lost himself in the fathomless depths of those eyes.

"As to what we were laughing about," Roldan began, ignoring the tender absorption of the man and woman standing before him, "it seems your lady is much the better sailor than you."

Aaron's head swiveled toward Roldan and his eyes narrowed. "You told her—"

"What the admiral so tactfully kept from her, yes, I did," Francisco said gleefully. "We were speculating if that might not be why you owe the Genoese such unswerving loyalty," he added with bushy eyebrows raised.

Aaron felt a chuckle trembling in Magdalena's throat. "I have come to reclaim my wife. I did not think to discuss your accursed feud with the Colons, Francisco —at least not at this moment."

"Ah, see you how he evades the subject?" Roldan said to Magdalena, causing her to loose the laugh that she had been suppressing.

"You indeed must have come to rescue me, not just to revenge yourself against Guzman, else you would not be so upset over petty matters," she said, sobering as she inspected his sweat-drenched, filthy body. His shirt was bloodied and torn, his hair matted to his head, and his fist clamped tightly over his sword hilt. Never had he looked more beautiful to her, damn him!

"Guzman did you no hurt?" he asked quietly, his fingers stroking a long strand of silky hair away from her cheek. *She had been touched by no man but me. Pray God it is yet so!*

"He did not use me, though he would have once we arrived here but for Don Francisco," she replied, staring into his piercing blue eyes, willing him to believe her for once in their mistrustful relationship.

Something tightly coiled, twisting deep in his gut,

seemed to unknot with her words. He let out his breath and turned to Roldan. "I owe you a great debt, Francisco." Then a lazy smile curved his lips. "Perhaps I shall think on a way to repay it one day soon."

"Peacemaker between the outlaw and the admiral?" Roldan replied, also smiling. "I, too, will think on *that* matter."

"I would speak in private with my wife," Aaron said, ignoring the outlaw's insinuation.

"I have been given quarters nearby. We can go there." As she led Aaron outside, she wrinkled her nose and added, "You need a bath."

He followed her across the crowded street to a small *caneye* guarded by two Taino warriors. Aaron's eyes swept the compound and he tightened his grip on his sword. "Is Guzman or any of his companions about? I would not be caught naked in my bath so he can slit my throat."

"Roldan has sent him to look at the caravels in the bay. He will return by darkness tonight, not before," she replied with increasing nervousness as they were left alone in the small cane hut. "When I recognized Lorenzo's voice that night in the garden, I knew he was the one in league with my father, but—"

"But Diego Colon would not believe you," he replied with a scowl.

"Do you believe me, Aaron? When I tried to tell you earlier, you thought I only made up lies to cover my father's monstrous deeds."

Aaron took a shaky breath and extended his hands, clasping hers and drawing them to his lips. "I have been a fool, Magdalena. You always spoke the truth, but I was blinded by old prejudices and new hatreds. I could not see who, what you were." He released her hands and turned to pace the hard-packed earth floor. "I have always desired you—and fought against it. But it was quite useless."

"I was quite determined," she whispered, afraid yet eager to have him continue.

"You tried to win Navaro for me. When I learned that, I began to consider many things on my journey back to Ysabel. You were determined to have me to husband even after I had lost everything. This is a dangerous wilderness for a lady from the royal court."

She smiled sadly. "This is paradise compared to the dangers for a lady residing with the royal court. I did not wish to repeat my mother's mistakes, Aaron."

"I know that now . . . that and so much more." He looked at her, studying her innocent beauty, the strength and integrity in every fiber of her being. "My father was a far better judge of women than I, but perhaps a poor judge of his own son's worthiness. I found his sealed document among your books. Even in taking your virginity, I accused you of sins of which you were not guilty."

Her face flamed as she met his eyes. "My pride kept me from showing it to you on our wedding night . . . only in part because of what you said."

"I was cruelly unfair and unfeeling, Magdalena," he said in a stricken voice.

"I had another reason for not showing you the document. The accident that Benjamin witnessed was my fault. I schemed to meet him and was injured because of it. . . ." The whole story of how she plotted to meet Aaron's family came tumbling out, the words like torrents from a bursting dam. Finally, she raised her tear-streaked face to his. "I came to love your father and mother, to wish, to imagine they were my family, rather than Bernardo and Estrella Valdés. But by becoming their friend, I was part of their deaths!"

"No! You tried to save them," he cried, reaching out and enfolding her in his embrace as she broke down, sobbing. He rocked her gently in his arms, his hand smoothing and caressing her silky hair. "All your life you searched for love, seeing in me and then in my family what you never had from those who owed you their devotion," he said hoarsely, beginning to understand the loneliness and pain of this proud, spirited woman. His father must have understood it from the first time he met her.

"Bernardo Valdés is probably not even my father. I know not who is—nor in all likelihood does my mother." She sobbed against his shirt, burying her face against his chest as he held her.

"That matters nothing, Magdalena, for now you are mine—my wife—and I love you with all my heart. Is it too late to ask you to forgive me? I would build a life with you here, raise children, and let all the old hates die . . . if you are willing?"

She looked up at him through tear-sheened eyes, trembling and realizing that he, too, was trembling with uncertainty, with fear that she would reject him. "I have waited a lifetime to hear those words. I love you more than life, Aaron Torres, and never will I leave you," she replied, pulling his head down to seal her vow with a kiss. She wrapped her arms about his neck, raising up on tiptoe as her lips moved from his mouth to his eyes, then down, brushing the raspy whiskers on his unshaven cheeks, lower yet as she licked at the salty skin of his neck.

"I am bloodied and filthy," he murmured hoarsely into her hair, smelling the tangy citrus fragrance of her clean satiny body.

"I care not," she said, sliding his torn tunic from his shoulders. Then, seeing the insect bites and abrasions across his chest and arms, she gasped. "You will take a fever if I do not tend these." She realized how long and hard he had ridden in search of her and felt her throat tighten with love all over again. Oh, the sweetness of this new feeling growing between them!

Aaron looked at the door of the small *caneye*, outside of which he knew the guards stood.

"Is there not some place near the compound where we can bathe in safety and privacy?" he asked in a heated voice, recalling the time he had made love to her beneath the waterfall.

Magdalena nodded, releasing her embrace only long enough to scoop up several lengths of cloth from the bed and from a peg on the wall a small sack which held her medicines. "Have you any other clothes? These seem to be beyond mending."

He flashed a boyish grin of deviltry that made her heart stop beating. "I could borrow from Francisco, but he is a bit bigger in girth than I."

Magdalena chuckled. "His hose would fall from your hips, exposing for all the world what is only mine to see. We will borrow a tunic from him and a pair of hose from his captain who looks to be of a size with you."

"And you, of course, have such a practiced eye," he said with a warm, teasing smile.

"'Tis all these months living among the Tainos who go naked as their mothers bore them. A woman learns the size of all things very quickly that way," she replied saucily.

"Bold wench," he said as he again crushed her to him in a swift, fierce kiss. "Let us gather those clothes and be off to bathe lest I lose all sense of decorum."

Within a few moments they were outside the compound. Magdalena led Aaron to a secluded place upstream from where the women of the village bathed their children and washed food utensils and cookpots. The shallow, swift-running stream was not nearly so luxuriant as the pools near Guacanagari's village, but it served them well enough.

Magdalena watched Aaron rip off his tunic, hose, and boots after carefully placing his sword and dagger close

371

by the stream's edge. Even injured and filthy, he was splendid. He paused with one foot on the bank and reached out his hand, palm up, unashamed of his nakedness as any Taino warrior. "I have made you stink with my sweat, love. Come."

Her trance broken, Magdalena quickly unfastened her cloth wrapper and let it float silently to the mossy bank. Beneath it she, too, was naked. The skin of her body was still pale and untouched by the sun that had turned her face and arms golden, while virtually all of him was bronzed, but for his member now standing so proudly erect. She approached him boldly, stopping only to pull a cluster of fruit soap from the bank. Rubbing it into a thick lather, she placed one of her small hands in his and let the other clasp his rigid staff. As her slippery little fingers curled about it and slid up and down, she was rewarded by his sharp intake of breath.

"Little witch, you always fill my thoughts. I cannot live without you," he murmured as she melted against him, her busy hands at work soaping and caressing all over his body.

"Kneel so I may wash you quickly," she said as she pulled him down into the rushing current. The cool water felt incredible as it rippled over his sensitized skin. They rolled in the shallow stream until he lay on the soft mossy bottom and Magdalena reclined atop him with her hair floating down her back with the current. "You will drown ere I can bathe you this way," she whispered as his head nearly submerged beneath the surface.

"I will risk such a sweet death," he replied, pulling her down for an underwater kiss. Their feverish mouths moved, opening, brushing, tongues dueling. The rush of water lent a sensuous urgency to the kiss until he sat up gasping for air. Magdalena, too, coughed and gulped breath into her lungs.

Aaron held her securely against his thighs with her legs scissoring his hips. "That was a most unusual way to go about a kiss, but I think it will last longer if we stay above water," he said, pulling her into his embrace once again.

"And be sweeter without the water robbing me of your taste," she whispered, opening her mouth to his kiss.

He rimmed her lips with his, then plunged in to explore. She returned the caress, splaying her fingers in his thick wet hair and pulling his head close to hers. He reached up and cupped a breast in each hand, letting the water slick his fingertips as they teased the pebbly nipples. She arched against the tantalizing torture, wriggling her buttocks against his straining staff until he seized her around the waist, raising her up and then lowering her to envelope him.

Magdalena let out all her breath as the exquisite sensations raced through her body. Throwing her head back, she closed her eyes and began to move with his hands on her hips, raising and lowering her in a slow, languorous rhythm. "The water, oh . . . it . . . ooh," she moaned.

His soft, breathy laughter rippled over her like the water. "Oh, yes, the water is very . . . very . . . good." He punctuated each word with a slow, deep thrust.

Aaron could feel her nails digging into his shoulders as she clung to him, moving with him to the rhythm of the rippling stream. As they ascended to that higher plane of sweetest union, she opened her eyes and met his. Piercing blue and luminous green mirrored their souls' love as he quickened his strokes. He was as hot as the water was cool, now ablaze with the splendor of his love for this small, russet-haired woman in his arms. Magdalena, too, felt the fiery beauty of the moment and drew him deeper into her, holding him fast, wanting the moment to last forever. Yet this intensity could not last, lest it consume them. Together they spun out of control into a whirlpool of heat. He poured life into her body as the currents eddied softly around them, enveloping them, cooling the shuddering ecstasy of their release.

Magdalena's head fell on his shoulder and she collapsed against his chest, holding him tightly. His hands moved up her back, softly stroking her wet mane of hair as he murmured love words in her ear. How long she had waited to hear them!

"All my life," she whispered against the hollow between his neck and shoulder, "all my life I have loved you."

"And I shall love you, my fiery little temptress, all the rest of my life, upon my soul I shall."

"'Tis not possible! Only yesterday he was healthy as could be," Francisco said, looking at the fat, shiny tears trailing down Aliyah's cheeks.

She stood before him clutching a small jar. "When he died, I had him burned. Here is his spirit jar. I will save it for his father. You may tell his *wife*," she spat the word, "that no one but the *zemis* own Navaro now."

"You may give the jar to Aaron yourself, Aliyah," Roldan said with a sigh. "He only this morning arrived in search of Magdalena. He will be desolate. Do not let your hate for her prevent you from remembering what you and Navaro's father once shared," he added with surprising gentleness.

Aliyah did not raise her eyes, but her mind raced. "Aaron is here? Would you send word that he come to my dwelling? I wish to tell him without that woman being present."

"It shall be as you request," Roldan said simply. As she turned to leave, bearing her small, sad trophy, he added awkwardly, "Aliyah, I am sorry."

She nodded and departed.

When Aaron was escorted to Aliyah's *bohio*, he felt a strange sense of forboding. The soldier sent to escort him would say only that the *cacique's* mistress desired speech with him and Roldan had dispatched him as messenger. As they crossed the compound, he stepped over several yiping dogs and two small boys playing with them in the muddy streets. *Navaro!* Magdalena had told him only a few moments before he was summoned that the boy had been ill—or that Aliyah seemed to feel he was ill, although Roldan said he was quite well. Surely it could be nothing serious . . . yet there was fever in the village, as in Ysabel. Everywhere the white men came their diseases decimated the Tainos. *But Navaro is half white. He must be safe from these maladies!*

Aaron approached the *bohio* and discreetly called out. Aliyah's voice was soft and low as she bade him enter. She was facing a corner of the room, seated on a plain low stool. Dressed in a simple grass skirt, her head was bowed toward the household *zemis*. Aaron knew with a raw surge of pain what she would say to him. "Navaro is dead." Her voice was choked with pain. "Your white man's sickness killed him."

Aliyah stood up and faced him with a small jar of ashes in her hands. She thrust them at him, saying, "Here is your son, the only one you will ever have if you stay with that barren stick you have wed! Keep Navaro's spirit to comfort your old age!" Jealousy and hatred flashed from her dark eyes, once so warm and lustrous, now cold as obsidian.

Aaron took the jar in trembling hands and said in a hoarse voice, "I will take our son's spirit jar to your brother's village, where he was born. It is fitting that he rest with the *zemis* of Guacanagari." He hesitated a moment, wanting to offer her comfort, to share their grief, but her body radiated such intense anger that it struck him like a wall. There was no consolation they could offer each other. "Good bye, Aliyah." He turned and walked away with his son's remains clutched to his heart.

Aliyah saw the tears in those wondrous blue eyes, magic eyes she had once thought, eyes exactly like Navaro's. A hard, bitter smile froze on her face as she watched his retreating figure. Soon, all the hated white men and their skinny women would be dead, especially that pig Roldan who had banished her husband, the royal Behechio!

Aaron walked slowly back to the small *caneye* he shared with Magdalena, feeling in need of the comfort, the understanding that he now knew only she could give him.

The moment he stepped into the hut, clutching the small urn, she knew what had happened. His eyes were sheened with tears as he silently knelt in the corner near the window and reverently placed the urn on the floor. "The first light of sunrise should strike it here," he said softly. Magdalena placed her arms around him and held him in a wordless embrace of consolation.

If only she could give him a child, a son—not to replace Navaro, but to fill their lives after the void of his loss. She had hoped for the past month, but could not be certain that at last she did carry her husband's babe. It would be cruel to raise his hopes after this painful loss and then have them dashed. After all the times they had come together over the past three years, she had not conceived. Perhaps Aliyah had been right. Maybe she was barren. Magdalena forced that thought from her mind and clung to her dream as Aaron began to speak.

"I never realized how bitter she is. Her love has turned to hate. Perhaps it never was love. She is not like her brother Guacanagari. He is noble and wise, tolerant of other's feelings, but Aliyah will ever be a spiteful child. I did not wish to wed her, even when I knew Navaro was mine. Some instinct made me want only my son, not his mother. She must have sensed that much. I am not even certain she truly mourns his death."

"I think you are in enough pain for two parents," Magdalena said, her voice muffled by her tears as she softly massaged his arms, trying to absorb some of the agony from him.

"You loved him, too, in spite of everything." He said it not as a question, but a fact, which he now freely acknowledged.

"Navaro was your son. How could I not love him?" she said simply.

"I must return his ashes to Guacanagari's *zemis*. That is the Taino way," he said after a few moments of silence.

"I will go with you . . . if you wish it."

He turned and placed his hands on the sides of her face, framing it gently. "I wish it, Magdalena, my wife. I wish it very much."

At Magdalena's insistence, Aaron rested for a few hours that afternoon, although he would eat nothing. He had ridden for three days across Española with little sleep, none at all the night before he had arrived. She knew when Lorenzo and Peralonso returned, there would be a fight. Roldan would encourage the two enemies to battle to the death. Even if the *cacique* did not, Aaron would insist on his vengeance against the man who had killed his family and abducted his wife. As Aaron finally drifted into a restless sleep, Magdalena prayed he would be victorious.

She could see the gray lines of fatigue about his eyes and mouth, even in repose. Perhaps if she asked him, Roldan might hold Lorenzo prisoner for a few days so Aaron could regain his strength before the duel. Praying she might have such influence, Magdalena decided to

approach the enigmatic Francisco Roldan, *cacique* o
Xaragua.

Roldan's bushy eyebrows beetled over his shrew
brown eyes. "You realize this will change nothing
Aaron will not be denied his revenge, nor would
withhold it."

"What revenge if Lorenzo kills him, Francisco? He i
so exhausted and stricken with grief for his son he migh
well be the one to fall, not Guzman!" Her expression
implored him as she leaned across the table with he
palms pressed on the rough surface.

He hesitated a moment, then said, "As you will. I wil
have Guzman and Guerra placed under guard for a fev
days. I warn you, Aaron will take it ill when he learn
what I have done." He paused and then smiled at her
"But as I am the *cacique* here, I may do as I wish and h
will abide by my decision." His humor mercuriall
shifted then, and he said sadly, "He is distraught ove
the boy's death."

"More, it would seem, than Aliyah. I saw her leavin
the compound as I came here. She did not look to b
mourning the loss of her only child." Oddly, she fe
none of the old jealousy, but only pity for a woman wh
was so shallow a mother.

Francisco scratched his bushy hair and shook hi
head in perplexity. "I still do not understand it. The bo
was well enough when last I saw him." He flushed, the
added self-consciously, "Aliyah had him brought her
each day when it was time to feed him. Yesterda
morning he had no fever."

Magdalena's heart skipped a beat. In a cold, stiff voic
she asked haltingly, "Do . . . do you think she killed he
own son in revenge . . . because of me?"

Chapter Twenty-Three

"What can you mean by this? I will have that murdering butcher! Why do you protect him?" Aaron shouted at Roldan.

Last evening, when he awakened from an exhausted sleep, Magdalena and Francisco had convinced Aaron that Guzman would return to the compound by midday following. When Lorenzo did not appear, Aaron began inquiries and found the *cacique* had imprisoned the couturier in a *caneye* under heavy guard.

"I will hold him until you are fit to do battle," Roldan replied.

Aaron's eyes narrowed and his expression hardened. "Magdalena is behind this. She fears for my life and has pleaded with you to keep me from that scum."

Roldan shrugged, neither denying nor admitting the accusation. "When it suits me, you may slash each other to bloody ribbons."

"And when will it suit you?" Torres grated out.

"Mayhap at sunrise tomorrow. Does that please you?" the *cacique* asked indifferently.

"No! Every hour he breathes is an affront to the House of Torres."

Roldan looked at the blazing fury etched in every line and angle of Aaron's taut body. "You had best save your ire for the morrow and focus it on Lorenzo Guzman." He waited until Aaron nodded and turned to leave, then said softly, "Have no fear. The fop will die soon enough."

"You seem quite certain of the contest's end," Aaron said, studying the shrewd brown eyes of the white *cacique*.

Roldan grinned. "I have seen him duel at court—and I have seen you hack down half a dozen Moors at one time, any one of whom was the equal of Guzman. Yet do not be overconfident. He has skill with a blade and he is crafty."

Aaron leaned his shoulder on the door frame of the *cacique's bohio* and replied consideringly, "He is not the only one who is crafty, Francisco. You play a dangerous game, rebelling against the crown. Even if you like not the Colons, they are the magisterial authority on Española."

"Perhaps I should allow you to return me to their good graces?" Roldan suggested, knowing what Aaron intended.

"Because you saved Magdalena, I will intercede with Cristobal for your pardon," Aaron replied. "If you in turn mend your ways." He looked at the burly Castilian measuringly.

"The idea of reformation has played about my mind here of late," Francisco said. He sat down on the carved *cacique's* chair and ran one large, calloused hand over the smooth wood, pausing at the inlaid gold carving on one arm. He looked up at Aaron. "Let us see what tomorrow brings. Then we will talk more. Do not deal harshly with Magdalena, Torres. She loves you well."

Aaron sighed. "Already I have dealt far too harshly with my wife. She wants only my safety. I will not fault her for asking this boon of you."

Aliyah looked behind her at the flickering fires of the compound. The orange flames danced through the slits of the cane walls like slivers spun off the sun. The gathering blackness of the jungle quickly enveloped her. Long ebony hair and dusky skin blended with the whispering palms and low-hanging flame vines of the dense undergrowth. Good. No one had seen her leave and no one followed. She made her way to the rendez-vous, her eyes glowing like a cat's in the night.

The moon was rising when she reached the clearing. She gave a low trill and waited. Nothing broke the silence but the hum of insects. Then suddenly, without warning, a set of calloused fingers bit into her shoulder, pulling her around.

"You are late," Behechio hissed.

Aliyah lowered the thick lashes over her glowing eyes. "I was forced to endure a meal with that pig Roldan before I could slip away unnoticed."

"A meal and what else?" the muscular, dark-skinned man asked, his harsh, angular features contorted with bitterness.

"Nothing tonight, but you know he takes me." She made an obscene gesture, then looked at him defiantly. "I hate him."

Although little taller than she, Behechio was barrel-chested and his powerful girth made him seem to menace the woman's softly rounded curves. "You say you hate white men, yet you have a white child," he accused her. "You are my wife now. No one should touch you but me."

She placed one hand placatingly on his hard, smooth chest. "No man but you ever shall again, my lord, once this is finished."

"What of the Golden One and his woman? My men tell me they are here. Once you went willingly to him."

Aliyah tossed back her long mane of hair as she raised her head. The handsome planes of her face were twisted with hatred. "Once it was my right. Now I would see you kill him and give me his skinny, red-haired wife as my slave. Will you do this for me, Behechio, husband?" she asked sweetly.

"Yes, I will kill him, but I will keep his woman as *my* slave, I think," he said consideringly.

"No!" she stamped a bare foot on the mossy carpet of fecund earth.

A cruel smile spread across his face. "So, you do not like me to have a white woman, yet you lay with two white men. Even now you may have that usurper's baby growing inside you." The smile was gone.

"You know this was part of our plan. I had to stay with Roldan if we were to succeed. I can rid myself of his seed as easily as I did the other . . . if it is necessary," she added carelessly. Then her eyes locked with his and she asked, "How went the battle in the north? Does Caonabo come to join us in driving the whites into the sea?"

Behechio's expression altered swiftly from jealousy to fury. "That traitorous dog you call brother has joined the enemy! He rules over more Tainos than all other chieftains, yet he fought with the whites. Caonabo and our friend are all taken. No help comes from the north."

"Then we must wait no longer. I overheard Aaron speak of the battle but could learn little. Once we kill Roldan and all the whites here, we will march north. I will make my brother, the ruler of Marien, see the justice of our cause," she vowed in a passionate voice.

"No more will white men kill us with their diseases and make us dig the accursed yellow metal," Behechio said, his voice rising. "You are certain Guacanagari will heed you and join us?"

"Yes, but I will plead your cause only if you do not touch the white woman. Give her to me when we take the compound," she implored.

"I will think on it," he replied, his male vanity pleased by her jealousy. It never occurred to him to question whether she was jealous over him or Aaron.

"When do we attack? Now that we know no help comes from the north, we must move quickly."

"My warriors are ready. Just before dawn three of the stealthiest will slip in and use their *bejucos* to strangle the guards. Return to the compound and wait. You must keep watch to be certain no one gives an alarm before we are inside."

"I will do better than that," she boasted. "A leaderless band of men fights ill. I will kill Roldan as he sleeps."

He smiled and nodded. "Let it be so. I will join you at sunrise."

Lorenzo Guzman paced his cell in the damp pre-dawn air. "God's balls and blood of all the martyrs! What am I doing in this hellish nightmare?" he muttered beneath his breath as he swatted at a mosquito intent on extracting what small measure of moisture remained inside his sweat-drenched body. When he next met Alonso Hojeda, he would kill the posturing little peacock! Sending him to this barbarian—a comrade in arms of Torres!

He shuddered as he considered the impending fight. It would be to the death. Torres knew he was Valdés' co-conspirator. He had not only abducted the swine's wife, but was responsible for the death of all the House of Torres. "And look what all my striving has gained me!" he hissed bitterly. "A prisoner awaiting a primitive gladiatorial combat to appease the blood lust of a pack of howling barbarians. I am their amusement in this god-forsaken hole!''

Peralonso watched his companion pace and mutter, swearing and sweating. From his reclining position on the crude pallet in the corner of their dingy prison, he spoke. "You but waste your strength on useless fear. Direct your anger. You are accounted a good swordsman. So is Torres, but he will attack with blind fury for revenge. Use cool determination against him and you may well take him.''

Guzman ceased his pacing. "Well enough for you to say. You will not be facing his blade!''

"I share this ghastly colonial prison with you, do I not? What madness to abduct that woman and flee here! I only wish—''

Guerra's speech was cut short when a dull thud sounded outside the door. A body had dropped to the ground. "What goes there?'' he whispered nervously, climbing to his feet as Lorenzo waited by the side of the room's lone entrance.

Hojeda's Taino slave slid into the room with a broad smile on his face. He bowed, a length of supple *bejuco* cord still wound around one brawny fist. "Come," he said simply, then added in broken Castilian, "I help you escape. Soon all whites be . . .'' He gestured with the cord, making his meaning abundantly clear.

Guzman and Guerra followed him past the strangled guard outside their cell.

Roldan's instincts had been finely honed over years of fighting Moors on the battlefield and brawling with his compatriots in the streets. He opened his eyes but did not move or alter his breathing as he lay in the *hamaca*. Someone was in the room with him. He swore silently for the unusually close night that had led him to sleep in the cooler but confining hemp sling. His sword and dirk lay across the room by the raised pallet in the corner. He was trapped, trussed up like a hog at butchering time!

The room was cast in darkness. The moon had set. Dawn was near. He strained his ears for another sound, but heard none. Then he caught the scent of fruit soap and the vanilla fragrance of the leopard orchid. Aliyah!

She approached the *hamaca*, knife raised high, gleaming dully in the darkness. *For all the times you rutted on me, white pig—as fat and dirty as the vile, squealing animals you brought to pollute our land!* She stood beside the *hamaca* ready to bury the knife in his throat. Then she saw the glow of his eyes—wide open, staring up at her in bemused surprise. Cursing, she plunged the blade downward on a swift, sure arc.

Roldan's reflexes were amazingly swift for a man of his size. One brawny arm came up to deflect the blade, smashing against her wrist. The knife went flying from her hand. Aliyah dove after it as Roldan rolled from the confining *hamaca*. By the time he had freed himself, she again held her weapon and ran at him, screaming like a deranged thing. He tried to seize her wrist, but the strength of her blind hate fortified her. As they struggled, she turned her body to the left while he twisted downward on her wrist. She held the blade at just such an angle that it slashed across her breast and embedded itself in her belly.

Aaron was restless and half awake. Something was amiss. The instant he heard the scream, he leaped from the pallet, awakening Magdalena. She sat up, rubbing her eyes as he slid on his hose and reached for his sword belt.

"What has happened?" she asked with apprehension. "'Tis not yet dawn. You cannot face Lorenzo now."

"I am not concerned with that filth. I heard a scream—a woman's cry. It sounded from Roldan's quarters."

"Surely we are safe in the compound," she said with a bravado she did not feel.

"Probably only a lover's spat," he said, his teeth a white slash in the darkness as he grinned affectionately at her. "Stay indoors until I return."

With that, he was gone. Magdalena felt an eerie sense of uneasiness pervade the room. She rose and wrapped her body in a length of cotton cloth, securing it tightly above her breasts. Such would have to serve until they returned to Ysabel. "I am only overwrought because of the duel," she murmured, trying to shake the tension holding her prisoner.

Aaron ran toward the *bohio* of the *cacique*. Already several of Roldan's men, night sentries filled with wine and none too alert, milled about the doorway to the big hall. He quickly shouldered past them and then stopped, frozen in shock. Aliyah lay on the floor, her head cradled in Roldan's lap. Both of them were covered with blood. It ran in a red river from the raw, slashing wound high on her stomach.

"I cannot staunch the flow," Francisco said quietly.

"How did this happen?" Aaron asked as he knelt beside the *cacique*.

"She tried to kill me. We struggled and her own blade turned on her," Roldan replied, puzzled and regretful.

Hearing Aaron's voice, Aliyah's mind cleared from the haze of pain and her eyes focused on him. One hand reached out and clutched at him with amazing strength, staining his bare arm with her blood. "I gave you a splendid son, yet you wed with a barren rack of bones, all for her precious white skin."

"Aliyah, please, do not—"

"No! I am going to the *zemis* of my ancestors. From the spirit world I will return to curse that red-haired bitch, but know this now, *white* man," she grated out in a low burbling rasp as red frothed on her lips, "I curse you with these words . . . you think your son dead . . . Navaro is alive." She glared at Aaron and watched with satisfaction as he blanched in the dim dawn light.

"I saw his ashes. . . ." Aaron's voice broke. "Where . . . ?"

"I sent him away. You will never find him, such a small babe of mixed blood. There are many such now, like the shells along the beach. Your son is as good as dead to you. Get one on your cold white wife, Aaron . . . if she can give you one . . ." She coughed once, then her eyes glazed over, glowing dully. She was still.

Aaron trembled as he stretched out his hand and touched her cheeks, then softly closed her eyes. "I had no idea . . . the strength of her hate . . . to send her own son off with strangers."

"'Tis a fearful, unnatural woman. How could a mother do such?" Roldan said as he lowered Aliyah's body to the floor.

Aaron crossed the room to get a length of cloth with which to cover her. Gazing numbly at the still form, he said in a low voice, "I will find you, Navaro, my son. I will search every village, every band of Tainos on Española until I do!"

Roldan clasped his shoulder. Just then a chorus of wild yelling broke the dawn silence. One of the Castilian soldiers ran into the *bohio* crying, "Behechio's Tainos are attacking—hundreds of them!"

"Magdalena!" Aaron said as he spun around. "I must see to her safety."

"Go!" Roldan said as Aaron raced through the door. Then he turned his attention to the men assembling haphazardly before him. "It seems my mistress was but the harbinger of more misfortune. Her husband Behechio must not be the craven coward I thought him when he fled Xaragua." As he spoke, he strode outside the *bohio*, hefting his sword. He issued curt instructions to all the assembled men, then walked toward the wall of the compound, where a horde of Indians was swarming in after having cut a wide hole in the heavy thatch barrier with stolen swords.

"How clever of these primitives to learn such a use of Toledo steel," he muttered as he sliced one warrior almost in half with his blade.

Magdalena heard the cries of alarm and sounds of fighting from the western wall of the compound. Seizing her dagger, she ran from the *caneye* and padded swiftly down the streets toward Roldan's large *bohio* in search of her husband. Suddenly two men materialized from the shadows. Instinctively Magdalena knew they were enemies and drew her dagger as one reached for her.

"Well, what have we here? The Jew's vixen," Lorenzo snarled as her blade drew blood from his arm. He moved quickly to her left, distracting her as Peralonso came up behind her, but this time Magdalena had learned the way they worked. She ducked as his heavy sword hilt came down, hitting her shoulder. It was a painful, glancing blow, but it missed her head. Without wasting a breath on a scream, she darted between the two closing assailants and dashed into a narrow passage between the *caneyes* still deep in dawn's shadows.

"After her! She is our means of escape," Lorenzo cried as he pursued his quarry with Guerra racing just behind him.

Magdalena turned corner after corner, twisting and turning in the maze of huts until she was thoroughly disoriented. All about her the cry of battle was rousing the inhabitants. She collided with men hastily arming themselves and stumbled over women and children huddled terror-stricken in the shadows. "Which way to the *cacique's bohio?*" she panted in Taino to one woman crouching in a doorway, shielding a whimpering little girl.

The woman pointed back the way she had come, but
wing to the vague glaze of terror in her eyes, Magdale-
a was uncertain of whether the direction was accurate.
Iaving nothing else on which to base her flight, she
uickly back-tracked in a circuitous route, praying to
void Guzman and Guerra.

A Taino warrior, fully armed with lance, knife, and
arts suddenly stepped in front of her with his long
pear outstretched to block her escape. She whirled
nly to run into Lorenzo and his minion. The Taino fled
nd the two Castilians closed in on her as she stood her
round, dagger moving this way and that, fending them
ff.

Please, Aaron, please—where are you?

All around the compound, Behechio's Taino warriors
acked their way through the walls and fell upon
Roldan's men and their Taino allies. The hiss of darts
lended with the swish of slashing swords. The
Castilians quickly employed their arbalests, letting fly
uiver after quiver of bolts, reaching their targets with
eadly speed and accuracy. Taino women shrieked,
lutching children and running for cover as men yelled
vith fear and battle lust, engaging in chaotic skirmish-
ng all round the large, overcrowded village.

Soon smoke began to curl from the dry thatched
oofs of the huts. The compound wall, in spite of its
recautionary drenching, was already smoldering in
everal places. The brilliance of the golden orange
unrise on the eastern horizon was already exceeded by
he crimson inferno inside the village. Orange flames
nd red blood blended, covering and consuming the
rown and green world that had been Roldan's capital.

Aaron fought his way down a street crowded with
nemy warriors, fleeing villagers, and sword-wielding
oldiers. A dart whistled past his head as he ducked
etween two huts. When a Taino lunged at him with his

lance, Aaron parried the thrust and slashed into th
warrior's arm. Quickly freeing himself, he raced towar
the *caneye* where he had left Magdalena, never lookin
back on the carnage behind him.

When he reached the *caneye,* he raced inside, callin
Magdalena's name. Over the cries of men, women, an
children, the din of battle and the roar of flames, n
voice answered from within. Quickly he scanned th
room and found no sign of violence. His wife was
fighter. No one could have taken her from here withou
her putting up a fearsome struggle, but that offered littl
consolation as it meant she was somewhere out in th
streets trying to reach him amid the pitched battle.

Swearing, he turned and retraced the path t
Roldan's *bohio* far less swiftly than he had when th
streets had been deserted. All the while he cut an
thrust, he called her name. Finally one of Roldan
Taino guards, his head bleeding profusely from a nast
gash, reached out to him and cried, "You search fo
your woman?"

"You have seen her?" he asked, heart stopped wit
dread.

"The two men my *cacique* had imprisoned—the
have escaped. I gave chase and saw them seize her. The
went toward the chamber where my lord keeps his grea
beasts."

"The horses," Aaron said with dawning horror. Th
bastards had Magdalena and they were going to escap
with her if he could not stop them! Wordlessly, h
turned, praying Guzman had not the brains to stamped
all the terrified beasts and leave him afoot. The bay h
rode had good endurance—if he was yet there to b
ridden!

Behechio's Tainos would not go near the fenced-i
area where the Castilians kept their mounts. Of th
friendly Tainos who lived here, only a few were not i
mortal terror of horses. He slashed and hacked his wa

across the village square toward the enclosure. When he reached it, a sob tore from his throat. The gates were open, and flames licked about the fence. It was empty.

He collared a soldier nearby just as the man dispatched an Indian with his sword. "Two white men dragging a red-haired woman—my wife—have you seen them?"

When the baffled man shook his head, Aaron released him and began to search further, seizing friend and foe alike, questioning in Castilian and Taino. The only white woman in Xaragua and no one had seen her! Just as he despaired, one of Roldan's captains came loping up, breathless and bloody with several minor wounds.

"Your lady—with two white men—those Don Francisco held prisoner. I saw them ride south—the trail to the caravels in the cove."

Nodding quickly, Aaron asked, "Know you of a single horse left in this village?"

At the negative reply, Aaron cursed, praying for his faithful Andaluz, lost back in Seville a lifetime ago. No one could have taken that steed from him when he called. Did Rubio remember only a bit of what he had been teaching him? He worked his way to a clear place in the compound wall, not as yet afire, and hacked his way through it, then circled warily away from the embroiled village. Already Roldan's men were routing Behechio's. He headed toward the coastal trail, which he had never before traversed.

How far was it to the sea? Would the ships take Lorenzo and his captive aboard? How could Guzman get the sailing master to cast off? As he considered these frightening questions, he whistled for Rubio, calling the big gelding by name. Just as he was about to abandon hope and begin to run after his quarry, he heard a snort, then the soft pounding of hoofbeats. Across the curve of the river in a planted clearing, half a dozen of Roldan's horses milled about, grazing aimlessly. Once free of the

terrifying smells of blood and smoke, they had cease
their blind run.

He whistled again and the bay resumed his trot awa
from his companions, heading toward his master. Aa
ron's clothes were blood-spattered, and he himself ha
more than a few nicks and minor wounds. When the ba
shied, he crooned to him in soft reassuring cadenc
until the horse came up, nosing him uncertainly.

Once he had a firm hand hold in the bay's mane, h
moved slowly to the left side and pulled himself up i
one swift, smooth movement. How fortunate that th
jungle heat had led him to practice riding bareback
Riding without a hackamore, however, was quite anoth
er matter. The horse shied backwards, skittered side
ways and generally resisted this strange new exercise
but Aaron's determination finally won out.

He forced himself to be calm as he controlled the bi
bay's pace and direction with his hands knotted in th
mane, his knees working into the horse's sides. Finall
he had Rubio plunging into the jungle along the trail t
the coast.

Magdalena sat in the cold, sticky mud, her hands an
feet numb, her body bruised and scratched from th
swift and terrible ride along the overgrown, twistin
pathway to the hidden cove where Roldan's caravel
bobbed on the morning tide. Twice she had nearl
escaped. Certainly she had slowed their progress, onc
by bolting her mount into the dense underbrush unti
they had overtaken her. Then she again had broken free
back-tracking and knocking Guerra from his horse a
she did so. But she nearly killed herself when her mar
slipped in the mud and pitched her several yards int
the air. Fortunately, the jungle floor provided a sof
cushion and she landed without hitting any trees. The
mare was less fortunate and broke her leg. Guerra cu
the poor beast's throat with his sword.

Guzman had her complete the ride with her hands
nd feet bound, slung across his saddle. Although
iserably uncomfortable, she knew that riding double
reatly slowed their pace. She had bought all the time
he could when Lorenzo dropped her like a sack of
ams onto the ground of the bare promontory where
ae signal fires for the caravels were laid.

Hojeda's Taino had run through the jungle on a more
irect route than the horses could pass. He had arrived
t the site ahead of them and gathered wood for the fire.
Iow he waited patiently with his small pile of dry twigs.
Iext to the kindling sat a bucket of pitch beside a deep
sh-filled, blackened hole. This was where the smoky
gnal was made which would draw the distant caravel's
ttention. Then a ship's boat would be let down and sent
⦁ the narrow band of wet sandy beach.

Guerra cut her bonds to allow circulation to return to
er hands and feet, but he stood directly over her,
nenacing her with an arsenal of weapons pilfered from
ae bodies of dead soldiers in the village.

Guzman commanded Hojeda's Taino servant to pour
ae black sticky pitch over the small mound of wood. He
aen produced a flint and set the sparks to ignite it as the
idian jumped back, still in awe at the magical ways
hite men had with fire. The leaping flames quickly
lled the dimness of the dawn sky with billowing black
noke, alerting the morning watch aboard the caravels
⦁ the fact that Roldan had sent an urgent message.

"Think you they will believe us when we tell them the
llage is overrun by Behechio's savages?" Peralonso
ked as he kept one eye on Magdalena.

"Aye. Only look at us, cut, burned and scratched from
ur flight. What earthly reason would we have to return
ut a few days after our last visit to the cove if not to give
arning?" Lorenzo noted with grim satisfaction that
ae ship's boat was being lowered into the water.

"What will we do with her? She will blurt out that we

are escaped from their *cacique* if given the chance, Guerra stated.

Lorenzo looked at the half-naked woman crumpled on the sand with her hair flowing like dark fire about her shoulders. He said with a shrug, "I suppose we must kill her. A pity we have never had the chance to use her."

Chapter Twenty-Four

"Of course, we could let you live . . . if you kept silent," Lorenzo added silkily as he gazed down at Magdalena. Her eyes blazed like emerald flames and she spat on his boots.

"I suspected as much. But then, if you are in a swoon from the anguish of the Taino attack, the captain will surely understand." He motioned for Guerra to move away. Then he knelt down and drew back his fist.

Realizing his intent, Magdalena's still numb hands, played in the soft mud, clawed deeply as she grasped fistfuls and hurled the sticky black grit full into his face. With an oath, Lorenzo swung at her in spite of his burning eyes, but she ducked. Before he could raise his fist to strike at her again, Magdalena rolled to her feet and began to run, forcing her cramped limbs to obey her.

Guerra gave chase until he heard the crashing sound

of a horse breaking from the undergrowth. Aaron's bi
bay gelding thundered into the clearing. He swun
down and clasped Magdalena as she stumbled into h
arms.

"My legs betray me. Aaron, beware!" she crie
Peralonso's sword gleamed evilly as he lunged at h
adversary.

Quickly shoving Magdalena behind him, Aaro
ducked Guerra's first clumsy slash as he unsheathed h
own sword. He met the next onslaught, and the lou
clanging of tempered Toledo steel rang across th
awakening jungle. The Taino quickly stepped bac
eyeing the combatants, ready to vanish into the unde
growth if the battle went ill for his masters. He stoo
near their horses, guarding them, a feat that definitel
marked him as one who had lived with the ruthles
Hojeda. Still the Taino would not dare to join the figh

Guzman, seeing how well his mentor was occupyin
Torres, smiled coldly as he drew his own blade. "This
a battle you will not win, *marrano*," he said with a
eerie laugh. He lunged, but Aaron's big broadswor
flashed in an arc from right to left, holding both men :
bay.

Magdalena frantically scanned the area, searching fc
a weapon. Lorenzo had taken her dagger. The cowardl
Indian had one, but she could not hope to wrest h
weapon from him.

Aaron fought with amazing speed and agility, fendin
off both his deadly and desperate adversaries. But as h
ducked, jumped and parried their blows, holding the
was all he could do—until he made one mistake an
they closed in for the kill.

Magdalena coughed as the wind changed directior
and smoke blew in her face. Instantly the idea came t
her. She raced around the fire pit and seized a lon;
slender piece of green wood lying to the side. Sh

shoved one end of it in the fire to let it ignite, keeping her eyes on the combatants.

Magdalena knew she took a terrible risk as she struggled to heft the heavy pitch bucket. If the flames came near her, she would die just as Benjamin and his family had. The thought fortified her. With a loud curse, she screamed at Guzman.

Instinctively he turned, just in time to have a generous splash of the tarry paste hit him square in the chest. Magdalena dropped the bucket and picked up the firebrand with lightning speed while Aaron and Guerra continued their fierce duel.

Careful not to get her pitch-covered hands near the flame, she jabbed the stub at Lorenzo, who, divining her intent, paled and backed away from the other combatants. "How like you this, Inquisitor's minion? You, who have sent saints to their deaths in the flames?" she grated out in loathing.

Icy sweat poured from his skin, and his gray eyes turned dark as pewter with terror. He could taste the ugly metallic fear in his mouth as he slashed at the torch, attempting to hold her back. Struggling to breathe, he ducked the firebrand's deadly strike once more. Then, recalling Guerra's advice to him about goading Aaron to make the man careless, he let a sneer curl his lips and spoke. "You will burn yourself, stupid little *marrano's* slut. Look you, the flames eat their way up the spear to your own pitch-soaked hands."

Her green eyes narrowed in quick calculation. "You called it a spear. So 'tis," she replied as she threw it with a swift, hard thrust.

Although Lorenzo tried to deflect the flaming instrument of death, it caught his billowing shirt-sleeve. His scream ripped through the air as the fire flashed across his upper body with a hissing whoosh, transforming him into a human torch. He dropped his sword and began uselessly beating at the flames. Smeared with pitch, Magdalena realized her own danger. She quickly dashed away from Guzman, but he was beyond thoughts of catching her.

"The sea, the sea," he shrieked, running headlong from the clearing down the rough, rocky pathway to the cove far below. His screams echoed up to where Guerra and Torres still fought.

Aaron had been cut several times before Guzman was taken from the fight. One slash on his sword arm particularly weakened his striking power. The older swordsman was a far worthier opponent than his young charge and now he closed in for the kill. But Aaron, bloodied as he was, still possessed the survival skills so hard won in the Moorish wars.

"You tire, my young friend, eh? You have lost much blood," Guerra taunted.

"And you have lost your helper. One on one I will take you, Peralonso."

"No, 'tis I will take you—and then your fiery woman. A dangerous piece, that one," he said as he thrust boldly, only to be met by Aaron's parry.

Although the blue eyes darkened, they did not flame with the unreasoning passion that would give Guerra the edge he needed. Torres attacked with precision, nicking Guerra's arm before the older man could retreat.

"Now, we grow more evenly matched," Aaron grated out grimly.

As they dodged and slashed, Magdalena picked up Guzman's discarded sword and kept an eye on the Taino across the clearing. After Lorenzo's cries died away, the Indian melted silently into the jungle, abandoning the nervous, shying horses. Magdalena debated attempting to catch them, then decided that was better left until the duel was over—and Aaron was victorious. She possessed no skill with the heavy broadsword and feared it

he attempted to intervene she might accidentally harm
her husband instead of helping him. She drew nearer
he combatants, warily searching for a way to clearly
lash Guerra if Aaron looked to need her aid.

They continually circled, back and forth, moving
about the smoking fire in the pit, both now drenched
with sweat and blood. Suddenly Aaron appeared to
tumble on the uneven ground. Guerra quickly moved
in for the kill, raising his sword in an arc of death as his
foe went down on one knee.

Magdalena screamed and raised her heavy weapon,
but before she could do more than take a step, it was
finished. Aaron's sword blocked Guerra's and the dagger her husband had extracted from his belt slashed into
Peralonso's soft belly. With a look of perfect astonishment, the courtier dropped his sword and fell to his
knees as the knife ripped yet higher before Aaron pulled
it free with a final twist.

"An old battlefield feint, but one apparently never
called into use when noblemen duel at court," Aaron
said as he stood up, breathing heavily.

Guerra toppled to the ash-covered ground, dead.
Magdalena dropped the sword and flew into her husband's arms. They held tightly to each other, sparing the
dead man not a look. Then shouts from below on the
beach interrupted them. Disengaging from Magdalena,
Aaron carefully led her from the proximity of the fire.
"Take care till we can get that deadly stuff washed off
you," he warned as he strode across the clearing and
collected the saddled horses. He whistled and Rubio
came trotting back into the clearing.

"How did you ride him without even a hackamore?"
he asked in amazement.

"'Twas not a simple matter," he replied grimly as he
helped her onto the smaller gelding that Guerra had
ridden. He then took the hackamore from the skittish
larger gray that had been Guzman's and placed it on

Rubio. All three horses were nervous because of the smell of blood and death permeating the air, but when Aaron swung up on the bay's back, the horse obeyed him. "Leave the gray here while we greet Roldan's men below and see to Guzman." He watched Magdalena pale as she remembered the flames licking at Lorenzo's face, enveloping his body as he ran down the hillside to the water.

"I wonder if he made it," she said softly.

"'Twould go easier on him if he did not. I have seen men live for days with pitch burns during the sieges in Andalusia. 'Tis not an easy death."

"Would you wish him to have one?" she asked as they rode carefully down the trail.

Aaron shrugged wearily. His arm throbbed and he was too tired to think straight after all that had befallen them during the past few hours. "I once wanted him to die in the slowest, most horrible manner I could devise . . . and after what I had seen during the war, I could devise much. But now . . . I have had enough of death, Magdalena. I would rather have life."

"So would I and so would your father, for us both," she replied simply.

When they reached the cove and dismounted, the *gromets* and one officer from a caravel stood around Guzman's body. He had died but a few yards from the water's edge. As they approached the hideously charred remains with arms outstretched toward the lapping waves, Magdalena felt her bile rise and turned quickly into her husband's arms. Aaron shielded her from the grotesque sight and stroked her tangled hair, soothing her as the ship's master approached them.

"Who was he? God's bones, what a way to die!" He too, looked away from the gruesome sight.

"Lorenzo Guzman, late of the ducal house of Medina Sidonia. You made his acquaintance but a day or two ago, I believe," Aaron answered.

"How came this gentleman to such an end?" the sailing master asked, looking at the bloodied man and pitch-stained woman before him.

"'Tis a long and twisted tale. Don Lorenzo and his companion Guerra, who lies dead at the signal fire, were prisoners of Roldan. They escaped during an attack by the followers of Behechio. The battle yet raged in the compound when I rode off in pursuit of them, for they had taken my wife." He held Magdalena close.

"I killed him," she said in a clear, surprisingly strong voice, gesturing to the remains of Guzman. "I poured pitch on him and set a firebrand to him, and I would do it again before I let him kill my husband."

The sailing master, a tall, portly man with a florid complexion, blanched at the iron determination in the small Castilian lady's expression. He averted his eyes from her and asked her husband, "You say Behechio's Tainos attack Roldan's stronghold?"

"Yes, but by the time I left, Roldan's forces were regaining control, although Behechio's men had fired the village. This offal and his companion wanted to flee Española in your ships. Doubtless they hoped to convince you the savages were hot upon this trail so you would weigh anchor at once and sail for Cadiz," Aaron replied.

Juan de León looked alarmed. "Mayhap we should return to my ship. Although several other caravels have put in here and taken on brazilwood, then sailed for home, I have not the supplies."

Aaron smiled grimly. "You would need to be able to return to Ysabel and secure them first—and as rebels you cannot do so." He watched the sailing master bluster and redden nervously, then added, "Don Francisco and I had recently discussed his, er, return to the good graces of the governor. I will speak with him about it, but before I can return to the stronghold, my lady and I could use your assistance. Food and medicines, perhaps some cloth to bind this accursed wound," he gestured to the dark red of congealed blood on his arm.

Magdalena could feel the way he leaned on her and suddenly realized that he was far more seriously injured than first she had thought. At once she took charge. "See you fetch clean water. There is a stream but a few dozen yards that way," she pointed toward the hillside they had just traversed and sent one young *gromet* to fetch a bucket from the boat to do her bidding. Then she turned to the sailing master. "Have you bandages and medicines aboard your ship?"

"Our surgeon can be fetched forthwith, but might it not be safer to take you both to the ship?" León asked.

"We will be safe enough here. I am not incapacitated so badly that I cannot ride back to the compound. Nothing and no one puts me aboard a ship again," Aaron added grimly as he walked stiffly over to a large flat rock, where he took a seat and then glared balefully at Magdalena and the sailing master.

"He is quite stubborn, as you can see. Please, fetch the surgeon and his wares quickly," Magdalena said with a hint of a smile on her lips. She turned and walked toward Aaron. As she knelt and began to examine the wound on his arm, she whispered, "Never again aboard a ship? 'Twas as bad as Roldan said, then."

He flinched, then replied, "We will sail to France to visit my family one day, mayhap, but there is no need now to board that ship. I must return to the stronghold."

"You are certain Francisco will be victorious?" she asked nervously as the ship's boat grew smaller on the horizon and the *gromet* trotted up with the bucket of fresh water.

"Yes, he will triumph. The man has more lives and wiles than a score of black cats." He paused a moment, then said, "Aliyah attempted to kill him just before the compound was attacked. He was asleep in his *hamaca* when she came in the darkness. He struggled with her and her own knife turned on her."

Magdalena's busy hands ceased their cleansing of his wounds. She looked into his eyes. "Aliyah is dead then?"

He nodded, a deep melancholy now pervading his expression. "Yes, but before she died . . ." His voice broke for a moment and he reached out and clasped Magdalena's hand with both of his. "Before she died she told me Navaro was not dead."

She froze. "But how could that be—the ashes, the burial urn—"

He loosened his tight grip on her hand and shrugged helplessly. "I do not know. She said that she sent him off with Tainos to a distant part of Española where I could never find him."

"But we can! Surely his looks will be remarked on—he has your eyes and features, Aaron—the Torres stamp. No matter how many half-caste babies there may be, he will always stand out."

His eyes warmed with love as he caressed her matted, tangled hair. "You would help me search for Navaro? How extraordinary you are, my lady, my love, my life," he whispered. "If only Aliyah's hate did not lead her to tell one final lie. Mayhap we will search in vain. . . ."

She swallowed, then said in a shaky voice, "I feared when Roldan said Navaro had been well the morning before his fatal sickness that she had killed her own child. That is possible, but I think she spoke truly. How much sweeter her revenge to let him live and yet keep him from us." She reached up and caressed his cheek. "We will find him, my lord. We will!"

Guacanagari sat very still on his mahogany throne, his face sad, yet its noble expression infused with dignity that belied his years. When Aaron finished telling the story of Aliyah's death and the defeat of Behechio's warriors by Roldan's army, the *cacique* nodded. "Hate consumed her. Even before she departed on her marriage journey, I feared the end would come this way. I am most saddened that she has used her own child in her poisonous schemes. We will begin a search at once. I will send runners to every village on this island . . . and if need be to every other island the Taino people have ever inhabited."

"You are a good and true friend and do me great honor, Guacanagari," Aaron said as he sat beside the *cacique*. They were alone in Guacanagari's private retiring room. Magdalena was with the village women, bathing and refreshing herself after their long, arduous journey from Xaragua. Although healing nicely, Aaron's arm still ached abominably after the long ride from Roldan's stronghold.

"Aliyah was buried according to your customs, with the full honors due a royal princess. I watched the elders in Xaragua do it properly."

"You do me great honor, too, my friend," Guacanagari said. "We have spoken enough of sad things. Let us now plan how we may find Navaro." He clapped his hands and summoned several nobles.

Finding the beautiful babe did not prove an easy task. No one in even the remotest village had heard about or seen a blue-eyed Taino boy. Aaron and his Taino friends traveled the length and breadth of Española, from village to village. Since the great battle in the Vega, the countryside was mostly pacified. The searchers were accepted freely everywhere they went as emissaries of the great *cacique* of Marien, but no one could aid them in their quest for the boy.

Perhaps Aliyah lied. Magdalena may have been right when she voiced her fear that Aliyah had killed her own child. This dying tale was merely her way of leaving me to ope for the impossible for the rest of my life. Aaron rode into Guacanagari's village, more dispirited and exhausted than he had felt since learning the fate of his family.

Magdalena watched him dismount at the fenced-in area where the horses were kept. He began to unsaddle Rubio and rub him down. She knew his search had been in vain. Sighing, she clutched the missive she had been carrying to her breast. Perhaps it and her other news might hearten him. She called out his name just as he gave Rubio an affectionate swat and released the great bay into the confines of the enclosure.

He turned at once and opened his arms to embrace her, crushing her to him and burying his face in her fragrant hair. "Magdalena, I have missed you so, my heart," he murmured. Then, feeling the paper she held crushed between them, he held her at arm's length and asked, "What have you here?"

She smiled. "Something to cheer you, I hope, for I know the search goes ill. 'Tis a letter from your uncle Isaac, all the way from France."

"Have you read it?" he asked eagerly, taking it from her.

"Of course not. 'Twas addressed to you," she replied primly.

He returned her smile, broke the seal, and unrolled the parchment. Quickly he scanned the contents, then his smile broadened. "He has Mateo's son Alejandro safely out of Barcelona now. Isaac and Ruth will raise the boy and Ana's little Olivia with all the love and care they lavish on their own grandchildren."

"I am so happy for them. Part of Benjamin and Serafina lives on in those children," she said, working up her courage for her next announcement.

He again pulled her to him and they began to stroll leisurely toward the village. "Uncle Isaac also says he

wants us to return to live with them. There is wealth
aplenty and much I could do to help him with the
importing business he has begun."

"Us? I know you wrote to him of our marriage, but
word of it cannot have reached him yet. And besides,"
she added uneasily, "I am outside their faith. Somehow
I suspect Isaac is not as tolerant as his brother."

"Isaac and Ruth will love you, I promise. The life
there would be much more comfortable than here,
Magdalena. You and I cannot return to Castile, but in
France we would be safe—able to live with all the
amenities of wealth that you gave up to pursue me."

She touched his lips with her fingertips to silence him
as they paused in the middle of the open clearing, a
man, sun-bronzed and dressed as a Taino warrior, and a
woman with loose, flowing hair spilling over her shoulders, robed in soft folds of gold cotton cloth. "I was
raised with few of the amenities—only stubborn Castilian pride and it takes naught of wealth for me to keep
that! When I lived at court, amid all the finery my
father's stolen money could buy, I was most desperately
unhappy. Aaron, I—"

A loud cry of greeting and the pounding of hooves cut
short her words as Francisco Roldan galloped up to the
embracing couple and swung down from his heaving
mount. He made what passed as a courtly bow to her,
then clapped Aaron on the back heartily. "God's bones,
I am mightily weary. 'Tis good to see you safe returned.
My Taino friends to the south said you were making for
Guacanagari's village."

"Yes, again without a word of Navaro," Aaron replied
soberly.

Roldan shook his great shaggy head in sorrow. "I, too
must report that my search the length and breadth of
the peninsula of Xaragua has yielded nothing. I am
certain the boy is not here. If Aliyah sent him away, she
sent him to a tribe far distant."

Magdalena watched Aaron control his emotions with great effort. He, too, had noted Roldan's use of the word "if." "We are grateful for your aid in the search," she said, then added, "Please, I go to prepare our evening meal. You will sup with us and I will have Guacanagari's servants prepare you a *bohio* in which to sleep."

"And any other accoutrements you may need will be readily available—if you but ask the women of the village yourself," Aaron added as the two men led Roldan's horse to be rubbed down and put to pasture.

As Magdalena walked toward the village, both men's eyes followed her. "I envy you your lady, my friend."

"Would you turn from your roistering ways and settle down to honest toil and matrimony?" Aaron asked half in disbelief.

"I would have a measure of peace, yes. I grow weary of the bloodshed. Once I thought I could protect the Indians who allied with me because as a white *cacique* the government would respect my claims, but even if I could keep the Colons out, I cannot maintain peace. Each month more ships arrive filled with gold seekers." He sighed heavily.

Aaron watched Roldan work the big chestnut with powerful strokes of the rub rag. "Are you saying you will agree to my good offices as mediator with the Colons?"

Francisco paused and turned, his shrewd brown eyes glowing as they met Aaron's level blue ones. "Back in Xaragua you offered such, and I said I would think on it . . . and I have. Yes, I would make peace with the Admiral of the Ocean Sea and his *adelantado*, if they will hear reasonable terms."

"Which are?" Aaron prompted.

Roldan rubbed his neck. "First, I would value not having this stretched. I hear they have kept the gallows in Ysabel quite busy here of late. And . . ." he hesitated as he resumed rubbing down the horse, "I have two caravels loaded with prime brazilwood—which as you

know I cannot sell in any port in Castile unless I giv
over a share to the governor and he allows the ships t
sail."

"There is also the royal fifth to be paid," Aaror
reminded him.

"Done—if I am allowed to keep the ships for futur
ventures. The crews are loyal to me."

"They mutinied when sent from Cadiz to supply th
colonists at Ysabel," Aaron said.

"You know how unpopular the Genoese are and wha
chaos reigned in Ysabel when first they arrived. But
have kept the ships safe and gathered a highly profitabl
cargo in the meanwhile. Surely that should give me
share of ownership." He waited, his shrewd gaze study
ing his companion.

"You drive a hard bargain," Aaron replied grudgingl

Roldan laughed. "That should make the Genoes
admire my skills all the more!"

Together the two men returned to the village for foo
and rest, but a runner from Ysabel had arrived jus
before them and Guacanagari summoned him to hi
audience chamber. After all the introductions wer
completed, Aaron read the missive from Cristobal.

A frown marred his forehead as he said, "Hojeda ha
escaped to the interior, where he will doubtless stir u
more grief."

"This news distresses you, my friend. Surely one man
even one such as this can do no harm before he i
captured by Don Cristobal," Guacanagari said.

"Let us hope so, but we must act quickly before h
can break the peace so hard won in the interior.
Aaron's gaze shifted from Guacanagari to Roldan an
then a smile twitched at the corners of his lips. "Perhap
this is your means to redeem yourself. You know Alons
well."

"A cocky little bastard but a hell of a man to have o
your side in a fight," Francisco replied.

"I would as leave never turn my back to his blade, bu

if he trusts you . . ." Aaron let his words fade suggestively.

"I catch the drift of your idea. Yes, I suppose I might convince Alonso that service under the Colons beats service over a gallows. If I can be pardoned, mayhap so can he."

"Only if he will cease his butchering of Tainos. I think it best if he sailed for Cadiz as soon as he is properly received back into the good graces of the governor. I shall send Magdalena ahead to treat with Cristobal and Bartolomé. She has more influence with them than anyone. If we bring Alonso to heel, I think things will go well for you both."

"I think Alonso will be delighted with the prospect of returning home. He can wring little gold from the Tainos and since Caonabo, Behechio, and even the formidable Roldan are all brought to recognize the crown and its representatives, he will find Española a tame and useless place indeed!" Roldan replied in the Taino tongue.

Even Guacanagari joined their jovial smiles.

If the men were all well pleased with their plan, Magdalena was not. When they returned to their *bohio*, Aaron sat down and extracted his writing instruments from his saddle bags. Before he could begin to pen a letter to Cristobal, Magdalena rounded on him.

"Men, pah! You and Francisco will go off chasing that vicious little cur while I must lobby for him with the governor. Let Francisco risk his life on Hojeda. Why should you?"

He looked up at her in surprise. "You were fortunate that Roldan championed you against Guzman and Guerra. Do you not wish to see him pardoned?"

Magdalena knelt by his side, earnest entreaty in her eyes. "Of course I do. I am most grateful for his help, but I do not see why we must include Alonso Hojeda in the bargain—or why you must go chasing after him. He is dangerous, Aaron." *And there is so much else I long to share with you, if only the time is right.*

"I am the commandant of the interior, at least for now. 'Tis my duty to apprehend an escaped prisoner."

Magdalena sighed. "I suppose you must do this, but what after? I would have you resign as commandant." She held her breath.

"I owe Cristobal much. Let me think on it. Will you to Ysabel to plead Roldan's cause?"

Her soft smile was his answer as she framed his face with her hands and kissed him. "Tomorrow you ride after Hojeda. Tonight I will ride you."

Chapter Twenty-Five

Cristobal Colon was a weary man. He sat at the heavy wooden table in his private office, staring at the charts and navigational instruments as he ran his gnarled fingers over the smooth pages of his log book from the first voyage. "Such beauty, such strange lands we chart among these islands, but where lies Cathay? Where Cipangu? Where is the great mainland of Asia?"

He ached to feel the rolling rhythm of ship's planks beneath his feet. How he hated the flat calm of the cold stone floor upon which he now spent his days. The letters and instructions arriving with disturbing regularity from the Majesties indicated their extreme displeasure with the fiscal return from his explorations, and more particularly their displeasure with his colonial policies in governing Española.

The enslaved, rebellious Tainos sent as tribute to the monarchy mostly died enroute. They made poor servants, being of weak physical constitutions in the colder climates of Europe. Everywhere, in Castile and on Española, they perished from the most minor of European diseases. The queen had been able to send pitifully few clergy to convert them to the true faith. He sighed, recalling the butchery when men with cannon and arbalest fired into the human walls of Tainos armed only with puny darts and wooden spears. "We offer them only death and that without salvation for their souls."

If only he could find the mainland with its vast wealth, great cities, and brilliant civilizations. Then all his failure here on Española would be forgotten, but as long as the contentious Castilian nobility poured in and out of Ysabel, fighting among themselves and abusing the Indians, he was chained to his civil post.

His eyes, red-rimmed from a recent bout of inflammation, again scanned the royal missive. Soon his enemies at court would be gratified, for a royal chamberlain, Juan Aguado, was on his way to investigate all the claims of malfeasance laid by Buil, Margarite and a host of other Castilians against the Colon family and most especially against him as governor. He had already sent his youngest brother back to plead his case at court, but it seemed Diego had little effect on the royal politics.

Just then a soft knock on his door brought Cristobal from his sad reverie. "Enter," he commanded, expecting a servant or some supplicant in trouble with the law. His face softened with a gentle smile as Magdalena entered.

"Am I disturbing you, Cristobal?" she asked, eyeing the logs, letters, and other official-looking documents strewn about his office.

"Of course not. I am most heartily happy to see you returned safely to Ysabel. What of the boy?" he asked, knowing well how long and arduously Aaron had searched for Navaro.

"I fear Aliyah lied and Navaro is dead. That, or else she keeps her promise from beyond the grave. She told my lord he would never find his son, even if he searched forever."

"And, of course, knowing Aaron, he will never relent," Colon said gently. "Is he yet in the interior going from village to village?"

"No. He has received word of Hojeda's escape from Bartolomé and given chase." Magdalena debated how to broach the subject of Francisco's desire for a pardon. "While he searched the interior for Navaro, Roldan visited every village in Xaragua for us. The boy is not there."

Cristobal's watery blue eyes took in her earnest face as he escorted her to sit at the table and poured them each a mug of wine. "You like this rebel rascal," he said, prompting her to speak.

A slight smile curved her lips as she sipped the wine. "Aaron said you were ever a genius at reading people's thoughts. Yes, I owe him my life. When Guzman brought me to Xaragua, I shudder to think what might have befallen me but for Don Francisco. Now Roldan has gone with Aaron. Together they will capture Hojeda. I would wager on it."

Colon sighed. "If only that would end the dissension."

"Once the Castilian malcontents are subdued and civil order restored, Bartolomé tells me you wish to return to the royal court and plead for more funds to find the mainland."

"In truth, I go to court to plead my own case. Buil, Margarite, many another good Castilian, Argonese, even a Catalan has gone before me to slander how I have governed. I fear I am competent only aboard ship. Life on solid ground does not sit well with me."

Magdalena smiled. "Quite the opposite of my husband."

"Surely he did not confess such. He was always at

413

pains to hide the seasickness from all," Cristobal said with evident surprise on his face.

"He could not hide it from Francisco, who revealed it to me in Xaragua," Magdalena replied with a chuckle. "My lord did not take it well that we made merry of his affliction."

"I can imagine that," the admiral said, some of his humor returning for a moment as he recalled the seasick young fleet marshal. "Aaron would rather have paddled a *canoa* across all the islands of the Indies than sailed aboard ship for a few weeks. Yet he crossed the Atlantic in a terrible gale and returned again with me to Española."

"And you will return to the court. I know your courage, Cristobal. You will plead your case with the Majesties and win their support anew." Magdalena prayed such would be the case as she studied the weary, prematurely aged man who sat before her with the glow of a visionary still lighting his eyes.

"I will return to Castile of a certainty. My sons are there, as is Fernando's mother, a woman I hold in great affection. Yes, I will try again. There is so much yet to do, to explore, places no European has seen in hundreds of years—some places where no Christian has ever trod. I would be the one to see the great Khan." His shoulders slumped as he touched the compass sitting by his hand amid the clutter. "But until the civil unrest on Española is quelled, I am a prisoner to this land."

"If Aaron and Francisco bring Hojeda to you—and if both rebels pledge to support you, would that not provide the tranquility you need to then set sail?" Magdalena asked.

"You are persuasive, my lady. Yes, perhaps it would allow me to return, but first—"

The loud sound of cannon fire followed by the blare of trumpets interrupted his speech. Both Colon and Magdalena leaped to their feet and walked to the door. A

messenger from the harbor came racing down the long
stone hallway, his booted feet echoing on the bare floor.

"Don Juan Aguado bids you come to the beach! The
royal emissary direct from the king and queen has
arrived aboard a fleet filled with food and wine! We are
saved!" the fat little Catalan said, not looking in the least
as if he had suffered a day's privation while on Española.

"Royal emissary, indeed. He is a court chamberlain of
no particular rank who sailed with me on the second
voyage and returned home fast enough last fall. I
requested that a trustworthy judge come to Española, a
man who would study the problem and then report
back about the rebellion and laziness of the nobility
here," Colon muttered as he and Magdalena walked
into the hall. He turned to the messenger, and instructed him, "Bid Don Juan come to the governor's
palace. 'Tis much cooler here and I would not have him
overtaxed awaiting me on the beach in this hot climate."

Magdalena watched Don Cristobal turn stiffly and
bow to her. "I fear I must make ready to receive one of
Queen Ysabel's peacocks. I would not take it ill if your
husband and his friend Roldan returned to Ysabel with
a subdued Alonso Hojeda thrown in to sweeten the
bargain."

"I devoutly believe they will return quickly, your
excellency," Magdalena replied, praying what she said
would come to pass. The governor needed a miracle—
and quickly.

The interview between the Colons and Aguado went
poorly indeed. The chamberlain quickly set his scribes
to recording the testimony of every malcontent in
Ysabel. All blamed the Colons for everything from crop
failures to Taino rebellions, even for the dwindling
amounts of gold found in Española's rivers!

The miracle arrived early the following week, and
none too soon. Two caravels bobbed into the sparkling
water of the bay, sending off a shot of cannon as signal.

Before the ship's boats were lowered, the clatter of horses' hooves in front of the governor's palace announced a bearded, dusty rider's arrival. As he leaped from the saddle, Aaron tossed Rubio's reins to a startled Taino servant. He climbed the wide, flat steps with ground-devouring speed and was greeted by Bartolomé Colon with a hearty bear hug.

"From the look on your face, I would say you know whose ships those be entering the harbor with such boisterous display."

Aaron's eyes rounded in innocence. "Why, 'pon my soul, Don Bartolomé, know you not that they are the governor's ships? Slightly delayed by way of Xaragua, but now filled with a valuable cargo of brazilwood—and bearing two loyal sons of the crown who long to return to their governor's fatherly embrace."

"You and Roldan took Hojeda—and convinced that arrogant little prig to swear allegiance to Cristobal?" The *adelantado*'s eyes glowed with pure delight. "God's bones, 'tis time something went well for my brother!"

"I heard rumors as far away as Guacanagari's village about a royal visitation. Let us hope this token of tribute from Roldan will win us royal favor," Aaron replied grimly. Then, looking down at his dusty clothes, he added, "If this emissary from court is one for ceremony, mayhap I should bathe and dress for the occasion."

"Magdalena is at your *bohio*. She left after the midday meal for a brief nap. I think she will be well pleased to see you returned," Bartolomé said with a wink.

"What? She is not tending the sick at Chanca's hospital?" Aaron asked, surprise, then worry flashing across his face. "She is not fallen ill?"

"The lady seemed in the bloom of health. Only go and see for yourself. I shall arrange to greet our visitors and escort them to the governor's palace. You have earned our gratitude once again, my friend," the *adelantado* said. Then he could not resist adding, "'Tis passing strange that you would ride overland when you could have joined Roldan and Hojeda upon the caravel's grand entry."

Aaron turned and fixed Bartolomé with a level stare. "By the twenty-four balls of the twelve apostles, has she told *everyone?*" Then, unexpectedly, he threw back his head and laughed. "To hell with it. I shall pass precious little time on sea ever again, so I care not."

Aaron walked across the plaza toward home. Odd, the small neat *bohio* was scarce the home of his dreams, certainly not pitched amid the squalor and disease of Ysabel, yet he realized that home was now wherever Magdalena dwelled. Together they could make any place tolerable, even this colony.

He called her name as he entered the door. Stepping inside, Aaron allowed his eyes to accustom themselves to the dimness. It was a hot day, the sun dazzlingly brilliant outdoors. The *bohio* was empty. With a muttered curse, he turned back toward the door and nearly collided with Analu.

As if reading Aaron's worried mind, the Taino smiled and said, "The mistress is at the river with other women washing clothes."

"She has two servant girls handsomely paid to do the scrubbing," he grumbled, looking at the fire pit outside the *bohio*. Nothing bubbled in the empty pot over the unlit pile of kindling wood. "Welcome home!" he muttered sourly. Then an unholy light gleamed in his eyes as he rubbed his beard-bristled chin. "Analu, send to the palace for Rubio."

Several minutes later, the laughter and chatter of Taino and Castilian dialects was broken by the splashing noise of a horse's hooves churning through the water. The Indian women and a smattering of tradesmen's wives, along with a more numerous group of women from the Sevillian waterfront, ceased their labors to admire the tall, golden man mounted on the big bay horse.

"Is he not grand?" one young whore whispered in awe to her companion, letting a length of linen tunic drop from her hands into the water with a splash.

"He is the governor's commandant, no one for the likes of us," the older woman replied bitterly, thinking of all the maravedis lost to her enterprise when Aaron's red-haired lady arrived from Castile.

All eyes, Taino and Castilian, turned from Aaron to Magdalena, who stood waist-deep in the clear rushing water, with a mound of scrubbed clothes piled on a large worn rock. She was wrestling with a length of cloth when Rubio came charging through the deep water toward her.

"I have already warned you about consorting with these women. You have servants aplenty to do manual tasks. All I ask is you oversee a hot meal for your husband. Is that too difficult?" he called out as he reached down to toss her across his saddle.

Magdalena raised her sodden cudgel of heavy cotton and swung it with a lusty plop against his chest. "You want washing more than these clothes. Also you want manners!" she cried as he ducked and Rubio shied, splashing her with a torrent of water. She snarled a remarkable oath as he again turned the bay toward her, but this time when he reached out his arm, she was unable to avoid his grasp. As the river's swift current caused her to lose her balance, she all but fell into his embrace. Aaron lifted her up and swung her across his saddle, then took off amid the catcalls and cheers of the Castilian women. The Tainos stood in round-eyed wonder and a few hid giggles behind their hands. They all watched Magdalena wriggle on her precarious seat and Aaron swat her buttocks until she let out a fierce oath. By that time the lovers had disappeared from sight around a curve in the river where the jungle claimed a patch of hilly ground.

Aaron slowed Rubio's gait long enough to pull his soaked wife up onto the horse in a sidesaddle position. "You have soaked me and my horse!"

"Good. You both need a bath," she said breathlessly, pushing away from his grasp and eyeing his bristly golden beard with distaste. "You have been gone for a fortnight. Hojeda must have given you good sport."

His face creased in an arrogant grin. "That the little popinjay did, but Roldan has him well in tow before the governor now."

"They sailed in, all bathed and ready for an audience while you, of course, could not accompany them aboard ship." She could not resist the taunt, knowing how sensitive he was about his affliction. Male vanity was such a whimsical thing.

"I may not fare well on the ocean, but I can take care of myself—and you—right here on dry land," he replied, reining in Rubio before the great spreading branches of a silk cotton tree. Cooling shadows and a soft breeze from the distant ocean beckoned them to enter the canopy. He slid from the horse and pulled her down into his arms where he held her fast. "I mislike coming home to find you gone."

"I mislike tending a cookfire week in and out waiting for you to reappear from the jungle," she replied angrily, aching to fling her arms about his glorious neck.

"I have told you not to consort with those whores. Only the lower classes do such difficult labor. I know I am no longer a rich man, but you are a lady and my wife. I have provided servants—"

"'Twas fearful hot and I needed cooling off. Naomu has been ill with the fever and could not do the washing. I merely wished the diversion. Since, as you pointed out, I am a lady—the only one of such rank in Española, whom am I to talk with when all the men are off playing at war and politics?'' By this time her hands had crept up to tangle in his shaggy golden hair.

He let his hands glide up past her slim waist, cupping the water-soaked curve of her breasts. ''By the staff of St Peter, you are all but naked in this wet linen,'' he whispered as his fingers splayed around her buttocks pulling her fast against him. When he lowered his head her fingers dug into his scalp and her lips opened for his kiss. ''I stink of horse and sweat and jungle,'' he murmured against her lips.

''And you know I will not care,'' she murmured back as they sank onto the carpet of soft grasses. Eagerly her hands began to unfasten his belt, tossing it and the weapons attached to it against the tree trunk where they fell with a clatter. Then she yanked free his shirt and ran her tongue around his sweat soaked chest, teasingly circling both hardened male nipples until he muttered an oath of endearment. Aaron began peeling the wet linen tunic from her body. She helped him raise it up exposing her sleekly curved calves and satiny thighs. His hands and mouth caressed each new inch as he unveiled it.

Magdalena reveled in his hungry touch, but even more in the possessive way he made love to her showing her by words and gestures that she was his woman, the only one he loved and desired. Her fingers began to unlace his hose, freeing his hard staff from the tight confines. Lovingly she plied it with deft caresses and rough strokes until he gasped in an excruciating conflict of pain and pleasure.

''By the rood, wait! My boots!'' he cried, rolling free of her long enough to yank off the soft kidskin riding boots and peel down his hose in a few swift movements.

Magdalena used the time to finish pulling off the encumbrance of her soaked tunic. Her hair, hanging in tangled wet masses about her shoulders, looked almost black. Small rivulets of water ran from it, dripping onto her arms, breasts, and thighs. Aaron began to lave them with his tongue, whispering, "I have a fearful thirst to quench."

A frisson of heat coursed through her as his silky tongue and magic mouth worked their way down one arm, then across her breasts, taking each in turn to suckle and tease. When he moved down to the soft indentation of her navel and lapped the droplets accumulated there, she arched against him, pulling his head up to hers for a fierce, sealing kiss.

Their tongues glided about each other, tasting, savoring, devouring as they rolled, arms and legs entwined, across the grass, finally coming to rest with him cradled between her open thighs. Boldly she reached down and took his staff in her hand, stroking it roughly, then stopping and squeezing it gently. "You said you had a thirst. Now I have a hunger," she whispered.

Aaron gently pushed her down onto her back and then let her guide his entry into the wet heat of her body. For one shattering moment he held very still, not daring to breathe lest he lose control. Then he rasped out, "I, too, have that hunger. Take care lest you glut yourself too quickly and ruin the culmination of appetite."

With that he began to move slowly, guiding her hips as he stroked deeply. Magdalena matched his rhythm, rising to meet each thrust, letting her hands roam up and down his back, one moment tugging at his hair, pulling his head down for a kiss, the next digging her nails into his buttocks, urging him to move more swiftly, to plunge deeper, harder. Her tongue snaked out and licked the salty sweat from his chest, then she raised the silky skin of her face to rub it against his bristly beard, reveling in the hard maleness of his body.

The noises of rustling jungle, the roar of the distant ocean all faded into oblivion as she felt the shattering crest. Crying out his name incoherently, Magdalena felt him swell and stiffen, pulsing his seed deeply into her body, adding to the rapture of the moment, more golden than the metal wrested from the soils of Española could ever be.

"This is the gold, the treasure, this is our world," she breathed raggedly against his chest as he collapsed on top of her, spent, at peace.

Aaron cradled her head in one hand and kissed her eyelids, then her cheeks, nose, and lips with soft, satiated caresses.

They lay together on the grass for several moments while the earth returned to life about them. Then he rolled from her body and pulled her to lie beside him, gazing into her clear green eyes. "You said this was our world. Would you be content to spend the rest of your life on Española?" He considered her gravely.

Magdalena smiled gently with a teasing light dancing in her green eyes. "'Twould be far better than cold France."

"Not long ago you were complaining of the heat, as I recall," he said with a lazy smile.

She shrugged saucily. "I grew hotter yet. Now I am cooled off . . . for the moment." Her face grew serious. "Aaron, I would live wherever you will. Only say what you wish to do, where you want to go, and I will follow."

He caressed her cheek with one calloused fingertip. "I love you, Magdalena. I would have us begin anew here in this land—away from Ysabel and its feuds and pestilence. When Roldan and I journeyed into the interior after Hojeda, I chanced upon some of the most marvelously beautiful country you could ever imagine—a paradise of open plains set in a wide, fertile valley, filled with lush grass and rich soil. We could raise horses and cattle to sell to the colonists, even grow food crops for ourselves. I spoke to Guacanagari about my dream. Many of his people are eager to go with us, knowing we will deal fairly with them and protect them from marauders like Hojeda."

"What will happen to the Tainos, Aaron? How long can we protect them?" Magdalena asked sadly, already fearing the answer.

"I do not know. They die of the diseases our colonists bring. Each new wave seems to decimate them more surely than sword or even slavery. We can offer to protect those who would go with us. Luis Torres and several of the men in Ysabel who have taken Taino wives would join us, I think." He paused and looked at her.

Magdalena smiled. "I think it is a splendid plan. We cannot save the whole Taino society, but we can preserve their blood, their customs—something for their children and grandchildren." Her eyes took on a misty glow. "You are so like your father, Aaron."

He looked at her with a puzzled expression on his face, sad and wistful. "I never felt worthy. He was a healer. I have only been a killer."

"Who now proposes to shelter helpless Indians and protect them from civilized rapacity? I see much that makes Benjamin very proud of you."

"You always speak of him in the present tense, as if he knows all that has transpired since his death," Aaron said softly.

"And you write in your diary to him still, do you not? Come, let us return to Ysabel and begin recruiting our farmers and stockmen," she said, pulling him up as she rose from their bed of grass.

Together they dressed and rode Rubio back to the settlement to plan their dream.

Later that evening Aaron sat on the carved chair in one corner of their *bohio*, writing by the light of a single flickering candle. The haze of twilight gathered outside as his pen scratched across the smooth, heavy paper.

Shirl Henke

My Dearest Father,

My heart is overflowing with both joy and sorrow, all together a bittersweet mixture, but a cup I would not have pass. My good friend Guacanagari plans to relocate his vast city farther in the interior, away from the diseases of the white men. With a few loyal men and true among my soldiers, we will protect them.

If only you could see this place where we will make our home—how vast and fertile, a paradise of fragrant flowers and sparkling waters.

I miss my firstborn son most intensely. Although I fear his mother's dying words were false, I will never cease my search for him even though I know now how unlikely it is that Navaro lives. I regret Aliyah's death and the destruction of her people and their way of life that brought it about. Yet I can not turn back history here any more than I could stop the wars between Christian and Moor in Andalusia.

Perhaps in time I can grow to accept Navaro's loss . . . or if God favors me with his richest blessing, I shall find my son. . . .

Aaron broke off writing as he heard Magdalena enter the room. "The bread is warm on the hearth and a savory chunk of freshly killed iguana roasts on the spit. Will you eat, husband?"

He put down his writing instruments and stood up as she stretched out her hands to clasp his. Rubbing her cheek against his freshly shaven chin, she said, "I think I liked the beard."

"Greedy wench. Your passions blinded you. I was filthy. No proper court lady would ever have taken such a one into her embrace."

"Do you seek compliments? Very well. Any court lady

would take you, bathed or no, bearded or no, and well you know it, Aaron Torres!"

They shared the simple meal and discussed their plans for the future, as well as what the shifting political winds would bring the Colon family. Finally, as Magdalena left their servants to clean the dishes they strolled to the edge of the settlement and sat on a low hillock overlooking the ocean, now glistening silvery black as the moon rose over its depths.

"We should perhaps see if Tanei's sister wishes to relocate with us," Magdalena said as they spoke of who among the settlers and Tainos might join them.

"She is accounted a fine midwife. I suppose in time that would be useful. Luis and his wife expect another child in a few months," Aaron said, nodding approvingly.

Magdalena held her breath for a moment, then said softly, "I know you will always grieve for Navaro, Aaron, and no one will ever take his place in your heart . . . but Luis' wife is not the only one who will be needing a midwife in the spring."

Aaron stiffened in amazement, then turned to her with a mixture of joy and anger on his face. "You are with child and you went down to the river to do heavy labor like a scrub woman? I threw you across my horse and then . . ."

"And then made fierce, wonderful love to me. Both the babe and I are well, Aaron. Your father was a learned physician who believed in hearty exercise for women carrying children." She hesitated with eyes downcast, then raised them to meet his in the bright white moonlight. "Are you truly happy that we are to have our first child?"

The moonlight etched the handsome planes and angles of his face, making his expression unreadable for a moment. "Magdalena, beloved wife, do I still give you cause to doubt how much I love you." He took her chin in one hand and raised it, then softly rained kisses on her eyes, nose, cheeks, lips. "You have known this for a while, I would wager. Did you fear to tell me?"

"I feared to have you hurt more. After we could not find Navaro, 'twould have been cruel to raise hopes if proved mistaken. I waited until I was very certain. Then you were gone with Francisco in the interior."

He smiled. "So that is why you were so cross when came riding up to sweep you from the river."

"Sweep me from the river, indeed! More like t chastise me as an errant wife acting like a spoiled girl rather than a lady of quality."

"Back in the marshes of the Guadalquiver, tha spoiled girl made me a promise, or so you told me— that she would be beautiful for me and make me lov her."

"Was her promise fulfilled, husband?" Her voice wa low and velvety on the balmy night air.

"More than ever she could have imagined, my beaut ful lady, my beloved," he murmured.

The lovers embraced as the moon overhead beame down its benediction on the paradise around them an within their hearts.

Epilogue

March 1496

The two small caravels rode low in the water, burdened with people and supplies. So many adventurers were eager to return to Castile that they were willing to sleep in shifts on the decks of *India* and *Niña*. As the final cargo and passengers were loading, Cristobal Colon took one last look at Ysabel. When he returned to Española, the colony would no longer be inhabited. His brother Bartolomé was already making plans to relocate on the southern coast of the island where the soil was richer and the harbors far more accommodating in time of storm.

With the prospect of again commanding a ship, the admiral's jaw was set firmly, his step sure, his purpose once again certain. Even if the two caravels were old and overworked, they would make the crossing. He surveyed his friends and family gathered at the shore to see him off.

Aaron and Magdalena Torres had journeyed from far

inland where they now resided. So had his old frien
Guacanagari and his entourage.

"We are agreed upon the harbor," Bartolomé said
the chart still in his hand as the brothers stood by th
ship's boat, which was waiting to cast off.

"Yes. I know it well, the place we named in honor c
the day on which I discovered it. Santo Domingo it wil
be. As soon as I have put matters to right with th
Majesties, I will return to you with more men an
supplies."

"Only win against your foes at court," Aaron said a
he clasped Colon on the back. "We will keep the peac
here on Española."

"And keep adding to the population," Cristobal sai
with the old twinkle in his pale blue eyes, as he looke
from Aaron to the small bundle in Magdalena's arms

"As soon as young Benjamin is old enough to with
stand the rigors of an ocean voyage, we will visit hi
great uncle in France. Then we will return to our hom
on Española," Magdalena said to the admiral. "Ou
ships may pass each other in crossing, but one day w
will all be reunited here."

"And by then, who knows how many more childre
my wife and I may have contributed to the population?
Aaron said with a chuckle, delighting in the pretty blus
on her cheeks.

Cristobal, too, noted how motherhood and their nev
life on Española had caused Magdalena to bloom. 1
only more such settlers could be found and brough
from Castile. "I wish you both, and young Benjami
here, Godspeed on your journey to France and back.
He turned to his brother and said, "As *adelantado*, yo
bear a heavy burden relocating the whole colony to th
south. I entrust you with it, having every faith in you
abilities."

Bartolomé clasped his brother in his arms, then said
"Guacanagari, Aaron, and their people will help us. B

he time you return, the new colony will be a city for you
o be proud of. Commend me to Beatriz and the
hildren."

"I, too, wish you a swift and safe journey across the
vaters where your family awaits you," Guacanagari said
n carefully rehearsed Castilian. Colon embraced his
aithful young ally.

"Tell that young rascal Diego that I long to see him
nce more, when he tires of court life and would come
ee the wonders of the lands his father has discovered,"
aron added.

"We all of us await your return, Cristobal," Magdale-
a said as she handed young Benjamin to his father and
mbraced the tall old man.

His piercing blue eyes agleam with tears, the Admiral
f the Ocean Sea gave them each one final farewell
mbrace, then stepped into the ship's boat to be rowed
o the Niña. On the tide, he would set sail for Seville, and
nother chapter in history.

Author's Note

Researching such vastly divergent and alien places a
15th-century Castile and the Greater Antilles was a
daunting undertaking for Carol and me. After our firs
background readings were completed on Columbus
the Trastamaras, Torquemada, the Sephardic Jews, and
the Taino Indians, I had threads of plot enough to weave
not merely a tapestry, but a whole tent! Rather than
become a prisoner of history, I made some arbitrar
choices, which I would like to explain.

To unify the plot and make events flow smoothly
have collapsed time to speed up the chaotic historica
events on Española. Thus Roldan's revolt, which did no
begin until 1496 and end until he made peace with the
admiral in 1499, has been incapsulated into a perio
concomitant with the Taino uprisings during 1495. The
number of caravels shuttling from Castile to the Carib
bean during the 1490's was staggering; I have adjuste
the dates of ships' arrivals to facilitate my story line. Th

marvelous speech of the *cacique* Caonabo was not, alas, his, but that of a Cuban *cacique* of a generation later. Since both men were motivated by the same injustice and met the same fate, I felt it justifiable to move the event forward to 1495 Española.

Although I have taken liberties rearranging events in some instances, I have striven to present all the historical figures as accurately as my sources and the passage of half a millennium allow. The men and women who fill these pages lived in the exciting Age of Discovery at the apex of the Renaissance. But we must bear in mind that they were prisoners of great violence and fanaticism that also shaped their world. If there is any purpose to *Paradise & More* beyond entertaining the reader, I hope it is to tell a story in which the love of Magdalena and Aaron triumphs over the hate of Torquemada and his inquisitors.

The figure of Christopher Columbus both drives the plot and haunts it. After reading Samuel Eliot Morison's masterful *Admiral of the Ocean Sea*, Carol and I were both in awe of the single-minded vision and navigational genius of the man, but we found him also bedeviled by physical infirmity and administrative misjudgment, and thus I have portrayed him. The traditional *gromet's* song to greet the dawn in chapter six of our book was taken verbatim from Morison. The *Journal of Christopher Columbus*, translated by Clements R. Markham, gave me some additional insights into the admiral's personality as well as his sense of delight in the beauty of the New World he unknowingly discovered. *The Columbus Dynasty in the Caribbean 1492-1526*, by Troy S. Floyd, depicts the strengths and weaknesses of this remarkable family during their rise to power. No work of fiction dealing with Columbus would be complete without consulting the garrulous yet fascinating accounts of the apostle to the Indians, Bartolomé de Las Casas. I used his *History of the Indies*, translated and edited by Andrée

Collard. Also excellent for a general overview of the age, and for pictorials, is the first of the Time Life Seafarer Series, *The Explorers* by Richard Humble.

Christopher and his intrepid brother Bartolome haunted the courts of Europe for years seeking financial backing for their quest. The Spains—for Castile and Aragon were not unified in these formative years—were ruled by a man and woman willing to gamble on the unlikely venture. If I have departed from the traditional depiction of a selfless and beauteous Isabella, it is only because in the real world neither Trastamara, Isabella nor her cousin Ferdinand, was at all noble. They were frequently ruthless, sometimes brilliant, and always self-serving. Felipe Fernandez-Armesto's *Ferdinand and Isabella* portrays the monarchs masterfully, as does Gabriel Jackson's *Policies in the Making of Medieval Spain*. For a solid overview of the making of Iberia, *Imperial Spain 1469-1716* by J. H. Elliott is a fine source. I highly recommend *España, Pueblos y Paisajes*, by Jose Ortiz E Chague, for its brilliant pictorial essay on the look and feel of Spain.

The darkest side of the unification of Spain during the Age of Discovery is, of course, the persecution and ultimate expulsion of the Jews. Spain itself paid a bitter price for this calamity. John E. Longhurst's *Age of Torquemada* and Rafael Sabatini's *Torquemada and the Spanish Inquisition* are excellent standard reference works on one of the most tragic chapters in human history.

Much of *Paradise & More* takes place in the Indies, as the Admiral of the Ocean Sea steadfastly called them. I would recommend a number of sources for further reading on both the Indians and their exotic and wonderful lands. Among them are *The Early Spanish Main* by Carl Ortwin Sauer and *The Caribbean* by W. Adolphe Roberts. Of particular interest is *The Columbian Exchange* by Alfred W. Crosby, Jr., which outlines the profound and surprising ways in which the New and Old Worlds gave and took from each other. The book covers everything from food and drink to epidemiology.

Numerous sources including Sauer and Morison, not to mention Columbus' diaries and Las Casas' history, discuss the now extinct native cultures the explorers found in the Caribbean. Additionally, I found the best anthropological source for details about daily life, religion, social organization, and economics was the work of Irving Rouse. *The Handbook of South American Indians,* volume four, gives a fascinating account of the Arawakan culture, especially the advanced society of the Tainos, who ultimately were doomed to a fate even more terrible than that of the Sephardim.

Carol and I hope you have enjoyed our first book commemorating the 500th anniversary of the discovery of America and will want to read its sequel, *Return to Paradise,* to be released early in 1992. The prologue from it is included as a preview at the end of this book.

I love to hear from readers:

Shirl Henke
P. O. Box 72
Adrian, MI 49221
(Please enclose SASE for reply)

Prologue

Château Oublieux, August 1524

The comtesse raised one milky white arm and traced his
scar with her long, tapered fingers. It was a casual,
elegant gesture, yet Rigo knew it betrayed more curiosity than was her jaded wont. He arched one heavy black
brow in sardonic amusement as he watched her compare their flesh, hers so softly pale, his so exotically
dark. "Still you speculate about my ancestry," he said
with a trace of bitter humor in his voice.

Louise of Saint Gilles shrugged her shoulders in
Gallic indifference, knowing the movement raised her
large, luminously white breasts provocatively. "'Tis no
matter that you are dark for a Castilian, but rather that
the Moorish strain in your blood gives you away as
enemy to France."

Rodrigo de Las Casas laughed aloud. "Since when
does a Provençal worry about loyalty to France? Charles
of Bourbon sold his soul to my emperor and now
declares himself Count of Provence to sweeten the
bargain."

Louise made a moue of distaste. "One never knows when the winds of politics will shift. Today your Spanish emperor holds sway, tomorrow perhaps King Francois will retake Provence. I only worry for your safety, beloved," she whispered, draping one plump, pearly thigh languorously across his lean, dark hips.

Rigo gave a feral growl at her invitation and rolled their entwined bodies across her bed to plunge into her wet, eager flesh for another bout of pleasure. He could feel her long nails dig into his back as she arched hungrily beneath him.

Louise gazed up at his dark countenance with passion-glazed eyes. She had always been aroused by the contrast in their coloring. The first time he had undressed her and run his swarthy hands over her pale skin, she had nearly swooned with the forbidden excitement. He was the enemy, a mercenary in the pay of King Carlos of Spain, but also the most exotically striking man she had ever seen. Louise was entranced by his classically sculpted features framed by shoulder-length, blue-black hair. His tall frame was sinewy with the muscles of a man born to horse and weaponry. Louise gloried in his scars, symbols of the hard, dangerous life he led, so unlike Henri's. Poor dear Henri, her pale, fat little husband, was in Aix feting the conquering Imperial Army. She gave a feline smile of anticipation as she pulled on Rigo's thick, straight hair, drawing him down to devour his mouth in a harsh kiss. *I, too, am honoring the victors.*

Later, as Louise slept, Rigo untangled himself from her lush curves and rose to dress. He pushed the heavy red brocade bed curtains back impatiently, then placed his bare feet firmly on the thick Turkish carpet. Saint Gilles provided handsomely for his lady, Rigo thought with grim amusement. The lavish wall hangings, intricately carved teak tables, and jewel-encrusted wall sconces attested not only to the Comte's wealth, but

to the Provencal trade with the Moslems of North
Africa.

Having broken his long sexual abstinence, he began to
dress, finding no exotic allure in Louise's milky flesh.
Over the years he had bedded too many beautiful
noblewomen, French and Flemish, English and Spanish, all possessing pale skin and a marked absence of
morals. As a callow boy of fourteen, he had been
seduced by the wife of an Argonese duke. Life had
taught him that the same alien blood that forever closed
to him the doors of political and economic advancement opened the doors to women's bedchambers. The
duchess had been twice his age and very inventive in the
arts of love. He had proved an apt pupil.

Hearing the rustling whisper of fine linen as he
donned his under-tunic, Louise awakened and peered at
him with heavy-lidded eyes. He had left the satin
coverlet undisturbed, but now she let it fall artlessly to
her waist as she sat up. Unable to restrain a note of
petulance in her voice, she said, "You need not depart
so soon. Henri will not return for at least another three
days."

"Henri is not the only man needed in Aix. Pescara
awaits my report and I have dallied long enough in the
countryside, Louise," Rigo replied soothingly. Always
he hated the leave-taking. Were all women so pettishly
intent on holding a man until they did the dismissing?

"Ah yes, Pescara, that little Italian fop you spy for,"
she said in silky insult. When her remarks caused no
even a twitch of irritation as he continued dressing, she
changed tactics. "Please, the marquis has no need of
you until the army leaves Aix. Bourbon enjoys the
adulation of the city, and he, not Pescara, is in command of the army.

Rigo snorted in disgust. "More's the pity. That little
Italian fop, as you so charmingly call him, is ten times
the soldier your puffed-up Frenchman will ever be."

Louise sensed that she could not sway her lover, yet refused to relinquish him so easily. He was such a splendid barbarian. "I do not want to discuss military matters or politics or the men who decide such things. You know I have been lonely these past months since we met in Naples. I thought never to see you again and then you arrive at my gates, bold as one of your Moorish ancestors."

He smiled with his lips but not his eyes. "'Tis you who say I am of Moorish blood. I never have."

She knelt at the edge of the bed and placed one white hand against his swarthy cheek, then ran her nails lightly down his throat and buried her fingers in the thick black hair curling at the opening of his linen shirt. "And what Spaniard as dark as you could claim aught else?"

His eyes darkened in pain, which he quickly suppressed. "Yes, what Spaniard could," he echoed expressionlessly.

"Does it yet disturb you so much?"

"My inferior blood has kept me from advancement where my bastardy would not have done. Many a capable soldier has risen to high rank and won land and titles, even if born on the wrong side of the blanket. But only if his parents possessed *limpieza de sangre*." He spoke in the Provençal dialect, all but for the words "purity of blood," which somehow required Castilian.

"The Spanish are such barbarians," Louise cooed, trying to soothe and seduce him. "I have told you of the sorry tale of my life, wed to a fat stupid boy when I was but twelve years old. Yet you have revealed almost nothing of yourself." She twined her arms about his neck and rubbed her large breasts provocatively against his chest.

Firmly disengaging her arms, he replied, "There is little to tell. You see me as I am. A mercenary in the pay of the Imperial Army. I grew to manhood on the plains of Andalusia and was first blooded serving old King Fernando in the conquest of Navarre. By the age of eighteen I had already learned I had no hope of earning my way but by my sword. I was raised by a pious family whose eldest son took Holy Orders, a vocation denied me because of my bastardy, even as my mixed blood kept me from studying law or medicine."

Louise let out a small trill of laughter. "You, a priest! Or a healer?" She appeared to consider. "Well, perhaps a lawyer, but only if women were allowed to sit in judgment!"

"Born with wealth and position, you may easily jest about such matters," he said tightly as he turned away from her and resumed dressing.

"I meant no offense, Rodrigo. For all your fine sad words about being illegitimate and of mixed blood, you have the devil's own temper. Hot Moorish blood, yes," she purred.

"Not Moorish, for they are civilized, far beyond the comprehension of Europeans. I am a savage scorned even by the barbarous Spanish—my mother was a primitive from the Indies, too mean and insignificant for my proud Castilian father to wed. God curse his soul, whoever he may be!"

Louise looked astonished for an instant, a most unusual expression for the sophisticated comtesse. Her hazel eyes grew round and her cheeks pinkened with a flush of renewed excitement. She tossed her tangled mane of amber hair over her shoulder and twisted one curl nervously in her fingers. Studying the methodical way in which he was donning the light armor of his profession, she said with a sigh, "Now I have made you angry with me. I care not a fig if your mother was chief wife of the Caliph of Bagdad or an Indian slave from the New World. I want you, Rigo. Do not leave me with such rancor between us. When can you return?"

Rodrigo de Las Casas turned to face the beautiful

blonde kneeling on the bed. She was right. If only women, not men, held the reins of social advancement in their hands, he would prosper indeed, but such a dishonorable thought gave him no comfort at all. If he could not prove himself on the battlefield, he would not dance attendance on unfaithful wives to secure his future. With a cynical smile he said, "The army marches south to lay siege to Marseilles. If all of Provence falls under the Imperial yoke, mayhap I shall return, Louise . . . if you are yet certain my savage blood does not frighten you."

"You may frighten me at times, Rigo, but 'tis the kind of fear a woman comes to relish . . . like rare sweetmeats from hot foreign climes," she added with a breathless chuckle as he scowled darkly.

Benjamin Torres combed his fingers through the long gold hair plastered to his head by the driving summer rain, then quickly grabbed for the oilskin-wrapped bundle of books in danger of tumbling from the pitching boat. Two stout *gromets* rowed against the pitiless wind that was driving the small boat farther out into the Bay of Lions, away from the dim lights flickering on the Provençal coastline.

"What a mission of mercy this has turned out to be," he muttered beneath the howl of the wind and roar of the waves swamping the tiny boat. The fat caravel he had sailed on from Genoa bound for Marseilles had gone down seemingly hours ago, all its desperately needed cargo of food, gunpowder, and weapons lost to the angry sea. The only items salvaged were a few medical supplies and the equipment that the young Jewish physician had carried onto the ship's boat. Now it seemed that both the remnants of the cargo and even his own skills were to be lost as well.

"I see fire—a campfire on the beach," the boatswain cried out over the din.

Several of the seamen cursed as one Genoese said, "They will be Imperials, ready to cut our throats. We have been blown too far north of Marseilles to reach Frenchmen."

"'Tis a fire and dry land. I care not what army holds it," another replied, renewing his rowing with vigor.

"You, Physician, can you speak anything but the Latin and Greek from your books?" the Genoese boatswain asked in his Ligurian dialect.

Benjamin smiled in spite of the danger. "My family was from Seville. If you say nothing of my being Jewish, perhaps I can deceive the Spanish soldiers into believing I am a loyal subject of King Carlos on my way home to Málaga, blown off course in the storm."

The boat had finally been turned, catching a strong current that drew them nearer the beaches. If only they could get past the jagged rocks jutting out like the enormous gray fingers of Poseidon.

Benjamin prayed for deliverance, not only from the sea and the rocks, but from the Imperial Army as well. In his medical books were inscriptions written in the Ladino dialect of the Sephardim, the Jews expelled from Spain by King Carlos' grandparents in 1492. He fervently hoped these soldiers were as illiterate as the general lot, not educated as was his father Aaron.

The rocks loomed nearer, then the boat was literally pitched past them by a giant wave. The boatswain was thrown into the frothing waters, as were several of the *gromets*. Benjamin held tightly to his precious medical gear as another powerful wave crashed against him. Then all went black . . .

He awakened with a splitting headache, made worse by the insistent shaking being given his bruised body. A small, thin man with a brushy red beard was attempting to awaken him, jabbering rapidly in some dialect that Benjamin could not understand. Should he attempt

Castilian or Provençal? Listening to the words over the dazed pounding in his head, Torres decided the language was some form of German. The man was dressed in the coarse woolen hose and quilted armor of a foot soldier, probably an artilleryman. Benjamin Torres was a guest of the Imperial Army of the Emperor Carlos V. He chose Castilian. "Where are we? Have any of the other men shipwrecked with me been saved?"

The little man replied in a badly mangled version of that language. "A few, yes," he replied holding up three fingers. "They no broken. They say you doctor. We have wounded. You come? Help?"

"My bags—they had instruments, medicines—were they lost?" Benjamin asked as he sat up and looked around. He was sheltered in a crude tent of oiled skins, lying on a lumpy pallet of moldy-smelling damp wool, probably lice-infested. After a rapid inventory of his extremities, he decided to attempt standing up, as it seemed he was not seriously injured.

Before the small German could answer his questions, another man shoved open the tent flap, bringing with him the harsh salt tang of ocean wind. "Your bags, physician, if so you be," the thickset older soldier said, handing Benjamin his precious tools and books. He had the dark eyes and rounded face of an Argonese and spoke far clearer Castilian. Benjamin accepted his satchels, grateful they were intact. "Yes, I am a physician. Who requires care? Take me to them."

"General Pescara's best field officer is the first you must see. Don Francisco says he has taken some shot in his side and the bleeding is fierce," the gristled veteran replied as he led the younger man from the tent.

The beaches were littered with crude lean-tos and other shelters. Campfires flickered in the dim gray light of dawn. The sea was once again glassy calm as if the previous night's storm had never occurred. Benjamin made his way past the rough men huddled around their

fires, breaking their fast with meager rations of hard
biscuit and watered sour wine. His stomach growled
but he ignored it. Burly blond Lutherans from the Baltic
Sea sat beside uneasy black-haired Sicilians. Fair-
skinned Castilian hidalgos haughtily ignored both imperial allies as they ate.

"Where are we?" Torres asked his guide.

"Look you up the coast," the Spanish soldier replied.
"Beyond the low hills lies the great seaport of Marseilles. We have battered and scarred its stone walls with
our cannon, yet the city remains secure as long as
supplies come to her from the sea," he added bitterly.

If the imperial troops learned his was one such supply
ship sent out through neutral Genoa, Benjamin realized
his life would be forfeit. He made no reply. Worse yet,
his family lay within the walls of the besieged city. They
were doubtless as frantic with worry for him as he was
for them. "My ship was bound for Malaga. We were
indeed blown far off course," he said grimly. *So near, yet
so far from deliverance.*

"Where is this commander of yours? I see many men
who could use my care," he finally felt bold enough to
ask as they walked up the gentle slope of a hillside
toward a small wooden hut with several guards sta-
tioned in front of it. The hard-looking Spaniards parted
as the Argonese led the physician inside.

Benjamin let his eyes adjust to the dim light as he
heard fluent cursing in Castilian. Recalling some of his
father's more remarkable oaths, he decided the commander must be a native of Seville to have acquired the
same unique idiom. "Bring a lighted torch," Benjamin
ordered. "I can see naught." As he approached the low
pallet, he saw the man lying on it, a large red ooze
soaking through his heavy tunic. His armor had been
removed and the injury bound crudely. The man lay
still, his breathing labored, his face turned away from
Benjamin.

Some instinct made Torres pause before he opened his bag with a loud click of the latch. The man was as swarthy as the Argonese, perhaps more so, yet what Benjamin could see of his features—slim straight nose, high forehead, and bold jawline—were classically chiseled. And disturbingly familiar.

The Argonese, who obviously had never before seen Pescara's favorite young officer, now stared in gape-awed amazement, first down at the wounded soldier, then up at the physician kneeling over him. Just then the wounded man let out another oath and his eyes snapped open as he turned his head to stare at the physician.

Two identical pairs of brilliant blue eyes fastened each on the other. "Like unto a mirror held up to me, bathed in light . . . while I am caste in darkness," Rodrigo said in a rasping voice.

The man lying before Benjamin had his face, the same full arched eyebrows, the same wide, sensuous lips, the same square jaw with its cleft chin—but above all the eyes, bright blue Torres eyes!

"You are golden and I am black. Think you it signifies our morals . . . or our fates?" Rigo asked, stifling a wince of pain as Benjamin began to remove the bloody bandage with trembling hands.

"I know not your morals, nor can I read our fates, but I do know your name." Benjamin felt the injured man tense as those unsettling light eyes in that dark face searched his own expression silently. "You are Navaro Torres, my brother!"